SUPERMODEL

JUDI JAMES

Supermodel

HarperCollins*Publishers*

HarperCollins*Publishers*
77–85 Fulham Palace Road,
Hammersmith, London W6 8JB

Published by HarperCollins*Publishers* 1994

A catalogue record for this book
is available from the British Library

ISBN 0 00 224464 0

Set in Linotron Sabon by
Rowland Phototypesetting Ltd
Bury St Edmunds, Suffolk

Printed in Great Britain by
HarperCollinsManufacturing Glasgow

For Jimmy

1

Chelsea, 1994

Oliver Zweinfeldt slithered backstage, a dewy young thing of ambiguous gender clamped to his side like a genital wart. His nerves jangled as furiously as small change in a pervert's pocket. He walked like a man who has just had his piles cauterized – which in fact was the truth – although Oliver had always walked that way, long before BUPA got their hands on his derrière.

'Darling! Kissy kissy! Mwa! Mwa!' He air-kissed the first black face he chanced upon. The young thing with him let out a small hoot. The black man merely nodded. There was an unsightly pause. Oliver felt obliged to conduct introductions.

'Luvvie, this is Lawrence M'Tambo – you'll have read that little piece I did on him for the *Observer*? Lawrence is from Soweto, darling. Courtaulds flew him in and sponsored his first collection. Lawrence, this is . . .' He had completely forgotten the name of his companion. Had he ever known it? How had he found *la petite créature* in the first place? He had a feeling it had suckled up to him as he had made his way through the pack of rabid journos outside the marquee.

Oliver shuddered, reminded suddenly of a swim he had taken one night, many years before, in the balmy, honeyed waters off the island of Cos. As he was towelling down he had discovered, to his horror, a small black leech supping off a vein on his thigh. A local boy had burnt the leech off with the tip of a cigarette. He wondered whether the same trick might work this time.

– Unfortunately he didn't smoke.

Pas de problème, though – the androgenous youth smiled charmingly, despite the snub, exposing milky, faux-diamond-studded teeth.

'Simmy Cartlet-Jones,' it lisped, extending a consumptive hand from the depths of one sleeve of a Vivienne Westwood tartan and ermine shirt. 'I'm researching a half-hour slot for Channel Four. It's part of a series called . . .'

But Oliver had no desire to hear more. The words 'Channel Four' were to nausea and boredom what a warm cowpat is to the average bluebottle. No matter, though, poor sweetie-pie Lawrence would no doubt be impressed – he had been fawning over Jeff Banks not ten seconds before. Oliver's lizard eyes had spotted fatter flies to lash his tongue around.

'Dee-Dee! Daaaarling!' Waving security aside with his press pass he sashayed across to a Tussauds-faced model holed up away from the crush in a corner of the vast room. The girl had been created for the catwalk from the moment of conception and would have looked out of place anywhere else, with her viscous white limbs and her luminous, Daffy-Duck face.

A broken ampoule of amyl nitrate lay on her table beside her Tupperware lunchboxes. As Oliver bent to kiss she exhaled a held breath and a cloud of sweet-smelling smoke billowed from her minuscule surgically-restructured nose. Versace was showing Seventies retro that season so everyone was back onto pot – naturally.

'Where is she, where is she, where is she?' Oliver was all wound up like a clock. There was no need to refer to his prey by name. The show was due to start in minus five and he still hadn't as much as a sniff of his exclusive interview.

'Steady, Ollie, old fruit!' Dee-Dee's broad cockney was always a revelation. She prised open the corner of her lunchbox with a french-manicured fingernail and pulled out a lettuce leaf, folding it into a small ball and swallowing it like a pill. She burped and then giggled. 'Roberto says she ain't goin' to show.'

'Why ever not?' Oliver's eyes lit like twin flames. He bent to peer under one of the dress rails – sometimes the models fell asleep down there.

Dee-Dee checked out her false eyelashes in the mirror. The glue was making her lids itch. Her agent would sue if there was lasting damage. A photographer elbowed past Oliver and snapped a shot as she picked her nose with a Chanel tissue.

'*Ça suffit! Ça suffit!*' she screamed but she didn't mean it – a breast popped out as a come-on as she waved her arms in mock-despair.

'He's using them transvestites again,' she called to Oliver, '– For the bridal scene this time. You know she won't work with them – says they spoil it for the rest of us, poncing about up there. It gets right on her tits. She hates them about as much as she hates any new girls – mind you, I'm with her all the way there. "The new breed of Supermodels," Oliver – look at them – look at that Italian cow over there – designer stubble on her bikini-line, for chrissake. They don't know their arse from their elbows some of them.'

Oliver sighed. 'What's the collection like this season?' he asked.

Dee-Dee posed reading a volume of Proust's *À la recherche du temps perdu* for the photographer from *Hello!* Oliver noticed the book was held upside-down but a sudden yawn prevented him from saying anything.

'Brilliant. Bloody great.' The photographer was gone. Dee-Dee blew a bubble of pink gum from between her front tooth-caps.

'What?'

'The collection – shit-hot. Bubonic.'

Oliver nodded and stretched.

'Then she'll turn up.' He looked at The Cat's empty chair and smiled. Catarina Kirkova would know instinctively the right moment to arrive. She would wait until the press caught the whiff of warm plasma in the air. She would wait until another model had been plucked from the raw ranks of relative obscurity and primped up ready to take her place in the show. She would wait until the designer had rent his follicly-challenged scalp and swallowed his fifth Valium, and she would wait until the audience bubbled and blistered in the searing heat of the auditorium. Only then would she arrive. Oliver could feel it in his water.

Dee-Dee didn't mind the delay – it gave her time to light another joint. She offered it to Oliver but he waved it away.

'There is really no space in here – seriously no space, Dee-Dee. I can barely inhale as it is and my ribs feel as battered as a cod fillet. What is that you are wearing, by-the-bye?'

Dee-Dee examined the outfit she had just been thrust into with an overwhelmingly obvious lack of interest. Oliver thought she would go out on the catwalk stark buck naked if nobody bothered to dress her. She looked at the description on the label.

' "*Faux* plastic zippered lounger" is all it says,' she told him.

'*Faux plastic*? Are you sure?'

Dee-Dee nodded and blew more gum.

'Not *faux leather*?' he fingered the cloth, '*Leather* made to look like *plastic*? What for? To save the cow's feelings?'

'It's five-and-a-half thou whatever it's made from,' Dee-Dee told him.

The room was filled with green smoke and hysteria. Only the models were immobile, which made them easy to winkle out – like flies caught in the aspic glare of spotlights and camera-flash – Linda, Jani, Christine, Kate, Shenaz, Bindi and Robyn – they smoked, they read, they listened to Walkmans, they telephoned their beaux – if they farted a soundman would have broadcast it to the nation, only they didn't fart because they didn't eat – a row of prize queen bees, each surrounded by their own workers and drones.

One drone pulled at her model's hair while another painted her mouth and a worker hummed and sang as it rammed shoes on her elegant feet. Choreographers buzzed in their ears and all the time the camera crews filmed them, scorching their wings with their red-hot lights. They gave interviews half naked, they ate, they slept, they posed for *Elle* with their superstar lovers.

As Jani, the six-foot-four Czech with the cute smile and the big, upwardly-aimed tits, rose shimmering from her canvas chair the drones backed off a second to re-group before moving in for the kill. She shrugged them off long enough to throw on her first outfit – a cherry-red tart's frock with matching impossibly-stacked-heeled shoes. Vulgarity was the name of the game that season – designers were tripping over themselves to produce the tackiest look.

Jani's breasts had so far risen manfully to the occasion – heaving, thrusting and overflowing their way along all the major catwalks in Europe. Westwood had her, Ozbek wanted her and Laurent would throw a fit when they discovered she was doing Chanel. Rumour had it she was also screwing one of the Stones when spare time permitted.

'Where's mah personal trainer?'

A man-mountain in puce lycra rushed forward to administer to Jani's stress-knitted pecs.

They were all dressed now – all the queen bees teased and tarted into their finery. They pouted, they meditated, but mostly they gazed into mirrors, never tiring of the sublime sight of their own breathtaking beauty.

A horizontally-advantaged body in a thick film of sweat approached Oliver – a walkie-talkie babbling gibberish into its ear.

11

'I'm afraid you'll have to leave, sir, the show's about to start.'

He was marinated in Kouros – positively reeking of the stuff.

Oliver waved his pass ineffectually in the space between their heads.

'Sorry, sir. Press too. Everyone out of here apart from the gold cards.'

Oliver smiled – charming but deadly.

'The show cannot start yet. How can it? The star still has to arrive. I have been promised an interview with The Cat and I shall wait right here for her. No-one need know, apart from us chickens.' He gave a conspiratorial wink.

'The show's starting now,' the body argued. 'The audience won't wait any longer. This isn't Paris or Milan, you know. They won't hang about in London. They've been in there an hour already. They think we're all crap as it is.'

Oliver folded his arms.

'Oh, I believe you'll find they will wait, darling. They'll wait to see if The Cat turns up, just like they used to wait to see if Garland was pissed or if Monroe would fluff her lines. Just as they need to see if Lizzie Taylor's fat again or if poor Michael Jackson's face has started to melt. The public adores its drama queens, you know. They like being around when the serious fissures start to appear.'

But the body had a severely restricted attention span. His idea of a star was Arnie Schwartzenegger and there were no cracks in that man's armour, nowhere, no sir!

'Sheeza beetch, darlink, a great beeg beetch.' Jani towered over Oliver, smiling her pouty, little-girl smile. 'Even Kaiser Karl say he'll cancel her if she turn up late once again, Oliver, and heeza sweetie really, you know.'

A make-up artist stood on tiptoe to press a large black beauty spot next to her left nipple. Jani pretended to swat him away.

'I thought you two were chums, Jani!' Oliver asked.

'Chums?' She let out a throaty laugh, taking care not to damage her crimson lipstick. 'No-one is poor leetle Catarina's chum. She has no chums. She ees alone. Like Garbo: 'Ah vant to bee al-ooone' understand?'

Oliver smiled.

'Do you like my new arse, darling?' Jani asked. 'I 'ad it lifted a little. It cost three thousand dollars but it vas worth every last cent.'

Oliver allowed his gaze to fall below the waistline.

'Your arse has not been lifted, my dear,' he told her, 'it has been completely removed. Where have they resited it? Up between your shoulder blades? Do you walk with a hump now, like Quasimodo?'

'Where are the dogs? Where are the fucking dogs?' A panicking woman piled into them, knocking her headset askew but still screaming at someone via the lopsided mouthpiece.

'Look around you, darlink,' Jani told her. 'All I see in here is dogs!' She laughed her famous throaty-dirty laugh. 'Some of these models is so ugly it look like Cruft's on a bad day.'

The woman appeared not to have heard.

'Twenty poodles, dyed bright pink to match the dresses,' she shouted. 'They were here at eight. They can't have vanished! Julian? Julian! Speak to me, sweetie!'

Jani smiled at Oliver.

'Ah, the real pooches! They wee everywhere, darlink! Even on my shoes, look! A man take them away somewhere to drain their bowels.'

This time the woman heard her.

'But we need them for the first scene! Jesus Christ, Julian, where are they? You should never have let them out of your sight for one second!' The woman continued the assault on her mouthpiece.

A camera crew appeared and Jani was suddenly luminous in the arc-light. Always the character, always the card,

13

she pouted and bent to reveal more acres of white breast. Jani could ham it up happily for hours — as long as a camera was present.

Did models exist out of the sight of a camera? Oliver wondered. If a tree falls in a forest and no-one is there to hear it, does it still make a sound?

'Hey, Oliver!' Jani shouted as he ducked out of the glare, 'Why you don't interview me instead of that beetch? I fuck royalty, you know!'

Oliver sighed.

'Of course I know, darling,' he called back. 'The whole world knows. Only the royals themselves seem unaware of the fact.'

She grabbed him before he had got three yards across the room.

'Hey, Oliver.' Her voice was more serious now and her tone had dropped. 'You want the truth about Catarina Kirkova? You want to know how The Cat really ticks?'

Oliver looked up at her. Her fingers had left imprints of make-up on the sleeve of his cut-price Armani.

Jani bent until her delicious face was level with his ear. He could smell the piece of white spearmint gum she turned over and over in her mouth.

'The Cat is a sham, darlink, that is the truth. Everyzink about her is a lie,' she whispered.

Oliver looked her in the eye. The irises were a peculiar shade of citrus. He thought he saw the unmistakably faint ring of tinted contacts but she straightened again before he could be sure.

Jani was laughing now. Had she been serious before?

'Look!' she cried, waving an arm at a group of sobbing models, 'She make the poor drag queens cry wiz her lateness. Soon Roberto will have a heart attack for the damage she does to his collection and we will be carrying his corpse on stage for the finale. Sheeza bitch, Oliver. I 'ate her!'

The dogs returned and ran wild among the rails of frocks.

The lights dimmed in the auditorium and the sound system ran out of fill-in, producing a queer silence that made the ears hum. The atmosphere in the tent was stifling – already heavily polluted by Poison and Eternity, it sagged with frustration and suppressed anger.

Outside, the masses grew fractious. A fan ran amok clutching a hank of long dark hair in his fist like a sacred relic and claiming it was one of Naomi Campbell's extensions. Another man grabbed at it and a slap-fight broke out. Someone shouted that Madonna was arriving around the back but when the paparazzi stampeded round there they found it was Princess Michael instead.

The audience stood to ease their skinny buttocks from the torture of the hard gilt chairs and to see who was present apart from themselves. Fanning frantically with their programmes they rose like moles out of holes, peering blindly through their opaque shades to see who else shared their discomfort.

Mag hags and celebs in the front rows, buyers behind, ducking and diving like fighters to see between the gaps – and behind them who knew? Even the B-listers in the back tiers had stopped smiling – no longer so grateful to have been invited to such a snazzy event.

There were murmurs of revolt among the great unwashed and uninvited too – the freeloaders and gate-crashers that squatted in heaps along the aisles, all claiming to be design students who had somehow mislaid their free passes.

'I'm off,' said someone from *Homes and Gardens*, and it was at precisely that moment that the lights went out and the marquee was plunged into a pit of pitch darkness like the day of the dead. The first few notes of Wagner's *Tannhäuser* skittered overhead like a trapped moth. Once

15

mutinous arses slapped back down onto seats like wet kippers. Against all the odds the show had begun.

Catarina Kirkova sat crouched in the back seat of her fat limousine, watching and waiting. Through her dark tinted windows she had seen the crowds arrive at the marquee and the unholy scuffle to be the first through the entrance once the doors were pulled back. She had watched two young journalists being felled by photographers whose jobs depended on getting the right shots from the right place and she had seen the fashion editor of *Vogue* nearly knocked out once the fists had started to fly.

She waited while twenty pink poodles piddled over every available lamppost in the King's Road and all the while she was shaking so badly that she could barely stay in her seat. She thought she might be sick again and she tugged the window down to let in a little air.

Pulling two small white pills from an envelope in her purse, Catarina threw them into her mouth and swallowed them dry, closing her eyes until she could feel their effect.

She whispered to herself – something quiet in Russian that her chauffeur could not understand. Then the dogs were gone and the street was still. Suddenly the lights went out in the marquee. She had to go in now, she had no option. With a sigh, she pulled her thick coat about her shoulders and threw open the door of her car.

There was a movement backstage – a barely discernable change in mood – like the vacuum before an explosion when a bomb goes off – then a rushing and pushing, but all directional this time, not like the silently-swelling eddying panic of before.

'She's here! She's arrived!' Oliver caught the buzz – though in the crush he was unable to tell who had shouted.

16

He shark-smiled with the satisfaction of being the one who was right all along.

Swaddled in sand suedette and wet-look zebra, her head swathed in yards of cashmere and her face concealed by the largest of large dark glasses, Catarina Kirkova cut through the backstage crowds like a warm knife through soft butter. Taller than the rabble by at least a head, she appeared not to notice the scrum around her, or the noise that emerged from it.

When she reached her seat she threw off her coat and unwound the scarf from her hair. Underneath the coat she was naked, apart from a white G-string. When she bared her head she looked bald, although when she moved, the lights shone on the soft down of her ash-blonde crop.

Devoid of all make-up, the skin of her face was like a child's skin – pale, fine and bloomy, with a small spit of pink on either cheek. Her eyes were very much those of an adult, though. Large, slanted and long-lashed, they appeared to show every emotion. The high, Slavic cheekbones gave the face its famous nobility and the haughtiness was there, too, in the straight, narrow nose and the full, bloodless mouth.

Catarina Kirkova was unique. It was little wonder the designers were prepared to wait around for her.

As she eased herself into her canvas chair the make-up artist pushed a bottle of Evian into her hand and set about painting her face. A wig was pulled over her scalp and a dresser crawled belly-up under the table to stretch cherry-red stockings over her pale thin legs. Oliver spotted an empty chair beside her and almost did himself a nasty in his hurry to vault into it.

'Catarina?' Her extraordinary dark eyes flicked open chameleon-style. She took a second to focus on his face.

'Oliver – Oliver Zweinfeldt. I was promised an interview. Your agent . . .' He was mesmerized by her nose. Was it real?

'Mister Zweinfeldt?' Her voice was so quiet he had to

lean across to catch her words. Its tone was rather thin — she would need coaching if she were to do a Pfeiffer and go into movies. Her accent was delicate, though — not deliberately hammed-up, like Jani's. 'Yes, of course I remember the interview. I read the piece you did on Dylan for *Q* Magazine. I thought you would be younger, Mister Zweinfeldt. Most journalists are, these days.'

Oliver was twenty-eight. Now he felt nearer fifty. His father looked just like Ted Heath and so he dreaded the onset of old age. It was like a hereditary disease and he lived in horror of the appearance of the first symptoms.

The Cat's face barely moved as she spoke. She lifted the water to her mouth and sipped it through a straw. Her hands were steady now. The make-up artist completed one eyebrow — a perfect, jet-black arch — and danced around the back of her chair to start work on the other.

Oliver nodded, even though he never had and never would write for *Q*.

'We can do the interview now, Mister Zweinfeldt.'

Oliver's eyebrows arched as high as Catarina's newly-painted ones.

'Now? But the show is running late already. I thought perhaps after it's finished?'

Catarina yawned. 'They can wait. They can all wait. We will do the interview now, while I am in the mood to talk.'

Jani was right, Oliver thought, Catarina Kirkova is a prize bitch. He pulled his tape machine out of his pocket and, after a quick test, placed it on the table between them. Catarina's eyes darkened.

'No tapes,' she said, quietly.

Oliver sighed and shoved it back in his bag. He had a notebook and pencil somewhere. It was just as well he could still remember his shorthand. Sometimes it paid to be that little bit older.

There was a silence.

'Tell me about your childhood in Russia.'

Catarina glared.

'I thought everyone knew about that already.'

'I've read three versions. I hear there are more.'

'Perhaps there are, Mister Zweinfeldt. Which one would you like to hear this time?'

'I'd like to hear the truth, Catarina. And please call me Oliver.'

She sucked more water through the straw.

'Which of the three stories did you like the best, Oliver?'

He thought a while.

'The one in *Paris Match* was very entertaining, though I must say I read it with a sense of *déjà vu*. Were you always a fan of Monroe's, Catarina? Your upbringing and hers were awfully similar.'

Catarina smiled. 'You are too lazy to ever be a great journalist, Oliver. A good journalist should always check his facts before he accuses someone of telling lies.'

Her mouth was finished now – a perfect painted heart of squalid red. The make-up man held a tissue in front of her and she bit on it to blot the colour.

'Ask me some questions then, Oliver, I feel I should like to tell you everything.'

'How old are you?'

'– Except my age. You are impolite to ask it. I thought British men had more manners. But then your name is not really British, is it, Oliver? Zweinfeldt. What is that, German or Austrian? Or did you just make it up?'

'Was your father in the KGB?'

Catarina laughed aloud.

'Have you had plastic surgery?'

More laughter.

'Why do you refuse to travel back to Russia?'

Her laughter stopped at once. Her eyes became chips of black ice.

'That's ridiculous.'

She rose sharply before him – a thin, half-naked woman in scarlet stockings and stacked shoes – her stone eyes almost obscured beneath the ridiculous false lashes and her

19

blonde hair totally covered by a three-feet-high red wig.

'Your agent turns down every offer that is put to you,' Oliver persisted, 'Italian *Vogue* offered anything to fly you back for a winter shoot. Your agent said you were busy but you had nothing that couldn't be cancelled. Then Moschino wanted you out there in '92. American *Vogue* wanted shots of you with your parents, in their old hunting lodge, for their society pages. The Japanese asked you to film that car ad. In '93 . . .'

Catarina pushed past Oliver roughly, sending the contents of a box of loose powder spewing over him. He bent quickly to minimize the damage, patting the marks on his trousers and tutting at the mess. By the time he looked up again, Catarina was gone and he was surrounded by three Kouros-scented goons instead.

Oliver smiled and shrugged. 'Don't accuse me of not checking my facts, madame,' he said, snapping his notebook shut.

Catarina Kirkova was first out on stage. She was there when the spotlight flicked on in a great white pool that was big enough to drown in. The audience shielded their eyes from the sudden light. Some thought she had been there all the time, standing there in the pitch darkness, watching them wait.

There was no music now, just silence. The strong light made the darkness more profound. Then it snapped off again, the strobes came on and the loud high whine of Hendrix's guitar screamed like a gull from the vast bank of speakers, grabbing the audience like a hand to the larynx and shaking them until their teeth rattled in their skulls.

Catarina had vanished – the audience blinked with shock, then they found her, already half-way down the catwalk, and they roared with admiration at her bare-faced cheek.

They had waited so long for her they could all call themselves fools if she was not worth the wait. They were forced
to erupt, to make her a star if for no other reason than to
qualify their own status. There were other reasons for their
excitement, though. The Cat was good. She had star
quality. She was something special on the ramp.

She watched them all scrambling below her. They were
old and ugly and small and squalid and demented. What
were they fighting for? Why had they waited? She would
never understand her audiences' motives. Photographers
called her by name and then laughed when she ignored
them. She saw women in their fifties dressed like skeletal
children, their faces apparently stuck on like masks. Their
skirts were so short their dignity was pared to the bone
and they owned so many outfits they would never live to
wear half the amount. Yet still they searched for more.
Women of that age in her country were fat and grey and
wore long black frocks.

How many outfits had her grandmother owned? She
never knew – they had all looked alike. Maybe one, maybe
a hundred. She had made them herself, too – from the same
cloth in the same style. Why did fashion mean nothing to
her grandmother when it was the very essence of life to
these old women?

She reached the end of the catwalk and stood quite still,
closing her eyes and basking in the spotlight as though it
were the Mediterranean sun. Her lids looked red from the
inside and she could see the tiny veins that pulsed there.
She opened her eyes again and a thousand flashlights
exploded in her face. She didn't wince or blink. That was
a trick she had learned early on.

'Catarina! Hey! Cat!' They still called to her but she
would not smile. She would never get used to that name.
It was not her name. It was the name of the monster that
she had become. How had she been, all those years before,
before the trouble started? A small girl with a face as white
and round and bare as an egg was conjured up in her

21

memory and her eyes filled instantly with tears, for the child was as good as dead.

Klara and Luisa Kuznetsova. She saw two young girls standing in the Moscow snow, hand-knitted mittens on their small hands and a bunch of bright red ribbons in their hair. She smelt the hot green tea and breakfast dumplings their father made. She saw the spires of the Kremlin and the birds that flew about their ruby stars.

'Catarina!' They called her back from the past and she looked about her, at her present. Why was she here? They scared her – they all scared her. She felt stretched out and skinned before them, like an animal prepared for dissection. Then she remembered why she could not leave – why she could never run away. It was her sins that kept her there – that kept her from her country. She hated them all.

'Bastards!' she whispered at them, and the audience screamed out for more.

2

The small Soho winebar had gone seriously downhill. A favourite haunt of local blaggers and young, snot-chapped villains in the Sixties, it had lain sadly fallow during the Seventies, becoming the nicotine-stained watering hole of an assortment of old farts – several of whom had literary pretensions and all of whom were intent on pickling their kidneys in copious amounts of Gilbey's or Bell's.

In the Eighties the magic had happened. The place was bought up and transformed. Chrome and cast-iron replaced mock-timbered beams and coal-effect gas fires and gin-and-its and pork scratchings gave way to tequila slammers and corn chips. You couldn't move for the crush of Gaultier rubberwear and you couldn't breathe for the smell of Giorgio and Gitanes.

Rick Palimo had liked the place then. He hated it now. It was a mongrel of a hole now – neither fish nor fowl. It was a bomb that had done it – just a small incendiary in the men's loo – courtesy of the IRA. Nothing crucial, but enough to scare off the punters. You didn't want to go out for the night all togged up and come back minus a leg.

The recession hadn't helped, of course. They couldn't afford the Bollinger now or, at least, they couldn't afford to be seen to afford it. When Rick breathed in now he smelt Old Spice and Fisherman's Friends. The old farts had returned with a vengeance to reclaim their birthright. They stared at Rick queasily and he scowled back.

Still only in his early twenties – handsome in a swarthy sort of way, Rick's attire was nevertheless yuppie circa 1986: pure wool DB Next suit, white button-down shirt,

Oxford brogues, waxed raincoat. And hair gel, loads of hair gel. Of course, the leather-bound Filofax next to his pint. And the mobile phone. Fashion didn't matter one whit to Rick – it was the overall effect that counted and this look worked for him every time.

It made the old farts twitchy. It reminded them of the years of suffering under enemy occupation. There was James Last on the jukebox now and an empty magnum of scotch, filled with coins, on the bar. The horse-brasses would be back next, round the flame-effect fire. The old 'uns wouldn't budge an inch now, not once that Plough-man's was back on the menu and all the bloody tapas had gone.

Shrivelled, bleary-eyed and white as the underbelly of a snake, they dyed their hair the colour of Worcester sauce and dressed like Jeffrey Bernard out of Dunn & Co.

Rick Palimo upset what little equilibrium they had. He wanted out of this dump just as badly as they wanted to be rid of him.

He looked at his watch. Oliver was late. Shit. He flipped his beermat with his thumbnail and it landed quizside up.

'Name three British inland waterways beginning with the letter "R".' Depressing, that. He slipped the Mont Blanc out of the spine of his Filofax then quickly replaced it again. He wasn't that bored yet – he still had over half of his warm pint to go.

The 'barperson' smiled at him. She had dyed rat-black hair and a hint of a bleached-out moustache. She was young, though, the only moist-looking thing in the place. Rick thought about checking her out. She looked the talkative sort. Perhaps some names still came in from time to time – by mistake, as it were. There might be something he could use. Oliver would no doubt be a waste of time and airspace and he needed to earn his dinner-money somehow.

'Rick?' Speak of the devil and there she was.

'Oliver Zweinfeldt, as I live and breathe.'

'Breathe, Rick? You? Aren't you taking this human-cloning thing a bit far? You'll be telling me you'd bleed if I cut you next. Ha ha.' Oliver laughed a weak skinny laugh and fell into the seat opposite via a small gap down the side of the fruit machine. Rick yawned in the direction of his fake Rolex, just to rattle him a little.

'Drink?'

'G and T – Slimline, please, no ice.'

The barmaid had ceased smiling now. She had clocked Oliver and obviously assumed the two men were an item.

Oliver was messing about with some papers by the time Rick got the drinks back to the table. He had a sudden, sinking feeling that the lunch might last hours. He studied his watch again, for effect.

'Look, Ollie, this will have to be snappy-*tout-suite*, I'm afraid. I've got another meeting coming up and some urgent copy to get done. The deadline was yesterday – you know what it's like.'

Oliver licked his lips in a way that made Rick feel faintly freaky, and leant across the table. Rick stretched back as far as his stool would allow, refusing to play ball.

'I'll come straight to the point, Rick.' Oliver's breath smelt of catmeat. Perhaps he had had lunch already. 'It's an idea for a story – what I think you would call an exposé. Something I stumbled upon last week. Just as sniff, you know, but I'm not often wrong.'

'Who?' Rick's stories had come from stranger sources – Hairdressers, toilet attendants, hard-up medical staff. Not many from other journalists, though. Not that he could remember, anyway. Close to the chest was usually their motto, which was why he had guessed he was wasting his time the minute Oliver phoned to arrange the meeting. Oliver was famous in Wonderful Wapping for his arse-licking stories on the royals. Rick doubted he was looking at the next Deep Throat.

Rick was famous in Wapping too, but for an entirely different reason. Oliver was sharing a drink with the Man With No Scruples. Rick Palimo had taken the job of gutter journalism and had single-handedly elevated it into an art form. Rumour had it there was nothing he would not do and no-one he would not shag in his eternal quest for the million-dollar story.

Whether the rumours were true or not was another matter — no-one had yet done an exposé on the king of the genre himself. Rick liked to see himself as a moralist — which was why he didn't smoke.

Oliver looked like a man who was about to sell his own mother for a shilling.

'I was interviewing someone last week — someone famous,' he added, noticing Rick's eyes beginning to glaze. '— And I noticed they became, well, rather twitchy when I mentioned certain aspects of their childhood.'

'So?'

'So?'

'Is that all?'

Oliver blushed.

'Yes, I suppose it is.' He leant forward again. 'She shut up, Rick. She shut up like a clam. It was very odd. They faxed me a typed account of her childhood the following day. It's the usual well-known story but somehow I don't think it's the truth. I believe she's hiding something.'

'She?'

Oliver licked his lips again. A nerve in his eyelid started to twitch. Jesus, how he hated asking this slimeball for help. He knew he had no option, though — Rick was king rat of the very slimy gutter and Oliver just didn't have the stomach for sloshing around in the mire. He had a reputation of sorts, too. If he was found dirtying his lily-white hands in this way he would lose all hope of a job on *Hello!* Better to do some sort of deal with Rick Palimo and get a quiet cut of the profits than to shelve the idea altogether and watch some other lucky sod fall over it.

'As you know, Rick, this type of exposé is not really my thing,' he said, 'I am happy to hand the details over, but we shall have to come to some sort of financial arrangement first. Shall we say fifty-fifty if I am right and the story is published?'

Rick shook his head slowly.

'Sixty-forty?'

Rick stood up to leave. 'I've got a meeting to go to, Oliver. You're farting me about.'

Oliver pulled him back. 'What then?'

Rick shrugged. 'Depends who it is. Depends what you know.'

'It's Catarina Kirkova.' Oliver's eyes glittered.

Rick looked unimpressed. 'The Cat?' he asked. 'A fashion model? Are you pulling my plonker, Ollie? What could I do with that? You'll be feeding me Page Three girls next!'

Oliver threw some papers across the table.

'Read these,' he said, 'This is the official version, the stuff her publicity office sent me. Then there's the other stuff – the stuff I've researched so far. I made a couple of phone calls. They're all recorded there. No-one could trace her so-called aristocratic connections.'

Rick laughed. 'They're Russian, Ollie, they're not the House of Windsor, you know! They're all over the bloody place out there! They've got white Russians coming out of the bleeding woodwork these days!'

Oliver narrowed his eyes.

'She's a model, Ollie, not an MP. They all lie about their backgrounds, it's good PR – it makes good copy.'

Oliver looked him straight in the eye.

'She's hiding something important, Rick. I'm sure of it.'

'Bullshit! You're pulling my bloody leg.'

While Oliver sloped off to the lavatory Rick pulled a small camera out of his pocket and photographed each page of Oliver's research, just in case. By the time Oliver got back the papers had been replaced and Rick was flipping his beermat again, looking suitably bored.

'Sorry to have wasted your time,' Oliver said huffily as he buttoned his coat.

27

'*Pas de problème*.' Rick was smiling again now. 'Call me any time you've got an idea. Doesn't cost anything to listen, you know that. Maybe another time, you never know.' He swilled down his pint and winced at the bitter taste.

3

The room was vast, hollow and ninety-five-percent empty – an account executive's dream and an agoraphobic's nightmare. What little light there was came from a chrome-plated quartz spotlight and the warm flickering glow of a bank of Sanyo computer screens. It was the room Rick Palimo worked in. It was also his home.

Verdi's Requiem bounced off the four walls like a trapped bird in a cage. It banged around the painted iron pillars, rattled against the picture windows and skidded its claws down the gleaming pine of the bare varnished floorboards. Rick reached for the headphones but thought better of it and stuffed them back in the drawer. Sod the neighbours. It was three-o-five in the morning. He turned the volume up a little higher.

Rick liked to work at night – he liked the feel and smell of the darkness. Behind him the sky was a shade of bruised black, while below him the lights from the barges glided along the Thames in sparkling clusters.

Catarina Kirkova. The name gleamed alone on his terminal screen, suffusing his face with a dull, eerie light. Flexing his fingers like a concert pianist he bent over his keyboard and prepared to start work.

Oliver had come up with very little in his profile that wasn't already common knowledge, although the story had made good reading. He had tapped into the files of a couple of tabloids and come up with the same tale, regurgitated many times over.

The Cat was a very private person – something of an enigma in a business where the innermost secrets of one's soul are usually laid as bare as one's breasts. No boy-friends, no nightlife, no spreads in *Hello!* No shots, apart from for work. He had had a selection faxed through and studied them closely, Blu-tacking them onto a wall. He didn't like women with short hair, yet he found himself drawn back to the wall of photographs many times that night, listening to the music and studying her face.

He ran a finger down the length of her body and a pulse began to beat somewhere down in the dank depths of his groin. Strange, that. Worrying – deeply worrying.

Her eyes went well with Verdi. *Appassionata* – the eyes of the Madonna – caring, sympathetic, sacred and some-how scared. The woman all men longed for – mother, lover and little lost child. Yet she was known to be a prize bitch. That was why Rick hated models, they were an act, a depressing facade – good at depiction and duplication alone – the photocopiers of the emotions, spewing out shot after shot.

Oliver said she was lying. About what then? Her age? So what? Her face? 'No plastic surgery,' was the story. Rick pulled on a pair of wire-framed glasses and peered more closely. Then he picked up his portable phone.

'Bernie?' Bernard D'Arcy-Green. Philanderer, paedo-phile and eminent Harley Street consultant. Always good for a tale or two and often at bargain basement prices, on account of his little predilections. He took more than a decade to answer the phone.

'Richard? Christ, man, it's five o'clock in the morning!'

'I need a favour, Bernie.'

There was silence, then a sigh and the sounds of move-ment at the other end.

'Just a minute.'

Rick waited. He could hear Bernie padding across the floor of his flat, then the sounds of running water.

'Go ahead, Rick. What is it?'

'What's that noise, Bernie? It sounds like you're taking

a pee. You're not talking to me from the toilet, are you?'
There was a lot to be said for portables, but they had their
downside, too.

'What do you expect when you awaken a man of my
advanced years from his slumber, Rick? Only the young
have bladders like tyre rubber. At my age the call of nature
demands to be treated with considerable respect and
urgency.'

Rick closed his eyes.

'Look, Bernie, I need to know if someone's had plastic
surgery done on their face. I've got a few photos and I'm
going to fax them across. Can you tell from a fax? This
machine's state of the art. The quality's not bad.'

Another drawn-out sigh. 'Who is it, Richard? Ronnie
Biggs?'

'A model, Bernie, a common-or-Covent-Garden fashion
model.'

Another pause. 'Naked?'

Rick flicked furiously through the shots.

'She doesn't appear to do nudies, Bernie. There's something in some sort of pyjamas, though. That'll have to do
you for now.'

It was ten minutes exactly before the fax began to chatter
into life again. Rick held the page to the spotlight and read
it quickly. First he whistled and then he laughed.

The Cat was a phoney. According to Doctor D'Arcy-
Green she *had* been surgically enhanced – at least her nose
had, anyway.

Bernie was the business, alright. Not only had he detailed
the work that had been done in full medical jargon, he had
also had a stab at exactly who had done it – some shit-hot
butcher from Colorado, evidently. The truly great plastic
surgeons were like artists, apparently – they could
recognize one another's handiwork just as surely as if it
had a signature in one corner. Rick picked up the phone
again.

'Thanks, Bernie. I owe you.'

31

'No trouble, old chap. By the way, I take it you had no interest in the other stuff?'

'What other stuff?'

'The rest of her delicious body. You only asked about surgery to the face.'

A prickle went up Rick's spine.

'You mean she's had her boobs done? That sort of thing?'

The doctor coughed, an old man's morning cough; loud and gut-wrenching. Rick held the phone away from his ear.

'No, old chap,' he said when he had finished. 'Not enhancement exactly. Your beauty – and a beauty she certainly is – has had some problems in her time. Scar tissue. Quite extensive, I should say. Well concealed though, from the looks of it. You'd never know now, unless you were of the profession, of course.'

'Scar tissue? What sort of scars?'

'The bad sort, old boy. The sort that hurt. On the arms and the legs and a couple more on the abdomen.'

'Caused by an operation or some accident?'

'That I can't tell you.'

Rick ran a hand through his hair.

'You can tell all this from a fax?'

The doctor sounded smug. 'No, old boy, I can tell all this from the flesh. The lady is a patient of mine – or was once, anyway. I saw the handiwork for myself.'

Now it was Rick's turn to sigh.

'Why didn't you tell me, Bernie?'

'You didn't ask.'

'Anything else I might have forgotten to ask about?'

The doctor laughed.

'Nothing special comes to mind, I'm afraid. It was the quickest consultation on record. Some magazine editor brought her in to look at a small rash she had developed as a result of the make-up they had used. I merely gave her a quick once-over and some antihistamine and sent

32

her on her way. Extraordinary-looking young woman, I remember, though. Something about her — barely caught by these snaps, I must say. Sort of thing you used to see once in the old stars, like Garbo. A sort of larger-than-life presence, I suppose you could call it. I take it you'll be meeting her before long?'

'Dunno.' Rick was impatient to be off and doing.

The doctor laughed. 'Dare say you'll end up screwing her as usual, lucky sod!' He coughed. 'Must be a curse, being so handsome. Do they still fall for the charm? Lucky bastard! Must want their stupid little heads examining! Us mature types have far more to offer.'

But Rick had already hung up. He was going off Bernard D'Arcy-Green in a big way. He hated to see old men behave like idiots, it spoke badly for the entire sex. Perhaps he would dig out that file he had on him, after all. The old bugger deserved it, he got more disgusting by the day. If Rick didn't do for him some other eager young hack would, sooner or later, and Rick hated to be beaten to the draw.

He took a magnifying glass from his desk and inspected Catarina's legs more closely. No signs of the scars that Bernie had mentioned. Still, the good doctor knew his job, if nothing else, and he rarely told lies, except under oath.

So The Cat was a liar. So what? They all were, all models. That meant she had lied about her age, too. What about her background? Rick smoothed out the papers he had photocopied. The story was there:

Catarina Kirkova. Born in Russia, near Moscow, the only daughter of Russian aristocrats. Her mother died when she was a child and she was brought up by her loving father in their exquisite country house.

Sent to Europe to improve her English, she was spotted by an American photographer and the rest is history. She was flown to America, where she was introduced to her agent and friend, Beth Parker. Beth saw her potential immediately and got her her first booking, for Italian *Vogue*. Since then she . . .

There was a lot more – pages of the stuff, but nothing to interest Rick. He flicked through them once more, though, and through all the other stuff he had filched from the files. Certain words kept reappearing, annoying him: 'Haughty,' 'Aristocratic,' 'Aloof,' 'Private,' 'Regal,' 'Charismatic' . . . did all journalists have to be so bloody boringly brain-numbingly predictable?

Then there were the 'other versions' that Oliver had been so eager to show him – an interview in some American rag, quoting her as an orphan – some quotes from her earlier days, when she was just making it, saying she had lived in the wilds outside Odessa – and yet another implying she came from a large family and that her mother was very much alive.

So what? Journalists got their stories from funny sources and what they couldn't research they often made up. If Catarina was so wary of giving interviews then perhaps they had got this junk by word of mouth and, as Rick knew only too well, people will tell you all sorts of bullshit just to get their names into print.

So what, so what, so what? The two words kept repeating in his head. Why was he sitting there until the sun came up, scratching his arse over some story that probably didn't even exist? Because Oliver had a hunch? Since when had he listened to the likes of Oliver Zweinfeldt? The likes of Oliver Zweinfeldt wouldn't know a good story if it jumped out and bit them on the bum. Why her, then? Why Catarina Kirkova? Stuck-up bitch, she was playing the press for all she could get with this private persona thing she had created. Even Oliver had to know it was the oldest game in the book, though still guaranteed to get the press sniffing round like dogs on heat. 'Leave me alone.' – the greatest request for publicity anyone could make. He was damned if he'd fall for it like all the other suckers. But then . . .

Rick looked at Catarina's photos once more. Scar tissue. The arms, legs and abdomen. The prickle ran down his spine again. An accident? A car crash? Falling off a swing as a child? He picked up the phone.

'Bernie? How old were the scars?'

Only a couple of years. Interesting.

He could just look back through the files to see if there was any record of an accident. It wouldn't take too long and there was no point going to bed now the sun was up. And, after all, what harm could it do? A beautiful woman. Scars. Violence. Secrets. The combination was irresistible. It smelt of money. Positively stank, in fact. The sweetest smell in the whole world.

Rick turned the air conditioning to ice-box to keep his face awake, threw on an extra jumper and got down to work.

4

Catarina woke, shivering, in the middle of the night. Her hands reached out to snatch at the comfort of empty air above her head – she had a recurring dread of being buried alive. She had no idea where she was or what she was supposed to be doing. She rolled into the foetal position, her head curled into her hands. Her head ached. She remembered one thing; a phone number. She felt for the phone by the bedside. It was a long time before anyone answered.

'I had that dream again.'

'Catarina?'

'Where am I?'

'I'm your analyst, Catarina, not your booker.'

'I don't know where I am!' – Her mouth felt funny, she was having to chew at her words to get them out.

There was a pause the other end. She listened to the static of long-distance. She heard some papers flicking. She heard him put his hand over the receiver so that he could sigh in secrecy.

'Milan. Your list says Milan. You flew there straight after Paris. From there you go on to London and then you're back in New York. You're safe in the arms of a five-star right now, baby, so go back to sleep. Do you want me to wait?'

Catarina said nothing, just replaced the handset. She had dreamed of the woman, hanging from the tree. It was minus twelve degrees in the dream and the snow stretched on for many kilometres, yet the woman wore a thin cotton dress – her best dress – and her feet were bare and blue.

Her boots stood where they had been placed, side-by-side behind the trunk of the tree. The woman had been too vain to wear them, even to hang herself.

The tree was a popular one for suicides – it was easy to climb and had a branch at the right height. The woman had torn her stockings on the bark, though. She must have been distraught because stockings were hard to come by. She must have saved for them, for the occasion. She would have been sad, of course, when she died, but she must have been mad about the stockings, too.

Catarina fingered the invisible scar that ran from her eye to her nostril. She reached for a switch by her headboard and when she pressed it a dim light came on in the room – the sort of light that ageing executives use to fuck their mistresses by – and she could see where she was at last.

She had two performances that day – one in three hours' time. The thought made her sick again. Perhaps she wouldn't show this time. Perhaps she would allow herself one day off.

Her purse lay on the bedside table. She opened it and pulled out a Polaroid. It was well-fingered and the edges were curling. It showed the face of a young girl, her eyes wide with fear and her mouth stretched even wider. She looked stupid, thick and funny but she wasn't laughing – she couldn't, because she had a man's penis stuffed half-way down her throat.

'Sonofabitch,' Catarina whispered. She lay back onto her pillows, still staring at the photo, and a tear slid the easy way, from her eye to her ear.

She touched a finger to the girl's face. Red lipstick from her mouth formed a smudged ring around the penis. Like a child sucking seaside rock. Like some dumb Russian kid being forced to give a blow job to a guy who had talc caked between his balls. He had smelt of Cuticura. She had never been able to stomach the smell since.

'Poor crazy little cow.' But it would never happen again. Not while she had the photo to remind her.

Catarina looked at the clock. Two hours forty minutes. She would have bags under her eyes again tomorrow. But she would do the show. She was OK. She had no choice.

5

The girl felt the toe pushing at the gusset of her pants. What should she do? Close her legs? Part them? The toe was inside now, pressing on her privates. Was this what people did for fun? Were they all doing it beneath the table? All of them? Did you eat at the same time? Or should you put down your spoon and smile? She liked the soup. It seemed a pity to let it go cold. There was cream in it too, piped into feathers on the top. She was eating around the cream feathers, leaving the best till last. She would tell her mum about it when she got home. She smiled because she had been taught to smile and because it was polite.

The toe was touching bits of her she had never touched herself. So what? She was fifteen, she had a lot to learn. Was it supposed to feel this uncomfortable, though? Perhaps if she moved a bit it might not feel so rough. The others were talking, something about scripts and treatments. The man talked too, you would never even know the toe was his. Perhaps it wasn't. Perhaps it belonged to itself. Had he arrived without socks on? Or had he slipped them off under the tablecloth? Were his feet clean? And where had he left his shoes?

The bill appeared and the toe vanished. They all stood up and the girl felt funny because her knickers were on crooked now. If no-one had been looking she would have fished them straight with her finger but people were smiling at her and saying goodbye.

Did she go home now? Her mum had told her to get a cab, her dad would pay. But no-one had mentioned the film part again, there was nothing cut and dried. Then the man said he had the script up in his room and she almost cried with relief because he hadn't forgotten her after all.

In the lift he suddenly leant forward and pressed his tongue into her ear.

'Lucy,' he whispered. 'Little Lucy. Juicy Lucy.' It was all so strange. He was so important. Why was he bothering with her? Were her ears clean enough or were they waxy? She blushed deep red, suddenly ashamed.

His room was OK – special really, twin beds with matching covers. And a fridge. She stood there like a lump in the middle of the carpet and he told her to close her eyes and when she opened them again he was standing there naked. It was strange, he had thrown his clothes onto the floor. He had looked so smart before, she would have thought he would fold them.

Was he supposed to look sexy? There was so much hair. She had never seen a man naked before, only boys. She found herself staring at his balls. They were hairy too. She felt rude, looking there, but she couldn't look him straight in the eye.

'I'm going to bed.' His penis bounced on his balls as he walked across the room. He was bored with her, then. What was the polite thing to do? She had obviously overstayed her welcome. You didn't stay when people were sleeping. She felt clumsy and foolish. What if he turned off the light? She could end up standing there all night. She felt such a child.

'Are you going to stand there forever?'

She wanted to cry. What was she supposed to do? It would look rude just to walk out and he hadn't shown her the script. They would all ask when she got home, they would all be expecting something. She had been so excited when she left. This seemed like a let-down.

'You can sit here beside me, if you like.'

She almost laughed with relief at being offered an alternative. He had patted the twin bed opposite, too, not

40

his own. Perhaps he was lonely. Perhaps he was scared of the dark.

The girl sat down, pulling her lycra skirt down as low as it would go. Not because she didn't trust him, but because she didn't want to look fast. He might have thought she was trying to seduce him, or something.

'Little Lucy.' His voice sounded drowsy, like a child's. His hand reached for hers and he closed his eyes. It was quite nice, like that. She didn't feel so awkward any more, just a bit odd, holding hands with a sleepy adult. She looked at his face. Was he handsome? She was too young to tell. He looked old, very old. As old as her dad, perhaps. How many girls at her school had been taken out by an older man, she wondered? And offered a film role? She was desperate to appear adult, too.

The man groaned.

'You're making me ill, Lucy – d'you know that?'

He spoke American, like the actors on the telly. The room was so dark. Her eyes became wide and round with wonder.

'Do you want to know what you're doing to me, sitting there like that?'

She hardly dared breathe. What was she doing to him? He was making her feel guilty. He pulled at her hand and pressed it onto his face, near the eyes. There were tears there, real tears. How had she made him cry?

'It's your beauty, little Lucy, little child. It makes me weep to have you so near.'

The girl had always believed in her own beauty – had always known of its power. This objective view made her melt down inside. It was true, then. She was special, unique. Her beauty made her so – her special beauty.

'What will you do with me?'

The man was asking her. She had felt so stupid and childlike yet all the time she had this power over a grown man. She had upset him. She must make amends.

She leant forward and kissed his cheeks, where the tears

41

had been. He smelt of Pernod and expensive cigars. He groaned as she kissed him and she melted some more, like butter in the sun.

'Tell me please, Lucy. I can't stand it any longer. What will you do to me? You're killing me, my darling child.'

'Anything,' she whispered, and so her fate was sealed.

Catarina Kirkova leant back in her seat and braced herself for the flight. She hated flying – she felt trapped and claustrophobic inside a plane, however large it was. This one seated two hundred, yet she still felt the urge to get out before take-off.

She looked like a boy, dressed in grey Oxford bags and a plain white cotton shirt. Her pale face was clear of any make-up and her eyes looked swollen and tired.

The stewardess had seen phobics a million times before. She had finished catering to all the wealthiest-looking men on the flight and now had time to notice the women. She smiled her extra wide sympathy smile and touched Catarina on the arm. As she had been taught to. As the flight manual told her to.

'May I get you anything, miss? We have a tape of relaxation techniques we can play through your headphones if you're feeling nervous.' The smile again, head cocked with concern.

'You may fuck off.'

The stewardess recoiled.

'If you're sure.'

'I am very sure, thank you. Never surer of anything in my life.' Catarina needed to be alone with her fear. She had long since stopped caring what others thought of her manners.

Sometimes they sent what the staff called stooges on these flights – in-house customer-care supervisors in a plain wrapper, just to test you out, to see if you were doing your job. They were always difficult and abusive, just to test

42

your reactions. The stewardess was as steady as a rock, just in case.

'Very well, Miss. Call me if you want anything.' The smile never wavered.

Catarina always booked two seats side by side on a flight to make sure she sat by herself. The spare seat was piled high with magazines and newspapers. Sometimes she read them, sometimes she didn't. It was difficult to concentrate when you thought you might be about to die. There were a thousand ways to end your life and crashing into a mountain had to be one of the least attractive alternatives. All the same, she was glad to be leaving London. Too many memories – too much chasing her tail. She shuddered and closed her eyes.

'Excuse me, is this seat taken?'

'What do you think?' She pointed to the clutter beside her.

The man did not appear to have moved – she could still hear him breathing. Catarina opened her eyes reluctantly. He was still there, smiling politely. He was very handsome and quite young.

'Look, would you mind very much? Just for a moment? Only the plane's about to take off and the seatbelt lights are on and I appear to have got myself lost. That snooty cow of a stewardess has vanished to god-knows where and I really hate flying.'

He smiled. His teeth were white against his dark skin. Catarina pushed her books onto the floor and he sat down gratefully, buckling his seatbelt and resting his head back and closing his eyes.

'It's the take-off I hate the most,' he told her. 'It reminds me of starting the car first thing in the morning and that never bloody goes. Still, what is there to be scared of? What's the worst scenario we're looking at here?'

Catarina leant her head back.

43

'The engines could fail and we could crash straight into the sea and our bits be scattered to the four winds,' she said.

He shrugged. 'Like I said, what is there to be scared of?'

'Do you get sick?'

'Never. It's matter of honour.' His eyes were still closed. Catarina found herself studying his face. He had good, clean-looking skin. His dark hair was combed straight back off his forehead and ran to small black curls along the line of his collar. He was strangely dressed for his age. Too smart – too conventional. He opened his eyes suddenly and caught her staring. His eyes were bright blue – the same colour the sea is in holiday brochures after they've airbrushed out all the mud and effluent.

'Do *you*?' he asked.

'Do I what?'

'Get sick.'

She shook her head.

'Good.'

He closed his eyes again. 'Good – for you, I mean.' He added, 'I wouldn't mind.'

'I believe we are airborne now,' she told him. 'The smoking lights are on.'

He stood quickly, politely.

'Thank you. Thank you very much. Have a good flight.'

Catarina closed her eyes without comment.

Rick Palimo returned to his seat in Club class with a satisfied smile on his face. So that was The Cat. And she had even spoken to him. He could, of course, have talked his way into that seat for the entire flight, but he had chosen not to.

Rick was a professional hunter – he preferred to watch his prey from a distance, and that was exactly what he did for the rest of the flight. He had chosen his aisle seat with care – it gave him the perfect vantage point.

Catarina obviously intended to sleep her way across the Atlantic. She spent a few minutes flicking through what looked like her schedules for the next week's work before switching off her light and pushing her seat to full recline. Rick enjoyed watching her sleep. She curled into a ball like a child and slept deeply and profoundly until the stewardess woke her, exactly an hour before they were due to land. He watched her stretch and look at her watch. Then she pulled a few of her newspapers onto her lap and started to study them. He saw a copy of the London *Times* and a tabloid he had once written for.

Catarina flicked through *The Times* and was about to do the same with the tabloid when a story seemed to catch her eye. She studied it furiously, shaking her head in apparent disbelief. Her hand went to her throat and she looked to be in a panic. Then she lay back in her seat, her hands covering her face.

Once the plane had landed at JFK, she pushed past other passengers in her desperation to get out. Rick noticed she had left the newspapers behind with the other magazines and picked them up as he walked down the aisle. Once he was through customs he bought a decaff double espresso in the airport lounge and settled down to skim through them. He didn't have to look very far. The tabloid was still open at the offending page.

MISSING CONVENT GIRL
FOUND WANDERING IN STREET
AFTER SEX ATTACK

He read on:

> The police hunt for convent-educated Essex school-girl Lucy Anne Hall was called off yesterday after she was spotted wandering through the streets of the West End, twenty-four hours after her parents had reported her missing. A passer-by said her clothes

45

were torn and she appeared to be in some distress.

Fifteen-year-old Lucy is currently being interviewed by the police but a spokesman said she had so far given few clues to the identity of her attacker. The extent of her injuries is still unknown, though a member of the public who came to her assistance said she had lacerations to her arms and legs and what appeared to be cigar burns on her abdomen and back.

A taxi-driver who was earlier said to be helping police with their enquiries has since been released without charge.

Was this it? Was this what had upset her so much on the plane? Rick's eyes skimmed the rest of the page but he saw nothing else there that would have had such an effect. Did she know this girl? Was she a relative – was that what had made her so upset? Yet how could a Russian like Catarina who spent most of her time in the US have close bonds with a kid from Essex?

'Lacerations to her arms and legs.' '. . . what appeared to be cigar burns on her abdomen and back.' Rick suddenly felt cold, despite the temperature of the coffee lounge. He rubbed his own arms in sympathy. According to the good doctor, those were the places where Catarina had had her own plastic surgery. Was that what it was? Some kind of shared sympathy? Forget the theory of an accident then.

Rick thought of Catarina's smile and of her haunted eyes. He was hooked now – he knew that. He would see this story through to the end, even if it evaporated into fine mist somewhere along the way. He could read a person's soul from their eyes. Catarina Kirkova had something to hide, he was sure of that.

6

Beth Parker had never seen her star model looking so ragged. Catarina's face was pale and bleary and there were slate-grey shadows underneath her eyes. She was still beautiful of course — in fact more so, if you liked fragile-looking women. Beth didn't. Beth liked her girls to be strong and sassy — the American dream come to life. She was prepared to make an exception with Catarina, though. In the last quarter Catarina had earned more than the rest of her other girls put together. For that sort of money she could be as ethereal as she damn-well liked.

'How was Londinium?'

Catarina shrugged, threw off her heavy coat and settled into the nearest chair. Other, newer models peeked at her through the door. Beth wished they wouldn't stare. It was like some fan club, for chrissakes.

'Cold.' The answer only came after a long pause. Still, at least she was speaking.

'You must have felt at home, then.'

'Perhaps.'

Sometimes Beth wondered exactly what type of monster she had created in Catarina Kirkova. Even she was afraid of her now, though she took great pains not to let it show.

'Did you get your schedules for next week?' she asked.

Catarina nodded. 'I read them on the plane. You've got me down for a provisional. You know I don't do provisionals.'

'I thought even you might make an exception for Prince, kiddo. He's got a tight schedule but they have to start filming the video . . .'

'*I* have a tight schedule. Tell them not to treat me like shit.'

'Catarina, who taught you that kind of language? Do you know what those words mean?'

'I like the sound of them.'

'Fine, but I think perhaps . . .'

'Was it inappropriate?'

Beth drew a long sigh. 'Under the circumstances, no – but . . .'

'Good.' Satisfied with her argument, Catarina rose from her chair and started flicking through the directories.

'Do you have a list of British newspapers here, Beth?'

'Of course. Why?'

'Can I look through them? I need to make a few calls.'

It was three a.m. when his phone rang. The cheap hotel room was quiet, soundproofed. Just the faint wail of a siren to remind him he was in New York.

'Mr Palimo?'

It had to be London. Someone had got their time zones all fucked up again.

'Speaking.' There was a long silence, during which he had time to wake up.

'Who is this?'

'What do you want, Mr Palimo?'

'What?'

'I asked you what you want.' The voice came through a scrambler – he couldn't even tell if it was male or female – spooky, he thought.

'What do you mean?' He felt nervous for some reason and he hated himself for it.

It spoke to him as though he were a retarded child.

'You are following someone. I wondered why.'

'Following who?'

'You know very well,' it said. 'Why else would you have booked on that particular flight when you could have travelled cheaper on the one before? Why else would you have paid that stewardess to disappear just before take-off? Why else would you be staying in that shabby hotel you are in? Is it just coincidence that its window overlooks the agent's offices?'

'Who are you?'

There was a laugh. 'Did you think you were the only one who could discover people's secrets? You want a story, am I right?'

Rick cleared his throat.

'My paper will pay for the truth . . .'

'Oh I don't need your money, Mr Palimo. You may have the story for nothing. You want the truth, you say? You want to hear the truth – the real truth about Catarina Kirkova?'

'Yes.'

The mouth was close to the receiver now, he could hear the steady breathing.

'The truth about Catarina Kirkova, Mr Palimo, is that she does not exist. She never has done.'

And then it hung up.

7

Luisa's Story – Moscow, 1982

The tram fare to school was two kopeks a head and that was exactly the amount their father had given each of them but the Kuznetsova sisters chose to walk instead, which meant they could save the precious coins. Luisa would have preferred the tram but Klara had the business brain and was stronger if it came to a fight and so, of course, they walked.

Luisa always did what Klara wanted. That was just the way things went. Luisa didn't mind at all – in fact she was happy to follow along. It saved on thought and it saved on effort and, besides, Klara was always right – which made arguing very difficult.

Walking was no easy feat in the early snow. Luisa kept stopping because her socks were wet but Klara grabbed her hand in a way that would have hurt had it not been so cold, and then she somehow pulled her along.

Luisa didn't mind this either – Klara knew best. The snow stuck on the rim of Klara's hat but Luisa didn't laugh because her mouth would get cold if she did, and then her teeth would ache. Klara only let go once, to throw a stone into the Moskva for good luck and when she did Luisa thought she had lost her – she vanished right away in a blanket of white.

'Klara?' – it came out as a scream.

'Booby, Luisa, you're such a little booby!'

But it was OK. Klara had her firmly by the collar this time. Luisa squirmed for the hell of it but she would have died if Klara had let go again.

It was September 1 – the first day of school and there were children everywhere. Like all the other girls they passed, Luisa and Klara wore little black dresses with white lace collars beneath their coats, and Klara had tied a mass of red ribbons in Luisa's fine hair – though she refused point-blank to wear any in her own. The boys looked less stupid. At least they had suits, even if they did have a red kerchief tied around their necks.

They fell in with the steaming crowds that spilled from the Metro and then they were through the black iron-grille gates and into the Alexandrovsky Garden. The snow was thicker there – it came and went with the wind. First you saw where you were going and then you didn't. The wind was like a magician, throwing a sheet over your head and then whisking it off. Close your eyes. Make a wish. Now open them. See! The scene before her was different every time.

The ochre walls of the Kremlin loomed over them and then vanished. She forgot herself and laughed. Her teeth started to ache.

Klara had begun to swear now – not truly bad words, just naughty ones, but that was OK too, because she was ten years old. Luisa was only seven. Klara would have hit her if she had dared to say such things.

Klara could be vicious when she wanted but she could also, sometimes, be caring. She would pull Luisa's hat on in the cold and button her coat right up to the neck. The collar would choke her and the peak of the hat blind her but she was happy to suffer just to have the momentary concern of the sister she adored.

They crossed the Troitsky Bridge and made for Red Square.

The snow eased a little and they saw people standing about. At first they thought they were queuing for hot tea and blinis at the samovar in the street but the vendor wasn't there today, he had moved round to Marx Prospekt where there was some shelter from the winds.

'Look, Luisa!' Klara sounded excited. She pointed to a circle of bird cherry trees. Luisa stood on tiptoe to see better.

Behind the circle of trees stood a large granite statue of Lenin. A tall woman in a fur coat had just climbed the statue and was balancing on the cold little ledge. The people around them were looking but not looking — definitely not staring, but shuffling their frozen feet and watching from the corners of their eyes.

'Is she mad, Klara?'

'I'm not sure. I don't think so. She is very beautiful — look. And there are other people with her, on the ground.'

'Who, Klara? Who are they? Put me on your shoulders, I can't see down here!'

Klara cuffed her ear to shut her up. The others had the right idea — it didn't pay to show you were looking.

'There's a man shouting up at her,' she told Luisa. 'He has a camera on a stick. There are others, too — a boy with a silver sheet that he keeps turning to catch the sun. There's a girl with some brushes — a couple of other men too, I think.'

But Luisa could only see the woman who clung to the statue. Suddenly a loud shout went up and she threw the heavy fur coat to the ground. Underneath she was naked — totally, utterly, bare-assed naked. There was a flash, like lightning, then another and then several more. Then someone threw the coat back up and the woman covered herself again.

Klara stared at Luisa.

'Did you see that?' her eyes asked. There was a dewdrop on her nose but Luisa was too shocked to tell her. Besides, it was no good talking as the wind had blown the snow back again. They were both freezing now — truly cold from standing still so long. They couldn't leave yet, though. They would rather have died from the chill.

The woman was down now — they moved slowly closer.

52

The rest of the crowd dispersed and the wooden benches quickly emptied. None of the adults had been shocked by the nudity — it was not the Russian way, but the queerness of the event made them go off shaking their heads from side to side.

Klara was bold, as usual. Leaving Luisa near some bushes she marched towards the strangers and asked them right out what they were up to. Luisa was so proud of her sister — nothing scared her, she was as brave as any man.

There was a brief conversation and Luisa saw one of the men laughing as he explained something to Klara. The man with the camera smiled at her and wiped his nose. Luisa prayed the dewdrop had fallen off Klara's. The men had to be foreigners, they were dressed so wrong for the cold. Luisa heard her sister call 'Thanks!' and wave back at the men as she walked away. When she returned, her face was red and her eyes gleamed with excitement.

'Foreigners,' she said, puffed up and triumphant. 'They had to get someone to interpret. They thought I was asking for money — can you imagine that? I soon told them what was what! The woman is a model. I saw her close to, Luisa. You should have seen her skin! Her face, too. She was exquisite — really special. They photographed her for a calendar, for England. The photographer is a Lord, a member of the British aristocracy. You could tell from the way he looked, even if the interpreter hadn't told me. The model must be very rich too, Luisa — just look at her coat. She earns over three hundred dollars an hour — just imagine!'

'You asked them?'

Klara snorted. 'Of course I asked them, how else was I to find out?'

'You asked her earnings?'

'I needed to know, Luisa. It's important. You never know . . .'

'You never know what, Klara?'

'Anything, booby. You never know anything.'

Luisa grabbed her sister's sleeve. 'You mean you might do that?' she asked. 'You might become a model?'

Klara stroked her chin like their father did when he was thinking. 'Like I said, you never know. It's good money, Luisa, it's something to consider. Look. Watch her carefully.'

She hoisted Luisa onto her shoulders now, so she could see the woman again. She was beautiful, even though her skin was turning blue. She had her hands around the cup of a thermos. She took a sip of the drink and then she started to complain. She waved her arms and paced about and the photographer lit a cigarette and stared down at the ground.

'We'll be late, Luisa,' Klara tried to pull her down. 'We will freeze if we stand here any longer.'

At least that much was true. Nobody else was watching now, they had all gone about their business. Even the foreigners were packing up quickly, hauling boxes into a Land Rover and falling over themselves in the rush to be off. A black limousine pulled up behind their line of cars. Even before it had stopped they were ushering the model inside like a precious package. The photographer kissed her quickly on the cheek and she touched a hand to his shoulder before disappearing into the deep leather seats. There was a spume of white exhaust and the huge car was gone.

'Did you see that chauffeur?' Klara asked, 'Seven roubles an hour to hire a car like that!'

Klara was clever with money, their father was always boasting about it, even to strangers. Luisa jumped to the ground and looked up at her. There wasn't much to see, her hat and her scarf hid most of her face. What did show was red and white and pinched with the cold.

'You're every bit as beautiful as she is, Klara,' Luisa said. 'Me? No!'

But Luisa could tell from her sister's smile that she had

said the right thing. She thought Klara was the most beautiful creature alive — when she was warm, that was. Thawed out, she had oatmeal-coloured skin and great dark eyes, like wet brown pebbles. She knew Klara hated her dark eyes because they were Uzbek eyes, inherited from their father's side of the family. The sisters shared the same pale hair colour and that fact alone made Luisa extremely proud. She prayed it wouldn't darken like their mother's had, when she grew older.

Why had their mother married an Uzbek? Theirs was the only mixed-blood marriage the girls knew of. Their mother was dead now — she had killed herself two winters ago, so they would never have the chance to ask her. Luisa could barely remember her — her face had seemed to fade from her memory with each month that passed. She was just a haze now — a pale blur — a blob in Luisa's mind, though Klara always said she had been kind and beautiful. Why had she killed herself then? That wasn't an act of kindness, it had made both the sisters very sad.

Luisa had a sudden dark thought. 'Where will you live, Klara?'

'What?'

They were hurrying again now, almost flying along.

'When you are working like that! Will you still live in Moscow?'

Klara let out a loud laugh. 'Moscow? I shouldn't think so! You know the score, Luisa, who is paid money like that in this country? America, that's the place to go. I want to become a millionaire, Luisa. For that I will have to go abroad.'

Tears welled up in Luisa's eyes, blinding her as badly as the snow.

'America?' All her hopes of future happiness dissolved in that one word. 'Klara, you can't!'

'Why not?'

'Papa would never allow it!'

'Then he'd better not know,' Klara said, and there was

55

a warning in her voice. 'No little boobies had better tell him then!'

The GUM Department Store rose up before them like a liner lost in fog. Its windows were ablaze with light and a smell of warm bread made Luisa feel hungry.

'You'd never get a visa!'

Anything – she'd think of anything. There had to be some reason to stop her beloved sister from leaving her.

Klara shrugged. 'Peter Kulakov can arrange it. His father is in Immigration.'

'Peter Kulakov is a liar, everybody knows that!' It was the wrong thing to say. Her sister had a soft spot for the boy.

'So?' Klara yelled. 'He wouldn't dare tell me tales, that's all I know!'

The worst thing was, she was right. No-one at their school would ever dare cross Klara. Tall and quick-witted, she was the best fighter in the place and she feared absolutely no-one, including their teachers. As thin as a stick and with the hands of a proper lady, Klara nevertheless packed a punch that would floor an ox.

Luisa was safe with her sister around – none of the boys would dare bully or tease her for fear of a pasting. But if Klara were ever to leave, as she was threatening to . . .

'Coming, Luisa? Or do we get double detention tonight?'

'I'll follow you, Klara! I'll come to America with you! You can't leave me here, I'll die without you! I'd have to live alone with Papa and you know I couldn't bear that! Say I can come!'

'Suit yourself. I don't care.' Klara never even broke her stride. She shook her head and the snow sprayed out from her hat.

Luisa smiled again. It was OK then, after all. Klara wouldn't leave her, she could tell by her tone. Luisa splashed in the sludge by the kerb but she hardly noticed the cold and wet now. Beautiful Klara was going to be rich

56

and famous — a model, like the woman in the fur coat. And she, little Luisa, the one with the fat nose and the big feet, was going along for the ride.

8

Joseph Kuznetsov finished his shift at the textile factory at three and was back in his apartment exactly forty minutes later. The walk took only twenty minutes but he would stop to visit his friends at the Uzbek bakery en route and share a bottle or two of Aleatiko wine, washed down with some hot kvass.

His father had been a baker and he liked hanging around the place, watching the flat loaves of raw dough being thrown onto the sides of the clay ovens, then smelling the bread as it cooked. He would have stayed all day if he could, but he had his daughters to get home to.

Joseph Kuznetsov was a drunk. He knew it, his pals knew it – even his daughters knew it, but no-one blamed him, because of his circumstances. Everyone knew his story and everyone treated him with tolerance and kindness, even when he became abusive or violent. His one mistake in life had been in marrying outside his race, but then who could have blamed him at the time? Polina Lemskaya had been a beautiful girl and talented too, with her singing and her poetry. They had met at college and Joseph had moved from his home in the country to live with his wife in the town.

They had worked together at the textile factory and Polina had presented Joseph with two lovely daughters. Then, one day, she had taken a trolleybus into the country and hanged herself from a blue spruce in the forest.

The reason for her suicide had soon emerged. Polina had been given the honour of collecting the party subs at the factory each week. Three weeks before she killed herself the funds had been ten kopeks short. Polina had not stolen them – another worker had soon confessed, but she had been unable to bear the shame, nevertheless. Ten kopeks. It sounded incredible, but that was the sort of woman Polina was. She had always been the same, really. No-one who knew her would have expected her to do otherwise, or at least they all said so once the terrible deed had been done. Polina Lemskaya had been a perfectionist from birth. Everything about her had been perfect – she had made sure of it.

Her one big deviation from the path of perfection had been her marriage to Joseph and no-one knew exactly why this had occured – least of all Joseph himself.

It was soon after the wedding that he had noticed his wife's frequent bouts of depression but then he had considered them understandable enough – perhaps she was realizing her mistake at last. It must have been an awful shock, finding yourself married to Joseph Kuznetsov, that ugly bastard. The idea came into Joseph's head that Polina had loved someone else – some handsome man that her parents had disapproved of – and then had married him to cause her mother further grief. He had never found proof of the idea but it had stuck in his head nonetheless and in the end he had believed it an unshakeable fact, bringing it up in all of their many fights.

Polina's death alone had been hard enough for Joseph to bear, but then the letters started to arrive.

He hadn't known about them at first. At first all he had noticed were the many smaller plans Polina had made for her suicide. The way she had ironed all their clothes for the week and left them in neat piles in the apartment, with labels attached, saying what day they should wear what. The way she had ordered black dresses for the girls so that they arrived promptly the day before her funeral. The way she had sent all her own clothes to the orphanage and placed her few kopeks' savings in an envelope beneath Joseph's pillow.

Each one of these things could have sent Joseph into a state of madness, but then the letters came.

They arrived once a month. At college Polina had been a fan of the writer Kuprin and had copied a story in one of his books. She had found the story desperately romantic. Before her death she had written god-knows how many letters and arranged to have them posted to Joseph on a regular basis. They were letters of love, reminding him of their few happy times together. She wrote that she had arranged for them to be sent so as to help him cope with his loss after her death, but all they did in reality was drive him to the bottle.

At first Joseph had tried to discover who was posting them to him, to beg them to stop before he was driven completely mad. Polina's elderly mother denied all knowledge of them, though, and there were no other relatives he could think of. So, he was forced to suffer for as long as they came. He had to read them – they were from his darling wife – yet each reminder of her wounded him like a knife to the heart.

When Klara and Luisa returned from school they saw their mats put out on the table and a bottle of Starka vodka in their father's place and they knew another letter had arrived. Klara sniffed the air. There was a smell of spiced broth and dumplings, so at least they would eat before the trouble started.

They ate in silence and then the two girls went to bed, although it was barely dark. Sometimes they wished their father would kill himself, too. It was very difficult to love him when he got into such a state.

The apartment was small, even by Moscow standards – just two rooms, the room they lived in and the room they slept in. Their father slept in the living room, where the girls had slept when their mother was alive. That was the only good bit, having the bedroom, though there was a sink in the corner where the washing-up was done, so it was hardly private.

There would have been more room in the place if their father had agreed to throw out all their mother's old books. There were hundreds of them – lining the walls, under the chairs, the sink and even the toilet. No-one knew what was in them because no-one was allowed even to touch them. Klara could barely make out the titles now, because they were so thick with dust. They could not go, though – their father just wouldn't allow it. Instead the family had to make a life around them and do the best they could.

There was a small mirror over the stone sink and Klara studied her reflection in it. Their father was playing music now, and they could smell a brew of green tea. It would not be too bad if he kept the noise down, but if the music became loud the neighbours would be round to complain.

Uzbek eyes, lips – their mother's hair and nose. Klara's hair was long, the longest in the school. She lifted her sister up and now there were two faces in the mirror. There was no mistaking they were sisters. Their colouring was odd – unique, even. No-one else they knew had such pale skin and dark eyes. But then poor Luisa had the fatter nose and flatter face. It made her look comical, like a monkey, while Klara looked haughty and elegant. Luisa didn't care. As long as she could look at her sister's face she didn't worry that her own was not so pretty. Besides, her sister was to make a career of it, while Luisa had plans to work in the factory, like their father.

He had taken them there one day, soon after their mother had died, and Luisa had been entranced by the noise and the busyness and all of the beautiful fabrics they made. The women who worked there had given her sweets and made a fuss of her. Luisa wondered whether they had such places in America. Perhaps she could make the fabrics for the dresses Klara would model. To Luisa it sounded like the perfect plan.

'I will need a new name,' Klara said. She rolled her long hair into a bun and piled it on top of her head.

'A new name?' The thought had not occurred to Luisa.

'Yes. All models have beautiful names. Klara is hardly beautiful, and neither is Kuznetsova. There are thousands of Kuznetsovas in Moscow alone. It is a common, horrible name. Klara Kuznetsova. It sounds like a stone rattling in a tin can. I will need something better. I'll have to think about it.'

Klara thought for three days before she came up with a name she liked. In the end they found it together, while watching the television.

Catarina. It was the name of an actress in one of the plays. Both girls knew as soon as they heard it – it was one of the rare things they agreed upon at once. Luisa looked over at Klara, her eyes big with the question: Is that it? Is it good enough? I think it's lovely. She could not speak because their father was with them. Klara did not even turn round but she nodded her head once. Yes, that's it, we've found it. Luisa was so excited she rocked silently in her seat.

The surname was almost as easy. It came from a book in the library. Kirkova was the name of the young countess, whose husband had died in the war. She was noble and proud and refused all other suitors to keep her handsome husband's memory sacred. The story made Klara cry, which was an unusual sight, to say the least.

So that was it, then – Catarina Kirkova. Beautiful and noble. It sounded exactly right.

9

Klara was an excellent story-teller and Catarina Kirkova became a favourite fantasy figure for the two girls and the heroine of many of Klara's best stories. As they lay in bed at night listening to their father, drunk, muttering to himself in the next room, Klara would whisper her account of Catarina's latest exploits.

The only daughter of an elderly Count and his beautiful young bride, Catarina was arrogant and proud, a highly-paid model whose work took her all over the world. She lived in the best suites in the best hotels and she ate only foreign food, like burgers and tropical fruits. All the photographers fell in love with her but she had a passion for only one man — whose name she never disclosed. Every time Klara introduced a new man in her stories Luisa would ask: 'Is this him? Is this the one?' but Klara would always shake her head. 'He is not nearly handsome enough or good enough,' she would say. Luisa saw Catarina's secret lover as a great dark man, a man who lived in the shadows and whose face she hoped to see one day.

They scoured any magazines they could lay their hands on for new fuel for their fantasy. There were sometimes Western magazines at the library that they could use to study the fashions. They found a small bag of cosmetics that had belonged to their mother, tucked away in a drawer in their bedroom and, when their father was very drunk and snoring, they would try the make-up out.

They were surprised to have found them — Klara said she could never remember their mother wearing any. There was some perfume too, but they dared not open the bottle in case the smell lingered and their father found out.

Klara tried some on the way to school one day, when they were out in the open air, but the smell clung to her clothes and Luisa was almost sick with fear. The smell of the perfume did not remind them of their mother at all. Perhaps she had never worn it.

On her fourteenth birthday Klara asked for some perfume of her own, but their father swore at her and said he would never allow it. Perhaps that was what had happened to their mother, then – perhaps he had not allowed her to wear her scent.

'Does Catarina wear scent, Klara?' Luisa had never grown out of the stories.

'Scent? Of course! What do you think? Catarina wears the most expensive perfume in the world. It costs thousands of roubles an ounce and it is also the most exclusive. France's leading perfumer fell in love with Catarina last year and presented her with the perfume as a mark of his adoration. She is the only woman to own it and the only woman to wear it. The perfumer has vowed to tell no-one of its recipe.'

'What does it smell like?'

'Like nothing you have ever smelt before, Luisa. Imagine the best smell there is and multiply it a hundred times. Even then it wouldn't be good enough. Women have begged the perfumer to give up his secret. Even the Queen of England paid him a secret visit and commanded him to make some for her, but he refused everyone. He still loves only Catarina, and will until the day he dies.'

'What does the Dark Lover think of this?'

Klara shook her head and whistled. 'Catarina does not wear it when she sees him. She wouldn't dare.'

'What would he do if he found out?'

'I don't know. Kill the perfumer, maybe. Beat Catarina up. Rob her of her beauty.'

'But she hasn't done anything wrong!'

Klara laughed at Luisa. 'You are such a child when it comes to men. They don't need an excuse, don't you know that? The dark lover is the most passionate man you can imagine. He would be unable to help himself.'

Luisa shuddered. Klara seemed to know so many terrible things. She tried to imagine the Dark Lover in such an impossible rage. All that came to mind was her father, ranting and screaming in a drunken temper. Would he ever have hurt their mother? The thought seemed impossible.

Klara was a young woman of fifteen when she finally discovered the means of their escape. She threw a magazine down in front of Luisa.

'Look! That's it!' Her face was pink with the effort of concealing her excitement.

'What? Luisa had been studying. She was trying hard at school. Klara never made the effort, except in English classes, but Luisa had to work twice as much just to catch up with her.

'There! Look!' Klara stabbed her finger onto the open page.

It was an advertisement, among many others for second-hand cars and holidays in the country. There were many advertisements in the magazines now that the foreigners had arrived. There were Americans setting up all over the place and this was another of them.

' "The American Dream Modelling Academy" ' she read, ' "Foremost two-year courses in model skills plus interviews and auditions with leading US model agents at graduation. Success guaranteed for the suitable candidates." '

Klara went to see them the very next day, using money they had saved between them for the train fare. She returned red-faced and inflated by her own importance.

'They have accepted me,' she told Luisa.

'Accepted you? Just like that?'

Klara smiled an annoying smile and pretended to read her paper. 'Have you finished your homework yet, Luisa?'

'Klara!' Luisa knew she was being wound up but she couldn't contain her impatience. 'What happened? Tell me the truth! Did they like you? What happens now?'

'I wait until I finish school and then I begin the course, that's what happens. They told me I am too young at the moment. They'll take me in a couple of years' time. You too, if you're lucky.'

'Me?'

'Of course you! I thought you said you would kill yourself if I ever left you behind! You little actress! I suppose you are going to tell me you don't have the guts for it now!'

Luisa looked for the words but none came out of her mouth.

'Babushka!' It was Klara's favourite insult recently. Since Luisa had become so engrossed in her studies Klara had taunted her with the word, saying she would do nothing with her life and end up a fat old Babushka like all the other women around there, in their knitted cardigans and woollen stockings – with their red and white headscarves tied tight under their wobbling chins. Luisa ignored the taunts, but they hurt, nevertheless.

'Do you want to stay around here all your life?'

Luisa shook her head, though the truth was she loved Moscow and dreaded the thought of leaving it. All the things that Klara dreamed of – the modern cars and high skyscrapers of New York – had begun to fill her with a sense of unease. She would look at the tall golden spires of the Kremlin, topped with their ruby red stars that rotated slowly in the wind and wonder if anything anywhere else could ever be as beautiful. Did they have jasmine trees in New York? Did it snow there? Would they have fried curd-cheese cakes for breakfast every morning, as they did at home? Did they follow the same customs, like

66

leaving their beds unmade on important days and throwing pebbles into the river, for luck?

There was something Klara still had to tell her, something important – although she tried her best to make light of it.

'Oh, by the way. One other thing about the course.'

'Yes?'

'It costs two hundred roubles for each place.'

'It's not free?'

'What did I just tell you? Don't be so stupid, Luisa. Why should it be free?'

– So that was all right then. They would never find that sort of money if they saved as long as they lived. Luisa felt a little happier, though she remembered to look downcast for her sister's sake.

10

London, 1994

Rick Palimo sucked at his thumb and stared at the wall of photos. The drawing pins had left dents in his skin but he'd run out of Blu-tack so dents it had to be.

His stomach ached with hunger but the thought of another delivery pizza sickened him. Where did those guys come from? Where were they cooked? Why take so much on trust? Who knew what had happened to that smug-faced little black olive before it was was popped in the middle of all that cheese? What was its history, anyway? No-one had sex with strangers these days but that didn't stop them ramming anything down their throats that a leather-clad biker cared to thrust through the door at them.

He chewed some old crust anyway and looked back at Catarina's face. He'd pinned a shot of himself next to her, just to see how it looked. He thought it looked good but then he was half-way pissed on Pils so what did he know?

The shot had been taken by a snapper-mate of his to sit atop a column he'd once had in the Dark Ages, before he'd won his spurs as the Wild Man of Wapping.

It made him look like the sort of bloke other men would want to be mates with and women would want to fuck. Catarina, on the other hand, was not looking as though she wanted to *fuck* him – Catarina was looking more as though she wanted to fuck him *around* – which was precisely what she was doing and had been doing for several weeks now.

Dead ends. Everywhere. Start at the beginning. Go back to basics. Catarina had no beginning. As far as he could find out she had never been born at all. And Rick had searched – Jesus, how he'd searched. His brain ached from all the searching he'd done. And all he'd managed to find out so far was that he hated Russians – that they were all meatheads, and that Catarina Kirkova was a grade A liar – either that or, as the voice on the phone had told him – she didn't exist at all.

Trying to trace people over the phone to Russia was like trying to bite your own ass – you rolled around in circles for hours on end getting nowhere and getting madder by the minute. The Russians sounded so bloody efficient – they would cheerfully promise anything and then – nothing. Some names – if he pushed it. A couple of addresses. No phone numbers. It all sounded vague and bitty.

Perhaps he should go out there. To Russia. The thought of chasing one name round an entire continent made him shudder, though. That was what modern technology was all about – it stopped you having to do things for yourself. With his phone and his fax and his computers Rick was a master of the universe – he didn't have to go out there cutting it with all the plebs any more.

America was different – the US was the centre of the universe and always good for a visit. Not that he'd got too far over there up till now, though. Catarina's agency had rattled off the usual well-rehearsed crap about their star model. No one working there had enough of a grudge or greed to give him a story. A couple of other models claimed to know things but they'd turned out to be nothing more than expensive dinner dates with empty heads – why did no-one even lie well these days?

He had the story in the paper, though. He had clues. He had some leads that maybe smelt right. If he couldn't start at the beginning then he'd just start at the end and work his way backward. He fingered Catarina's face in the photograph.

'Don't worry, I'm getting closer,' he whispered. 'Can you feel it? I'll find you somewhere.'

The face seemed to smile at him but it could have been the light.

11

Russia, 1988

They waited until their father was asleep and then Klara
turned to Luisa and told her it was time to go out. Her
face looked strange in the yellow electric light. She had
blue shadow on her eyes and her lips were a matte cherry
red. She had pink rouge on her cheeks, though they were
also bright with excitement. Klara looked like a stranger
– not like Luisa's sister at all. She looked frightening. Some
lipstick had smeared on her teeth. Luisa told her and she
quickly licked it off.

'It will get better when I am used to it,' she said.

She looked at Luisa before she turned off the light. 'Are
you sure you have to come?' she asked. Luisa nodded,
lying. She would have done anything to have stayed at
home in her bed but she didn't want to be left alone. She
was afraid of their father. Afraid he might find out and
she would be the only one there to face him when he
did. It was his mouth – the shouting and the swearing.
He had never hit them, but the noise he made was bad
enough.

She pulled on her coat – her summer coat, because it
was late spring and therefore not so cold. Their grandmother had made her the coat for her thirteenth birthday.
Klara had celebrated her sixteenth a few months earlier
and she had been given an identical garment. The coats
were black with a blue satin lining and Klara had refused
to wear hers any way other than inside out. She didn't care
when people laughed, she said that black reminded her of
death. That night she went out without it, even though her

teeth were chattering before they had reached the end of the street.

Luisa wore her coat as her grandmother had intended it to be worn and she didn't mind the black because it made her feel like nothing more than Klara's shadow – which was all she wanted to be. As she had grown older she had grown taller and, as each inch was added to her height, she had also grown quieter and more shy. People stared because she was so tall but she felt she had little to offer to make her worthy of their attention. It was as though her height called out to them: 'Hey! I'm here! Look at me!' but then they were cheated – she had nothing to say – unlike Klara, who could talk the legs off a mule.

So to be Klara's shadow was no hardship – she liked it like that – it was what she preferred.

People stared at them on the tram, alright – at Klara at least, with her dress and her bare arms and legs. Luisa was impressed by her sister, though. Klara just stared straight ahead, ignoring them all. She even stopped her teeth chattering somehow, though there were still goosebumps all along her arms.

Then she did something so wonderful that Luisa almost burst with pride. From the depths of her handbag she pulled out a cigarette and lit it and smoked it even though she had never smoked a cigarette before in her life! She didn't cough and she didn't blink, though the smoke brought tears to her eyes.

It was a wonderfully disgraceful thing to do and Luisa felt less scared after that.

They got off at Sverdlov Square and walked up to the Metropol Hotel. Klara paused by the entrance, watching the people come and go, not minding the funny stares they got from some of the men.

'Too many Americans,' she announced at last and they walked on further in silence. Luisa was feeling the cold now – even through their grandmother's black coat. She wondered why Klara walked so slowly. It never occurred to her that her sister, who was afraid of nothing, could be trying to build up some courage.

There was a smaller hotel nearby, one with a revolving door.

'Wait outside,' Klara told her.

Luisa looked shocked. 'I can't! I'll die of the cold!'

'Booby! How do you think I feel?' But Klara pulled her inside with her, nevertheless.

The hotel lobby was well-heated and grand enough, in a shabby sort of way. There were plastic-upholstered armchairs everywhere, even behind some plants, which was where Klara sat Luisa.

'Sit here, I'll get you a hot chocolate to thaw you out.'

Luisa looked about the place while she waited. A couple of waiters came past and stared but she looked at her feet for so long that everyone finally ignored her. She was the shadow again – Klara's shadow.

The chocolate had whipped cream and cinnamon on top. Luisa was so happy she hardly noticed Klara had vanished.

Klara had never been in a lift before. She had never been in a hotel room before. She had not dared to look at the man at first but she had seen him in the mirror and he hadn't looked so bad. He had a kind face, even though he was fat. Not all fat, though – his legs were skinny when he took his trousers off. His fat was all on his stomach but that was OK – most Russian men got fat when they got older. In a way it helped – it meant she couldn't see so much of his cock.

'Have you got something for me?' She spoke in English. She had learnt the phrase from a girl she had got chatting to outside The Cosmos.

'Sure.' He pulled the packet of condoms out of his trouser pocket and threw them onto the bed.

73

The room was a good one. There were narrow twin beds, padded chairs, a small, wall-mounted desk and even a heated towel-rail in the bathroom. There was even piped radio and music playing when Klara came out of the toilet. She washed herself in the sink with the hotel soap, just in case. She wanted to smell good – she didn't want to put the man off. There was a tear in the wallpaper and the picture over the bed was crooked. Perhaps it wasn't such a good room after all.

'Drink?' Did the man only speak one-word sentences or did he think that was all she could understand? Klara nodded and he pulled a bottle of vodka out of a brown paper bag. It was Stolichnaya – not the Starka their father liked. He unscrewed the top with a strange little grunt and offered the bottle straight to Klara. She took a large swig and her eyes bulged with the attempt to stop herself coughing. The man laughed, but not unkindly.

'How old are you?' Four words this time. She smiled and tried to giggle like she had seen the other girls do when the men spoke to them.

'Eighteen.' – only a little lie.

'You look younger. I have a daughter at home. You look as young as she does. Look – here is her photo.'

The man opened his wallet and showed Klara a colour photo of a young girl. There was a thick wad of notes behind the photo. The man saw Klara looking and snatched the wallet back. So now he thought she was a thief, too.

'Do you like the music?' It was hotel music – nothing she could name.

'Yes. It's OK.'

'Would you like to dance?'

They looked so ridiculous, waddling together in that room – she a good head taller than her partner and his great belly stuck out there between them. He pressed his head onto Klara's shoulder and started to hum. He pulled her tighter and she stooped to even the height. He was

74

wearing a wig – she had only just noticed. She stared at the narrow bed over the man's shoulder. The sheets were yellow nylon and there was a cigarette burn just below the fold.

'More vodka?'

'No – thank you.' She didn't want to drink out of the bottle after him – it was an unhygienic thing to do.

There was a couple making love in the next room – Klara could hear it plainly through the partition. She felt embarrassed at the sounds. The man called out obscene words: 'Bastard! Whore!' while the woman cried like a cat.

'Undress me.' The man wore only his vest, shirt and pants. The buttons were difficult and he watched her eyes as she worked.

She had to bend to remove his pants and he pushed her down kneeling onto the floor, pressing his naked body into her face and crying out loud for her to love him.

'Bastard-whore-bastard-whore!' The man next door was reaching his climax. Klara's punter forced himself into her mouth, grasping her shoulders with his two fat hands and pumping his hips at her until she thought she would choke. There was silence next door now. A quiet grunting in Klara's ear. She was screaming but no sound could get out.

'Ungh! Unnnngh!' His legs started to shake as he went into a seizure. He came in her mouth and she scrambled to her feet to spit it all out, retching, in the sink in the bathroom.

There was a mug by the sink. Klara filled it with water and rinsed her mouth many times. When she looked in the mirror her make-up had moved. Her lipstick was every-where, making her mouth look twice the size and her rouge had all gone – wiped off by the man's wet, grasping hands.

When she came out again the man was in bed and there was money for her on the desk. She thanked him politely but he didn't answer. She thought perhaps he was already asleep. The money was a note short but she could not wake him to ask for the rest. Perhaps it was just a mistake. She turned off the light and closed the door quietly.

Luisa was waiting in the lobby. Klara almost forgot her — she walked straight past and only stopped when Luisa called her.

'Klara! Are you OK?' Klara could still taste the bitter taste in her mouth. Luisa's breath smelt of chocolate.

'Of course! What do you think?'

Luisa caught up with her sister. She sounded alright but her face was a mess.

'What was it like?'

But Klara said nothing until they had rounded the corner and were crossing back into Sverdlov Square. Then she threw a few folded notes at Luisa, who had to jump quickly to catch them.

'There,' Klara told her. 'The first instalment. Our path out of this godawful place.' And then they waited in silence for the tram to pull up out of the darkness.

12

Luisa waited in many more hotel lobbies on many other nights. Sometimes Klara would be gone for an hour – sometimes for just a few minutes. When the job was quick she would be in a good mood but sometimes, after a longer session, she could hardly bring herself to speak. Once she turned up with bruises and a couple of times she appeared to be drunk. Then she leant on Luisa's shoulder on the bus and they made so much noise getting indoors that Luisa prayed out loud their father would not wake up and find them like that.

The drunkenness frightened Luisa most of all. The second time it happened she stood on the pavement outside The Cosmos and screamed at Klara and shook her until passers-by started to stare. Luisa could not bear to see her sister become like their father. Klara was shocked – Luisa had never stood up to her before. This new concept sobered her up a little and she staggered home in thoughtful silence.

Apart from those few scares Luisa found the whole thing something of a game. She was excited by their nocturnal walks and loved sitting in the grand hotels, watching the guests go about their business, sipping her hot chocolate and knowing no-one saw her. Sometimes she took a school book in with her and used the time to study for her exams.

At thirteen she had only a vague idea what went on in the hotel rooms between Klara and the men she met. Then one time someone did see her.

'H-h-how much?' He was little more than a boy – very young and very nervous. His features looked oriental, though he spoke pretty good Russian.

Luisa looked up from her school book. Her mouth went dry. She looked about for her sister though Klara had only just gone upstairs.

'Thirty roubles.' Had she really said that? But why not? If Klara could earn money for their course then so could she. It wasn't fair to expect Klara to do all the work. What could be the harm? If they both worked they would end up enrolling in half the time. It was no longer any use hoping Klara's dreams would come to nothing – she was almost half-way to saving all their money already. Luisa thought she might as well help with the rest.

The boy checked his wallet and, to Luisa's great surprise, nodded quickly.

'OK.' Thirty roubles! What a nerve she had!

He glanced at her in the lift and started to blush when she caught him looking.

'Sorry.'

'That's OK. Stare if you like.'

She didn't feel embarrassed when the young boy looked. It was adults that made her shy – anyway this boy was nervous enough for two.

'How did you get so much money?' Luisa had to ask him. She didn't want to find out he was broke after all.

The boy looked down.

'My father,' he said. 'For my birthday. He insisted. Tonight I will become a man.'

Luisa laughed. 'Your father has paid for you to do this?' It seemed such a comical idea – 'You mean I am your birthday present? Do you have to spend it all on me? Couldn't you use it to have a bit more fun?'

The boy shrugged. 'It's important to him.' Then he fell silent. The lift doors opened and he fumbled for his keys as they approached his room.

The room was the best in the hotel.

'Does your father stay here, too?' Luisa asked.

'No. He sleeps in the next suite – next door.' The boy was whispering and pressed a finger across his lips.

'You mean he's there now?' Luisa whispered back.

The boy nodded – miming a hand to his ear to show his father would be listening through the wall.

Luisa looked shocked. 'He has to hear us?'

The boy nodded again, looking depressed. 'He needs to know his money has been well spent.'

'But what would you really like to do most on your birthday?'

The boy thought. 'Dunno. Eat a good meal. Have some fun with my friends.'

'So how do you get the food in this place?' Luisa asked.

'By phone,' the boy told her. 'There is room service. There is a menu by the bed.'

They ordered caviar and salmon and blinis and cream cakes. Luisa barely knew most of the other foods on the menu, so she asked the waiter to bring up an assortment of the best stuff too. Up came intricate pastry cases filled with chopped egg and soured cream; dishes of salads and vegetables from all over the world and small bowls of ice-cream topped with nuts and spun sugar.

They ate until they were full and then Luisa ate some more until she felt sick. There was chocolate around her mouth and when she pushed her chair back the boy let out a small belch and that made them both laugh.

Luisa flipped a spoonful of cream at the boy and he retaliated by throwing even more back at her. Soon they were covered in the stuff and laughing so hard they could barely stay on their chairs.

When Luisa finally stopped for air she rose from her chair and led the boy towards the bed.

They lay there side by side, doing their best to keep their faces straight.

'You start,' Luisa whispered.

'Start what?'

'The noises! We have to make the right noises! Your father is listening, remember?'

The boy nodded. He lay still, staring at the ceiling for a minute or so.

'Go on then!' Luisa was getting impatient.

'I can't.'

'Why not?'

'I don't know what it sounds like.'

Luisa giggled. 'Haven't you ever heard your parents?'

'Never. The house is too big – have you?'

Luisa shook her head. 'My mother is dead.'

'Sorry.'

'That's OK. It was a long time ago.'

'So?' The boy sounded desperate. 'What do we do?'

Luisa shrugged. 'Make it up, I suppose.' She let out a small squeal, like an otter.

'How was that?'

'Good.' The boy yelled and bounced so hard on the bed that it banged against the wall. Luisa jumped up to help him and they hit the wall again, causing a lamp to fall out of its bracket.

'Darling!' the boy called out.

'Sweetheart!' Luisa replied.

They groaned and they laughed and they jumped up and down on the mattress. In the end they stopped when they were exhausted.

'Will that do, do you think?' Luisa whispered. The boy nodded solemnly. He handed her the thirty roubles and she kissed it for luck before pushing it into her pocket.

Klara was waiting down in the foyer. She took one look at Luisa, with her filthy face and her messy hair and grabbed her by the arm, dragging her out into the street where she slapped her hard on the cheek.

Luisa cried with the shock of the blow. Klara had hit

her so heavily her face turned pink where the blow had landed.

'What the hell were you up to?' Luisa had never seen Klara so angry. 'You little cow! What the hell got into you? I was frantic with worry! How could you? How could you do that? Look at the state you're in! What happened? Did he hit you? Did he give you anything? Make you take anything? Answer me, Luisa!'

Luisa pulled away from her sister. Klara was frightening her and she didn't want to be hit again.

'You do it!' She loved Klara so much – she had only wanted to help her.

'I'm sixteen, Luisa! You're only thirteen! You're just a baby! You don't know anything!'

Luisa pulled the money from her pocket, desperate for Klara's approval.

'I got thirty roubles . . .' she began.

'Thirty roubles! What did he make you do for that?' She grabbed Luisa's arms and pulled up the sleeves of her coat, searching frantically for needle marks.

Luisa struggled to get away. 'We just ate a meal. He didn't want anything more, Klara! He was just a boy, really.'

'You ate? He paid thirty roubles just for you to eat a meal? Don't be stupid, Luisa! Don't lie to me! Look at the state you're in! Do you think I'm a fool or something?' She pulled the collar of Luisa's coat and Luisa flinched, thinking she was going to be hit again, but then she saw there were tears on her sister's face and Klara suddenly hugged her, which was the first time she had done such a thing in her life.

'Promise me, Luisa,' she whispered. 'Promise me you will never do such a thing again, ever.'

Luisa nodded. Klara thought she was a liar. Suddenly she was crying too.

81

13

It was three weeks before term began at the modelling school and Klara was desperate because she was still several roubles short of their fees. She had enrolled the month before and paid both their deposits but full payment was due before the term started and she knew she could not get the money by then.

Klara's nerve had gone. She had lost what stomach she had had for prostitution. When she had planned the venture she had watched the other prostitutes behaving with their clients like young girls flirting at a party and had somehow imagined, like Luisa, that it would all be a bit of fun — but now she knew better. She could never have realized what she would have to go through. Klara felt one hundred years old now, instead of sixteen. She looked at her college friends and her sister and envied them their innocence. She wore make-up all the time — she no longer cared what her father thought. He was just another drunk and she had dealt with enough drunks by now to know what was what.

She paid another visit to the director of the school and, to her great relief, he agreed to take them both on the course if she signed a paper agreeing the money was owed. She would need to pay interest too, she was told, as the agreement constituted a loan, but Klara didn't care. Once she was on the course she knew nothing would stop her. She could leave Moscow at last.

The wind felt good in her hair as she walked back across the city. The school was in the suburbs — a long train ride from their home. They would be living in. Klara felt she would burst from all the waiting and wanting. She wanted to be away. She wanted the power that comes from freedom.

'Pack your case,' she told Luisa when she arrived home. 'We're leaving next week.'

The American Dream Modelling Academy was housed in some disused army barracks far on the eastern outskirts of the city. There was a small grey park and then a line of pine trees and from behind the trees rose the green roofs of the ten-storey accommodation block. The school itself was in a modern prefab nearby. This building consisted of twelve rooms only – the largest of which was the studio where they would learn to dance and walk and the smallest of which was the canteen, because the students were not encouraged to take their meals in public, but to eat alone, reflecting quietly on each and every mouthful.

Luisa burst into tears when they booked in and Klara was angry at the humiliation this caused. She had told Luisa she could cry on the train ride if she wished, but Luisa had stayed dry-eyed until they reached the school itself.

They had left home once their father had made his way to the factory that morning. Klara had written a business-like note for him, telling him they were gone for good and that they would contact him again once she had made some money. She did not, of course, tell him where they would be. She doubted he would even try to find out.

Klara had informed Luisa that she was to lie about her age. Luisa watched as she filled in their forms: Klara Orlova (Their grandmother's name, just in case.) – Eighteen years. Luisa Orlova – sixteen.

The receptionist turned the book around. 'You will need your parents' consent,' she told them.

'Our parents are both dead,' Klara said, staring straight ahead.

The woman sighed. 'Very well then.' She gave them the keys to their lockers and directions to the dormitory.

The intake that term was thirteen pupils in all – eight girls and five boys. The last group had graduated the evening before and the new recruits were informed that they had all reached the required standard and had all been offered satisfactory contracts.

The dormitory was mixed-sex, though there were small curtains between the beds for privacy. The curtains were printed with blue flowers, which provided the only colour or pattern in the room. The walls were stippled with ancient grey paint and the floor covered with brownish lino. There was a small woven mat beside each bed and when Luisa pulled her mat away she saw it concealed a worn patch at the exact spot where her feet would land when she got up in the morning. How many feet did it take to wear a hole like that, she wondered?

Pinned next to each bed was a typed list of rules and a timetable for the following week. Each student read the list quickly then sat on their bed in silence. They stared at one another, waiting for something to happen. Even Klara was quiet, though she managed to find a cigarette and light it without too much difficulty. She had been warned the course was tough but the schedule looked horrendous. She crossed her legs and gazed at the ceiling. If she looked at all shaken by what she had just read then Luisa would start crying again and that would be unbearable.

A boy got up off his bed and approached her.

'Mind if I have a puff?'

He was good-looking with a charming smile, though two of his front teeth were broken.

'Buy your own.'

The boy shrugged. 'OK. I just thought I'd ask.' He didn't go, though, and that was the way it was with Klara – the ruder she was the more they seemed to hang around.

'I said I only thought I'd ask,' he repeated.

Klara looked up at him. 'And I only told you to push off.'

The boy grinned. 'If you want.'

'I do.'

He sat down on the bed next to her.

'I have my own car, you know.'

Klara raised an eyebrow. Suddenly she was interested. 'What sort?'

The boy looked embarrassed.

'A Moskvich.'

'A pick-up? Hah! Where do you come from, a farm?' Still, it might be better than nothing, she had to admit.

Luisa watched the encounter carefully. Where did Klara get her nerve from? She could never be rude to boys as her sister was. She smiled at an older girl on the opposite bed but the girl gave an obscene sign and lay back on her pillows.

'Luisa?' Klara crept into her sister's bed that night. 'Are you OK?'

Luisa nodded, though she had been lying awake suffering from homesickness.

'Have you noticed anything strange?' Klara whispered.

'Strange?'

'Hmm – about the others. Did you look at them, Luisa? Did you get a good look? They didn't look too great to me. I thought they would all look rather special but they didn't.'

'Rudi was OK.'

'Rudi?'

'The boy who came across to speak to you, Klara. I saw his name on his locker.'

Klara thought for a bit.

'You thought he was good-looking? What about his broken teeth?'

Luisa nodded. 'Some of the girls were quite pretty.'

'Pretty? This is a modelling academy, Luisa! They are supposed to be beautiful!'

'I'm not beautiful, Klara.'

Klara tutted. 'You're better than you think. You should give yourself more credit, Luisa. Look at the way you walk about. They'll sort out that stoop of yours, if they know what they're up to! Anyway, you're here because you're my sister. The others don't have an excuse. Watch out for the boys as well, Luisa. Give me a shout if any of them come creeping around your curtains at night. I'll soon tell them where to get off! Do you hear me, Luisa?'

But her sister was already asleep.

They were woken at six the next morning and taken for a run around the grounds, followed by an ice-cold shower to step up their circulation. Then they were weighed and measured and each student was given a sheet, telling them how much weight they had to lose. Luisa was amazed to see she had to drop several kilos, even though she was already as thin as a young boy. Klara too, and she looked like a stick – you could count her ribs when her vest was on.

They were cold all day because the heating was kept down as they were told they would lose weight faster if they were chilly. The boys complained about their diets but the girls were more philosophical. If American models were so thin then they were happy to lose the weight to compete with them.

In the afternoon they studied deportment, then more exercise and they were back in their beds by seven at night. The routine was repeated each day for a fortnight and then a photographer came in to photograph each student in turn.

The photographs were strange. They were each shot in their underwear: front, back and sides – and then some

shots of their faces – though they were strictly forbidden
to smile. The following week the shots had been processed
and each student had to appear before the principal to
discuss future 'improvements'.

Samuel J. Lorenz's office had walls three-feet thick and
windows so high the light could barely make the effort to
shine through them. His desk used up most of the floor
space and whatever was left over was carpeted by erupting
piles of inferior-quality index cards. They looked like
stepping stones. A cabinet behind the desk was filled with
tarnished sporting trophies. The largest photograph in the
room was of Samuel J. Lorenz himself – taken in his modelling days, when his toupee fitted and his teeth were all his
own.

'Come in!' The smile was just as large but the face had
sunk around it. Luisa stepped gingerly across the floor and
Samuel held out a hand to show her where she was to sit.
She had not seen the school's principal before this moment.
They had imagined he would be exceptionally handsome.
Luisa felt disappointed and she knew Klara would have
been too, a few moments before. She had passed her
coming out from her interview but Klara had not looked
at her, keeping her eyes to the ground instead.

'Another little Orlova sister!'

Luisa smiled politely.

'How is your diet going?'

'Very well thank you, Sir.' They had semolina for breakfast, some salad for lunch and a milk jelly for their tea.
Luisa felt she was starving, but Klara had told her it was
important to be polite.

'Hmm. Stand up.'

Luisa stood.

'Let me see you walk.'

Luisa tried to remember all she had been taught in
deportment classes. The principal barely watched her,
though – he had pulled her photos out of the file and was
studying them instead. She was actually quite good – she

was tall enough and, like her sister, had the sort of bone structure you saw in French *Vogue*. She was not the one with the money, though — her sister took care of that job. Lorenz saw little point in bothering with the younger girl. Besides, he noticed when he did look up, she walked like a horse.

'You look quite a lot like your sister. Let me see your profile.' Luisa turned her head to the side.

'You do know the girls in America have perfect features?'

'Yes, sir.'

'So what are we to do about yours?'

He peered at her over steepled hands.

'Your sister has agreed to surgery to redress her imperfections.'

'*Klara?*'

'Why not?'

— Why not? Luisa could think of a million reasons. Klara had perfect features already! What fault could this man have found with them?

'Where does she need the surgery?'

The man sighed. She had annoyed him now with her question. Perhaps she should have kept quiet.

'Her nose is a little crooked, just above the bridge. Your sister is very ambitious. She knows the work will be worth it in the end. Your nose is flatter — a common-looking nose. Look at some of these. Do you think you would stand a chance against them?'

He threw some magazine shots across the desk. Luisa saw picture after picture of smiling models — all with perfectly shaped noses. Then he put her own shots beside them. The contrast was so absurd it was all Luisa could do not to laugh.

'What do you think then?'

Luisa cleared her throat.

'You're right — I wouldn't stand a chance.'

'So you agree to the surgery then? We might add a little silicone along the jaw, too.'

'How much will it cost?'

The principal turned his chair to look straight at her. 'I beg your pardon?'

'I said how much. How much will the surgery cost?'

The man sighed again. 'We have our own surgeon. The work is done on the premises. The cost is extremely reasonable. Why do you ask? Your sister told me your parents left you well provided for. She said your instalments came out of a regular trust fund – that was why I agreed to take the two of you without prior payment.'

Luisa thought quickly.

'I'll wait. I'll see how my sister turns out. Then I'll have the work done, thank you.' They could never afford it – better Klara got it than she.

'Very well.' The principal turned his chair away. Luisa realized the interview had ended.

She tried to ask Klara why she had agreed to the surgery when she had such a fine nose already but Klara grew angry and asked her what did she know about it anyway?

'They might spoil you, Klara!' Luisa was desperate enough to keep the argument going.

'Don't be so stupid!'

Klara went off to join Rudi. The two were close now – the other girls said they were sweethearts. Luisa suddenly felt very lonely. She missed her sister's company and she missed fried curd-cheese cakes and hot green tea. That night she cried herself to sleep like a baby.

14

The students were not supposed to leave the campus during term-time but Rudi sometimes drove out, undetected, at night. He had money sent from his parents and he would buy food for them all — slabs of sweet sponge-cake and hot spiced rolls. Luisa would set on the food like a starved animal but Klara always refused it — she was obsessive about her set diet.

'You're too thin, Klara!' Luisa told her. Even Rudi told her the same thing, but Klara was determined to reach her targeted weight. After five weeks she barely had the strength to get out of bed in the mornings but nevertheless she would be the first in her kit and out running around the grounds as though her very life depended on it.

Plastic surgery had been recommended for at least fifty per cent of the students and some had already had their operations. The place resembled a hospital as they went through their different stages of recovery. Some had bruised eyes and plaster covering their noses — others had bandages around their breasts or red marks on their bodies, where moles had been removed.

Klara could barely wait for her turn. The night before her operation she crept into Luisa's bed. 'This is it!' she whispered.

Luisa felt her sister's cold, bony body beside her and could barely suppress a shudder. Klara felt like a corpse.

'Are you sure, Klara? Are you absolutely sure?'

Klara's eyes glittered in the silver moonlight.

'Of course, booby! What else? Do you understand what I went through to get us here? Some of those filthy men,

Luisa! You should never have to know what they like women to do! But I did it for this and now we are here! I have made my sacrifices already, Luisa — what happens tomorrow will be nothing compared to what happened before. Besides, you saw the others. They came out of it OK. Rudi looks good now his teeth are fixed. Think how I will look once they change this ugly old nose of mine.'

'Your nose is beautiful, Klara! Leave it as it is!'

Klara laughed. 'You don't know what you're on about! I have to be perfect, or I don't stand a chance. Do you want all those other models in America laughing at me because of it? Mister Lorenz says I have wonderful potential. He says I could be world-famous once my features are corrected. Just think, Luisa, next year it could be me on that statue in the square, posing for that photographer and wearing that fur coat!'

When Luisa woke the next morning her sister had gone — vanished like she had in the snowstorm on that day in the Alexandrovsky Gardens.

'Klara?' But this time she did not reappear to grab her by the collar and pull her mittens onto her hands. The others were staring at Luisa — some were sniggering, she was behaving just like a child.

'They took her away early for her pre-med,' Rudi called out. 'She'll be back by suppertime tomorrow. You'd better watch out, Luisa — that anaesthetic can put you into a real black mood. Watch what you say or we'll all be for it!' He was laughing but Luisa could not force herself to join in.

Rudi sought Luisa out after exercises, sitting down next to her on the bench in the studio and offering her a sip of his water.

'Look, Luisa, Klara has told me you are not really interested in modelling. Is that true?' She watched his Adam's apple bobbing as he leant his head back and swigged from the bottle.

91

Luisa shrugged. 'I used not to be interested. Now I know more about it I hate it,' she said. 'I hate to see what it is doing to Klara. She looks so ill – she has lost so much weight.'

Rudi smiled, showing off his new white teeth. 'She is a true professional, Luisa. You have to understand something about the job. All of us here are dedicated – we need to suffer a little to get anywhere, that's all. So Klara goes hungry – that's not so bad! Look at the life of a ballet dancer! Some of them dance until their feet bleed and they all have to diet. The sacrifice is the same, I think – though a dancer will suffer for longer.'

'But you eat, Rudi!' Luisa was mad now – too mad to remember her manners.

Rudi ruffled her hair with his hand. 'And so do you, little one! Perhaps it's just as well Klara takes the whole thing seriously or none of us would ever get on! I believe you're fatter than when you started, you know!'

He was right – Luisa was not just eating the cakes Rudi brought for her, she was eating Klara's share as well. All the sugar had given her spots, too. She didn't care, though – at least she didn't faint during class, as some of the girls did.

When she was called to the principal's office late that evening she assumed it was because of her weight. She looked across at Rudi as she left the dormitory, thinking perhaps that he had reported her.

Samuel J. Lorenz looked harried. His toupee was not square on his head and he wore jeans and a pullover, instead of his usual suit.

'Take a seat,' he told her. He steepled his hands and stared at Luisa.

'There is a problem,' he said. 'Perhaps not too serious but . . .'

Luisa sucked her cheeks in, trying to look slimmer. If

they threw her out of the course she would be parted from Klara.

'There was an accident this morning – the sort of thing that can happen at any time but which, thank God, is still rare enough. Nevertheless, mistakes, rare or otherwise, can happen at any time to anybody – as I'm sure you'll agree, Miss Orlova. We're none of us perfect, are we?'

Luisa shook her head. He sounded very reasonable. Somehow she appeared to be being let off the hook. She smiled politely.

'Do you have any close relatives, Miss Orlova?'

'No – no one. There's just me and Klara.' She felt a moment of panic. Was she being thrown off the course after all?

'I see.' He touched the tips of his fingers to his lips. There was dirt under one of his nails. Luisa was shocked to see it.

'Do you have any kind of guardian?'

'No – nobody, like I said.' – She was going to be expelled! 'Look – please wait until my sister gets back! You need to speak to her, honestly!' Klara would put things to rights – she always did.

'I'm afraid your sister has had to be taken away from here, Miss Orlova.'

So it was Klara that was in trouble! What on earth could she have done? Refused the operation at the last minute?

'Klara? Where is she?'

'At a larger public hospital near Zagorsk, about seventy-five kilometres from here. The move was only taken as a precaution. You understand, we always do the best for all our students.'

'Zagorsk?' It could have been another country for all Luisa knew. 'What is she doing there? Has she had her operation? What's happened?'

The principal studied the ceiling. 'She had a bad reaction to the anaesthetic, that's all. It happens sometimes – every operation has its risks, everybody knows that. They are doing everything for her they can. I was out there myself this afternoon, waiting for news. She is a healthy young woman, Miss Orlova – she should pull round OK.'

Luisa rose from her chair. 'She's dead!'

The principal laughed quietly. 'Klara is not dead. She is just taking a little longer than usual to come round from the operation, that's all.'

'I want to see her!'

The principal sighed. 'It's a long drive. Of course you can go there but you will have to start out in the morning. There's no need for too much disruption. If you want to make a phone call you may use my line. I have the number of the hospital here . . .'

But Luisa ran from the room.

'Rudi! Rudi' He heard her screaming his name long before she had reached their dormitory. He tried to get up, his head still full of sleep, but suddenly Luisa was upon him, shaking him, slapping him, screaming his name out over and over again.

'Luisa! Stop it! What the hell is up?' He grabbed her arms and pinned them down to her sides. She stopped yelling and stared at him, her dark eyes bulging from her head.

'Get your car, Rudi! We have to drive to Zagorsk! Hurry!'

'Have you been dreaming or something?' Rudi could make no sense of what she was saying.

'It's Klara, Rudi, she's sick! The operation went wrong – they had to take her to another hospital. Hurry, please – she may be dying!'

Rudi leapt from the bed and pulled on some clothes. When he told Luisa to shut up she did – at last someone was doing something.

*　　*　　*

It was cold outside – well below freezing – and at first his pick-up wouldn't start but he finally kicked it into life and they set off on the road out of town.

The roads were thick with ice and Rudi insisted on keeping to a safe speed, despite Luisa's pleading.

'Do you want us all to be killed?' he shouted, and she finally kept quiet. He sounded angry. She looked at his face. It looked set and determined enough. Luisa sat back and let him take care of the journey.

The hospital was a new one – built less than ten years before. Rudi said that was good – they would have the most up-to-date equipment, but to Luisa it was just a reminder of the seriousness of Klara's condition. She wore Klara's coat for luck – the inside-out one their grandmother had made. It smelt of Klara herself and the smell was somehow comforting.

Rudi gave Klara's name at the reception and Luisa was thankful he was with her because her sister had been booked in under her school name and Luisa would never have been able to remember that in the panic.

Klara was in a small room on the fourteenth floor. The room was dark apart from a spotlight above the bed that shone onto her face. A nurse sat beside her, reading a magazine. Luisa looked down at the bed. It was Klara but it was not Klara. She let out a laugh of relief and Rudi looked at her oddly.

'It's not her!' She covered her mouth with her hands. When she looked at Rudi her eyes were bright with excitement.

'Calm down, Luisa,' Rudi said. 'Of course it's her.'

And of course it was. Luisa had forgotten the operation and the bandages and the bruising. Beneath the puffy flesh and redness it was her sister's face alright.

'Klara?' She heard Rudi start to cry quietly. 'Klara?'

'She may not be able to hear you.' The nurse had a kind voice – the kindest voice Luisa had ever heard. Luisa watched as Rudi knelt and grabbed Klara's hand. She couldn't touch her sister like that. Her flesh looked like wax. She did not want to feel it. The room smelt terrible, too. Luisa had had no tea that day but suddenly she wanted to be sick.

Rudi was stroking Klara's hair. The hair was matted with the blood that had run from her nose. It made the hair stick to her face so that Rudi could not stroke the full length, his hand kept getting stopped, but he went on with it anyway.

'What's that?' There was a tube in one of Klara's arms.

'It's to feed her while she's asleep.'

The magazine slipped from the nurse's lap and fell to the floor. Luisa looked at her. Her hair was frizzed like mattress stuffing and the same colour as the freckles on her face.

'Will it fatten her up while she's like that? She has got so skinny at the school.'

The nurse smiled. 'I don't think it will. Don't worry, though.' She did not make Luisa feel stupid.

'When will she wake up?'

The nurse shrugged and pulled a face.

'Who knows? Do you believe in God? You have to understand she is in God's hands now. He will decide that sort of thing. You just have to wait and be as patient as you can.' Luisa started to cry too.

'Don't worry. I'll be here to take care of her.'

They waited all night by Klara's bed but God did not decide the moment was right to wake her. Luisa stared at her face for many hours, trying to make sense of it. How long would it take to repair?

'Is she dying?' she asked the nurse, but the nurse only shrugged. 'That is for God to decide,' she said.

* * *

'We have to go back to the school,' Rudi said the next morning. His eyes were red from crying and he needed a shave. Luisa had not known he and Klara were so close. She was appalled by his distress.

'No!' She could not leave Klara alone.

Rudi grabbed her by the arm. 'We have to,' he said. 'I have to speak to that Mister Lorenz.'

They drove back in silence and this time Rudi appeared to spare no thought for their safety, speeding along the motorway and taking corners so quickly his tyres squealed and slid on the ice.

Luisa was badly shaken by the time they pulled up in the courtyard. She was stiff with the cold and her stomach was so empty it hurt. She had tried to sleep during the drive but the van had been rocking too much and her head had banged hard against the glass, making it ache.

'I need some breakfast,' she said, rubbing her eyes until they were pink. Klara would have made sure she was fed.

Rudi clasped her by the shoulders, making her jump. 'Look, Luisa, I know you're used to Klara looking after you but she's not here now – not for the time being, anyway. You have to look after her for now – do you understand? There's no-one else, Luisa – just you and me. You are going to have to grow up very quickly. I know Klara allowed you to act like a baby but you're not any more – you're a young woman. You have responsibilities now and so do I. We have to do what's right for Klara, Luisa – she can't help herself – do you understand what I'm saying?'

Luisa nodded – though she really had no idea. The nurse had told her she would look after Klara. What more could she and Rudi do for her?

But Rudi was adamant: 'We have to see to things ourselves, Luisa. We have to do what's right for Klara.'

They went straight into the principal's office, Rudi pushing into the room without even stopping to knock. Samuel

J. Lorenz was practising his golf putt behind the desk.

'She is very ill. She may even die.' Rudi came straight out with it, shocking the principal and making Luisa snuffle with grief.

'I think you're exaggerating, young man.' Samuel put his golf club down slowly, 'Look at the effect you're having on her sister with your emotional outbursts.'

'This is your fault!' Rudi said. His face was bright red and his hands shook with anger.

'Mine?' the principal raised an eyebrow. 'You should understand these things can happen to anyone, no matter how much care is taken.' He smiled, 'You must be tired. Why don't you both get your heads down for a few hours? I'm sure your tutors will understand. What classes did you have this morning? I'll let the appropriate people know so that you don't have any trouble.'

Luisa went to the dormitory and fell gratefully into bed but Rudi didn't follow her — instead he woke her a few hours later. Luisa jumped when he shook her. She remembered what Klara had said about men coming into her bed and her first reaction was to call to her sister for help. Then she remembered what had happened and her expression changed from one of fear to grief.

'What is it? Is she dead?'

Rudi shook his head, putting a finger to her lips to silence her. He placed something on the bed between them — something wrapped in a metre of old-fashioned dress fabric.

'We need to move quickly,' he said. Luisa looked bewildered. 'You agree that what happened to Klara is the principal's fault, right?'

Luisa frowned. 'He said it could happen to anybody . . .' she whispered.

Rudi tutted. 'Don't be so stupid, Luisa! I told you you have to grow up! Do you think this would have happened to her if she'd had the operation in a proper hospital, with proper facilities? Lorenz is a scrounger, Luisa — he saves every kopek he can! He probably gets the cheapest butcher he can find to perform the surgery for him and look at the way she was half starved in the first place. She was too weak, anyone could see that!'

Luisa shook her head. 'You told me she was OK. You said it was all part of the sacrifices models make! You told me . . .' But Rudi shut her up.

'Keep quiet, Luisa! You're doing no one any good with all that.' He moved closer. 'We have to put things straight. He can't be allowed to get away with it. Someone has to teach him a lesson.'

'You?' Luisa was confused. Rudi talked big but he was not really the sort for a fight. Klara could have beaten him without breaking into a sweat.

'You'll have to help.'

Luisa's eyes widened. 'Me? I can't fight!'

Rudi shook his head, making her feel stupid. 'I'll sort the old man out. I just need you there, that's all. Just in case. Can you be brave, Luisa?'

He didn't wait for her answer. He opened up the dress fabric that lay between them on the bed and inside it was a gun – an old revolver. It gleamed dull silver-grey in the light. Just looking at the thing made Luisa feel she might wet her pants. Rudi was right then, she was a baby – only babies wet themselves like that.

'My father's,' he said. 'He bought it on the black market last year. He said it was to protect the family if burglars broke into the home. He said we have too much money.' Rudi laughed as though he had made a joke but Luisa wasn't listening – all she could see was the grey metal of the gun.

'Are there bullets in it?' she asked.

'Look – I don't mean you to shoot the bastard,' Rudi told her. 'Just point the gun at him to keep him still when I hit him, that's all. It'll stop him calling for help or anything. Not that anyone could hear through the walls of his office, but you never know. You just hold it and I'll handle the rough stuff.'

'Can you hit him, Rudi?'

'Of course – just a few times – just to show he's not to do what he did again. I need to wipe that smug smile off his face for a bit, that's all. Once he goes down you can kick him too, if you like. OK?'

'OK.' It didn't sound too bad. Rudi was right – the man deserved a few bruises for what he had done to Klara.

15

In the end the whole thing was over too quickly. Rudi waited until the lights were out in the dormitory and then he shook Luisa gently by the shoulder and she jumped out of her bed immediately. There was a sour sort of taste in her mouth, as though she had been sick in her sleep. She checked her pillow quickly, just in case, but there was nothing there. She spat into a handkerchief to get rid of the taste but it was still there afterwards and she saw streaks of blood from her gums in her spit.

Rudi looked bigger and older somehow. She felt like telling him the truth about her age suddenly – that she was really not the adult he assumed her to be – but that would have meant making Klara out to be a liar and Luisa could never have done that, even though Klara was no longer there.

She should have been angry, like Rudi. Anger made you tougher than you really were. It was her place to be angry. Klara was her sister. Rudi was only Klara's friend. But the anger would not come to her aid. She thought about hitting the principal with her fists for Klara's sake but the thought only made her feel stupidly weak.

She was so nervous she found herself smiling at Rudi. She hoped he had forgotten the gun, or that it was all a joke after all but then she saw it, tucked into his belt. It was a crazy place to put it – if it had gone off accidentally it would have taken half his leg away. It was the sort of place a child would have put a toy gun. Perhaps it meant it wasn't loaded after all.

Luisa forgot how they got to the office. One minute they

were in the dormitory and she was worrying about her bleeding gums and the next they were outside the principal's room, studying the light that spilled out from beneath the door. The light was grey and flickering. Lorenz was watching his television. He had a small set in the corner of his office and a pile of videos stashed behind it.

Rudi pushed the door open slowly. Lorenz was sitting in his chair with his back to them. He hadn't heard them enter. It was an awkward moment – how do you introduce yourself when you want to start a fight? Rudi passed the gun to Luisa silently. It was heavy and cold, though there was a warmer spot where it had touched Rudi's body. Luisa laughed out of fear and her hands shook as she held it.

'What can I do for you?' – So the principal had heard them after all. The sound of his voice made them both jump like rabbits. He turned his chair slowly. On the screen behind him two boys were making love.

Lorenz looked straight at Rudi. He ignored Luisa with her gun – he ignored her totally, as though she didn't exist – Rudi's shadow now, instead of Klara's.

Neither of them spoke – neither of them could speak.

'I heard from the hospital, Miss Orlova is doing fine. I hope you're pleased.' Luisa's heart leapt at the news.

'Liar!'

Lorenz smiled across at Rudi and steepled his hands, pressing his index fingers onto his lips thoughtfully.

'Stand up!' Rudi's voice was a boy's voice, shrill and hysterical.

'So that you can hit me?' There was a close-up on the screen behind – a penis and a tongue, locked together like swords. Luisa watched, mesmerized.

Lorenz laughed. 'I don't think so, do you? Go back to bed, boy. You're tired, it's been a long day.' Then he leapt at Rudi like a cat, a golf club clasped in one hand, ready to strike. Rudi was caught unawares. The golf club came down on his head but he twisted away before it could fall and it caught him square across the ear, making him howl out in pain. Luisa screamed. Rudi looked up at her, an expression of shocked surprise on his face. There was no blood but his ear was as red as a flame. Luisa heard herself laugh, though her eyes were fixed on the TV screen.

Lorenz pounced a second time and Luisa laughed again. She didn't mean to laugh but the noise came out of her mouth nonetheless. The scream was bad but the laugh was worse. She no longer had control over her own body. She watched the TV in an attempt to sort out her mind.

Rudi was somehow ready for the second blow. He watched the iron fall towards him with something like a smile of resignation on his face. This time he was hit more squarely because he didn't move and his knees crumpled like tissue and the floor shook as he fell in supplication.

There was blood this time. It came in a spray that stained the model cards around their feet. The sight of the red splashes on the white cards shocked Luisa more than the video and more than the violence. She wondered what would happen to those cards now they were ruined and she wondered how many of them were ruined. Rudi's blood was deep, dark red – darker than she would have imagined. Would the blood seep through the paper to ruin the fresh cards underneath? She knelt on the floor, scrabbling about to pick the top cards up before that could happen.

Now she had blood on her hand. She stared at her fingers, telling herself the sight of the blood was not so bad – she saw her own every month, after all. But this was Rudi's blood. She wondered if Rudi was dead. She tried to look at her hand closely but it would not keep still. The other hand was quieter but that had the weight of the gun to calm it.

'Luisa!' Her name came out in a retch. So Rudi was not dead. Somehow she clambered to her feet. Rudi was standing again, too. How had he managed that? His face looked terrible, so she steered her eyes back to the screen and ignored his cries.

'Luisa! Help me!' Rudi was screaming now but they could have been the cries of a gull overhead for all she cared. She had seen too much. She could not move.

Lorenz got no third chance. Rudi summoned a strength that came out of sheer terror and felled the older man with one desperate blow. When Luisa finally looked back again, Lorenz was on the floor and Rudi was kicking him joyously in the stomach. Lorenz's teeth lay beside his head and his hands clutched at his wig as though it were a helmet that would protect him.

'You too,' Rudi shouted, 'kick him now, Luisa, while he is still on the floor.'

Lorenz's stomach would have felt soft against her boot. Luisa shuddered. Lorenz started to vomit.

'Luisa?'

Rudi stopped kicking and walked over to her. There was blood matting his hair, just like Klara's. He took her hand, the one with the gun in it, and pulled her across to him. Lorenz was like a wounded bird at her feet. The vomit just trickled from his mouth. Rudi pointed at him but then the bird's wing stretched out and a hand grabbed at Rudi's leg. Luisa heard Rudi's scream of fear and her hand contracted around the gun. So, there were no bullets in the gun. Otherwise it would have gone off right at that moment and she would have killed him.

Then there was an explosion and Luisa felt her hand whip backwards so quickly it could have been torn off the end of her arm. She saw nothing in her panic. She looked at Rudi and they were both deaf from the noise. Her face was wet. When she put a hand to her face it came away covered with blood. Not Rudi's blood this time. Lorenz's blood. The blood felt warm as well as wet. She opened her mouth to laugh again but a scream came out instead.

She heard Rudi's voice from far away: 'What have you

104

done, Luisa?' Then his hand came across her mouth in an attempt to silence her.

It was as well his hand was there. When Luisa looked down at Lorenz – when she could no longer keep her eyes away from the floor – she saw that he was no longer there. What lay where the principal had been was a blood-spattered body, dressed in his clothes.

Grey light flickered on Luisa's and Rudi's faces as they gazed at one another over the terrible sight. Rudi took the gun from Luisa's hand, holding it with the fabric it had been wrapped in. His face was so distorted with terror that it frightened her more than the sight of the body. She laughed again and the laugh became a cough and she was unable to breathe.

'You were not supposed to use it, Luisa!' Rudi's voice was high-pitched with hysteria. 'You weren't supposed to use it! Not really! It was just for show! It was just to scare him! We're dead now, Luisa – you do know that, don't you? We're dead when they find out what you did!'

Luisa started sobbing. 'I didn't do anything, Rudi! The gun just went off by itself!'

Rudi shook his head slowly. 'You shouldn't have done it. I didn't mean you to use it.' His voice fell away.

'Come on,' he said, suddenly, and Luisa followed him, running, from the room.

16

London, 1994

'What did you do, Catarina – what the fuck are you hiding from me?'

Catarina's face stared back at Rick, impassive.

Find me, you bastard – find me if you can.

Scar tissue. Arms, legs, abdomen. What had happened? Why the lies about her past? Why so many lies? Did she want to be caught? Was she really hoping to be found out? But Rick didn't believe in that sort of psychobabble crap.

What did people do that made them want to hide it so deep? Was she illegitimate? Was is drugs? Prostitution? Or was her past really only hidden because it was boring? Was she some middle-class princess or whatever passed for one in Russia?

What did he want her to be? Make up the story first then prove it – he'd done it before loads of times. So what would he make up for her? What was he hoping for? What would write the biggest paycheck?

He allowed his brain to swim around in the deep end of his imagination. Then he wrote on his computer screen:

BEST STORY: *illegitimate daughter of Gorbachov.*
MOST LIKELY STORY: *prostitute.*

Rick decided he'd run with the latter.

17

Russia, 1988

They fled into the night – hand-in-hand – weightless – laughing now, although nothing was funny to them – nothing on earth – their laughter was hysterical.

'Stop Rudi – please – I'm going to be sick.'

'Don't be so stupid, Luisa. We can't stop, we have to get away.'

The moon was full, so that their eyes were bright with reflected silver, like dogs' eyes – like mercury. The steam rose from their mouths as they ran panting towards the van. Rudi threw the gun into the river and they watched it sink. They hugged one another and Rudi's cheek felt cold against her own hot face. Then they realized what they had done and they started to shake.

A fierce wind hit them, bending them in two like a blow to the gut. Rudi groaned and Luisa gasped for breath. The air had gone from her. She could neither breathe nor speak. She thought she was dying, sinking like the gun. The wind stopped abruptly and they staggered, caught off-balance. Luisa was still choking. She looked towards Rudi but he didn't see her – he was lost in his own terrors.

'Oh no,' she whispered.

'What have you done, Luisa?' Rudi asked again. 'You killed him. You have committed murder.'

'No, Rudi!'

'You shot him. You killed him.' Rudi's voice sounded calmer, which frightened Luisa more.

'I was scared, Rudi! He would have killed you! Your scream made me jump – the gun went off in my hand!'

Rudi looked straight at her. 'The gun will have your fingerprints on it, Luisa. The water may not have washed them away. Who knows what scientists can do these days? You pulled the trigger. You know you did. You are in serious trouble now.'

Then they were in the van – though neither of them knew how they had got there, and Rudi was driving like a maniac – swerving and skidding. Luisa didn't worry, she just wanted to be as far away as possible, even as far away as death if necessary – she didn't care if they were killed along the road. She had other fears greater than that of dying.

And nothing happened – it was amazing. The van did not hit a tree. No police came. Nobody stopped them. They just drove along. Rudi settled in at the wheel and Luisa wiped the blood off his face with her hankie and after that they could have been anybody – anyone at all once the van was straight on the road and their breathing became steadier. It was totally unbelievable – they had both felt so sure that retribution would be swift.

Finally Luisa spoke.

'I must see Klara.' They were on the right road – she saw that now. So why not?

'We can't.' Rudi's voice had changed. She ignored it. Its tone asked to be ignored. They drove towards the hospital. She knew he didn't mean what he said.

He parked a few kilometres back down the road, beneath some trees. Luisa was to walk the rest of the way. Rudi said they would be looking for the van and for the two of them together. He gave Luisa some money before she got out. 'Ten roubles for the nurse and the rest for yourself, in case anything happens.' Luisa stuffed the money into the pocket of her skirt. She looked back at Rudi once and his face looked grey and flat. His hands were still on the wheel, as though the van were moving. She thought about waving but it was a stupid thought. Murderers didn't wave to one another like ordinary people.

108

She managed to stop shaking once she stepped inside the hospital. The place was empty and quiet and no-one stopped her on the way to Klara's room. She had blood on her face still, but in a hospital that was OK – if they saw her people would think she had been in an accident.

It was as though nothing had happened – it was as though she had just come for a normal visit. She went into the toilets and no-one saw her as she washed the blood away and pressed her hair off her face with her wet hands. She passed a row of women in wheelchairs – old women, skinny and drooling, their limbs bent like broken twigs. One of the women smiled at her and it was only then that her nerve broke and she almost screamed out loud.

Klara was alone. Unmoved and unchanged – more like a wax dummy than Luisa's wickedly clever sister. Luisa was glad she looked like that. If she had looked more like Klara then she knew she would have fallen onto the bed and cried and begged for her help and advice.

'Help me, Klara! Tell me what I should do!'

But Klara's dummy could never have told her, so she stood beside it, staring, instead. She made herself touch its hand. It felt like wax. Was Klara inside there, somewhere? Luisa wanted to say goodbye but there seemed little point. There was more of Klara inside her own head than there was lying out on the bed.

'Goodbye.' It was a little-girl whisper. Klara would have been mad to hear her use such a voice.

'You're going away then?' The nurse stood behind her, her coiled-twine hair bouncing like broken bedsprings as she nodded her head.

Luisa sucked at her lip. She wanted the nurse's sympathy desperately. She wanted her to touch her on the arm as she had before. If she had she would have told her everything – everything! It would have been so easy!

Nothing happened, though. The dice had been tossed and the moment had passed. Should she tell Klara? 'Darling, I killed the man who put you here.' So what?

What use was it to her? All Klara wanted to hear were the little machines pumping by her bedside and the liquid food dripping into her veins.

'I've got to go away,' she said.

'Trouble?' Perhaps the nurse understood after all. Luisa nodded.

'Can I help?' The nurse was plain – almost ugly – but she had the kindest smile. Luisa felt tears flood her eyes.

She looked up at her. 'I have to leave for ever. I don't believe I'll see my sister again.' The tears began in earnest now.

The nurse moved towards her. 'Don't worry. Keep in touch when you can. I'll watch her for you – I've grown fond of her while she's been here. She's very beautiful, isn't she? I believe God must have more in mind for her than a short inconsequential life. Some people are special, you know. You get a feeling for these things when you work in a place like this. I was watching her tonight – just before you came in. Her face under the light . . . I'll do all I can, I promise you that much . . . it's just a pity . . .'

'What?'

The nurse smiled. 'It's best to keep an eye out in these places. Do you want anything extra for her – if you're not going to be here, that is?'

'Extra?' Luisa could not think, only repeat.

'You'll need to pay, I'm afraid. Do you have any money you can leave with me?'

So Rudi knew what was what, after all. Luisa pulled the money from her pocket. 'I thought it was all free . . .'

'It is.' The nurse took the money from her. 'The basics, anyway. Your sister needs extra care, though. They'd leave her lying here if they could. This will help to grease the wheels a little – get her a few little bits, like flowers and books for when she comes round. Don't worry about anything else, I'll see to it all.'

'You'll look after her for me? See that she gets the best possible? Don't let her die, will you?'

110

The nurse shook her head and more hair escaped from her cap. She had the kindest eyes. Klara was safe with her – she had their mother's blob of a face.

'Here's my name if you want to write to me – or you can phone if you like. Do it at night, though. It's quieter and I'll have time to talk. Don't forget the money, though – and you'll need to keep the payments regular. One day she'll answer the phone for me, you'll see!'

Luisa laughed with delight at the thought, but the laugh came out as a sob. She put her hand over her mouth to stop too much sadness bursting out. She read the name on the piece of paper she had been given: 'Nurse Olga Margolis'. Another ugly name – Klara would never have liked it – but it was just right, all the same.

The van was gone when she returned to the tree where it had been parked. Perhaps Rudi had driven to fetch them some food. Luisa sat on a rock by the roadside, waiting. She waited for over three hours and it had turned dark. Rudi had left her. She wasn't surprised. After all, she was the one who had killed the principal, not him. It was hardly fair that Rudi should suffer too. She rocked to and fro, hugging her knees to her chest. Her coat smelt of dust. Her feet ached. Her stomach was empty. Luisa didn't cry now, though – she couldn't, she was too scared even for tears.

18

A lorry driver picked Luisa up and drove her on several towns. The woman was tough and good-humoured; she gave Luisa advice about finding her own way in life and told her what was what when it came to searching for accommodation.

'They post notices on the trees in the parks – you must have seen them in Moscow sometimes. A young person will advertise, say for a roommate for six months. They write down how you should be – male or female, student or worker – if you fit the bill you tear the note down and call the number. Always sound polite and if you're a student then never admit it unless they ask specifically. Students come and go like fireflies – nobody trusts them.

'You look quiet – that's good. Too much noise is the worst thing when you're sharing. If they ask if you like pop music say no and shake your head. Tell them you read a lot and are not very talkative. You'll do OK.'

The woman laughed a lot. Luisa wondered how she could be so happy. She looked out for Rudi on the road. There was no sign of him, though. Perhaps he had returned to his parents.

The town she was dropped at was an industrial one – grey and bleak, with soot-splattered air that smelt of benzine and diesel. Luisa had no idea where she was. Moscow, with all its beauty, seemed to be on another continent. Luisa made her way to the nearest park and stared up at the trees. In Moscow the birds would have been singing and the tall trees alive with sticky-buds but the limbs of these trees were blackened by grime.

Luisa touched one of the trunks and the soot came away on her fingers. It didn't matter if she got dirty now, though, Klara was not there to nag her. She wished she was – she wished very badly that she was. Being nagged would have been a delight if it were the only price to pay for having Klara back with her again.

There was something very comforting about tears. They were hot – hotter than her face – and they ran down her cheeks like butter down warm toast. With them came a feeling of release.

Luisa considered pumping out some more but she bit at her lip and told her eyes not to. There was nothing tangible to be gained from them, she told herself – nothing at all. The people around her in the park would think she was strange and she did not need that, it was detrimental to her aims.

She straightened and pulled her head up. The pain of sadness was like a real pain, stabbing away at her gut. She was also hungry. Her feet were cold and her legs felt weak, like after a long illness. She ached from sitting in the lorry so long.

It was hard not to give up – but then she hadn't actually done anything yet – only hitched a ride and walked a few kilometres. It wasn't such a big thing after all, when she thought about it like that – a little walk followed by a long ride.

It was the strangeness that tired her, though – the strangeness of everything. There wasn't one thing or one person she knew there. It was completely bewildering.

When an Uzbek visited a new town they would be given names to look up – friends of friends, relations of acquaintances, cousins of uncles, in-laws of nephews. It made things easier – with a list of names you were never alone. Things became less strange once you had knocked on a door and presented yourself. Luisa had to be alone, though. She had put herself in that position when she had fired Rudi's gun. She didn't remember doing it now – only the noise it had made. The gun had looked hard to handle – a man's weapon. She couldn't believe her hand was capable of firing such a piece.

It had been, though, and now she had to lay low whether she liked it or not. If she was capable of using a gun she was capable of looking after herself. Then she remembered it was her fourteenth birthday that day and the tears came anyway, without pausing to listen to reason this time.

The truck driver had been right – there were notes advertising rooms to share pinned to the trees. Luisa read a few then found a couple that she thought might be suitable. In the end she took the first one – she had no more change to make phone calls.

The room was a small one, to be shared with a tiny, puppy-faced woman who worked at night, therefore Luisa was to have the place to herself when she slept. The woman asked few questions – she just needed the money in advance and Luisa gave her a good portion of the cash Rudi had left with her. There were many instructions about the heating and the shared bathroom and then the woman gave her the keys and left. Luisa thought her too trusting but then she looked around and saw there was really nothing there to steal.

There was red lino on the floor – worn to black in places – and the walls were so coated with grease and dirt that the pattern painted on it was almost indiscernible. The bed was a little like the one at home – a low metal cradle that could be folded away if guests came. There were blankets on the bed and then a thick rug – a good one – perhaps the woman had relatives who sent her such things.

The single armchair was old and covered in worn green plastic. On the chairback lay a snowy white lace doyley – perhaps from the same source as the rug. The woman's shoes still stood beneath the bed. Luisa pulled them out, blowing off the dust and buffing them with the sleeve of her coat. They were good shoes, but badly worn. Luisa tried to push her feet into them but the shoes were too small.

There was a small picture on the wall of a young man in uniform. The landlady's sweetheart, perhaps? Luisa took it down and pulled it out of its frame. There were words written in ink on the back: 'To Freya from Vitali' – would a sweetheart write in such a cold way? The ink had soaked through the paper a little, giving Vitali a blue bruise to the left of his cheek. Luisa shuddered.

She opened the drawer by the bedside. There was a pair of glasses in there; some cough lozenges, a comb with two hairs in it and a packet of contraceptives. Luisa got up from the bed and hung the picture back on the wall. Vitali looked cruel, suddenly. She pulled the rug from the bed and curled up on the plastic-covered chair. She was tired enough to drop but somehow the bed had lost its appeal. She imagined it to smell of cruel-looking Vitali and his was the last face she saw in her mind before she finally dropped off to sleep.

It was the following morning – after she had slept, bathed and eaten, and all other vital necessities of life had been dealt with – that Luisa first experienced a new pain in her soul. It was one she had never experienced before and she had some trouble identifying it. It was not like the pains of grief and homesickness – they had a strange sweetness about them, despite the bite they gave. This pain gnawed harder than hunger and grew just as quickly.

Finally she realized – the pain was called guilt. Guilt for what they had done to their father when they had left him alone, guilt for leaving Klara by herself in the hospital – and guilt most of all for taking another man's life. She hugged her knees to her chest and considered the new problem.

'We'd best get acquainted, you and I,' the pain said. 'After all, I shall be probably be staying with you for the rest of your life.'

19

'You can't walk in those shoes? Then you will have to learn fast. And what about your swimsuit? Don't you have one? I don't understand! Whatever are you playing at?'

A girl leant across to Luisa. 'Here — you can have one of mine.' She handed over a swimsuit — burnt orange spandex, which would make Luisa's pale skin look like suet — but a swimsuit nevertheless.

The girl smiled. Luisa looked away quickly. Kindness made her cry these days — anything made her cry these days — but kindness was the worst of all. When people were kind it was like an onion had been held right under her nose. Not that it mattered much — most people she met were more like the show organizer — bastards of the first order. Those sorts of people were OK, though. They made her angry, which was better than the tears. At least they paid bed and board for the contestants, plus some money for travel. Luisa had hitched to the competition and pocketed the money instead.

'Don't tell me, let me guess — this is your first beauty parade — am I right?'

Luisa nodded. 'Yes, of course you're right.'

The girl smiled again. 'Would you like a little help?'

She didn't wait for an answer. She moved right over onto the next seat and started painting Luisa's face.

'How old are you, sweetheart?'

'Eighteen.' Luisa had become used to lying about her age.

The girl looked surprised. 'Same as me. How do you keep your skin so good? Look at mine — a mass of lines

116

and wrinkles. I should wear lighter make-up but I need this heavy stuff to cover the whole lot up. It's stage make-up – my boyfriend's an actor so he gets it for me. It gives you spots if you keep it on too long but what can you do? Wrinkles or spots? It's not much of a decision, now, is it?'

Luisa shook her head. The girl tutted and wiped off some liner that had smudged.

Luisa had kept her head down for many months – almost a year, but then her money had run out and she had been warned by the landlady she would need to find a new place to live. She had found ways of making money over the year – selling change for the telephones had been one of them – but the money was not much to live on. She had even walked past the big hotel in the town, considering whether . . . but she had promised Klara. She would never try that again, even though she was older now, nearly fifteen. The girls she saw inside did not look much older. But she had made a promise.

Then she had seen the advertisement in the newspaper. There was to be a beauty competition held many kilometres away, near the coast. The prize was vast amounts of money and a contract for work in western Europe. Luisa's mouth had gone dry and her hands damp with sweat. Klara needed more money – the nurse had told her when she phoned.

She had looked in the mirror. A beauty? Hardly. All she saw were the great dark Uzbek eyes and the wide nose and mouth. Her hair was fair still – she washed it in lemon each day in case the soot turned it black – but so what?

There was no other way, though. She needed the money badly. Perhaps if she tried some make-up – but she had no money to buy some. She bit her lips to make them pink and patted her cheeks to get colour. She tried smiling but the smile looked terrible – far too false. She tried to remember when she had last smiled properly. You lost the knack with time, she decided. She stopped to watch a childrens' theatre in the street, hoping the puppets would make her laugh. That did the trick. She laughed out loud with the other kids and then tried to carry the smile back home with her so that she could see how it looked in the mirror.

She pushed socks down the front of her vest and the landlady caught her posing with them in the mirror.

'What the hell are you up to?' She appeared annoyed. Luisa tried the smile she had worn in the street.

'I'm thinking of entering for a beauty competition. Perhaps I could do something with myself. I need the money – what do you think?'

The landlady leant across the bed and turned Vitali's photo to the wall. If Luisa was *that* sort of a girl she did not want her boyfriend looking at her, even from a photograph.

'I think I would like you out by the end of the month,' she said, quietly. Luisa looked at the back of the photo and wondered what she had done wrong.

So now Luisa was there – at the finals. Being selected for the finals was no big deal – they selected the candidates from their letters alone without having ever seen them. Therefore, there were three hundred in the finals and not one of them could afford to be vain as they had not even been seen in the flesh yet. The good thing was that those who lived out of town – like Luisa – were placed in hotels for a week. The hotels were not grand but Luisa didn't care, she had food and a bed and, best of all, it was free.

It had occurred to her some weeks before that winning the competition might be a problem. The winner was sure to get her face in the press and then someone might recognise her and report her to the Ministry of Internal Affairs. She felt she had changed thoroughly since she had left the school but when she looked in the mirror she found the same face staring stubbornly back at her.

In the end, once she was picked for the finals, she had no option. Regrettably, she had to dye her hair black. Now she looked different. Now she looked as strange as she felt. She tried to cut it too but the hand that held the scissors would not obey her, so she told herself the dye would do the trick by itself.

Her face felt heavy and sticky once the girl had finished her make-up. She looked twenty-two now, instead of fifteen. She pouted her lips and the other girl looked pleased. She looked ridiculous. Her eyelids were emerald and glittered like snowballs. When she blinked her lids felt heavy because of the black mascara. She blinked one eye at a time to see how the other looked. The rouge had produced hollows in her cheeks. She sucked them in further and tilted her head back.

'Do you want me to curl your hair?' The girl had some electric rollers – all the other girls had used them.

'Do they burn?' Luisa asked. The girl laughed at her. Next minute she had hot rollers all over her head and was scratching at her neck when they itched the skin.

'Looks good – no?' Luisa couldn't reply. When the rollers were out, her hair looked ten times thicker. The girl sprayed it with lacquer too, so that it didn't move, no matter how much you shook it. The costume looked quite tasteful now, compared to her face and head. Still, the look was OK. It was how all the other girls looked – well, those who knew how these things worked, anyway. There were of course a few farm girls who were fat and ruddy-faced. And more than a few old babushkas who had lied about their age. Klara would have loved to have seen them – one of them wore a swimsuit that could not have seen the light of day since the war.

'Do you think I am in with a chance?' she asked the girl who had helped her. The girl just shrugged.

'Who knows?'

*   *   *

119

Luisa did not go out on stage when the false name she had given was called as she did not recognize it at first. Then somebody pushed her and she was walking into the light, dazzled by its brilliance – as blind as a moth banging about a naked bulb.

The lights made her sweat. She worried about what lay beyond them. She tried to walk as she had been taught at the school and to smile as she had done at the puppets in the street.

She counted her strides. There was a smell like scorching in the air. Twenty-eight steps and she was at the judges' table. They sat there in the dazzle – a row of indistinct faces that she was supposed to impress. She smiled. The soles of her feet were wet too. She had a bad desire to urinate, like a kid called up before the school board. What if she wet herself, there and then? The thought made her legs shake.

A piano had played her in and now it tinkled impatiently, ready to play her out again. But her legs wouldn't work. She turned towards the source of the music. 'Help me, play me off.' The piano became louder but her legs just wouldn't obey. Someone whistled in the audience and then a slow handclapping began. Her throat constricted badly, blocking her saliva so that she could not even swallow. She was choking.

The audience were animals. Someone threw a drink can. It hit Luisa on the side of the head but she didn't flinch – she couldn't, she couldn't move at all.

Someone took her arm – a firm hand – decisive, like a parent to a child.

'Come – let me help you off.' She looked up at the face that went with the hand but there was nothing there, just the same brilliant glow that blinded her wherever she looked. The piano stopped. She walked a few steps with the hand and the audience clapped gratefully, glad to be shot of her. Still smiling, she grabbed at the arm above the hand. It was a man's arm, warm and muscular beneath the fabric of the jacket. She smelt a wonderful smell of rich cologne. She would have followed that arm anywhere – to hell and back, if necessary.

The darkness off stage was as alarming as the light on it. The hand became a pair, guiding her by the shoulders. She was pushed into a chair. Someone gave her a glass of water. Her teeth began to clatter so hard she could barely sip at it. When she looked up there was a face before her, close to her own.

'Are you OK now?' It spoke in English.

'Yes – thank you.' Some reflex action enabled her to reply in the same language. Schoolgirl English. She saw the stranger smile and his eyes soften. He had the handsomest face she had ever seen – she was only just aware of that. He had a tan. His eyes were brown, like her own. When he smiled only one side of his mouth lifted. He needed a shave but then that was the fashion – the dark stubble set off his thin lips and white teeth. Even his ears looked good. He was staring her straight in the eye, looking down into her soul as though he already knew her.

'Thank you,' she repeated – it was the only English she could remember now.

'Think nothing of it.'

'Pardon?' she was back to Russian now. The man looked puzzled – it was obvious he spoke not one word of her language.

'Excuse me.'

'That's OK.' He stood up suddenly and she felt as though her world had just tilted on its axis.

'I have to get back to the judging.' He looked around for help – 'Tell her I have to get back, will you. She doesn't understand me.' He tipped a hand to the side of his head in salute and then he was gone. Luisa felt bereft.

'Feeling any better?'

He was there that evening, walking through the foyer of

121

Luisa's hotel. She could not believe he was there – she thought she would never see him again.

He wore a beige suit and an open-necked shirt. His hair looked wet, as though he had just washed it and combed it through damp. He was tall – tall enough to make her look up at him when they spoke. She breathed in hard when he stood near her, so that she could smell his cologne again.

'I am good, thank you.' She could not stop herself smiling. He laughed at her broken English.

'"Good" – that's good. I'm glad you are good. Number two hundred and six is good. That's wonderful.'

Two hundred and six had been her number in the competition.

'So what are you doing down here in the foyer? You appeared to be looking for something or someone. Was it your lover? Has he run away from you?'

She looked down at the floor. 'I came down to look for some butter.'

'Some butter?' He took her arm and they walked together towards the desk, 'Ah, now that sounds much more interesting. Not a lover but some butter. And so late at night.'

'I need it to take all this off.' Luisa pointed to her make-up. The man laughed. 'Here, come here.' He took a large white handkerchief from his pocket, wetted it under the drinking-fountain and wiped it gently across her face.

'So there you are in there,' he said, quietly. 'I wondered who I might find under all that. So you are real, after all. Try soap in future, butter will make your skin stink. Are you hungry?'

Luisa nodded. She was always hungry. Even when she was full she felt hungry at the same time.

'Good – then I'll buy you dinner. Go and change, I'll be down here again in an hour.'

She had no other clothes and was ashamed to admit it.

122

She sat in her room and chewed her nails for a while. Then, when the hour was almost up, she prowled the corridors in desperation. Several rooms had open doors. She crept into a few, just to look. One had a couple inside but she just said she had the wrong room number – it was easy enough if you kept your wits about you. In the last one she found what she was looking for.

The room was empty but the cupboard was full – lots of dresses, too many for the occupant to miss one for the night. Luisa pulled out the plainest one she could find – less identifiable if the woman should see her – and fled back to her own room to change. She would put the dress back in the morning. No-one would ever know what she had done. It was hardly like stealing.

'You look good, number two hundred and six.'

Walking into the restaurant was almost as bad as walking out on stage. The man kept his hand on her elbow and she realized with gratitude that he was steering her, keeping an eye on her.

'My name is Alex, by the way – Alex Head. Easy to say. Is it easy for you to pronounce?'

Luisa repeated the name. Alex smiled in a way that told her nothing. Had she pronounced it right or not?

Alex chose her dinner for her and ordered her Pepsi to drink with it as he said wine was bad for the complexion. When she ate everything on her plate he whispered that she should have left some or she would get fat when she was older.

'Don't you care?'

Luisa shrugged. 'Why should I? Russians learn to eat whatever they are given.'

Alex leant across the table. 'What about your career?'

'Career?' Luisa thought she might choke.

'You want to be a beauty queen.'

'No!' He was joking with her. But he didn't smile when he spoke. Surely he could never suppose after that terrible experience . . .

'I lost! I must have come last – or lower! How could I ever . . .'

Alex looked angry. 'You got stagefright, that's all. It can happen to anyone. You'll grow out of it – you'll have to if you want to do better next time.'

'Next time?' It sounded so absurd.

Alex pointed to the right knife for her to use for the cheese. 'You have a lot of promise, number two hundred and six. You could do well.'

'But I didn't win.'

'You couldn't have won, even if you hadn't bottled. The thing was rigged, do you understand? No? Money changed hands – bribes – do you understand the word? You were good, not bad. You could be better. But even if you were better you would still have lost.

'I was a judge, remember? We were told who should win. Your friend – the one I saw doing your make-up – she knew she would win, it was decided before. Understand?'

Luisa nodded, though she did not really understand at all. Still, she was happy just to watch him as he talked.

'I want to ask you something, number two hundred and six – something important. Would you like to get on as a model? I can help you if you would. I think you have something. But you have to be keen.'

Luisa chewed on a breadstick. 'Do I earn money for this?' It was her only consideration. Money meant Klara could be kept more comfortably.

Alex looked at her oddly. 'Yes – thousands, if you want.'

'Thousands?'

'Of dollars – not that funny money you play around with here.'

Thousands of dollars – the idea made her feel sick. Alex was still looking at her strangely. She wished she had not eaten so much food. Perhaps he was right – perhaps you should leave more on your plate. It was his eyes that were making her feel strange. She tried to avoid their gaze, though she could feel them on her all the time. When she

124

looked up she felt the buzzing in her stomach. She put down the breadstick and sipped at her Pepsi instead.

'Are you interested?'

Luisa nodded. 'Yes.'

'Good.' Alex placed his hand across hers. She thought she might throw up there and then.

20

Alex took Luisa to dinner every night and when her free room at the hotel ran out, he paid for another two weeks. Luisa had never seen so much wealth. He ordered the best food each night and gave such big tips to the staff that Luisa became embarrassed at the way they looked at her. They obviously thought she was up to no good with the rich Englishman, though, in reality, Alex had not even attempted to kiss her.

If he had tried, Luisa would have let him – she had decided that many days before. She was drawn to him – she yearned for his strength and protection. The only time she felt safe was when she was with him. He somehow banished all her bad feelings – apart from the guilt, and even that seemed less fierce when she listened to him speak.

Alex had contacts that Luisa could only dream of. He fixed her a passport and documents so that she could leave the country and travel with him to England. He must have paid a vast amount to get such things on the black market.

In England she would be safe. No one would find her so far away. Alex told her to sit up straight when she ate and she did so gratefully. He made her stop dying her hair and she did that too – no longer fearful of the MVD. If they found her Alex would bail her out somehow, she was sure of it. She washed her hair in the bath twice a day to make it the colour Alex wanted. The dye came out quickly and she scrubbed at her scalp until the skin was raw.

Then, one night he came back to her hotel with her in the taxi, instead of sending her off alone from whatever restaurant they had eaten at. He said nothing as he did so and Luisa was too frightened to question him. When the taxi stopped he paid the driver and Luisa heard his footsteps following her as she made her way into the foyer. The night porter looked at her over his glasses but when he saw Alex he smiled politely.

Luisa could barely breathe. The air seemed heavier, suddenly. She wanted to turn to Alex, to talk to him as usual but his silence was overpowering and she knew it was right to keep quiet.

She could not find her room key. She fumbled in her bag – dropped it on the floor so that its contents spilled across the lino. Still Alex said nothing, just watched her scrabbling about, throwing her paltry bits back into the sack. The key somehow found its way into her hand. She was inside the room and so was he and the door was shut fast behind them.

'I have to stay here tonight,' was all he said. He switched on the radio.

'Do you know this song?' Luisa shook her head.

'It's by Eric Clapton.' – He hummed a few bars – 'Why don't you take a bath?'

'Yes.'

Luisa took her bath. The water was so hot it turned her skin pink. The soap smelt bad to her – she wished the hotel had provided better. The running water was so noisy she could hear nothing from the other room. Perhaps he was listening to more music. Perhaps he was already asleep. She scrubbed herself hard between the legs, rubbing the soap into her pubic hair until she thought she must smell as sweet as the soap would allow.

Alex had ordered some champagne. His shirt was open at the neck and Luisa could see his chest. It was as brown as his face. She had not thought there was so much sun in England.

He passed her his glass and she took a sip and coughed. It was the first time he had allowed her to drink alcohol.

'We're celebrating,' he said, as though he had heard her

thoughts. 'I'm to become your manager. You're going to be famous.'

Luisa smiled. She did not understand the last word but she smiled because Alex smiled.

'You must be tired.' He leant across and ran a finger along her cheek, just beneath the eye. 'Why don't you get into bed?'

Luisa had never felt so embarrassed before. Alex was staring at her yet she had to get undressed. Her dress was old but her underwear was older. What would he think when he saw it? She had no robe so had dressed again after her bath.

Alex would want to know only beautiful women with beautiful underwear – all she had was the stuff she had owned as a kid. The girls in the beauty pageant had all laughed when they saw it. Alex would be disgusted. She looked towards the bathroom. She could take her clothes off in there but then she would never be able to run naked across the room to the bed.

Alex saw the fear in her eyes. 'What if I go and clean my teeth?' he asked. Luisa nodded. It was a wonderful idea – the best she had heard all day.

Once he was gone she pulled off her clothes so fast she almost ripped them, then threw herself into the bed – turning the light off as well for good measure. Now Alex could not even see her. Her teeth began to chatter even though the room was warm.

She could feel Alex's presence in the room again even though she couldn't see him. It was like listening for an animal in the dark and knowing it was there even though your ears couldn't hear it. She pressed her knuckles to her mouth, sucking at them like salt-covered pebbles. There was a slight noise as he walked across the floor and then he was on the bed beside her.

Alex ran his finger down the length of her nose and Luisa shivered at its touch. He shushed her gently like a child. His finger pressed against her lips. She could not tell if he was naked too – the blanket lay between them. She had climbed between the sheets but Alex had only thrown the top quilt over himself. She could neither see him nor hear him – she could just smell the heat and the tension of his body in the blackness.

'Do you know what you are doing to me, number two hundred and six?' His voice was dark and gentle like velvet.

He took her hand.

'Little one.'

Her hand was damp and it shook, like an animal. She allowed it to be led towards his warmth. It was guided past his chest, brushing the hairs there, down past his stomach and then – and then it stopped. He let out a low groan and she imagined his eyes had closed. Her hand touched nothing, only his hand. What had she done? How had she given him pleasure? Or was the groan a groan of pain? The heat from his body was massive.

'This is what you do to me.'

He pulled her hand upward, to his face. He pressed her fingertips against his cheek. The cheek was damp. Was he crying? Why? Luisa felt a rush of compassion that smothered all but a few of her fears.

He released her hand suddenly. She wanted to caress his face, to stop the tears, but instead her hand hovered like a hawk. Should she touch him again? What did he want?

When his finger touched her its touch was so light and yet it came with an electricity that made her gasp with surprise.

The finger paused, then moved to her chin and ran down the arch of her neck, tickling as it passed the soft flesh beneath the jaw.

He pressed his lips against her ear. 'Trust me,' he whispered. She did trust him. But she could not stop the shivers.

The hand moved so slowly that she could have screamed out from the tension. There were knots inside her and they were tightening. Her heels dug into the mattress and she would have squirmed out of the way if she had not been

129

so mesmerized. What should she do? Was she allowed to move? She lost all sense of perspective – there was only the finger and her in the darkness.

It caressed her breastbone but did not touch her breasts. Would it? She had no control. She did not even know if she wanted it to.

The fingers ran lightly onto her shoulders and down the length of her arm. Her own fingers stretched and the skin of her forearm pimpled in a reflex.

'Close your eyes, number two hundred and six.'

Luisa closed her eyes. The fingers were disembodied now, moving gently, rhythmically. She felt her spine start to relax. They circled her nipples, as light as moths' wings and her back arched slightly, willing them down, seeking them out. They discovered each rib at a time and then ran in a line down her middle, from her breastbone to her navel.

'Breathe the air, little one.'

Luisa breathed deeply and the air smelt so sweet she could almost taste it. There was a warm breeze from the window that ran through the jasmine trees in the court-yard.

'Breathe with me.'

She picked up his rhythm. It was slow and deep and her hips moved in time with it. He ran across each of the bones of her pelvis and drew circles on her stomach that made her gut ache with a contraction deep inside. His palm brushed against her pubic hair and that slight touch was electric, so that she leapt with the shock.

She felt Alex's smile against her ear.

His palm was rubbing circles now, though barely touching her flesh, just hovering above the brittle hairs. She felt a warmth begin to grow inside her along with the ache. She tried to speak – to say something – but Alex stopped her with the fingers of his free hand.

Her hips rose slightly from the bed but his hand rose with them, keeping the touch unbearably light.

130

There was nothing else in the room with her now – just the hand and the darkness and the sound of her own deep breathing. Luisa made fists with her own hands and then splayed the fingers wide. Her head tilted back and her lips parted. The palm of the hand moved faster, but still in its rhythmical circles. She felt it on her flesh now.

Her legs relaxed and opened slightly and she let out a small animal cry of desire.

And then suddenly the hand was gone. She gasped, but it didn't return. She squeezed her eyes harder shut and her fists beat against the sheets but nothing more happened. The mouth had gone from her ear too – her breathing was no longer guided by Alex's own. Luisa felt cold and alone and empty and hollow inside, as though something vital had been ripped from her. She opened her eyes.

Alex lay beside her in the darkness though she could not see his face to tell if his eyes were open or not. She waited, barely breathing now. Something had to happen. But nothing did. He was as still as a corpse. Not sleeping, though, there was no relaxation of his body. What was wrong? What had she done? She thought of her arousal of a few moments before and she felt ashamed. Alex must have been disgusted – or worse. She lay still on the bed until her bones ached with the effort of not moving. When she woke it was morning and Alex had already gone.

21

Nurse Olga Margolis put down her book with a sigh when her pager called her to the phone. It was early morning – barely light. She was off duty in less than three minutes and her childminder would leave the apartment whether she were home in time or not.

'Nurse Olga?' It was the young blonde girl – the one with the sick sister. The nurse took a breath. She still found these calls unpleasant – necessary though they were.

'Miss Orlova?'

'How is my sister?'

'I'll have to check. Can you hold?' The nurse had not been on Klara's ward for a week. When she got to the room she saw the bed was empty and the mattress turned back. She grabbed a passing orderly.

'What happened to the patient in here?'

The man barely stopped. 'She died last night.'

'The girl? The blonde one?' – but the man had said enough. Nurse Olga made her way back down to the phone. Luisa would be upset. Her money would stop. Klara no longer needed it but Olga did – badly.

'When are you coming to visit, Miss Orlova?'

There was a deep, tragic sigh from the other end of the phone.

'I told you, nurse, I can't. It's impossible. I can never go back there . . .'

'Your sister is the same – there is no change. Don't worry.'

'Are you still taking care of her?'

'Of course. I told you. I am like a sister to her now.'

There was a silence at the other end. Why did relatives always take so long to digest simple words? Sometimes you had to repeat yourself ten times over before they understood. It was as though dealing with medical matters somehow anaesthetized their brains.

'You haven't sent any money in a long while.' She disliked being blunt but the minutes were ticking away.

The girl let out a sob.

'Crying won't help her, you know.'

'I do know – you're right – but sometimes it's hard not to . . . Is she OK? Does she still have the things she needs?'

'It's not so bad. They came to take her to another room – a smaller one, without windows. They said she couldn't see, so what difference did it make?' The nurse looked at her watch as she spoke, 'I'm sure she can hear the birds though, Miss Orlova, so I paid the bit extra out of my own purse. I couldn't bear to see them move her.'

The line was bad but she was sure she heard the girl gasp.

'Thank you, oh thank you. I will pay you back – I promise! Someone has offered me work – well-paid work. I may have to go abroad to do it, but it will mean I can send regular payments. Please continue looking after her!'

'I don't know how long I can afford to keep paying, Miss Orlova. I have a family of my own, you know. Do you suppose I have much left from my salary at the end of the month?'

'Please! It will not be for long, I promise! I'll get the money somehow!'

'They only change her bedlinen once a fortnight now, you know . . .'

'Please!'

The nurse sighed again.

'Very well.'

'Thank you.' Luisa put the phone down slowly.

22

Alex appeared at lunch as though nothing had happened. He was the same Alex that he had been before – business-like, charming, authoritative – nothing had changed. And yet . . . but what had she expected? Something in his eyes, she decided. She had expected a change in his eyes. Some new warmth and intimacy. The glow of a little fire that had not burned there the day before. There was nothing, though. Luisa felt she had somehow let him down.

She picked over the events of the night before in her mind, like a vulture picking over bones. What was there to think about? What exactly had they done? Had he shown love for her? She remembered Alex's tears, that he had been so keen to let her see. Had he sought something more from her? How had she let him down?

She wondered if there was a new fire in her own eyes and, if there was, did Alex see it there? She felt embarrassed suddenly and kept her eyes lowered to the table.

Alex threw an envelope down before her. It held her passport, papers and airline tickets. She was leaving for Europe. She was going to be famous and make thousands of dollars.

She stared at a bread roll and her eyes filled with tears. She wanted to throw herself onto the ground and cling to it so that nothing could part her from her country. Klara was there, her father was there, the sticky-bud trees were there and the snow was there. But they were parted from her already. She could never go back to those things, so what was there to lose? There was a lump in her throat the size of a dough ball.

'We're leaving next month,' Alex told her, wiping his clean knife on his napkin. 'It will give you time to say your goodbyes and pack your things up.'

What goodbyes? She could never go to visit Klara and her father would not speak to her. She could have packed her things together in two minutes. She tried to smile.

'Thank you.' The words sounded squeezed when they came out of her mouth.

'Are you happy, little one?'

'Of course.' Luisa had never felt so confused before in her life.

Alex leant across the table and took her hand, pressing the fingers together so hard they hurt.

'Smile, then.'

This time Luisa smiled.

23

London, 1994

So Catarina had been married. That little fact alone had cost Rick five hundred in bribes. A reasonable investment, though, especially when he discovered how easy it was to track down information on the blushing groom. The guy had been a media junkie – his face popped up all over once you went back in time through the files. Then he vanished too, about the time Catarina appeared – give or take a year or so.

What was this then – a sex-change scandal? A man disappears and then Catarina appears? Was Alex Head really Catarina Kirkova? The idea tickled Rick but then it depressed him with its silliness. Then his depression depressed him even more because he knew a few years ago he would have run with that story for the hell of it and enjoyed himself in the process.

He looked at her picture again. He didn't want anything like that for her. He wanted something good and he wanted something that would destroy her. But nothing silly. He was going soft. But not too soft.

24

London, 1990

The Leica had jammed.

'Shit!'

Two thousand dollars' worth of fucking state-of-the-art fucking technology and the fucking thing had jammed.

Eve tore it from its tripod and threw it onto the ground. Now it was broken.

Happy now, Evie? No, not happy – deeply ashamed. She looked around for someone else to blame. You're being too New York. Take a powder. Calm it. Chant a little. Breeeeathe. You're in England now. They paid for a shoot, not for a fucking production number.

Her assistant picked the camera up gingerly, shaking it against his ear to hear the rattle of broken dreams.

'Load up the other one, Stevie-boy.' She turned her head away, like it didn't matter. Two thousand pissing dollars. Plus the lens. Bluff it out, though, never lose face. The Hendrix of the fashion world – 'Keep the equipment coming, boys, there's an artist at work here and she's trying to create.'

Create what? Eve looked across at the model on the backdrop. Sante Victoria – well-known bulimic-depressive: 'Sorry dear, didn't recognize you with your wrists stitched up.' She was only good till lunchtime – if they went on any later she'd fade away like the snow in summer sunshine.

The new camera stood loaded and ready. Eve stooped to look through the lens. Sante appeared stable enough, with her marshmallow skin and her burger-bun-brown eyes.

'Polaroid back?'

'It's on there already, Eve.'

Her mouth twitched as she turned to face Stephen but there was no hint of irony in his tone and his expression was pure one hundred percent Sistine Chapel angelic. Fair hair. Blue eyes. Pure Huckleberry Finn.

She bent again. The boy troubled her. He looked so cute, so young, so totally unsullied, yet she was certain he fucked like a rabbit. All the models lusted after him – Sante's mournful eye followed his butt across the studio, just as Eve was trying to focus . . .

Something was wrong.

She shook her head – looked again.

Simple techniques – one light, soft and bounced from a large white umbrella, a touch of fill-in to bleach out any shadow. Sante looked fit enough – the make-up artist had done his job well. She had looked like the walking dead when she had arrived at six that morning – one cup of expresso and a thrown-up bacon sandwich had brought the colour back to her cheeks, though. They had heard her being sick from the studio.

There was music playing – old stuff, from The Police. A ghostly guitar. Stephen sang along, in the wrong key.

'Shoot her, Evie, shoot her now, before she escapes.'

The lights around Sante exploded with a soft pop – the loveliest of all noises – the best sound on earth. Another picture taken, another photo in the bag. Sante looked startled, disorientated. 'Too late, my lovely, too late.'

Pull the Polaroid from the back of the pack. Stuff it under your armpit and look at your watch, though you never count. The time is in your head – the photographers' infallible watch. Smile at Stephen. It wasn't his fault.

He returned Eve's half-grin with interest – a corn-fed, Golden Graham, Wheat-O, Gung-ho sort of a smile.

'You should try more spit on your cowlick, boy!'

She was on top again now, back to cracking jokes. Steve laughed back, relieved the tantrum was over and not too young to take a leg-pull in good part.

Eve peeled back the paper, held the photo to the light and whistled through her teeth.

'By golly, Watson, I believe we have something here!'

'Good?' Stephen bent over her, smelling of fresh grass and sunburn.

'Indubitably! Yes – yeeees!'

They hit high five. The tension on the set evaporated.

Eve looked at the shot again.

'Jesus!'

The tension returned like a switched-on light.

'What's up?'

'Jesus!'

Concerned faces appeared out of the shadows – stylist, make-up, PR, client.

'Who booked the background models?'

Stephen shrugged. She watched as he bent down to look through the lens. It was a long bend. He was six-foot-one and Eve was over a foot shorter.

'What's wrong?'

Why did he always sound so goddammed reasonable? And always look so goddamned healthy? She'd been keeping him out of the daylight for three months now – ever since she'd first taken him on – but his skin still glowed with burnished rude health and his eyes still had that same Kellogg's sparkle they'd had the first time they'd met. He should have had a bad case of dark-room pallor by now and his eyes should have been filmy with all the serious rutting that came with the job.

'Come here, darling.'

There were two models in the background of the shot – a man and a woman. Entwined and naked. Both out of focus. Out of sight, out of mind. Not Eve's mind, though.

Someone gave the girl a wrap and she stepped gingerly

out of the spotlight. She looked stupid, as though she didn't understand what was being said.

'Darling?'

The girl nodded. So she understood some things.

'What's your name, sweetie?'

It was painful watching her think.

Eve tried to look kind.

'You're off the shoot, sweetie. I can't use you. Tell your agent to call me if there's trouble. Goodbye.'

The girl still stood there, blocking the way.

Eve turned to Stephen.

'Deal with her, Stevie. Those legs, Christ!'

Stephen smiled at Luisa.

'Do you speak English?' He had a soft voice. Luisa nodded. Stephen glanced across at Eve then back at Luisa. 'Come to the changing room. I'll try to explain.'

He made Luisa a mug of tea and her wrap slipped open as he handed it to her. He stared at the bruises on her legs.

'What happened?' Luisa blushed and closed the wrap again quickly. She wore too much make-up and she smelt of sweat. Who had booked her? Then he remembered. The client had booked her. There had been some hairy guy hanging around all morning who was this girl's agent. He had looked as though he were thick with the client for this shoot. Drugs, probably. The client was a well-known smackhead.

'I'm sorry.' He didn't know what for but there was something in this girl's face that asked for an apology. He looked at the bruises again and felt that he was apologizing on behalf of all mankind.

'Am I finished?' Her accent was heavy, her voice quieter than he had expected.

'Yes. I'm sorry.' Apologizing again. He was too young for this stuff but he had a kind face. He hunted for a lie that would keep the girl happy.

'She wanted a brunette.' It was the best he could come

140

up with. The girl's face was impassive. She worked a rubber band nervously between her fingers. Stephen wished she would put it down and relax a little. He had never been so close to someone who looked so sad.

'Dark hair – do you understand?' The girl shrugged now and sighed. She looked like a hooker. Then she unpinned her hair. Stephen watched as she greased her skin with cleanser and wiped the make-up off with a tissue. She stared at her own tragic face in the mirror. It reminded Stephen of a circus clown after a performance.

With a clean face she didn't look like a hooker any more – she looked like a fourteen-year-old child. He glanced down at her bare arms, praying there would be no needle marks on the soft inner flesh. The arms were clean, apart from a few pale mauve stains.

'Have you worked before?' He felt he had to say something – he had not forgotten how to be polite. He wasn't a kid any more and it was only kids who could stare without speaking.

'Modelling? Yes – for a year or two.'

'Who's your agent?'

She cocked her head towards the door. 'My husband. He is my personal manager.'

Stephen thought of the hairy man in the flashy suit and groaned inwardly. Her husband. Her manager. She was just a young snapper – not much older than himself. What had she got herself into?

'Where do you come from?'

'From Russia.' Her eyes filled with tears the instant she said the word. She looked up at Stephen and this time he felt free to stare back without speaking.

She shook her head. 'I love my country. I'm sorry.'

'Don't be sorry. I never knew there was so much to love out there.'

She spoke to him then – really spoke to him – talking for many minutes without drawing breath. She spoke so quickly in a quiet monotone that sometimes he did not know whether she was speaking English or Russian but it didn't matter – the spell was in her voice itself and in her large, liquid eyes.

She spoke of her country while the lights in the studio behind them flashed like lightning and when she had finished telling of the snow and the trees and the smells and the tastes, the tears had reached her cheeks and fallen to the floor like melting ice.

By the time Luisa had finished, Stephen was half-way in love with her, though he did not know it at the time. All he knew at the time was that he was embarrassed by his own insensitivity: 'I never knew there was so much to love out there.' Why had he said that? She must have thought him the greatest fool that ever drew breath.

When Luisa returned to the flat she shared with Alex there was a small square package waiting for her in the hallway. The package was wrapped in brown paper and tape and bore a bright yellow sticker with the name of the courier company emblazoned on it.

She studied the parcel like everyone studies a parcel prior to opening it – turning it around in her hands, looking for clues to the sender – delaying the actual moment of opening it in case the contents fail to meet the expectations.

These contents surpassed expectations. Once the wrapping was off Luisa found herself staring at a small glass dome. Inside the dome stood a painted figure of a girl in Russian national dress. She lifted the dome level with her eyes and the girl's face smiled out at her from behind the glass. Her arm was raised and she was waving at Luisa.

'Klara?' It was not her sister, of course. The eyes were bluer and the hair a different shade of blonde. Nevertheless . . .

As Luisa lifted the dome, the movement caused tiny particles of snow to tumble inside it. The snow became heavier. Luisa shook the dome some more and the figure inside it was lost from view in a terrific snowstorm.

'Klara!' She was back at school again and her sister was lost to her in the blinding snow of the Alexandrovsky Garden. The folder of photos she had been carrying fell, scattering its contents at her feet: headshots, full-lengths, some laminated, some in plastic folders – the only thing the shots had in common was that they were all bad. At least three of them showed Luisa in the nude – artistic shots, Alex had called them. Luisa nearly fell over herself in her hurry to pick them up. Underneath the shots lay the note that had come with her package.

'To remind you of home,' was all that it said. It was signed: 'Stephen'. Luisa pressed the note to her lips, closing her eyes until she felt dizzy and had to open them again.

The present was perfect – the best thing she had ever owned. She shook it again and watched the snow fall, more gently this time. It made her cry but that didn't matter – these were good tears.

The large door slammed behind her, making her jump. She had forgotten her key again. She would have to wait in the hall until Alex came home. She pulled her coat around her shoulders and slid slowly down the wall until she was sitting, crouched, upon the floor. She wiped the warm tears from her face with her sleeve and then wiped her runny nose on the sleeve too.

Klara. She placed the glass snowstorm carefully on the cold radiator so that it was level with her eyes. There was an envelope in her bag and a pen. She addressed the envelope to Klara's nurse and pulled some money from her pocket and counted it before stuffing it quickly inside. It wasn't much – only a few dollars, but it was all the shop would give her for the broken camera she had stolen on her way out of the studio.

She didn't feel guilty. Eve Horowitz had plenty of cameras – she had thrown it onto the floor in the studio on purpose, just to break it. That kind of disregard for

143

money made Luisa feel sick inside. It was like watching Alex lose at gambling – it was they who should feel guilty, not she. And anyway, Alex said she would be earning soon and have money of her own.

'Soon, Klara,' she whispered at the snowstorm. 'Soon I will send you all you will ever need.' The girl smiled and waved back. 'Hurry, Luisa!' – and then she was lost in the snow.

25

Of course, things had not started out that badly. When Luisa first arrived in London with Alex she had thought herself truly happy at last, despite the gnawing ache of homesickness that grew more spiteful with every day – and despite the longing to be with Klara, which she knew would never be possible.

As their plane had taken off she had looked out into the clouds and down at the country of her birth – which was by then just a small thing below her and not so great and frightening as it had been a few moments before – and Luisa had felt her mind clear a little so that she could think straight for perhaps the first time since she had left their father's apartment in Moscow.

Alex had unbuckled her seatbelt then reclined his seat to sleep. She felt that he cared for her as Klara had done when they were children. She felt safe. He was tough, like Klara, but she was happy in her dependence. It was easy – much easier than living on her own.

He was also an honourable man. Naive though she was, Luisa realized something inside her had changed back at the hotel when they had shared the bed for the night. Since then he had barely touched her and she had been left feeling ashamed and frustrated by her own desire. It was as though her whole body had been altered forever. Would it never heal again? Now, when she looked at his face, she felt herself liquidize, like butter in the sun. She wanted him to touch her again in all the places that he had before, but she would never have shocked Alex by asking.

His face was still, the eyes closed in sleep already. Could

anyone fall asleep so quickly? Luisa stared at him, studying him. The eyes did not move beneath their lids. He frightened her. She thought he knew things without being told. She thought he could even tell what her thoughts were. She wanted to touch his face. His eyes opened suddenly, making her jump. 'When we are married, little one,' he whispered, 'I will teach you it all when we are married.'

Luisa was confused by London. There was so much being offered there, yet its people looked so miserable and took so much for granted. Alex took her to the shops one morning, before they opened, and he promised to take her to all the smart restaurants, but only once she had learned how to eat and how to behave. The British had very strict rules of etiquette, he told her, and if she broke them through her own ignorance then he would be made to look a fool.

Luisa understood. She would have been embarrassed eating in the sort of places Alex showed her. She would have made a fool of herself just walking in the door. The staff inside spoke French, Alex told her, and the food had to be ordered in the same language. Even the toilets were marked in French. Luisa's English was only passable and she knew no French at all. She could not have even used the toilet in such places. It was better they waited until she had learnt how to behave.

In the meantime they went to the cinema to watch American films so that Luisa could understand the accent if they went to live in the US.

Alex had no home – Luisa realized that after a few weeks. They used a hotel for a few nights and then went to stay in a flat in Notting Hill that belonged to one of Alex's friends. The friend was away on business – they also had to walk his small dog.

The flat was OK – bigger than four Moscow apartments, though Alex called it a hovel and said they would be moving to a much better place. Luisa had her own room with a balcony window that looked out over a tree-lined street. The place seemed to make Alex restless and jumpy. He was out most of the day working but there was a stereo in the room so Luisa played music until someone banged on the walls and then she watched TV quietly instead.

The next flat they moved to was smaller and in a basement, so Luisa had no view. The place was rented and Alex said they were lucky to get it – there was a waiting list for that sort of area. The neighbours were more accommodating this time so Alex bought her a stereo of her own and she played music as loud as she liked all day.

She went out very rarely and then only with Alex because he told her she would only be safe when they were married and until then she should keep her head down because she was an illegal immigrant. Luisa had no grasp of the law, only memories of the regime in her home country. Alex said he could get papers for her and she trusted him because he could do anything. She didn't worry whether this was legal or not because she knew it was the only way she could survive. When she thought of being returned to Russia she became truly scared. She could never be sent back to Moscow. She wanted to get married as soon as possible to prevent it.

Alex, of course, sorted it. He got the papers and the documents and, as soon as he said things were legal, he married her. Luisa had no idea why he should want her. She was young and stupid and she knew she was a whole list of problems for him. She was a virgin and she had no idea if he loved her or not. She could not even be taken to restaurants. Her English was improving, though Alex told her she still made bad mistakes with the grammar.

Luisa thought she was lucky – there was no other reason why she should have fallen on her feet in such a way. She only wished she could tell Alex about Klara, then things would be perfect. Alex could sort things for Klara too, and maybe she could come to a hospital in England. But it was no good wishing for such things. To tell about Klara would mean having to tell about the murder. Some things had to be kept secret, even from a husband.

Alex was rich and he had promised she would be famous. She would get the money to look after her sister. She was doing the right thing.

They married in a registry office, with two strangers as witnesses. Alex had bought Luisa a knee-length frock of white chiffon and a posy of lilies and ivy. He plaited her hair and wove ivy into the plaits. It was October and she shivered in the cold. An elderly woman threw confetti as they left the office and Alex turned to Luisa and told her for the first time that he loved her. Then he told her to pick the confetti off her dress before it stained the chiffon.

Luisa's education began at once, on their wedding night.

Alex lay on the bed in their basement flat in a new peacock silk dressing-gown. He had bought an identical gown for Luisa – identical even in size, so that the sleeves draped over her fingers and the fabric was bunched by the belt.

'I promised to teach you all about sex, Luisa,' he said. 'There's a lot to learn and it cannot be rushed. Do you have the patience sweetheart? And the courage?'

He was smiling at her now. There was a glass of red wine in his hand and another for her beside the bed. She thought how much she hated the wine that he drank and wondered whether sex would be the same. She watched as Alex took a mouthful of the wine and then he kissed her so that the wine dribbled from his mouth into hers.

Could you be taught to find pleasure in things you hated? Alex told her once that all the great pleasures came from things you found offensive at first. First came the hate, he said, then the tolerance, and lastly the desire and unquenchable need and dependence. Was that how it would be for her?

He patted the bed beside him and she sat down with

148

dog-like obedience. A candle burned by the bedhead and she smelt the hot wax as it dripped onto the pillows.

Alex took another swallow of wine and turned to kiss her again, spitting the burgundy down her throat in a warm red torrent once her lips had parted. It oozed down her chin as she tried to sit up. It tasted of blood and looked the same on the white sheets. She started to choke but he shushed her coughing.

'Drink more.' She felt the cold glass neck against her lips and swallowed as Alex poured. The wine was strong and the effect was immediate. The walls of the room lost their structure. They looked silly. Luisa smiled nervously. She wiped at her chin with the back of her hand.

Alex leant back against the pillows, his body spread before her.

'Untie me like a present,' he said. She grinned like a retarded child. It was ridiculous – a grown man offering himself to her in this way. She became embarrassed and fluttery. She looked away.

Alex had her by the arms, his fingers pinching at her skin – playground pain. Bullying pain.

'I said untie me, Luisa,' he said. 'I'm giving myself to you – don't you understand? This is important! I love you, Luisa, and what I am giving you is sacred, do you understand?'

He leant back again, slowly, staring at her hard.

'Have you seen a man's prick before?'

Luisa shook her head.

'Haven't you been curious?'

She couldn't answer. She didn't know the right thing to say. Alex repeated the question patiently.

'Aren't you curious, Luisa?'

'Yes.'

'Good.'

His robe was tied around the middle with a cord. She moved her hands towards it and pulled at the knot.

'Slowly,' he warned. She tried to be careful but she was

149

clumsy and fumbling. She wished he would close his eyes or look away from her face. She wished the candle would blow out so that she could finish in darkness.

The knot fell apart but the robe stayed closed. Alex offered her his glass and she took another swallow.

'This is serious, Luisa,' Alex whispered. 'If you laugh I will have to hurt you – do you understand? You're not a child now, you're a woman.'

She barely touched the silk robe and it fell back from his body.

'Is it how you thought?' he asked.

She hadn't known what she thought. There was so little nakedness in Russia – the country was too cold. Bare flesh of any kind was frowned on for reasons of comfort and health. Even her own flesh was largely kept hidden from her. Seeing an adult undressed was like seeing an animal skinned of its fur. There was a shockingness about it that she could never have described.

His penis was unexpected and surprising – like a sudden wound – in its nest of dark hair. Brownly-veined and meaty-looking, like a raw ripe sausage. She thought it looked ugly – a deformity. It made her pity Alex – it made her glad she was a woman and more perfectly formed.

'There is pleasure all over a man's body, Luisa,' Alex told her, 'but that is the pleasure's core, just like a woman has her core. Touch it. See how it responds.'

Luisa touched it gingerly with her fingers. Its head lifted immediately and it began to stiffen, like a blind animal woken, stretching, from sleep.

'See the power you have over it?' Alex pulled her down beside him. She felt cold and awkward.

He kissed her behind the ear, where the pulse was warm, and then on the neck. His lips felt soft.

'You see, when I kiss you here, Luisa . . . and here . . . and here . . .' He knew her most willing places – places even she didn't know about herself – 'and when I stroke you here . . .' His fingers ran across her stomach and she

150

felt herself begin to relax. 'All that is fine, Luisa, all that gives you pleasure – but when I touch you here –' His hand clasped her so hard between the legs that she let out a cry and tried to push him away. His hand would not move, though its grasp became lighter and less painful.

'You see where your core is, Luisa? The core to your pleasure? Always remember there is pain there, too, though. Pleasure is only pain that we can tolerate. There is no pleasure without pain. Without that sensitivity there is only a dullness, remember that. Do you understand what I am saying?'

Luisa nodded. The hand tightened, then became gentler again. Luisa closed her eyes and tears spilled out the sides, like wine. She felt Alex move away and slide down the bed. When she opened her eyes again he knelt naked on the floor and his head was between her legs as though he was looking for something – like he had lost something there. She tried to close her thighs but his hands held them apart.

'Alex! No!' Why would he? How could he stand to do that? She tried to move. She felt his tongue on her, rubbing at her – wriggling away like a crazy worm. She pushed her hands against his shoulders but he did not budge, not at all. His tongue just worked away and she felt a scream or a gasp build up inside her.

She couldn't stop him. There was nothing she could do. She couldn't stop her body, either. Now she told her body to wait but it would not obey her. Her legs relaxed and pulled Alex closer downward instead. Her pelvis began to lose shape – like a jellyfish – and slid and slithered its wet way down the sheet. She felt her flesh begin to hum and sing like meat under the flame of a grill. Her eyeballs sizzled like eggs in hot fat. She was full of heat – ready to burst out pop.

A tight grip of pain and excitement seized her guts and a foaming wave of great sadness began to seep through her body from the toenails up.

151

As she relaxed to the pleasure that Alex had promised her — as she began to realize she didn't care if she did die or whatever in the process — his head moved away. He was gone — watching her now from a distance. She cried out for him but it was too late. The pleasure carried right on seeping but it was lonely and empty now and somehow it didn't feel right. She squirmed ridiculously, lonely on the bed. She felt the cold water of that ridicule but, like a mating dog, she couldn't stop.

Then it finally ended — faded to a different place. She would have gone right off with it — eloped, hand-in-hand down the beach — but instead she just lay there, staring back blankly at Alex's stiff face.

There was silence.

Then, finally — 'Lesson one, Luisa — you don't come without me — Never. Not again, not by yourself — understand?'

He grabbed her by the hair and twisted her neck until it hurt like it might snap. 'Do you understand?'

'Yes, Alex.'

She didn't but she could learn. She could do anything — she had to — she had no choice. He stared at her, but then his eyes softened.

'Good.'

Alex stroked her like an obedient dog. Then he held her to him gently and tenderly, rocking her to and fro until her neck stopped hurting and she slept.

26

The phone rang in Eve's studio. She was eating – she hated the phone ringing when she was eating. She had two rounds of corned beef on rye in front of her and a custard Danish so sweet it played kiss-chase with your cavities. Not bad for British cuisine.

The call was for Stephen. Wiping her hands on a paper towel (no napkin provided, as usual, she noted) she yelled out across the complex: 'Steeee-vieee-shit-where-are-you-boy?'

When she got back, red-faced with yelling, he had already taken the call. Now how did he do that? She decided to stare.

'Stephen?' He recognized her voice at once.

'Hi!'

'I phoned to say thank you – I have had no better present. Does your boss mind my call? Were you busy? You get the sack? I'm sorry. The snowglass is wonderful – too good a present. Too expensive. Please have it back. I adore it – so much just the right thing. I make you sad. You felt sorry for me. Thank you for making me happy . . .'

'Woa!'

'You do not realize . . . it reminds me exactly of my home . . . I cannot accept it . . . I'm so sorry . . .'

'Hey!' Stephen cut off the flow. He wished Eve wasn't staring. She had a sliver of pickled cucumber on her chin and she was listening to every word. He turned his back.

'Yes?' Luisa was breathless, eaten up by nerves and her own words.

'Can I take you to lunch?' Stephen asked.

153

'When?'

'Friday?'

'Friday. Yes.'

Stephen smiled, surprised. 'Twelve, then. At the tube. Covent Garden. Do you understand?'

'Yes.'

'Good.'

'Goodbye.'

'Your face is red, Stevie.' Eve pulled the Danish in two and offered him half. He shook his head.

'It's good. Try it.'

'Bad for you.'

'So is sex. Maybe you should try that too – or is that what you're planning with the little hooker you just spoke to?'

'She's just a kid, Eve.'

'Yeah, and King Kong was just a monkey. Be careful, Steve. Be sure to take a clean hankie and plenty of spare change for the machine in the john.'

Maybe he swore at her, she just couldn't tell. He certainly mouthed something but the sound got drowned by a voice on the tannoy, announcing the arrival of the next client. Eve pulled a Gold Spot from her pocket and airbrushed her grin.

Luisa had been married three weeks before Alex really hurt her enough to mark her. Pleasure and pain – he told her the words enough times but she never found the connection in reality.

Icecubes.

Alex held one in his mouth and let it drip onto her nipples. She felt her flesh scream out with the shock. Then he balanced the cube on the middle of her stomach, where the flesh was warmest and at first it felt funny but then it hurt and lastly it became unbearable and she tried to slide it off. It was then Alex took the cigar and placed the red tip on the exact spot where the icecube had been.

The flesh blistered and she didn't feel it but then she did. Alex put the ice back onto the blister like a mother placing a plaster on a small child's graze. Then he touched her until she came and he came too, though never inside her.

Stephen tried on three pairs of jeans and then settled on his leather pants after all. Then he changed his mind and got back into the first pair of jeans. Then he changed out of them again because he worried they were too much of a cliché, then finally he settled on them because otherwise he would have been late.

Luisa was there already, standing on the corner outside Covent Garden tube. A train must have pulled in because the draught blew her hair up around her face as he approached and he couldn't see if she was smiling or not.

The whole world meets in Covent Garden at lunchtime. Stephen hadn't realized. There were people standing every-where — stood-up, annoyed, looking sheepish, studying their watches for the thirtieth time.

Luisa didn't wear a watch. He wondered how long she had been waiting there. He wasn't late so she must have been early. She was badly dressed. She looked untidy and sad. If he hadn't known her he would have taken her to be a hooker.

'Hi!'

Luisa looked at him but didn't smile.

A man came up and stood beside her and took her hand. For a moment Stephen thought it meant trouble — that some jerk had taken her for a whore and that he'd have to have a face-off to get rid of him.

Then he recognized the man. It was the one with the client at the studio. The one Luisa said she was married to. By herself Luisa looked fragile. Together, as a pair, they looked tall and kind of weird, like something out of the Addams Family.

The guy showed his teeth and threw out a hand. He wore a suit and smelled of French cigarettes.

'Hi, Stephen. Alex – Alex Head. I'm Luisa's Personal Manager. Good of you to invite us to lunch. Where did you have in mind? They might squeeze us into Langan's if we hurry.' He flagged a taxi down out of nowhere and pulled open the door, motioning Stephen inside.

Stephen turned towards Luisa but she made no move to get in. Alex spoke to her quickly and handed her some coins before jumping in beside Stephen and yelling: 'Piccadilly' at the cabbie. When they drove off Luisa was still standing in the street.

'She gets the tube,' Alex said, looking out of the window. 'It's the only way she'll learn to find her way around.'

Langan's was full so Alex led Stephen round the corner to the Mayfair Hotel instead. Stephen had to remind him to leave a message for Luisa, to say that they had moved on.

Stephen was sweating by the time they were seated – he couldn't make the guy out at all. Was he playing with him? Did he plan to ridicule him for daring to ask his wife out for lunch? Yet he hadn't mentioned the fact they were married – only referred to himself as Luisa's Personal Manager, whatever the fuck that was.

Alex was posturing like crazy – getting on the waiters' tits – snapping his fingers at them and all that sort of crap. Stephen felt embarrassed and wished he was old enough and tough enough to get up and walk out before it was too late. Then he saw Luisa arrive and he knew the moment to leave had passed.

She looked lost. Alex made no move to help, allowing the waiter to lead her to their table instead. She sat down clumsily, jerking the table as she did so. The glasses rattled but nothing broke. Stephen saw her look quickly at Alex, an expression of fear on her face.

Was she a hooker? Alex Head certainly looked the role of pimp. Stephen smiled at Luisa but she looked away with a nervous laugh.

'How much?' Alex was smiling, still ordering their meal – still ordering for the three of them – ordering without asking. Arrogant bastard.

'How much?' His eyes flicked over to Stephen.

'I'm sorry?'

Alex leant back in his chair.

'Look – you're a photographer, right? My girl here is a model – OK? Photographers book models. Are you with me so far? So much for the easy part. Now the difficult bit. As we all know, models are not always the brightest of creatures. That's OK too – they're paid to look good, not to recite Homer. However, naughty boys like yourself will often see this slight deficiency as something to take advantage of. Take them out for a sandwich, get them to agree to pose for next to nothing – the promise of some free prints or the sniff of a better job, that sort of thing. Do you get my drift?' A small baked goat's cheese tart was laid in front of Alex. He lifted the lid with a fork and peered inside before pushing it to one side and lighting a cigarette instead. Stephen would have left but he was mesmerized by the man, almost willing him on to be more of a shit.

Alex's voice dropped to a conspiratorial whisper. 'So that's where I step in, my old darling,' he laughed. 'I take the bookings. I discuss rates. I know the market, you see, I know what my girl here is worth. Just like you do. Do you get me? No offence, Stephen. That's how we discuss things – professional to professional. That way she doesn't get ripped off, right? So – how much?'

Stephen felt his throat dry out.

'There is no job,' he said.

Alex smiled. 'I was told this was a business lunch.'

Stephen looked over at Luisa. Her eyes were fixed on the table. She was gripping her napkin hard. There were four pale sepia bruises across the fingers of her left hand.

'You're right,' Stephen said. 'I was after something for nothing. I wanted to do some test shots. I had some ideas in mind and I thought Luisa might fit the bill. There's no payment involved – like you said, I was going to offer her shots for her book. I didn't see it as a rip-off.'

Luisa's hand relaxed and the napkin fell to the floor. She bent to retrieve it but Alex stopped her, snapping his fingers at a waiter and pointing to where it lay instead. The waiter picked the cloth up and went to replace it on the table but Alex tore it from his hands.

'Bring a fresh one,' he said. Then he smiled again. 'Luisa's book is full. She doesn't need tests.'

Stephen took a deep breath and nodded. 'OK . . . fine.'

Alex leant closer. 'And she doesn't need young fuckers like you sniffing round her, either. Understand?'

Stephen looked into Alex's dark eyes and he understood why Luisa looked so shit-scared half the time.

Then Alex got up and left, dragging Luisa with him and leaving Stephen with the bill.

When Alex hurt Luisa she would think of Samuel Lorenz and wonder whether he had hurt as much when she shot him. He had to – he had to have hurt more. She felt it was somehow fair then that Alex hurt her in return. Maybe the pain could burn away her guilt – maybe Alex could help her in that way.

She tried to imagine how she felt about Samuel. She wasn't sorry he was dead but she was sorry she had killed him. So she concentrated on that particular guilt every time Alex hit her. If she closed her eyes sometimes it wasn't Alex hurting her any more, it was Samuel. She tried to make the pain worth it but she couldn't – she never could

158

– she hated it. It wasn't fair – even though it was less than she deserved.

When they got back to the flat that day Alex punched Luisa with his fist in the small of the back, before she had taken her coat off – before he had his keys out of the door. Then he flung himself at her, clinging to her waist and crying.

'Jesus, Luisa, I love you – don't treat me like this. I'm your husband, for chrissakes. I love you . . . I love you.'

He held her so tight he nearly pulled her over. She watched his wide shoulders heaving.

'You're going to leave me.' There was a terrible fear in his voice.

She shook her head slowly but he didn't see it.

'Luisa. You'll leave me. I know you will.'

She put a hand on his head. He fell lower, to her ankles. He was sobbing now – choking on his tears. He kept repeating something over and over but it wasn't till he raised his head towards her that she could make out the words.

'I'll . . . kill . . . myself.'

She thought of the tree in the woods – of the woman who was her mother hanging there with her boots left side-by-side in the snow.

'I'll . . . kill . . . myself.' Had her mother said that to her father?

Alex was staring at her now, his handsome face distorted with fear. He wanted her to speak, to tell him something to end his pain. She bent and kissed his wet face, like a mother kissing a child. Her back hurt, where he had punched her.

'Tell me you forgive me, Luisa.'

'I forgive you, Alex.'

He pulled her down beside him and kissed her on the mouth.

'Now kiss it better.' He whispered in her ear.

Luisa undid her husband's trousers. His prick was fat and erect — ready, keen and waiting for forgiveness. She cupped his balls in her hand and kissed his prick all over — like Alex liked it best — while he orgasmed. That was how they made love. After eighteen months of marriage Luisa was still a virgin. Her husband liked her that way.

27

'I'm a hustler, sweetheart – trust me, you'll make it soon.' Alex put the finishing touches to Luisa's lipstick and turned her chair around to face the mirror. Luisa looked at her own image. It wasn't her face. Nothing she saw there belonged to her. There was dark blue liner on her eyes and blue-pink lipstick on her lips.

She recognized the words Alex used – they had heard them in one of the American movies they had seen the week before. Was he trying to be funny? She was too afraid to laugh in case she was wrong and he was serious. Alex was always doing that – repeating large chunks of script. He had an ear for words – he could memorize whole scenes from a play and repeat them as they drove home.

She had no idea what he really did for a living. When she asked him he grew angry so she gave up questioning him and tried guessing instead. He had had an agency once – she had been told that before the beauty pageant in Russia. He mentioned films he had been involved in. She wondered if he was a producer. He seemed to know everyone in the modelling business but he grew mad when he phoned them and they didn't return his calls. In the end she even gave up guessing. She depended on him totally – that was all she needed to know. Alex had to be the hustler he said he was. She trusted him – she had no other choice.

So far, all Alex's contacts had come to nothing, though. The name Alex Head pulled no strings at all. Alex told Luisa they would have to go cold-calling. He didn't like it, but there you are – once they saw Luisa in the flesh they would know what they'd missed. He bought her a leather suit and a pair of shoes with heels so high she could barely walk in them. He taught her how to make herself sick if she ate too much, so she'd keep her weight down. He even stopped hitting her so that her bruises had time to fade. They were broke. Alex was desperate.

They went to magazines the first day and fashion houses the next. No one wanted them without an appointment, but Alex carried right on hustling. He hustled receptionists, security, assistants and even the cleaners. He was charming in one place and threw a temper at the next. His lies sounded more honest than the truth he sometimes told to appeal to their pity. Luisa was overwhelmed with embarrassment.

Someone, somewhere, either fell for Alex's cheek or took pity on Luisa's pathetic face and gave them five minutes, which Alex turned into twenty. The woman was new to the job and knew how they felt. She looked at the shots in Luisa's book and told her they were crap. She didn't want to be unkind, she explained, but the shots were crap. They had no place taking shots like those round the quality magazines. They were wasting everyone's time, including their own. It was the most constructive piece of advice they had had all day but Alex gave the woman three minutes of verbal abuse and they were thrown out by a commissionaire.

'She knew shit!' Alex was screaming by the time they hit the street. 'Bitch! Fucking bitch!' Luisa took him by the hand and led him home. He was like a child again that night. She had to wash his face for him and put him to bed, stroking his hair until he slept.

Then next day Alex went out by himself.

'You've got a job,' he told her when he got back. He threw an address card down onto the table.

'It's a photographer.' Luisa read the card out loud, to be sure.

'Well done.'

'. . . In Wardour Street.'

162

'Fucking brilliant.' Alex looked tired. He was unshaven – his beard was beyond the range of designer stubble. His head lolled onto the back of the sofa though his fingers still drummed on the arm.

'What's the job, Alex?'

He didn't open his eyes. 'It's for a book – a magazine.'

'They saw my shots?'

'They *loved* your shots.'

'Is it fashion?'

'No, Luisa, not fashion.'

'Beauty?'

Alex looked up. 'It's porno, darling, do you understand what I mean? Did we cover that term in our language education classes? Porn, porno, pornography. I fuck – you fuck – they fuck – we all fuck, get it? Every model's done it sometime or other – it's part of the rites of passage. Besides, it pays well and god knows we need the money.'

Luisa stared at her husband. His neck was bare. She wanted to slit his throat.

'You know I won't do it.'

Alex groaned. 'I know you will, Luisa. Don't fuck me around. You have no choice.'

'Because you'll beat me if I don't?'

He rubbed a hand over his forehead and groaned. 'No, darling, not because I'll beat you. Because you don't want to go home to Russia. Because that's where you'll be sent when our money runs out and we're starving. Because otherwise you'll be shipped back to dear old Moscow, darling, and I know just how keen you are to return there. You'll do it, Luisa, and then you'll forget it. One day when you're famous you will even laugh about it, that's how much it will matter to you then.'

'I don't want to do it, Alex.'

'Good. I should hate to think of you relishing every moment.'

'Alex . . .'

He was out of the chair in an instant. Luisa flinched but he didn't touch her.

'Who do you think's suffering, Luisa? Who do you think's feeling the pain this time? How much do you think *I'll* enjoy it, knowing my wife's giving some strange faggot a blow job in front of a camera? Jesus, Luisa, you think you've got problems? We need the money, darling – end of story!'

Alex was gentler to her that night than he had been at any time during their marriage. He poured her bath, put lavender essence into the steaming water, and carried her to it. He bathed her like a child, using a big soft sponge and scented soap, and he carefully shaved her legs and beneath each armpit. Then he washed her hair and dried it for her as she sat in front of the fire.

He massaged her feet and he fed her honey yoghurt from a spoon.

She looked golden in the firelight.

'You're so beautiful,' Alex told her. 'The most beautiful girl in the world. I can't believe you're mine, Luisa, I can't believe you're my wife, my child bride.'

He looked kind and handsome. His skin looked like suede. He smelt so good. Luisa cried quietly, wishing he were different.

Luisa did the job the following day. It was the only time Alex did not go with her. As she walked off to the tube she suddenly turned back and saw him looking sad, watching her from the window. Neither of them waved.

28

The studio was a small one but it was full of people. It was on the sixth floor, over an Indian restaurant and Luisa was panting by the time she got up there.

'You're wearing a bra!' A short guy in jeans took her bag from her and led her into the changing room where he peered at her face under a naked bulb.

'Sorry?'

He heard her accent then and spoke more slowly.

'A brassiere, dear – under your T-shirt. Didn't anyone warn you? Do you have pants on too? Oh dear. They leave marks – lines on your body. Very unprofessional. Oh sugar, now what, I wonder? No undies next time, understand? Is this your first time, sweetie? Don't get upset, then, you weren't to know. Smile! OK? Better! Good!'

He sat her down in front of a mirror. He was about fifty and wore a threadbare velvet jacket over denim jeans. He was going bald but had covered the top of his head with hair from the side. He had a cold and kept sniffing.

'How old are you, sweetheart? No – don't tell me, I'd rather use my eyes. Try not to be nervous, honey, we'd all rather be doing something else. Better off mowing the lawn, eh, on a day like today?' He was moving her hair around, trying a bun and then plaits. 'Better off on the 'pick 'n' mix' in Woolie's, eh? Your manager told me you're still a virgin. That's OK. That's good. It'll show in your face. Bunches, I think – tied with red ribbon. Something about bunches and red ribbons that makes the average wanker go wild, can't say why. We'll stick to heads, then. You'd best meet Alberto, sweetie – or VO5, as I call him.'

There was a young Italian man waiting on the backdrop, stark naked apart from trainers, but very polite with it. He shook hands with Luisa and asked if his breath smelt of garlic. The camera was moved for a close-up and Luisa was given a chair to sit on. Alberto's cock was placed in her mouth and some Polaroids were taken. It took ten minutes to do the shot for real and then she was told she could go.

Alberto shook hands and smiled and Luisa just made it down the stairs and outside into the street before she threw up. Passers-by must have thought it was the curry.

When she could straighten she wiped her mouth with a hankie and walked back up the six flights of stairs again. The photographer looked surprised. Alberto was fucking a young boy in front of the camera, apologizing politely all the while.

'You threw the Polaroids in the bin,' Luisa asked. 'May I keep one?'

'Sure, sweetie, if you want.'

Luisa picked out the top photo and put it in her handbag. She wanted to keep it forever, to remind herself just how much she hated her husband.

29

London, 1994

Rick had new pictures to add to his wall. New pictures of
Catarina that had cost him nothing. Pictures he could never
use, though, and this sickened him. You hit paydirt but
what you find is too bad to publish. Mr and Mrs Average
liked a good helping of filth with their Sunday breakfast
but these shots might just have Mr Average choking on
his bacon baguette. Like Catarina choking over what
she had in her mouth. Jesus. Rick could barely believe his
bad luck.

'So much for your class act, my darling,' he told the
photograph. The aristocratic queen of the catwalk, Miss
'Butter-wouldn't-Melt,' – all made up with goo and a
gobful of dick to boot. Oops.

He looked again. Was it Catarina? The face was
younger, the features different. But then this would have
been before all the plastic work. The eyes were the same
and you couldn't change eyes. There was even that flicker
of fear that became less perceptible in her later shots, only
in this one it was naked fear – there for all to see.

Photo libraries were wonderful things and the one that
had churned these shots out of its bowels had done Rick
proud many times in the past. Eric, the little greasy-haired
manager of the place, would often spend his lunch hours
flicking through old records for shots of the celebs in their
leaner years when times were less cushy. He'd thought this
face looked familiar but that was all. Rick had just shaken
his head dumbly and thrown the shot into his bag. This
time, though, they didn't even know what they'd come up

with. This time they'd pulled out the big one and not even got paid for it.

Rick narrowed his eyes. Would anyone be able to print it? You could censor the odd naughty bit but in this case you'd run out of black ink. Still, it was a start. It showed he was on the right track. Catarina Kirkova – Porn Queen. It had a good ring to it. There was a studio number on the back of the shot. Rick picked up the phone and punched in the numbers.

As he did so his mobile started to ring.

'Rick? It's Oliver.'

Rick paused. It was a deliberate ploy to humble the caller. Silence. Full title please?

'Oliver Zweinfeldt.' – It never failed. Oliver sounded positively peeved.

'Oh, Ollie. Hi.' The other phone stopped ringing in Rick's ear and he heard an answerphone begin its dull litany.

'Thank you for calling Mortimer Photographic Studio. Unfortunately there is no-one available to take your call but . . .' Rick tutted and put the phone down.

'Rick? Rick are you still there?' Oliver was an impatient squeak in his other ear.

'Still here, Ollie. What's up?'

Oliver cleared his throat. 'Did you get anywhere on the Kirkova story, Rick? Did you do any research?'

'No, Ollie. Like I said, no interest. No story. Dead ends. You were right.'

More throat clearing.

'Only I heard on the grapevine that you'd been asking the odd question, Rick. I just wondered . . .'

'Well wonder no more, old chappie. Unfurrow that brow. Not worth the time spent scratching, I promise you.'

'Are you screwing me around, Rick? I . . .'

'Screwing *you*, Oliver? No ta.' Rick slammed the phone down, laughing, and redialled the studio to leave a message this time.

30

Eve Horowitz gazed out at the Manhattan skyline and breathed a deep sigh of relief.

'Hullo, Legoland.'

'Welcome home, Evie.' She'd been back in New York for a year yet she still greeted it passionately every morning. Never take a lover for granted – that's when the rot begins to set in.

Eve hated to travel. The only good thing about travelling was that it made returning all the better. She was a New York photographer – New York was where she worked. Half-a-million-dollar trips to the UK were just a diversion – a little affair on the side. She was always glad to get back. A few moments of chanting and all would be well with the world. Jewish Buddhists have all the fun.

Her coffee breathed steam all over the window. Her cheese Danish tasted cardboardy-good. The smog smelt good. Her husband, when she caught up with him, would feel good. The steam cleared and she saw her own face looking back at her. Hair like Harpo, only dark. A face like a camel. Not ugly – just, well – just like a camel. Perhaps ugly – it depended on your opinion of camels. Eve thought camels had beautiful faces, as long as they didn't smile. Eve rarely smiled – it made her look goofy. She had had enough goofy pictures taken as a child to fill an album three times over. She was forty now – well, forty-seven really – and the hottest photographer in New York. A legend. Legends shouldn't go around looking goofy.

London made Eve nervous. She was glad to be home. She wished she could say the same about her trusty Boy

Wonder. Stephen's chin had been scraping the floor ever since they'd made it back to base camp.

'Are you suffering PMS, honey?' That hadn't raised even half a smile. Stephen hadn't heard her, he was gazing off into space. Eve studied his profile. He was mellowing – growing up. *Tristesse* suited him, it gave his good looks an edge – brought a little gristle to his boyish cheeks. Even his hair was laying flat these days.

'The Leica's bang to rights again.' One good thing about the British – they knew how to repair cameras. Eve picked it up, cradling it carefully in her hands.

Stephen had seen Luisa steal it from the studio – followed her to the shop where she'd sold it and had bought it back, returning it before Eve had even noticed it missing.

Eve threw the camera across to Stephen and he caught it, startled.

'Here – take the day off. Be Henri Cartier Bresson for an afternoon. Roam the streets taking shots of dogs and things – all that sort of arty crap you like. Get a few in focus and you might even sell them.'

There was a guy begging by the entrance of the building. His nose and his right leg were missing. Stephen thought he might as well start there as anywhere. He wished it was the left leg that was gone – the light was better in that direction. The guy spewed out abuse while he shot him but that was OK because it distorted his face in a way that was interesting.

Stephen smelt Alex before he saw him. There was no way the beggar would be using Eau Sauvage. Stephen inhaled the smell and he froze like a rabbit that smells a fox, missing the best shot as the beggar spat at the camera. He could have freeze-framed the spittle as it caught the sunlight in a glorious arc. But his finger ossified instead and the spit fell to his feet with an impotent splat.

He turned slowly. Alex stood there behind him, patient, smiling. A hand offered in friendly salute.

'Stevie! Hi! Surprise! How-wow-wow!' He took Stephen's hand, pulling him by the elbow and grasping him to his chest.

'Stevie-Stevie-Stevie!'

'Mother-fuckin'-cock-suckin'-shit-eatin' . . .'

The beggar continued his coke-ad litany of abuse behind their backs. Stephen admired the man's judgement.

Alex pulled away, still clasping Stephen's elbow – scanning his face for signs of delight and surprise.

'Alex.' There was nothing more to say, short of joining the beggar's chant.

'Stephen.'

Alex let out a loud laugh, as though he had just cracked a rare joke. 'We're here, Stephen, we're here in New York, looking you up, just like you said.'

'We?' Stephen was sure the words 'look me up' had never passed his lips during his conversations with Alex.

'My girl and I. She's going to make it here – they'll love her – you know it and I know it. Wait till they hear that Russian accent! We need to talk, Stephen. Are there any bars around here? We need somewhere quiet, somewhere discreet. You know the sort of thing. Just a minute.'

He emptied out his pockets and threw a handful of dollars into the beggar's cardboard shoebox. The abuse stopped faster than a pig in a spam factory.

Stephen got the impression that this was all the money Alex possessed.

'Thanks, friend.'

'You're welcome,' Alex grinned broadly back at Stephen.

'Come on, young man,' he said, 'let's talk business.'

Luisa was waiting for them, standing round the next corner, her portfolio in her hand. Stephen was surprised to see her there – she looked so wrong for New York, somehow. There was a look of relief in her eyes when she saw the two men together and Alex placed an arm around Stephen's shoulders after patting him soundly on the back. 'See?' he seemed to be saying to his wife, 'There's no problem! We're still mates!'

'We need contacts and we need work,' Alex said, as soon as their drinks had been placed before them. He was in good form. New York seemed to suit him. He was playing the old-time hustler, a role tailor-made for the young Jack Lemmon. Stephen could almost have liked him if it hadn't been for Luisa's great dark eyes watching him from across the table.

'I came by some money, Stephen,' Alex was saying, 'enough for our fare here and a little present for my girl.'

As if on cue Luisa held out her left hand. There was a large sapphire ring sparkling on her finger.

'An engagement ring,' Alex explained. 'The first time I've been in a position to get her the sort she deserves.' He leant across and kissed Luisa on the cheek. She blushed and so did Stephen. She had looked pale before she blushed. Her hair was longer and duller. Alex ordered another round of drinks.

'So?' he looked across at Stephen expectantly.

Stephen sighed and ran a hand through his hair. 'I'm just an assistant, Alex. I don't book models for work. I don't even have any contacts.'

Alex's smile widened. 'You're only the assistant of the best goddamn photographer in New York,' he said. 'We're friends, Stephen. Put in a good word. That's all.'

Stephen looked embarrassed. 'Eve wasn't impressed with Luisa on the shoot in London. I really don't think . . .'

Alex was on a long fuse for a change. 'Fine. Tests, then. You offered to do tests. She needs new shots, she looks hotter than she did before. You're the man, Stephen, you've seen how the great lady works. Some of that magic must have rubbed off. Test her, Stephen. Then let me do the magic with the results.'

The pleading in Alex's eyes was nothing compared to

that in Luisa's. He could say no to Alex but he could never have said no to his wife.

'Monday,' he said. 'Come at nine. The studio's empty then.'

Alex leant back in his chair, delighted. Luisa looked as though she might cry with relief.

Nurse Olga Margolis picked up her daughter, grunting with the effort as she did so. The child was heavy for her age which was surprising, as she ate so little. Her father had been a big man, though – at least until his illness. He was thin when he died. What a bastard, leaving them alone like that! How had he thought they would cope?

There were tears in her eyes as she thought of him. He had been elderly when they'd married – her friends had told her he was a poor bet for a secure life. She only had herself to blame – falling in love with a man old enough to be her grandfather. He'd managed to sire a kid, though, and that had surprised them all.

There was a knock on her door. She knew what it meant. The girl was on the phone again. No-one else phoned her much these days. She put the child back in its crib. The phone was down five flights and she couldn't carry it that far.

'Nurse Olga?' It was time to get tough. They were short of food and clothing. She was tired of making do. The girl had been sending a pittance. Now the money was arriving in envelopes marked US MAIL. There was no way she could be poor and still afford the trip to America. Olga thought of telling her her sister was dead. She was tired of the lies. Then she heard her baby crying, echoing from five storeys overhead.

'Your sister needs an operation,' she said. 'The money you send is not enough.'

'An operation?' There was a note of terror in the girl's

voice. If the bitch was so worried then why didn't she send the money?

'Only a small one – to make her comfortable. It's routine, don't worry. You owe me money, though. Please don't forget.'

'I'm getting it, I promise. Don't give up on Klara – please. I will have the money soon. Things are looking better for me. I should have some work, good work. Please.'

Olga sighed. 'OK.'

She was too soft, that was half her trouble. People took advantage. She had to be stronger in future – it was the only way to survive.

31

'Not bad . . .

 'Not bad . . .

 '. . . Shit – even you should know something about fill-in by now! See those shadows? Ugly, ugly ugly!

 'Good – *almost* good. Very, very, closely, definitely nearly good.'

Eve pulled out a magnifier and bent over the lightbox to get a closer look at Stephen's contacts. Her hair fell in a circle. She looked like a prostrate floormop.

'Do I know this face?' she asked. Stephen didn't answer. Eve had a mind like a flea, always hopping from one question to the next. Sometimes forgetting what she'd asked in the first place.

Sod's law. She looked up at him, the lightbox glowing out under her chin, direct eye contact. Smiling. Interested. Quizzical. Waiting for an answer.

'Only she looks familiar.'

Stephen tried to hold her gaze but his bottle went.

'She's new. They're just tests – you know, nothing special. I just thought she was good. I thought you should see her . . . sometime.'

'I've seen her before.'

'Maybe.'

'Maybe?'

Stephen looked like a man with his socks on fire, hopping from foot to foot. He stuffed his hands into his pockets and then took them out again.

'You threw her off the shoot in London.'

Eve went back to the floormop routine again.

175

'The whore? The one with the drugs problem?'

'No!' Stephen sounded angry. Eve looked up in surprise. 'No drugs, Eve, she's clean. And she's not a whore. She's still a kid. She needs help, that's all. I think she could be OK. She looks good in front of the camera, doesn't she?'

Eve looked back at the contacts again, smiling beneath her veil of hair.

'When did you fall for her, Stevie?' she asked softly.

Stephen's face turned a roaring radish-red.

'What about that pimp she takes around with her?' She heard the anger start again. 'Sorry. What about her Personal Manager? The guy's a shit. I spoke to the client after the shoot.'

'I can handle him.'

'*Sure* you can.'

'Will you test her, Evie?'

'– OK.'

Eve could have sworn it was the first time Stephen had smiled since they'd come back from the UK.

Stephen chose the music with care – something just right, not too loud, not too brash – checked the temperature of the room a thousand times – saw the lighting was OK – sniffed at his armpits until his neck cricked – moved potplants by one millimetre because it felt better – stared at his reflection in the mirror, willing his hair to lie flat – in the end Eve barked at him to sit still and chant beneath his breath because – hell – he was giving her the willies with all his twitching!

He watched from the window instead and saw Luisa arrive across the street, weighed down by cases – Alex following in the rear. Stephen thought he might be sick when he saw Alex. He had told Luisa to come alone. Eve would not stand the intrusion. The session would get cancelled.

Then he saw Alex kiss Luisa full on the mouth. He

176

looked through a telephoto lens to watch Alex's face as they parted. Stephen didn't know much about these matters but if it had been a photo shoot he would have guessed the guy had just been told to look as though he loved the girl. The thought was like an electric current, running through his body and aimed at his heart and his prick. He had forgotten to look at Luisa's expression. Her face was impassive as she crossed the street.

Alex ran after her, pulled her back, kissed her again. This time he let her go, watching from the doorway of a building opposite, his hands deep in his pockets. He looked distraught. Stephen realized he was going to wait for her. Now it was Stephen who had a bad attack of the willies.

'Ms Horowitz?' Luisa's eyes looked calm and her expression confident. She wasn't going to blow it a second time. Stephen was surprised at the certainty he saw in those eyes. It changed her whole face – it was like looking at a stranger.

She placed her bags down carefully in the changing room. She was wearing a smart brown suit that looked absurdly out of place. Nobody wore suits to Eve's studio – not unless they were paid to. When she straightened, the suit gave off a faint smell of mustiness, as though it had come from a thrift shop. Perhaps it had. Stephen could see Alex taking her there, choosing the suit and paying cash for it with the same smile he would have used if it had been an Armani. The suit didn't fit her, but then Alex would not have noticed details like that.

Luisa opened her cases and began to hang her clothes. The cases were almost empty – a grand gesture, just for effect. You could have put all those clothes into one medium-size bag and still have had room for your lunchbox.

'I arranged a stylist.' Stephen had pulled in some favours, using Eve's name as surety. Daniel Carl was popping round with a couple of Westwoods he'd filched from another

177

shoot. Daniel was the best in Stephen's book – a worker of miracles.

'I have my own clothes, thank you.'

Stephen started to sweat. Luisa just carried on hanging up thrift shop things as though they were Valentino exclusives.

'I suppose Alex chose them for you?' he asked.

'Yes.' Luisa flicked a skirt to get the creases out.

'Jesus, Luisa, the guy's borrowed from Westwood! You don't know the kind of start clothes like that can give you! You'll look terrific in them!'

'I'll look terrific in these, Stephen.'

'She's right, Stevie.' Daniel had arrived and was standing behind them. Stephen saw him watching Luisa through the mirror. The Westwoods landed in a pile on the chaise longue.

'Show me your things, sweetie.' Daniel flipped through the hangers quickly. 'This and . . . this,' he pulled out a couple of dresses and a long skirt. Old hippie stuff – pure crap, in Stephen's eyes – but who was he, anyway? He grinned and Luisa smiled. Jesus, her smile could have lit up the whole of Manhattan.

Daniel had The Face on now – the face he wore when he was into creating. The Fuck-off-and-don't-interrupt-the-old-creative-juices-are-flowing-like-honey sort of a look. Eve wore a similar expression when she was on a good shoot. It was sort of single-minded and determined – the sort of face you wear just prior to orgasm – when it wouldn't matter if Bush pressed the button or the Beatles launched a comeback right there and then in your bedroom. Stephen hoped to wear that look one day – then he would know he had made it as a photographer. Or as a sex machine.

'How's she doing, boy?' Eve was fingering through some magazine.

'OK. Daniel's with her.'

'Daniel Carl?'

178

'The same.'

Eve didn't look up but she pulled a face and nodded. 'What about the pet gorilla?'

'I told you I'd sort it, Eve. He's not a problem.'

Eve turned the page. 'Is that why he's waiting over at the building opposite looking very much like De Niro in *Mean Streets*? Because he's not a problem? I'd hate to see him when he is.'

Stephen sighed. 'You looked.'

'I looked. Just to see if he was armed, or anything. I hope you don't mind, only bullet holes might spoil the line of this little Donna Karan number I'm wearing.'

'Don't joke, Eve.'

'Are we under siege?'

'No.'

'Good. I'm down to my last Danish.'

Luisa appeared on set. She looked tall and skinny and lovely – but then so had every model that had ever stood there.

'She smells a little strange and she doesn't shave her armpits properly.' Daniel lounged alongside Stephen, watching, wondering if there was any magic there worth waiting for.

'She looks odd.' Stephen had that sick feeling coming on again. This wasn't going to work.

'She *is* odd, Stephen – I thought you knew that.' Daniel lit a herbal cigarette. 'Too odd for the Westwoods, even. I just cleansed her face and wrapped those rags she brought around her body. Do you think pit hair might work? It might be due for a revival, you know. I could ask Evie to try some arms-up stuff.'

Luisa wore a thin pink top, a long hippy skirt, a white ballet-wrap and layers of socks and leggings. On her feet were a pair of heavy boots. Her hair fell over her shoulders and down almost to her waist. There were ribbons plaited into it.

'Hair!' Daniel shouted so loudly they all jumped, even

179

Eve. 'Sorry, darlings, it's the hair – Lord, is it the hair!' He grabbed Luisa's arm and dragged her off into the changing room.

They were gone so long that Eve got bored and Stephen got worried. A nasty thought occurred to him. 'Daniel, I hope you weren't . . .' He stopped in the threshold of the changing room. It was as though he had been hit by a truck. Or as though Alex had finally appeared carrying a sawn-off and screaming obscenities. Luisa's hair was now lying all over the floor. She had been shorn, cropped. Things had gone too far – things that could never be put back as they were. Stephen felt bereft and terribly guilty.

'You should have asked . . .'

Daniel carried on cutting. 'I did.' He turned the chair, so that Luisa was facing him.

'I love it.' Her face looked small and stubborn. Her eyes challenged him to disagree. What had happened to her features? Her face was all mouth now.

There was a lamp of his grandmother's – something from the Fifties – a woman's head, made of plaster and painted black, like a negress. All full lips and cropped hair and slanting eyes. That was how Luisa looked now, only white. Her neck was so long and thin. Alex could have snapped it like a twig, with one hand. Who would look after her now – now that she looked like this?

'Jesus!'

'Exactly!' Daniel looked pinkly proud. Stephen wanted to kill him. He didn't know what he had done. She wasn't a joke. She wasn't someone to try out your stupid fantasies on. He could have picked any of a thousand other models to launch his new look. Any one of them would have been stupid enough to say yes when he offered to crop their hair. It was OK for him – he went home at the end of the session. He hadn't had his life ruined. Luisa would have to live with it.

Eve said nothing when she walked out onto the set. She stared a little, but then she always did that. Then she

180

frowned and moved one of the lights, but she always did that too. Apart from that it was as though nothing had happened.

Stephen walked across to the window and looked down onto the street. Alex was still there. His neck must ache from looking up for so long. What was he waiting for? When would he need to go off for a pee? Or food? He looked cold, even though the day was warm.

What would he do when he saw his wife's new look?

Eve had taken the shoot over now – she didn't scream for Stephen or even ask for his help. She took the camera off the tripod and held it in her hands. Luisa sat before her, cross-legged.

'OK, honey, I'm ready to shoot now.'

'What would you like me to do?'

'Whatever you want. Whatever you feel comfortable doing.' The lights went pop. The first shot was taken. Luisa blinked.

'May I talk?'

'Of course.'

Luisa talked. She talked as though there were just the two of them, just her and Eve, in the whole wide world. She talked non-stop and her voice never rose above a whisper. As she talked Eve shot and the lights were like an electrical storm above them.

'My real name . . .' she began, and Stephen was hooked, 'My real name is Catarina Kirkova. I was born in Russia, to wealthy aristocrats, and my childhood was so happy I believe no child could have been happier . . .' Luisa talked endlessly and the story she told was all lies from beginning to end. They were Klara's tales – perfectly repeated and told as though about herself. Stephen sat in the edges of darkness and he swallowed every word. Luisa gazed at something in her lap. It was only when she raised her hands that Stephen realized she was staring at her snowstorm. She lifted her hands close to her face and the snow rose in a blizzard and the girl that was Klara was lost to sight.

181

Eve shot Luisa's face in close-up as she gazed at it – the light from the orb reflected in the sad hopeful crystals of her eyes. When you looked at the photo afterwards you saw Luisa's eyes, as big as fishbowls, and the tiny figure in the blizzard reflected in them. Eve thought the shot one of the best she had ever taken, though she never once said so.

32

Stephen watched Luisa as she left the studio. She had been there five hours and Eve had taken fifteen rolls of film. Luisa swayed under the weight of the half-full cases. Her legs looked too thin for the stacked heels she wore. Alex was still waiting. To Stephen's knowledge he had not moved the entire time. When he caught sight of his wife he stamped out a cigarette and moved quickly across the busy street. When she got closer he stopped.

Stephen saw Alex embrace his wife as though he thought she had been lost to him forever. Then he held her at arm's length to look at her hair. Then he slapped her face. Stephen could not bear to watch, though he did not know which had been the hardest to look at – the slap or the embrace.

Eve whistled through her teeth, her face glowing softly like a boiled egg in the suffused light from the lightbox.

'Stevie?' He was unrolling some Colourama. What was he up to? Always fiddling around these days. 'Don't you want to see your little snow queen's contacts? I did them specially! Just the way mommy knows you like them!'

Stephen swaggered across slowly. Eve could have cried at his feigned nonchalance. He hadn't even asked her what she thought of the Russian kid. She hoped he would grow up quickly because all this adolescent angst was starting to vex her. She could even feel herself getting motherly towards the boy and that was an impulse best consigned to the nuclear wastebins.

She watched the vulnerable bit at the back of his head as he studied the shots.

'What do you think?' – His voice sounded strangled with concern.

'What do *I* think?' She placed a pair of glasses slowly on her nose. She studied the pictures again – taking her time – feeling the heat of despair emanating from his poor distraught body. If she didn't give her verdict soon he would spontaneously combust. She couldn't stop the wind-up, though, he was just a sitting duck.

'I . . . er . . . I think she's pretty good.' She took the glasses off again. End of conversation. Meltdown was about to commence.

'*Pretty* good?' – It was the dying croak of a man choking on ashes and cinder.

'Great, Stevie, she's great. Special. Weird. She looks like an alien. Are you sure she's just Russian? She creates magic with the camera, OK? Use your own eyes, boy – what do you think?'

Stephen's face became round with wonder, like a kiddie at Disneyland. He looked at the contacts again.

Luisa was magic. In the flesh her eyes took second billing to her wide, wide mouth but on camera they held you fast, like a fly trapped in amber. Her face came off the page. Eve had done it and Luisa had done it. Daniel had done it, too. The hair was right. He chewed on a fingernail. His cock twitched with pity and lust at the sight of her.

'It's more than you expected, isn't it, Stevie?'

'What do you mean?'

'I mean you thought she was good, but not this good. You wanted to help her. Now you can't – right?'

'*You* could help her, Eve.'

Eve looked at Stephen. And if I do help her you'll lose her, she thought.

'Just what do you have in mind?' she said.

'You find her an agent.'

'Sure, sure, and I find a zoo for her gorilla, too, right?'

184

Stephen grinned. His grins had become heart-rending.

'Are you sure this is what she wants, Stevie?'

Stephen just looked at her. Yes, there was no need for an answer — she had seen the look in Luisa's eyes too. Of course it was what she wanted. Even the camera had picked it up. Luisa looked young, she looked fragile, she looked innocent — but most of all she looked determined. It was a new dimension to her character — one that had been absent the first time they had met. And it suited her — that touch of feistiness gave a breath of life to the insubstantial bag of bones she would otherwise have been.

'OK,' Eve sighed. 'Give her a call and tell her to collect the shots — alone again, mind. I'll see what I can arrange.'

Luisa told Stephen she had slipped away while Alex was out making business calls. He would be gone for the afternoon, so she accepted Eve's invitation for lunch.

They ate at a sushi bar, because Luisa liked the decor and the raw fish. She was wearing a Fifties summer frock and a gallon of cheap perfume. Daniel turned up five minutes after they'd ordered, which had to be more than an I-was-just-passing coincidence. Daniel was as tall as a basketball star and as thin as a fishpole. He had hair down to his waist and Jim Morrison bare-navel-appeal. Stephen felt crowded and angry. Eve read his mind and gave him a look that said 'I told you this would happen.'

'Catarina needs an agent.' Daniel brushed breadcrumbs off his chest hair.

'Catarina?'

'Your real name, darling — you told us during the session. I love it — mucho, mucho better than Luisa. I like what it does to your tongue when you say it.'

Despite all the posing, Daniel somehow came across as a regular guy. Stephen watched Luisa — Catarina smile at him. There was a molecule of prawn on her chin. Daniel

185

lifted his napkin and dusted it off. Stephen wanted to throw up.

'So — where are we talking?' he asked, looking round. 'Ford? Wilhelmina? Elite?'

'I want her to see Beth at Bettina's first.' Stephen was surprised at the bossiness in Eve's tone. Suddenly it mattered. Suddenly she was taking a big interest.

'Bettina's?' Daniel raised an eyebrow. The agency was new but exciting. Beth was an ex-model who had a good name in the business.

'Don't you think Catarina is a little European for her?' But Eve just shrugged. End of conversation.

They went that afternoon. Strike while the iron's hot. Play while the cat's away — or while Alex had appointments, at least. Luisa-Catarina went as she was — no make-up, an old-fashioned dress — heels as high as the Empire State Building. Beth took one look and laughed. Then she saw Eve's tests and the smile wilted away like a desert rose at dusk.

'Your name again?' she asked. She had beautiful features that were fraying at the edges. The fraying looked good, though. The day she had retired from modelling she had stopped dieting and stopped dyeing her hair. Even the fat looked good on her, though, and the grey hairs could have started their own trend.

The agency was in vast empty offices above a dry cleaner's. You could see the steam go past the window in great cumulus clouds.

'Catarina. Catarina Kirkova.' So that was it — Luisa no longer existed.

'Green card?'

'Yes.' Alex could get anything, forged or otherwise.

'You'll need to look after yourself better.'

'Yes.'

'I don't normally take your type of look.'

'No.'

'It will just be a try-out. You'll do more tests, maybe go see a few people. If the photographers don't take to you, you're out, understand? You'll need shoes, jewellery, tights, better clothes, OK?'

'OK.'

'Good.' Beth looked at Catarina and smiled. 'You're on, kiddo.'

Catarina smiled back.

'Twenty-five per cent commission on all jobs.' Beth spread a paper napkin across her lap and peered at the innards of a tuna ciabatta. 'Gotcha' – she prised out two black olives with the tip of her manicured nail.

'Twenty.'

'Jesus!' An olive hit the floor with a small plop. 'Get outta here!'

This time it was Eve's turn to smile. Catarina was full of surprises. She could tell Beth liked her, though – she liked her girls to have balls.

Stephen was waiting in reception like an expectant father. Two models – black identical twins, Donnie and Lonnie – were staring at him dreamily and the receptionist had put a hold on lunch in case – just in case – he suddenly got hungry and asked her out for a meal. She realized it was highly unlikely but she believed very much in wish fulfilment – it was something her therapist was into that month.

'You have to want it bad enough,' her group had been taught to chant – well there was no problem in this case – the boy was so cute she could have eaten him whole with chocolate fudge sauce and a black cherry topping.

'Have him washed and sent to my tent,' she said and Donnie and Lonnie screamed with identical laughter.

'She's in!' Eve and Stephen slapped high five while the twins stared at Catarina – who was that bitch?

Catarina kissed Stephen full on the mouth.

'Thank you.' She smelt of coffee and boiled sweets. There was a loud grinding sound as the Earth stopped on its axis. Polar caps melted and tidal waves wiped out an entire sub-continent.

'That's OK.' Stephen wanted the moment fossilized – stored away forever like the last days of Pompeii – only without written records of those last crass words of his.

Catarina somehow vanished. It was Eve standing before him now, smiling up at him so that her teeth showed.

'Don't get carried away, lover, Russians kiss everyone – it's a national trait. I'm growing a moustache myself, to keep her at bay. It's a good tip, boy – you'll use it too, if you're smart.'

They went to The Russian Tea Rooms on 57th Street to celebrate.

'Twenty different types of vodka!' Daniel announced. 'Come on, Catarina, honey, talk me through them, I intend to get thoroughly rat-assed.'

Stephen wondered whether she had kissed Daniel on the lips yet, too.

They ordered blinis and sour cream and the taste of the vodka together with the food made Catarina cry, because they reminded her so much of home. Daniel started to hum the 'Song of the Volga Boatmen' into her ear. She laughed then, though the tears kept coming.

She looked at Stephen through her tears, so that her eyes reflected the light from the crystal chandeliers.

Do Russians cry at everyone too? Stephen wondered. The drink made him bold. He leant across the table and covered her hands with his own. Catarina's hand was cold, like the vodka. The coldness startled him for a moment, like touching a corpse. Daniel was laughing for no apparent reason. He'd seen some friends and soon there was a tableful. Catarina's tears wobbled but didn't spill, held in place by surface tension. It looked just like vodka, as though she was crying vodka tears.

Stephen took another slug and the drink thwacked against the sides of his brain. There was a drone of noise around them, like sitting inside a hive.

'I must tell Alex,' Catarina was saying. 'I must let him know what has happened. He'll be pleased.'

Stephen doubted that – he doubted that most severely. Even Catarina had to doubt it. Hearing Alex's name was a shock – he sort of thought he'd got shucked off like a snake's skin when Luisa changed her name and her image. Eve was looking serious.

'Wait till we're with you, honey,' she was saying, 'don't tell him while you're alone. We can have lunch at Le Cirque – he'll love it there, it's top of the list, you won't find better – the best sea scallops and truffles in town, I promise. Fois Gras to die for. Wait, Catarina? Promise?'

Catarina laughed. Stephen wondered if she had understood. She must know why Eve was worried, though – she of all people had to know. There were stars still in her eyes. She was so excited she could barely keep still, her heels were rattling on the marble floor and every time one of the table laughed she joined in loudly.

'Over lunch, honey, remember? When there are witnesses around and waiters trained in the martial arts. I'm not being funny. Wait – OK?'

Catarina nodded. Eve was wrong – she was being funny, only she couldn't see the look on her own face. If she had've done she would be laughing, too, by now. She looked so serious and the others all found it hilarious. Catarina couldn't understand what Eve was saying – her accent was too much and the vodka wasn't helping. Still, she would cheer up soon, Catarina was sure of it.

She was grateful to the woman, after all – however odd she looked – Eve had taken her to the agency and they had said they would get her work. Catarina had recognized faces stuck all over the walls there – top girls who had to

189

be earning top money. It was all that she wanted – money to pay for Klara's treatment and money to get her freedom and the power to breathe her own air for once. Catarina laughed again. Her life was looking good at last.

'He's taking advantage of you, you know. He's onto a good thing. He won't want to lose you. Don't let him use you, Catarina – I've seen it happen to so many other girls.' Catarina understood Eve this time. She smiled.

'You're wrong, you know,' she said in a quiet voice. 'Alex does not use me. It is the other way around – it is I who am using him.'

33

Alex was in the apartment when Catarina got home. She was happily squiffy. She giggled climbing the stairs, shushing herself now and again when she heard she was making too much noise. She only remembered there was a lift when she reached the tenth floor. From that point on it was easy, just step into the little room and press the button marked 14. All the rest would be done for her. She leant her head against the lift wall and her legs felt woolly and gave a bit so that she slid down, not standing exactly, though not crouching either.

'Luisa?' – Catarina wanted to tell Alex that Luisa was dead now – that Catarina had taken her place, but the words would not come out.

'I was worried, baby, where have you been? Christ, I thought you'd been killed or something!' – Alex smothered her with kisses. She felt the back of his head, where his hair was thickest. He smelt good. Alex always smelt good.

'Are you OK, baby?' He cupped his huge warm hands around her face. She nodded, her mouth covered with his spit from his kiss.

'You're OK?' He kissed her again. She touched her tongue against his teeth. Her hands were warm too, now, warmed by the feel of his thick hair. He pressed his mouth against her ear. 'Christ, I thought I'd lost you! You don't know how I felt. When I got back and found you were out . . . Jesus, Luisa!'

She was folded into him like a letter in an envelope and now he was licking at the gum, sealing her away for good.

'Do you love me, Luisa? Tell me you love me, baby, tell

me.' — His hands worked at her body, kneading, soothing, stroking. He had smoked ten cigarettes that evening — she counted the butts one-by-one, in the mirror.

'I love you, Alex.' He was holding her so tight she could barely breathe. He had an erection, but then Alex always had an erection of some sorts — or so it seemed. He was proud of his erections — he would press himself against her in crowded places just to prove their existence and make Catarina fondle them beneath tables in restaurants. Alex was very turned on by restaurants. He loved being felt beneath a napkin while he complained about the service. Catarina had to learn to eat with one hand but that was OK in the US because that was how most Americans ate anyway — deft with the use of a fork — it was one of the many talents Alex had taught her.

Even though she was drunk she could hear her voice sounded unconvincing. Alex seemed happy with it, though.

'Alex, I can't breathe.' Had she spoken in Russian? She was confused, she couldn't remember. His grip on her didn't relax — perhaps he hadn't understood. He pushed her hand into his pants and she felt the tip of his prick bounce beneath her fingers, hot, damp and rubbery, like a dog's toy bone.

'I have to tell you something, Alex.' It seemed like the right time. She knew what Eve had said but Alex loved her and he was in a good mood.

'What, honey?' He rocked her like a child, stroked her hair as she stroked his prick.

'I was lucky today, Alex. I found an agent — a good agent. I will get work now, the best work. They handle a lot of the top girls. I might earn big money with them. We can pay for a good flat then, Alex. You won't need to go out all day looking for work.'

Alex's voice was soft. 'I don't understand, baby.' At first she thought it was her English.

'You've got an agent. You've got me,' he laughed and she laughed too, like a parrot.

'I know, Alex, but Eve told me this woman will get me more work. You will still be my manager but I will get good jobs.'

'Eve? Eve Horowitz?'

'Yes.'

'She put you up to this, baby? She took you?'

'It's OK, Alex. Eve wanted to help me. She thinks I am good. They liked her shots. They . . .'

The first punch broke Catarina's nose. It came from nowhere. She felt Alex drop his arms and then she heard the honeycomb crunch of her own bones and sinuses.

He had never hit her on the face before. The blow blinded her and then it was like someone had released some valve somewhere in her head — like a dam had just burst and the blood broke free and she felt it run hot down her chest. She couldn't speak, she didn't know what to say. You can't see and your face has turned to liquid — what was there to say? There was nothing more left for him to hit.

She was wrong, though, Alex hit her again — a slap this time, which showed her the way to the floor, in case she couldn't find it. She felt the cheap shag pile against her fingers. If she clung onto it hard then perhaps he wouldn't hurt her again.

'Bitch!' She could hear that. She knew what it meant — she had looked it up after the first time.

'Fucking bitch!' A dog having intercourse. That had never made sense. She clawed the carpet some more. She could see again now. There was an old condom underneath the bed. Dust too, probably. Her father made her clean beneath the bed in their apartment in Moscow. She hated the job because the grey dustballs looked like rats and she was frightened one might grow eyes and move. Klara used to laugh at her.

Alex propped her up so that he could punch her face properly. It was a good move — all he had been able to do was kick her when she was lying down — there was an explosion in her jaw. She knew what he was doing – he was wrecking her face.

'You're going to leave me, Luisa – you're going to fucking leave me!'

'Yes!' she wanted to shout, 'I understand, Alex, I understand everything – anything. Stop now that I know what you are trying to tell me!'

He hit her twice more – she didn't know how – all she knew now was the pain. Her eyes were wide open but there were dark stains obliterating Alex's face. She fought the stains for a while, even while he hit her, but then she thought they might be friendly after all – perhaps they had come to take her away from the pain. She let the stains grow. The scene before her eyes burnt up like a map of the Ponderosa. She passed out and the pain went at last.

Catarina was swimming in a lake. The waters of the lake were thick and heavy like blood, so that floating was easy but swimming was difficult. Her limbs ached from the effort. Her mouth gaped open so that the water gushed inside, choking her. She tried to close her jaw – she knew it was slowing her down, but the rush of water was too heavy and it just hung there, slack as old elastic.

'You'll never leave me, Luisa.'

Alex's voice was constant because the water was silent. She would, though. She would swim away. She would find the strength from somewhere. She would swim for hours – for days, if necessary. She was crying with the pain. Her head was filled with firecrackers of agony and each time one went off she wailed some more.

She was carried to a bed. Alex's face was above her. 'You stay here, Luisa.' Covers were pulled up to her chin. She smelt lemon salts from the bath. The pillow hurt her head. She had to tell Alex, the pain was too bad. The pillow was killing her. Then she was swimming again.

A day passed. Alex was trying to force food into her

194

mouth. She tried to tell him she couldn't eat because she couldn't close her mouth but she couldn't speak either and, when she tried, the firecrackers started again so she just had to stop. The food was baby food. He was spooning it from the can. He was frightened that she couldn't eat, she could tell from his eyes.

Alex killed himself right in front of her. He did it three times a day. The first time he put the barrel of a shotgun into his mouth and pulled the trigger while he was staring at her. She knew it was her fault he had done it. The back of his head appeared on the wall behind – the sort of flat mess you see on a road when a bird has been run over. Only the mess contained Alex's hair. Catarina was sorry about the hair because she liked the hair at the back of Alex's head.

The second time he had been in the bath. He was naked and the bath was full of water. Even then he had a hard-on, she noticed. She was standing over him, watching. He took a silver dinner fork and stabbed at his wrists. The bath slowly filled with blood and he slid under the surface.

The third time they were in a forest. She saw the tree and knew what would happen. She saw his footprints in the snow. He took his boots off and left them side-by-side behind the tree. He was too big to climb the branches gracefully – she saw the frosted breath billow from his lungs with the effort. He tore his trousers in the climb and she knew that upset him because he was, despite everything, a dapper, tidy man. That was why he had placed the blankets so neatly around her and that was why she got upset when she felt someone pulling at them, ripping them, tearing them off her.

'Catarina! Catarina Kirkova! Squeeze my hand if you can hear me, honey. Squeeze it hard. Good girl. Are you in pain, honey? Don't try to speak, squeeze once for yes and two for no. We'll give you something for the pain, honey. You'll feel a little woozy but don't be scared by that. Just a little prick, honey, that's all – yeah, you go

195

ahead and laugh at me, all the patients like that line about the prick.'

She held onto a large black hand. It would pull her through the water, to safety. She didn't feel the needle – the firecrackers saw to that. Then the explosions stopped – it was no longer bonfire night. She began to swim more easily, although Alex was floating alongside in the water, his face distorted and bloated. He looked as though he was smiling at her, though his eyes were grey and filmy. The water cleared. She swam out of the way. She swam like a fish. She was free.

34

'Luisa?'

'Catarina.' She broke the surface, came up quoting her new name. The air felt fresh and good.

'Sorry — Catarina.' There was relief in Stephen's tone. He didn't mind being corrected, he didn't mind at all.

'You're OK. You're alive.'

She could open her eyes then. Stephen's hair looked dirty. He had spots on his face. Why hadn't he washed his hair? It looked darker, covered with grease like that. He held her hand like a relative. What had happened to the black hand?

'Alex almost killed you.'

'He killed himself, Stephen — I saw him, in the bath.'

Stephen looked worried — his gaze flicked across the bed. Catarina knew Eve was there, she could smell her scent. Only she couldn't possibly smell it — the scent had to be inside her own head. Her nose was packed with wadding, she was breathing through her mouth. She couldn't open her teeth, she spoke like a B-movie gangster. Her tongue felt small and lost, like a pearl inside an oyster.

Why had she said Alex was dead in the bath? She had seen him hanging from the tree. After he had shot himself. She closed her eyes again. Her thoughts needed an order — they had stepped out of line and got into disarray.

'Alex left, Catarina. When he realized what he had done he was gone like a scalded jack rabbit. He took money and a passport. He's not dead, Catarina — he's just gone, that's all. Don't be scared, he can't hurt you again.'

The thoughts formed a more orderly queue.

'My face?'

Stephen looked away again. This time she heard Eve's voice. 'He's messed you up, Catarina. Your nose is broken and he fractured your jaw. We spoke to the doctors, though. They're every bit as sick as we are. They say they can fix you up with plastic surgery. I spoke to the man myself and I'm sure he's no bullshitter. He showed me some of his work. I'm a photographer, Catarina – I know what they can do in a photo. This guy's good, though – he showed me noses I've photographed myself and never guessed, not for one minute. When I saw what he could do I almost booked in for myself. I'm talking too much. Hospitals make me nervous – always have. Give me an hour or two and I might shut up. It's the smell, I think, the medical smell. It hits you in the car park, the minute you get out of your car. Do they spray it about, do you think, like they spray the smell of fresh bread in a super-market? To make you buy more?'

'No!' Catarina cried.

'No? Well it was just a joke, anyway. Excuse me, my mouth runs away with me when I get nervous. Did you see that guy in the next room? I know you shouldn't stare but his door was open and I never saw so many machines and tubes and things – I mean, there must be a point where you think, "Well, we've gone too far this time, so let's just switch off while he's not looking." – I mean, what use can he be to society or himself . . .'

'No plastic surgery. No operation.' At least, that was what Catarina meant to say. What came out through her wired jaws sounded different somehow, but Stephen seemed to catch the drift. He also caught the look in her eye – like a lamb being led to the slaughter.

'Catarina . . .' he began.

'No operations!'

'You mean you're standing me up, honey? Why, this is just our third date and I thought we were getting on just fine.' The surgeon had come into the room. The man with the black hands and the deep sonorous voice. He bent over Catarina and smiled. His eyes were bloodshot but his teeth looked friendly.

'I've had you down to theatre three times already and you didn't even know it was happening,' he smiled. 'Surely one more time won't be asking too much? Just for me? I could have you looking pretty again.'

Eve patted her hand.

'No.' Catarina was adamant.

'Mind if I ask why? Was it something I said? My brand of aftershave?' He turned to Eve and Stephen. 'Perhaps you could leave us alone awhile to talk?'

Catarina turned her head away once they were gone.

'What's up?'

Catarina didn't answer. The surgeon sighed.

'Look, I'll be honest with you. I said one more time. I meant two – possibly three. Your fella knew what he was doing. He did a good job, understand? Nothing I can't put to rights, mind you, but I'll need a little co-operation, if you know what I mean. Are you scared? Is that it?'

He looked at Catarina's face. He had seen shots of how she used to look before. She used to be beautiful. He wondered if she had any idea just how bad the damage was. A lot of his patients guessed – they didn't need a mirror, they just knew. Others acted like they'd just been shot once the bandages came off and they saw for the first time. This girl was trying to act tough but who knew once she saw for herself?

'I can help you, you know.' The nose needed total rebuilding. He only had the photos to go on, he could never have guessed its shape from the pulp Alex had created.

'Will I heal without another operation?'

'Sort of.' The surgeon folded his arms. He wasn't used to women refusing his services. Women usually begged him to help them. Without his help this girl would look like a prize fighter the rest of her life.

*   *   *

199

'Talk to her,' he told Stephen when he was outside the room again. 'Find out what's troubling her. She needs that operation – I think she might still be in shock. Can you speak to her? You can see how she'll be if she doesn't change her mind.'

Stephen tried. Eve tried. Even Daniel tried but Daniel was no good – he hated hospitals more than Eve. He also hated ugliness, so Catarina's face was a problem for him, too. It wasn't that he could see much underneath the bandages but the shapes didn't look right somehow. He had developed a morbid fascination for those shapes. He wanted to pick her head up and feel it and rattle it to guess what was inside, like a wrapped Christmas gift. He pleaded with her to agree to the operation – for his own sake as much as hers. Daniel thought himself an artist – now he felt like a painter who'd had a canvas destroyed by a crazed knifeman.

'Just how bad is her nose?' he asked Eve a couple of days later.

'Well let's just say she'll never snort coke again,' the doctor cut in.

'That guy just isn't funny,' Daniel complained once he'd gone.

'No,' Eve said, 'but he's good – the best.'

'Please, Catarina.'

– But Catarina was adamant. She had seen what plastic surgery did to people. She didn't want to end up a living vegetable, like her sister.

35

They heard the music echo across the water long before the house came into sight. 'My Funny Valentine' by Nat King Cole — his father's favourite singer, according to Stephen. He was bringing Catarina back to his home, back to recover and rest.

Catarina no longer looked like the girl of his dreams. With her dark bruised eyes and her crooked, plaster-swathed nose, the only dreams she would have appeared in would have belonged to Wesley Craven.

Stephen's parents were rich. They lived on the coast just outside Boston and their sprawling white-painted house and its linen-clad occupants looked like something from a Ralph Lauren catalogue. Mr Van Doren — Hoogie — played polo and wore Herbert Johnson fedoras that he had specially imported. Mrs Van Doren — Aimée — was a notorious social agoraphobic who only left her own property once a year, to attend the Consul's Ball at the Copley Plaza — a white-gloves event that was invitation only.

They had five children — three boys and two girls — but only Stephen — the youngest boy — had made the lazy effort to fly the nest.

'Hail to the prodigal!' Mr Van Doren called as the cab pulled up in the drive. He clasped his son firmly to his chest. Stephen smiled, embarrassed and pleased. His hair started to stick up in a cowlick again and his skin started to sprout freckles in anticipation of his return to the land of his childhood.

'Miss Kirkova — welcome.' Catarina's hand was enveloped in another the size of a bear paw. 'You're the very first citizen of the USSR to set foot on this property to my knowledge – and this has been Van Doren land since the house was first built. We're honoured, Miss Kirkova. Come into the house before the mists eat you up – Aimée and the kids are waiting to meet you.'

The house rose out of the sea mist like a palace. Seagulls circled and screamed overhead. A butler opened the door. Aimeé was waiting, posed in the hall. She wore men's clothing and smoked Gitanes in a long holder.

'Stephen!' her voice was soft, with a trace of the South. 'You look thinner, Stephen. We'll have to feed you up and get you some sun.' She kissed her son on the cheek, then extended a hand towards Catarina. Her eyes flicked over Catarina's face, her badly-fitting brown suit and her bare legs and high heels. Aimée smiled. Her teeth were perfect, like pearls.

'Welcome,' she said.

The whole family were tall and fair and handsome like Stephen – even the women. Sport was their life and they broke off playing for just long enough to be polite and say their hellos, rough-house their brother a little and then they were gone again, either shrieking down to the beach or sprinting to the stables to saddle up. The sun burnt off the mist and Catarina saw the lawns like green velvet and the yellow beach that lay beyond.

'This is your home for a while,' Aimée said. 'Relax and enjoy it – you're here to get well.'

Catarina could never have relaxed in that place, it was just too marvellous. She would have let herself down – worse, she would have let Stephen down. She was glad of her injuries – they might excuse her manners.

They gave her a chair on the patio and pillows and a rug to make sure she was comfortable. Aimée placed some design magazines on her lap – any pictures of models had been surreptitiously cut out of the ads, Catarina noticed.

It could have been tact, or to rub salt in the wounds. From what she'd seen of Aimée, it was anyone's guess — the butler brought a tray of iced tea. Stephen sat with her a while, playing quietly with a large grey hound but the dog was soon keen to be off, finding pieces of gnarled driftwood and challenging Stephen to throw them. The shrieks from the beach grew louder.

'You get off down there, son,' Aimée said. 'I'll keep Miss Kirkova company for a while.'

She smiled at Catarina once Stephen was gone.

'I don't know why he has to be so stubborn, do you?' she asked.

Catarina was confused. 'I beg your pardon?' It was a phrase Alex had taught her. Good English manners.

Aimee's smile widened. 'Stephen, dear. Look at him — so ill and gangly-looking. There's no need for it, you know — no need for him to take himself off and work for a pittance in New York. Hoogie and I both offered him help when he started but he threw the idea back in our faces. I don't know where he gets his stubbornness from. I would never do anything so downright demeaning and neither would his father. We are a family who inherit, my dear. I see no point in being self-made when it is all laid out on a plate for you already, do you?' She leant forward to stub her cigarette out. 'Are you comfortable, dear? Is there anything you need?' She lit another Gitane. 'Does the smell make you ill?'

'No. I like it.'

'Good.' Aimée leant back in her chair, making the wicker squeak. Her skin was pale tan and her eyes a sort of washed-out blue — the only indistinct thing about her face. Her hair had been cut into a silken bob. She had changed into a swimsuit with a pair of faded white linen shorts worn over the top. Her foot tapped gently as she watched the others on the beach.

'You met Stephen in New York?'

'Yes.'

'He tells me you are – were,' she corrected herself quickly, '– a model.'

'Yes.'

'I'm sorry about your accident, Miss Kirkova.' She stared at Catarina's face now.

'I hear you have a husband.'

'Yes.'

'But you use your own name.'

'That's right.'

'You know my son has feelings for you, too?'

Catarina was silent.

Aimée tapped ash into a cut-glass dish. 'May I ask you two questions, Miss Kirkova?'

'Catarina.'

'Maybe.' Aimée shrugged.

Stephen waved at them from the beach but only Aimée waved back. He looked younger than he had in New York.

'Are you a hooker?' – Aimée was still smiling.

'What?'

'A hooker – a whore. Do you fuck men for money?'

'No.'

Aimée leant back again. The hound arrived, wet from the sea. She laughed and kissed its pink snout.

'You look like one, you know. You look like a whore that got beaten by her pimp. Looks go a long way, Miss Kirkova, first impressions count, I learnt that when I was very small. That was my first impression when I met you – that you were a young hooker in a spot of bother.

'When he was a child my son was always bringing home stray animals in distress and expecting me to tend to them. I think he might have taken on more than he can handle this time. He's a wonderful young man but too soft for his own good. Sometimes his father and I have to look after his interests. I hope you understand.'

Catarina shielded her eyes from the sun.

'What was your second question?' she asked.

Aimée poured iced tea into a crystal tumbler. The ice groaned and crackled.

'Are you in love with Stephen?' she said.

Catarina shook her head slightly. 'No.'

This time Aimée's smile looked genuine. 'Good. Then we can be friends. Do you play bridge? Whist? Blackjack? No? Wonderful! Then I can teach you. Do you ride? Play polo? Once you're up and about I'll have you on a horse. You don't resent my bluntness do you, Catarina? Only I see no point wasting time going through the niceties if we're to end up running you off our land at some point. It helps to know what people think when they meet you, don't you agree? Lord knows what people must think of Hoogie and me at first meeting.'

Catarina looked Stephen's mother straight in the eye. 'I thought Mr Van Doren looked kind,' she said. 'I thought you looked like a dyke.'

Aimée's eyes narrowed. 'An ugly dyke?' she asked, 'Or a good-looking one?'

'Oh, good-looking. No spring chicken of course, but good-looking, no question of that.'

'Your English is better than I thought.'

Catarina sipped her drink. 'Not really – you just pick up phrases in New York.'

'Did you ever hear the phrase 'smart-assed bitch'?'

'No.'

'Pity.'

Then Aimée Van Doren tilted her head back and roared with laughter. 'I knew you weren't as stupid as you looked, dear,' she said. 'I think we might truly be friends, Catarina.' She raised her iced tea in a salute. 'I saw it in your eyes, you know.'

'What?' Catarina sipped her drink.

'Call it intelligence, call it native cunning. You have it, whatever it is. Were you clever at school?'

Catarina shrugged.

'Why do you try so hard to play stupid, then? Is it the

205

language? Is that all? I can find you a tutor. Someone who will teach you everything, dear – not just the basics – your grammar is rather shop-bought but not bad – but the important things, like recognizing sarcasm in someone's tone. I'd introduce you to all my other girlfriends too, only I can't with you looking the way you do at the moment. Perhaps we can have a little shopping expedition and get you kitted out in something nice and tasteful. Show you to a few designer labels, that sort of thing. Then we'll get your face sorted out. You look like the Phantom of the Opera. What's all this about you not wanting plastic surgery? Nobody in their right mind could choose to be in such a state.'

Catarina closed her eyes. 'I knew someone who was operated on once,' she whispered. 'She never came round from the anaesthetic.'

Aimée threw a stick for the dog. 'Don't be a fool all your life,' she said. 'My father died having sex with his mistress but it didn't make me spend my whole adult years avoiding copulation for fear it might kill me. What if your friend had died choking on food? Would you have given up eating?'

She meant well, even Catarina could tell that.

Stephen arrived at that point, towelling himself down from a swim. He had a good body. The two women watched him in silent appreciation. His skin was burnished already and pale sand stuck to his legs and feet. He laughed and shook off droplets of salt water. Catarina wondered whether his mother was right – if he did have feelings for her beyond friendship. The tense was wrong though – Stephen may have *had* feelings for her but there was no way he would want her now with her face in such a mess.

The dog pushed round her legs, making the rug damp and sandy.

*   *   *

They all arrived for coffee – father, sons, daughters, more dogs. They were healthy and happy and noisy, Aimée's brood. Rough as puppies they jostled and fought and mostly they ignored Catarina because they didn't know what to say to her.

Aimée was at her best when there were men around. She became bright and loud and funny and when Catarina looked at her she found she had become almost beautiful, too. It happened most when she looked at her husband, but it was the same with all the men – it was an expression that transformed her face. Devoted and awestruck – how Nancy Reagan used to gaze at Ronnie.

'We're taking the boat out this afternoon – do you feel well enough to come?' Stephen asked Catarina.

'Catarina is too tired, Stephen.' Aimée cut in. 'She needs to rest. I thought that was why you brought her out here.' She passed Catarina a plate of biscuits. 'The creams are the softest if you can manage them, dear,' she said. 'Did you lose any of your teeth in the accident?'

Eve came to visit after a couple of weeks. She looked out of place in her black jumper and ankle-length coat.

'Who's she supposed to be?' she asked when Aimée had left them alone. 'Joan Crawford or Bette Davis? What a bitch, eh?'

Catarina laughed. Her eyes looked better now – almost perfect. She had a little colour, too, from sitting out in the sun and seaspray.

'I like her, Eve – I think she's wonderful. We have a secret deal – she teaches me how to look and behave like a lady and I keep my filthy little hands off her precious son.'

Eve felt a pang of concern. 'Does Stephen know about this arrangement?' she asked.

Catarina shook her head. 'There's no need for him to know.'

'So you don't have any feeling for the boy?'

'We're friends, Eve. I'm grateful for all his help, but that's all. I've got a busted face and a husband on the run. What else could you expect me to say?'

She moved closer to Eve. Her eyes looked excited. 'I made another decision, Eve – I have to get back into modelling. I don't have any choice – it's the only way I can make any money. It's money I need badly, too – I . . . I've got things I need to pay for – relatives back in Russia. It's all I can do, Eve – I'm desperate.'

Eve looked worried. 'Then you'll have to get your nose fixed, honey.'

'I know. Aimée has been on at me, too. She's offered to pay for the operation and she says I can use her surgeon in Boston. I'm going to do it, Eve, I've got no other choice.'

Eve let out a sigh and ran her fingers through her mop of hair.

'You know there's still a big risk you won't be able to model again?' she asked. 'The camera can be cruel, Catarina – it shows up any flaws and scars like a magnifying glass.'

Catarina looked at her hands. 'I know. Did you bring my photos?'

Eve passed Catarina a leather folder. Inside were the prints of Catarina's last session. Eve looked at Catarina's face as she studied them one by one and she felt like an intruder. The girl should have been alone with her personal grief. There were no words Eve could think of to give her comfort.

'I was beautiful, Eve.'

'Yes, Catarina, you were.'

The folio slipped slowly to the ground and the pictures fell out in a fan. Luisa looking straight into camera. Luisa gazing down at her precious snowstorm – the light from the ball sending a magical glow across her face. Luisa talking. Luisa with tears in her eyes. Luisa laughing. Catarina threw her head into her hands and wept.

36

Catarina's pony trotted round the paddock. The movement made her head ache like hell but apart from that she felt fine. She had had the last of her operations one week before. Now all she had to do was wait.

Aimée told her the devil found use for idle hands. She was learning how to cook cordon bleu, how to ride, how to play cards and how to shop. Aimée sent her own maid to make sure Catarina bought in all the best places. She taught her how to feel the difference between a natural and a synthetic fibre. She showed her how much better a bias cut hung. She made her recite a litany of all the best designer names from Armani to Saint-Laurent and she explained why handmade shoes from Bond Street in London far outclassed anything bought over the counter in New York.

They sat on the patio at sunset and Aimée would teach her how to tell a Chianti from a Claret. She played classics on the gramophone and, one evening, Catarina discovered that Elgar's Cello Concerto made her weep, although it was a happy sadness.

'Men are terrible bastards, dear,' Aimée said, handing her a handkerchief. 'But women can be worse. Why did you allow him to beat you so badly? Why did you believe he had the right?'

The sea sounded louder at dusk. The evening was cool – Catarina wore one of Aimée's cardigans around her shoulders.

'I know what I'm talking about, dear, believe me. Hoogie beat me once, you know.'

Catarina looked up.

'Yes, I thought that might interest you. But don't go spreading it – I've never told another living soul. He got drunk one night soon after we were married. I happened to laugh at the wrong moment and he was onto me like a bloody animal. He fractured my cheekbone with a bound copy of Mark Twain's Greatest Works.'

'What happened?' Catarina pulled the cardigan closer round her body.

'I shot him, dear. In the leg. I was aiming for his balls but I hadn't had contacts fitted in those days and was too vain for glasses, so I guess my aim was poor. You should be thankful that it was, dear, or there would have been no Stephen to help you out of your scrape.'

'What happened then?' Catarina was enthralled.

Aimée smiled and shrugged. 'Nothing much. Hoogie got stitched up. They told the hospital it was an accident while he was out shooting. No desire for scandal, you see. I was quite a name anyway in those days, before I retired from the social scene. The family would never have recovered if word had leaked out.'

They sat in silence for several minutes.

'Is that true, Aimée?'

'No, I was lying, Catarina. I told you the story just to cheer you up.' Catarina had no idea whether she was telling the truth or not.

The silence continued in a friendly enough way, then Aimée spoke again.

'Mind if I give you some advice, dear?' she asked.

'Would my minding stop you?' Catarina asked.

Aimée chuckled. 'I was going to tell you to be tough, Catarina – as hard as diamonds and then some. Don't allow them to screw you around again – never! Learn self-respect. Learn your own worth and then act accordingly. You have a spark of fire there already but I guess your husband has done a great deal to extinguish it. Fan the fire, Catarina – nurture the flames carefully. Become hard

210

– develop a shell. They will all act like bastards, you know – if you allow it.'

Her head fell back against her chair.

'I can teach you to be tough,' she said. 'On the other hand, dear,' she added, 'you can ignore me completely.'

It seemed like a decade before the plaster and the bandages came off for good. The doctor peered closely at his handiwork and then stepped back to take a longer look.

'Well, the bones have knit straight, at least,' he said.

Eve was there, holding her hand. She said nothing, just looked. She could have beaten Aimée at poker any day of the week with that expression.

'Do you want to see?'

Catarina nodded.

'Remember this is not how it's going to look. Remember it'll look a little strange at first.'

Catarina looked at her nose in the mirror and she screamed. Eve screamed a split-second after, because of Catarina's scream, which had made her jump.

The nose was swollen and bruised. It was hard to tell what shape it would be because it had no real shape at that time. They gave Eve a Valium for her nerves and told Catarina she would just have to wait.

'My lord, you look like you've just done ten rounds with Tyson, dear!' Aimée said when they got her home.

Stephen looked in to see her but he could find nothing more helpful to say so Aimée shushed him out again. Hoogie came in straight from polo. Catarina watched his legs all the time these days to see if he had any sort of a limp from Aimée's target practice.

'My my!' was all he could say.

Catarina stayed in the house now because her skin felt raw and the cold autumn winds seemed to bite at her face. It was over a month before she looked at her reflection

211

again and when she did she dropped the mirror in shock and it shattered to pieces at her feet.

'Klara!'

'Who, dear?' The mirror was French, eighteenth-century. Aimée tried to keep the irritation out of her voice as she picked up the broken pieces gingerly.

Catarina turned to her, her eyes bulging with panic. Her fingers fluttered in front of her lips.

'You look wonderful, dear, as I told you. Women would die for a nose like that, you know – I dare say Doctor Kling will be swamped with orders before the week's out. It's perfect – what's wrong?'

'It . . . isn't . . . *my* . . . nose . . .'

Aimée grew more irritated. 'The doctor explained, dear – he couldn't copy the one you got broken. He did his best, Catarina – better than his best, I should say. As cute as a button – in fact I should say that man has performed a miracle.'

Catarina was turned inside-out with emotion. It was not her face she had seen in the mirror – not her own. The doctor had performed a miracle – he had made her look like someone else. Klara had always had the perfect nose, not her. Klara's nose had been good even before her own operation.

She looked in the full-length mirror in her bedroom and it was Klara who posed before her eyes. She placed a mirror on the bedside table at night. Lying down she looked like Klara. She squinted her eyes so that they appeared closed in the reflection – it was Klara in the hospital bed, the last time she had seen her. She felt an unbearable sadness overwhelm her. She felt that she lived in her own sister's ghost. Klara lay in the hospital bed many miles away but she was also there with her, too. Klara's eyes looked out at her, disapproving. She held a hand out to the mirror. 'Klara, forgive me . . .' Her fingers touched glass, not flesh. Klara's eyes were crying now – great tears rolled down her face. Catarina tasted those tears in her own mouth.

*   *   *

212

She placed a wretched phone call to the nurse in Russia, late at night, when the house was asleep.

'Is my sister well?'

'What do you think?'

'Please!'

'It's late. I was asleep. My child is crying now.'

'Please, please can you tell my sister I love her?'

'You know she can't understand.'

'She might. Please!'

'Very well. Don't forget the money, though. She needs new sheets.'

– Then the line went dead.

Nurse Olga went back to her room. The baby had soiled itself again and she was tired of changing it because it was like work to her – it was like she never left the hospital at all, not for a moment. All she did all day was clean up shit. Old men, babies – it all looked the same after a while.

She washed the child carefully and dusted it with sweet-smelling powder. The child stopped crying and smiled at her. She picked it up and laid it carefully over her shoulder. It smelled good now – she loved that smell and the warmth of its little body against her face. If she sang to it softly it would sleep.

She carried it to the cot and laid it down carefully so that it didn't wake. How could it be so beautiful when its father had been so ugly? She laughed silently and shook her head. That was the thing about nature – it didn't bear grudges.

She switched off the main light in the room and switched on an old desk lamp on the table. She sat down with a sigh and pulled open one of the small drawers. In the drawer was a roll of rubber tubing and a tin containing a syringe and other stuff that she had stolen from the hospital. She rolled up her sleeve and bound the tube around her arm, pulling until a vein appeared in the white skin. Then she pressed the needle into the vein.

Olga was frightened. Security was becoming tighter at

the hospital. If she couldn't steal the drugs any more she would have to go out and buy them. She needed money badly. The dead girl's sister would have to pay up, there was no other way.

When Eve next came to visit she brought her camera with her. Catarina was riding around the paddock, her back straight as a rod and the rain squashing her cropped hair flat against her scalp. She was enjoying herself. Aimée was not around for once but in a way she was, because Catarina had acquired so many of the woman's mannerisms that watching her was like breathing Aimée's perfume long after she'd left a room.

The mimicry rankled Eve but at the same time she had to admit it suited Catarina. Now she looked like the aristocrat she had claimed to be – proud, confident – a tad aggressive, maybe. She never used to sit up straight – now she looked a whole foot taller.

Eve guessed Perry Ellis for the trousers and Norma Kamali for the T-shirt. Aimée's credit cards must have been hacking and flashing their way around Newbury Street like a set of knife-thrower's swords.

She smiled when she saw Eve, jumped from her horse and threw the reins at a stable-girl.

'Iced tea, dear?' she asked, in a close imitation of Aimée's throaty growl.

Eve looked shocked. Catarina laughed. 'Just joking,' she said. Eve laughed too, loudly, full of relief. For one minute, though . . .

She caught sight of Stephen, watching them from across the lawn. 'You wanna clean up the studio after you next time, boy!' she called. 'I thought we'd had a visit from the burglars when I got back late last night.'

Stephen smiled and shrugged an apology but Eve could see he looked tired. Commuting from Boston to New York each day was obviously getting to him. 'When are you moving back?' she'd asked him the week before, while they were working together.

'I don't know.' He had sounded evasive.

Eve was onto him like a hound that smells a rabbit. 'I prefer you to be on hand, you know. Just in case.'

'In case of what?'

'Oh – sudden jobs – last-minute calls – you know the sort of thing.'

Stephen chewed at his nails.

'So when're you moving back?'

'When Catarina is fit again.'

'Has your mother got the adoption papers through yet?'

'What?' – Stephen sounded annoyed.

'Well she has certainly taken our little Russian friend under her wing. I thought maybe . . .'

'My mother felt sorry for her, Eve.'

'Well of course, who wouldn't? I was sorry for her myself but I didn't feel like cloning her, too. It's like the bloody *Stepford Wives* out there! Look at the lot of you, all fit and healthy and with that ungodly tan! What happened to your New York pallor that I was working on, boy? What is it she feeds you all on? And now Catarina too! I never saw a Russian go brown before, Stevie! It's just not natural!'

Stephen looked at her. 'She looks magnificent, Eve. Go down and photograph her and you'll see for yourself.'

Eve looked at him from out of the corner of her eye, but she went all the same. Catarina did look good – there was absolutely no point denying it.

'Come down to the beach,' she told Catarina, 'And bring that ugly old excuse for a dog with you, too – the hound I mean – not dearest Aimée.'

'You should watch yourself down there, dear!' Aimée's voice came from behind her. 'With skin that colour you might get taken for driftwood!'

Eve gave her the finger and carried on walking.

'I'm not sure I'm ready for this, Eve.' Catarina was running along behind her.

'*I'm* the photographer – *I'll* tell you when you're ready. It's the camera that knows, Catarina – not you – and not Scarlett O'Hara back there. OK?'

'OK.'

Stephen was following them. Eve waved him away.

Eve started shooting the minute they stepped onto the sand. Catarina was nervous. The dog was a natural.

'You're being upstaged by a mutt, honey.'

The sky behind was charcoal. The sand looked the colour of chamois. The wind whipped Catarina's T-shirt out like a sail. The dog jumped up and pulled at it with his teeth. Catarina laughed. Things were looking better.

'More of that, honey, more of the same.'

Catarina drew pictures in the sand with a stick while the dog jumped joyously in the background. The wind blew up stronger and then Eve called a halt after an hour because the sand had become a problem. It was in her eyes, her ears and, worst of all, her lens. Eve hated sand almost as much as she hated brilliant sunshine – they were a photographer's nightmare when you were shooting on spec.

'You weren't happy?' Catarina walked across to her slowly, the dog still in tow.

'No – it's the fucking sand, it's killing everything.'

'Not me, then.'

'No, not you, honey.'

'Not even me a little bit?'

Eve looked at her. 'This was your first shoot since the operation. This was just a warm-up.'

'I was OK then?'

'Yeah,' – Eve unloaded some film – 'OK, you were wooden, Catarina. Better than before, though. That first time in the studio – those first few shots – I never showed them to you – you were wooden enough for a whole rain

216

forest then. You were nervous. You're still nervous now –
though for different reasons. Don't worry about it. Models
have to learn their trade just like any other profession. It
comes with time and it comes with hard work. Only a
handful of girls make good from day one. You don't expect
good sex on the first date and if you get it it's often the
last date. Do you understand what I'm saying? I'm telling
you the truth because you asked, Catarina – and because
I think it will help you to learn.'

Catarina nodded and chewed her thumb.

'I don't enjoy it, Eve,' she said.

'You will. It comes with time.'

Catarina looked out to sea. 'No, I never will.'

Eve shook sand from her hair. 'Give it up, then.'

'I can't.' There was a ship out at sea – a small peppery
dot on the horizon. Catarina imagined it was sailing to
Russia.

Eve followed her gaze and guessed her thoughts. 'Why
did you come here, Catarina?' she asked. 'Why don't you
go home if that's what you want? Alex is gone now, there's
no need for you to stay.'

'I can't go back.' Catarina whispered, 'I can never go
back. I will model because I need money and I need freedom and a life. Money most of all, though. What else can
I do? I'll be good too, Eve, even though I hate it.

'It was someone else's dream, Eve – never mine, someone
I loved back in Russia. Now she can't do it and I have to
do it for her. I think it will make her happy. I also think
it will keep her alive.'

'Who was it, your mother?' Eve didn't know if she
should say anything – Catarina seemed to have been talking to herself. Catarina shook her head. The dog jumped
up at her, no respecter of atmosphere or mood.

Eve felt uncomfortable around emotion. Her own childhood had been full of screaming, shouting and hugging.
You never spoke in the Horowitz household if screaming would do better. Talking meant shouting. Sarcasm

equalled affection. Quiet and moody equalled zilch – it just didn't arise. If you were quiet you were dead, as simple as that. Talking as Catarina had just done would have been unimaginable. Eve wasn't programmed to respond to such emotion and so she reached cut-off and just did nothing.

'Can I hear ice clacking around in tumblers of tea?' she asked after a long pause. Even the dog looked relieved.

They walked back up the beach together, Eve's little legs pumping to keep up with Catarina's long ones.

'Why don't you come back to New York?' she asked. New York was the centre of the universe. Boston was like a great black hole.

'Beth should see you, Catarina. She's been waiting to see how you turned out.'

'I know,' Catarina answered. 'She wrote.'

She paused, turned around. 'Do you think Beth really is the best, Eve? Are you sure I shouldn't see other agents before I decide?'

Ouch! Eve felt just as though Catarina had bitten her. Now where did that come from, she wondered? All models bit back at some time and most made a meal out of the hand that had fed them. Helping a model was like adopting a bear-cub – all cute and helpless and dependent one minute and the next they're ripping at your gizzard. Catarina had beaten all records with her turnaround, though.

'Try others if you like,' she said, trying to sound indifferent. 'Try them and weep!' was what she really meant. Beth had taken Catarina on on Eve's say-so. In the real world she would have been beaten up and left for dead. How did she start to get so hard-faced all of a sudden? Was it all Aimée's influence?

'Come back to New York, Catarina,' she said. 'Whatever else, you'll just fossilize out here in Aiméeland.'

Catarina nodded. 'OK.'

'Do you have money for an apartment?' Eve hated to ask. She hated to lend, too.

'I'll get it,' was all Catarina said in reply.

37

Catarina sat in her hotel room in the same brown suit she had worn when she first left New York – only now she was back and the suit fitted better because she'd put on weight in all the right places, as Hoogie had said. Her hands shook like leaves and she took a pill to stop the shaking. There had been a note waiting for her when she first checked in – just a folded sheet of card. She'd thought it would be from Stephen but then she'd read the words on it and the smile had died on her face.

'Welcome home – Alex.'

Just three words but the blood had drained so quickly from her face that the receptionist had run to get her some water before she passed out.

'Welcome home – Alex.'

He hadn't gone then, or if he had he was still looking out for her. He knew all about her – where she was – when she had arrived. She phoned Stephen to tell him but when she got his answerphone she knew she was alone with her fear.

She knew she had to do something – anything, so she counted out her cash on the bed quilt: four hundred dollars from the sale of the clothes Aimée had bought her; a thousand that she'd won off the girls, playing poker when Aimée wasn't around; two hundred that Hoogie had crushed into her hand as she'd got into the car to leave. That paid for the goosing he'd been doing since she arrived; two thousand for an antique snuff box that had got stolen while she was out shopping with Aimée's maid. It was the maid who had lifted it – Catarina had caught her and told her she'd return it to the store. She had never imagined it would be worth so much; fifty dollars Aimée had given her to tip the taxi; one hundred and eighty dollars' worth of tips from her new job as a waitress. She split the money into two even piles – one for Klara's keep and one for her keep. She owed the nurse some back pay. She took a few more notes off her own pile and then stuffed the lot onto Klara's.

'Welcome home – Alex.' She burnt the note but the words stayed alive in her head.

Beth had arranged the job for her. She had gone into the agency as soon as she got back – while she still had Aimée's clothes to wear. Beth had been impressed.

'You look good, Catarina. Are you ready to work?'

'Of course. I need the money.'

Beth had sighed. 'There's a way to go before we get to that stage, Catarina. Like I told you, you need shots, a card, a folder of work. Then you do the rounds of the circuit. Then, if you're lucky, you get onto the castings. *Then* you start earning money – if you get the jobs.'

'I need to earn straight away.' They all said that, even the wealthy ones. Like it was a game of leapfrog.

'Sit down.'

Catarina sat.

'Did you read the booklet I sent you?' – No, of course she didn't, none of the models did. Beth had published two small books – *A Model's Guide to the Business* and *A Model's Guide to Tax and the Law*. She sent free copies to each girl she took on and for years she had been puzzling over exactly what it was those girls did with them – use them as a door stop? Whatever it was they sure as hell didn't read them. They must have rated alongside the Gideon Bible as some of the greatest unread books of our time.

221

She watched Catarina try painfully to string a lie together. 'I had trouble with some of the English . . .' she was saying. Beth smiled at her and let her go on. Silence was the best reproach, she had learnt that from a class she had done in man management. Beth had done courses in everything – it was the only way to expand your mind.

Beth's mind was now expanded to near full capacity, like a hot-air balloon that is ready for take-off. She knew How to Shine in a Crowd, How to Get what she Wanted by Asking for it, How to Power Dress and Use Colour As A Communication. She never said yes when she wanted to say no and her Business and Body Politics were rated impeccable. She had learnt to control her anger, too, using yoga techniques – although right there and then in that office she felt like taking one of her own books and shoving it down Catarina's throat.

'You don't just go into modelling and start earning money, Catarina,' she explained. 'There are things you have to learn first. You start good but you get better. Super-models aren't supermodels from the day they start, they get there by dedication and hard work. You wouldn't expect a guy to start a career in politics one day and become president the next now, would you?'

Catarina looked unconvinced. Perhaps this one was going to be trouble. Beth readjusted her own body language – leant back in her chair and steepled her fingers – perfect for what she wanted to say. Who needed words when your gestures said it all for you?

'I need to work, Beth, I need the money.' Her Calvin Klein outfit shouted louder that she did not.

Beth raised her hands, palms outward, in a gesture of appeasement. Her nail varnish had chipped. She put her hands down again.

'I know how you must feel, Catarina, honestly I do. New York is an expensive place to live – all my girls have the same problem. I have thirty girls on my books at the

222

moment and at least a third of them are in exactly the same situation as you. Look – let me help, OK?'

Catarina looked less sullen.

Beth smiled.

'Now – we have one of three plans, right? First – the agency advances you some cash so that you can keep afloat while you're starting up. Second . . .'

'How much?'

'Sorry?'

'How much money do you lend me?'

Beth puffed air out of her mouth. 'I don't know! How much do you need?'

'Several thousand dollars.'

'Do you have a drugs problem, Catarina? I insist my girls are clean.'

'No drugs. At what interest?'

'What?'

'What interest do you charge for the money you lend me?' – Eve had told her to ask this.

'Look – let's skip over plan one and go straight on to plan two, shall we?'

'OK.'

'Good. Plan two – I try to get you a short contract abroad – say, three months? Maybe Japan – somewhere they will take new models. You fill your book with tear sheets while you're out there and pick up some money into the bargain. They pay quite well, you know.'

'Japan?' Catarina just stared.

'Well, I've got links with agencies all over the world. Germany, maybe. I don't know.'

'And plan three?'

'You stay in New York, pay your dues. Work your legs out on go-sees and work in the evening to pay your rent. That's what most models do. You can't get a drink any-where decent in New York without an out-of-work model spearing cherries into your glass or an actor resting between roles shaking your Martini. I can get you an

223

interview. I can also arrange a meeting with two other girls who are looking to share cheap accommodation. What do you say?'

Catarina started at Sidney's Downtown Blues Bar the following night. She wasn't ready to leave New York – not yet. She also met the girls with the apartment, just to keep Beth happy. Yasmina and Bonnie. Catarina hated them on sight. She moved in the following day, though – she had no choice – she was still running from Alex.

Yasmina and Bonnie were very excited about their new flatmate. They cleared cupboard space for her and gave her a list of the house rules. Yasmina was tall and black with aggressively-cropped hair and a gold tooth in the side of her mouth. Bonnie was a natural blonde with a shape like a Barbie doll. They were both heavily into star signs and told Catarina that hers checked out just right which was a great relief to all of them, especially to Catarina herself because she'd made up her date of birth when they asked her.

Yasmina only dated Leo men. Catarina misunderstood and thought the word referred to their names and called all Yasmina's dates Leo, which made her laugh at first and annoyed her later. Bonnie's dates were all called Ralph because Bonnie only dated one man and that was his name.

Ralph was what was known in the trade as an asshole. He came on to Yasmina the minute Bonnie left the room and he was heavily into coke, which meant his nasal passages were the consistency of moist toilet tissue, so he sniffed all the time. Catarina imitated his sniff but Bonnie didn't notice.

Stephen called round the night after she moved in. He looked round the small apartment with a strange expression on his face.

'What?' Catarina looked luscious. She'd been in the shower when he arrived. Bonnie had giggled as she'd shown him into the hall. He watched Catarina rubbing her hair with a towel. Her eyelashes were still dark and glued together with water. A pain rose inside him as he watched – a pain of longing and need to possess.

'What?' Catarina repeated. He'd forgotten to answer her.

'Nothing.' He stuffed his hands into the pockets of his jeans, which took some doing as they were as tight as a drumskin.

'You don't like the place.'

'Does it matter what I think?' – He knew he was sounding childish. 'Of course I like it. It's great.'

He felt pissed off but he didn't know why. Perhaps it was because she was becoming self-sufficient. He hated himself for thinking like that but he couldn't help it – the thought had just sprung up unannounced in his head.

'You don't like the girls then.' Catarina looked really concerned.

'They're terrific. Wonderful.'

'What then?'

'Nothing. I brought you some wine. A moving-in present. Shall I open it?'

Catarina took the bottle from him. 'Thank you but I'd better not. I've got to be at work by nine and I've got an appointment tomorrow – some photographer over on the Bowery.' She placed the bottle in the fridge.

Stephen bade farewell to the bottle as the fridge door closed. It was a good vintage – he hoped Yasmina and Bonnie didn't get their skinny little mitts on it.

'Orffman? Charlie Strauss?' he asked. 'Who's the photographer? I know a few of the names around there.'

'No – no – it's neither of those.'

'Who then?'

She looked surprised. 'I don't know.'

'You must do. You said you had an appointment. You

225

must have a name.' What was he doing? His mouth just wouldn't stop.

'You sound just like Alex.'

'Jesus! Thanks!' He knew he did and he knew he couldn't help it and that made him mad. He picked up his jacket and made his way quickly towards the door. Catarina watched him.

'What's the matter with you, Stephen?' She was close to him now – he could smell the shower gel. The smell started the first stirrings of an erection. That was it – his mind turned to Jell-O now.

'I care about you, Catarina, that's all.' It sounded clumsy and stupid. His voice sounded good, though – husky and just right, so he might get away with the corny crap he was saying to her. The sentence replayed like an echo in his head.

She bit at her thumbnail. 'Thank you.'

Stephen grasped her bare shoulders, taking care not to hurt, taking care not to come across like the animal Alex. Alex the monster. Alex the man she had loved enough to marry.

'No, Catarina, that's not the right answer. You're supposed to say you care for me too.'

'I do, Stephen, of course I do.'

'Now it's the tone that's wrong.'

'Tone?' – Stephen was stumped. He could never have explained a word like tone. He thought perhaps she understood – that she was just playing games with him. He kissed her on the lips – not a lovers' kiss, more a friend's kiss – the sort Eve said Russians did all the time.

It was Catarina who kissed him back – he would have sworn his life on it. It was *her* lips that parted first and it was *her* body that pulled towards him. He felt a hundred-year-old groan escape inside him. It was what *she* wanted – *she* wanted what he wanted – they both wanted the same thing. Her body felt soft. Her skin felt like petals. The phone rang but he didn't hear it.

226

'Catarina!' Bonnie was sniggering, holding the phone in her hands. Eyes all wide and blue — all oh-gee-whoops-am-I-interrupting-something? Stephen could have scalped her there and then. He could have scraped her fucking stupid blonde mane from her stupid pin-shaped head and then he would have . . . but when did he get so aggressive? He was the nice one — one of the ones that tipped their hats to the ladies in all the cowboy films. He just didn't feel nice at that moment, that was all. Even nice guys can have an off-day.

It was Aimée. Catarina took the phone into her bedroom, where Stephen couldn't hear her. The line was good but Aimée still shouted. She always shouted when she used the phone — it was as though she still had reservations about anything vaguely modern and scientific.

'Catarina?'

'Aimée?'

'How's the new place?'

'Desperate.'

'Good. Has my son come to visit yet?'

'No.'

'How long has he been there?'

'About forty minutes.'

'I see.'

'I have a job in a bar in the evenings, Aimée.'

A sigh. 'Remind me not to go there.'

'It's OK — not too high class. They'd let you in, Aimée, no problem.'

'I miss you, dear. I even miss your insults.'

'I miss you too, Aimée.'

'You can let Stephen out now.'

'Ok.'

'Aimée?'

'Yes, dear?'

'There's one thing I don't understand. If you wanted me to keep off your son then why did you try to make me so much like you? I thought all good sons married women just like their own mothers.'

227

Aimée chuckled. 'Not Stephen, dear. He might love me but deep down he hates everything I stand for, didn't you know?'

'Goodnight, Aimée.'

'Goodnight.'

Catarina went back into the lounge. Stephen looked funny, like a dog that has been knocked down by a truck and somehow managed to spring back onto its feet again to kid itself everything is still alright.

'I have to get ready now, Stephen.'

'I love you, Catarina.'

The words hung in the air – pale and limp, like strands of boiled spaghetti.

He watched the blush spread across Catarina's face.

'You shouldn't do, Stephen.'

'Why not?'

'There's no point.'

'Thanks.'

'I'm sorry.'

Stephen felt all at once like an open wound. His erection skulked discreetly from the room, shutting the door quietly in its wake.

'You don't understand, Stephen.'

'What don't I understand, Catarina?' He peppered the sentence liberally with sarcasm.

'Look at yourself, Stephen – you're young and you have everything. I've done so much – things you could never ever know about.'

'You make yourself sound like Errol Flynn.'

'Who?'

'It doesn't matter. Are you telling me I'm too young for you? That you prefer older men? Men who have been around a bit? Men like Alex? I'm not a virgin, Catarina.'

She laughed. She still was. Alex had always preferred her that way.

'What's so funny?'

'Nothing.'

'For fuck's sake!' — It was the perfect exit line. Stephen really left the apartment this time and without pausing or turning back. The door slammed behind him, creating a draught that ruffled the coats on the hall stand.

Yasmina and Bonnie appeared on cue from the kitchen, wide-eyed and innocent, pretending they hadn't been listening at the door. 'I'll have him if you're finished with him,' Yasmina said. Catarina laughed. It was all she could do. Somehow she felt more like crying.

38

Bar work was not fun. Catarina's uniform was short and tight and so were most of the customers. She hated to see men drunk because they reminded her of her father. She wondered about him sometimes. Was he still alive? She had written him a letter but was too afraid to post it. The police must have traced her back to their old home by now, looking for Samuel's murderer. What if there were fingerprints on the letter? She had put no address but what if they had some private code on them that gave the where-abouts of the sender? Besides, her father had had enough of letters by now — the ones from their mother had sent him nearly mad — what would new ones from a murdering daughter do to him?

The clients of the bar were mainly businessmen. Tony — one of the barmen — told her there were lots of celebrities, too, but she gave up trying to pick them out because she knew hardly anyone, anyway. She had never been to the cinema and she could not afford to buy magazines. Tony did both most of the time when he wasn't tending bar. He was also an actor but — like Catarina's modelling career and the assorted dreams of all the other bar staff — it was a subject best not mentioned on duty.

Tony's real name was Moon Starburst — his mother had been living on a commune when he was born, though she packed up her bags and went back to Illinois and a career in accounting six months later — but he'd changed it to Tony on his twelfth birthday because that was the day he'd been taken to see Tony Curtis swinging his way around a

230

big top in some glitzy circus film and it had been love at first hard-on.

He took Catarina to see the film. He adored it all and mouthed the lines as they were spoken. He also cried at the ending – uncontrollably and for no apparent reason. He had had his eyelashes dyed specially so his mascara didn't run.

Tony taught Catarina how to spot a smackhead and how to avoid the groping and bumchat that went on in the bar. He also taught her how to apply make-up because on some of his nights off he did a drag act in a gay bar. He took Catarina down there once a week and, although she was always shocked by the place, she thought he looked beautiful in his outfit.

Sometimes she sat backstage.

'Could I find an excuse for more sequins on this bodice?'

'There's always an excuse for a sequin, darling.'

'Jesus, these lashes make me look like Clara the Cow!'

'I have to tell you it's not just the lashes, dear!'

Catarina understood little of the banter but she laughed along with them all, just the same. Tony watched her with intelligent eyes and tried to translate the bits she'd missed, later. The performers were like nothing she had ever seen in Russia.

When the show was over and Tony cleaned off his make-up he looked young and vulnerable. He pretended to look after Catarina but she felt as though it was she who looked after him.

They ate cheap meals together and he warned her of the dark side of the modelling business. He was good at giving out warnings but bad at heeding his own advice. Tony was a romantic – he fell in love with everyone and liked to look for the good in everybody.

'You are always in love,' Catarina told him one day as they rushed through Central Park on their way to a go-see.

'So? It's a great feeling – the best there is.'

'But you can't love all your lovers.'

231

'Why ever not?'

Catarina thought. 'Because you can only love once in your life,' she said, 'Only one big love. Lots of little loves, maybe, but only the one proper one.'

'I have my Big Love, Catarina,' Tony said. 'And then I have lots of smaller loves, too. I am faithful in my way and in my heart. Who says you're only allowed one love? Whose rules are you playing by, dear? One love, forever, eh? Sounds a bit bloody dreary to me. Have you ever been in love, Catarina. No? Then you don't even know you're born. Did you love your husband? You must have done.'

'I thought I did.'

Tony looked triumphant. 'There you are, then – you *thought* you loved him, you thought *he* was the Big One, but he turned out to be an asshole. So, by your theory, that shouldn't make any difference – if he was the Big One you should still be loving him, right?'

Catarina was confused.

'Or if you don't – and heavens above I hope you don't,' Tony went on, '– then you are saying that that's it – you'll never love another man again – true?'

'Tony, you give me advice on modelling yet you have never done any yourself – you give me advice on men yet you fall in love with every man you set eyes on . . .'

'Not true – I never cared for redheads!'

'– You tell me to eat health food yet you live on hot dogs and cheesecake . . .'

'But I give good make-up, don't I, dear?'

'Stop calling me 'dear' – you sound like an old queen.'

'I *am* an old queen.'

'Don't be stupid.'

'Anyway – where'd you learn that term? I bet you don't even know what it means.'

'One of your friends in the bar says it all the time.'

'He knows what he's talking about – you don't.'

'You think I don't?'

'I know it.'

232

– They loved to bicker, it kept them amused for hours. They bickered right the way through a film one time, until they got thrown out for making noise. The film was *Now Voyager* and Tony was distraught at missing the ending.

'You've seen it six times already, Tony,' Catarina told him, 'Besides, anyone can see how it's going to end.'

'How, Missy know-it-all?'

'She dies, of course.'

'Catarina, your heart is made up of chips of Russian ice.'

'Yours is made of marshmallow.'

One night they sat in her room listening to show tunes. Tony was being Doris Day and she was being Howard Keel.

'Who bought you that?' he stopped short in the middle of 'The Deadwood Stage'.

'What?' Catarina looked up, surprised.

'That.' He was pointing to the glass snowstorm.

Catarina felt herself blush. 'Why?'

Tony turned around. 'Humour me. I'm curious.'

Catarina shrugged. 'It's just an ornament.'

'Wrong, Catarina, it's a possession. The only important possession you have, as a matter of fact. I want to know why it's so special, that's all. Did your husband buy it for you?'

'No!'

Tony laughed. 'Who, then? No – don't tell me, let me try and guess. Blond . . . tall . . . handsome enough, in a makes-one-horny-as-hell kind of way? Am I warm? Name begins with an 'S'? You look so young when you blush, Catarina, did you know that? No wonder poor Stevie adores you so much.'

'Stephen? You know Stephen?' – Catarina was stunned.

'Mmmmm.' Tony wandered off to change the tape, playing hard-to-get.

'How do you know Stephen?'

233

'Hmm-mmm.'

'Tony!'

'He came into the bar.'

'*Our* bar? Stephen was there? When?'

Tony looked at his nails.

'Oh, Monday . . . or was it Tuesday? Definitely Wednesday, anyway. I think he missed a day the week before last – or was that the week before that?'

'Stephen comes into the bar?'

Tony smiled. 'Not too much – only nearly every night. Just for a quick beer and a chat.'

'I never see him.'

'No – that's the point.'

'I don't understand.' – Tony's Cheshire-cat grin was beginning to get to her.

'He's looking out for you, dear, and he doesn't want you to know. He'd have my hide for a handbag if he found out I'd so much as breathed a word. What on earth did you do to the boy, you cow? Don't you know who he is?'

Catarina shook her head slowly yet it still didn't catch up with Tony's words.

'He's a Van Doren, Catarina! One of the Van Dorens of Boston! They're loaded, darling! His mother was the greatest socialite on the East Coast! She was a beauty, Catarina – she outshone Jackie O in her day – oh, don't tell me – the name doesn't mean a thing. There's you with just the fucking suit you stand up in and there's this boy – this deliciously tasty young boy – and he's creeping around asking after you because you won't give him so much as the time of day!' He stopped, panting.

'Stephen has been following me?'

Tony smacked his forehead and let out a loud groan.

'Did you not hear what I just said, Catarina? The guy is a catch! The ripe juicy melon in a basket of lemons! The glass of chilled champagne floating in a bucket of warm Lambrusco! What's wrong with you, girl? Didn't you see God pointing you out with his lucky stick?'

234

'Stephen has been checking up on me behind my back?'

'Oh Jesus, I'm out of here!' Tony made a move towards his coat.

'What does he want, Tony?'

'Just to know you're alright. Is that so godawful?'

'He's just a boy.'

Tony smiled – 'Look again, Catarina – I didn't see no nappies. Besides, child or not, the boy's loaded.'

'Not if he sticks around me he won't be,' Catarina whispered.

Tony grinned. 'Who told you that, his mother?'

Catarina closed her eyes. 'Not told, Tony – implied. As though that was all that I would be interested in. I didn't even know. I hadn't even thought about it. Stephen's just a friend, Tony, that's all he'll ever be.'

Tony shrugged. 'If you say so.'

'You don't believe me.'

'Does it matter?'

He came across and kissed her on the cheek. She always liked that, she liked the way he smelt.

'By the way,' he told her. 'Keep an eye on your little flatmate. I've heard things on the circuit.'

'Which flatmate? What sort of things?' Catarina was surprised.

'The blonde one – Bonnie. Watch she doesn't try any tricks – I've heard she's desperate for money.'

'So are we all, Tony.'

'Not as desperate as Bonnie, dear. I've heard she has a little addiction problem.'

'Bonnie?' Catarina laughed.

'Take my word for it. Watch her. Ciao.' Tony kissed her again and was gone.

It was ten weeks before Catarina realized Bonnie was ripping her off. She was taking messages for castings and forgetting to pass them on to Catarina, then turning up herself instead. When Beth started getting curious, Bonnie let it drop that Catarina was taking work direct from clients. The first Catarina knew of it was when Beth wrote saying she was off the agency books. Catarina phoned Beth but she was always in a meeting and didn't return her calls.

'Go in there!' Tony told her. 'Chew the rug a little! Find out why she's been such a shit!'

Catarina was desperate. If Beth blacked her now so would most of the good agencies in New York. She turned up without an appointment even though she was so scared her teeth ached.

Beth was chanting – Catarina could hear her through the closed door.

'Beth?' – It didn't seem right to bust in. Catarina yelled through the keyhole instead. The receptionist just stared. She would have called security only they didn't have any – they were still just a small business – healthy, but small – which meant no security guards and no cleaner, no dog-walker, no coffee-brewer and no plant technician, either. Sandie, the receptionist, did it all. The bookers were too busy, of course.

Beth helped out when the place was closed and no-one could see her. 'Bad for the image' was her excuse. Sandie was Beth's step-daughter and sometimes she wished she was Colonel Gaddafi's daughter instead. Things could hardly have been worse.

'Beth?' Catarina called louder and the chanting stopped. There were footsteps – annoyed sort of footsteps. The door opened. Beth was wearing jade. She had been diagnosed as an Autumn and jade was not in her palette. She had no place wearing it then – it made her look like sick. Which meant she was in a bad mood anyway.

'Catarina?' She sounded polite enough. 'Oh-what-a-surprise,' was the sort of tone she used.

'Can I talk to you, Beth, please? About the letter?' Catarina asked. Her voice let Beth know she was ready to beg.

236

Beth seemed to think it over. 'Come in,' she said finally. Catarina went into her office. Bath looked to see if there were other models waiting in reception. There were. She had to make an example of Catarina, then. 'Don't ever turn up again without an appointment!' she said, for effect.

She waved Catarina into a chair and sat down opposite her. Steady eye contact. Hands locked together on the desk.

'Why, Beth?'

Beth sighed. 'I told you you were only on trial, Catarina. I can't use you, that's all.'

'Why?'

Beth looked down at the desk.

'The photographers seemed keen – the ones on the go-sees. I thought you'd give me more time. You told me to take things slowly.'

'I did. You obviously didn't agree with me.'

'What do you mean?'

'I mean not turning up at castings. I mean taking work behind my back. That's the sort of thing that gets you thrown off any agency, Catarina. That's the sort of behaviour that can kill your little career stone dead.'

Catarina's eyes widened. 'I don't know what you mean, Beth.'

'Why, did I speak too quickly for you?'

'I understand the English. I don't know what you are talking about, though.'

Beth smiled. She hated these interviews. So many girls tried it on and they all lost out in the long run. She was surprised at Catarina, though. Even though she knew nothing should surprise her – after the years she'd spent in the business.

'No agent would keep you on their books after that, Catarina. Don't think I'm being unfair – it's normal prac-tice. It's in that book I gave you – the one you chose not to read.'

Catarina looked scared. 'I haven't done any work you don't know about, Beth. I haven't missed a single casting, either. You know how desperate I am for work. Do you think I just wouldn't turn up?'

Beth looked at her. 'What happened last Tuesday then?'

'Tuesday?'

'The video job. I know it wasn't much but I knew how badly you needed the work and they were happy to take someone without too much experience. They gave it to a girl from another agency in the end. I especially pushed you for that one, Catarina. I don't like to be made to look a fool when you don't feel like turning up.'

'I didn't know anything about it, Beth!'

'We phoned you, Catarina.'

'Nobody phoned me.'

Beth buzzed one of her bookers on the intercom. 'Delta left a message at your apartment, Catarina.'

'I didn't get it, Beth, I swear. Who did she leave it with?'

'Bonnie.' – Beth's eyes began to glaze over as the penny dropped. 'Bonnie. Shit – look, Catarina, can you just give me five minutes, OK?'

Catarina sat outside in reception, staring at the photos of successful models that hung on the walls. They all looked so perfect, so happy. She ran a hand through her short hair. Tony had lent her a pair of Levi's so that she didn't have to turn up in the brown suit again. The jeans were slashed at the knee and even she could tell they looked dated. One of her knees was dirty from where she had crawled under the bed that morning to find the jumper she had on. The jumper was Yasmina's – she probably didn't even know it was missing. Aimée would have a fit if she could see her protégée now.

'Catarina!' Beth was calling her back into the office. She wasn't exactly smiling but she didn't look grim any more, either. Even the jade frock looked better on her suddenly.

'Catarina, I've done some checking. Bonnie took both messages for you. She also told me you'd been taking work behind my back. I'm sorry – I should have trusted you more.'

238

'Bonnie?'

'I know – it was me who introduced you. Still – you've had your first lesson, kiddo – welcome to the world of modelling. That's what your colleagues can be like, so you'd better get used to it. Dump on them before they dump on you – that always used to be my motto!'

'She almost got me thrown off your books! Why? Does she hate me?'

'She's got problems, Catarina – don't be too hard on her. I gave her six months to sort herself out. That was obviously her way of doing it.' She handed Catarina a sheet with some addresses on it. 'Here – go on a couple of new castings. The first two are photographers who are as new to the game as you and the third's a designer. I would have sent Bonnie to him. You can tell her I said that, if it helps. Good luck.'

Tony knew someone who knew someone who knew Beth's step-daughter. The phone was ringing the moment Catarina walked in.

'Don't say I didn't tell you.'

'Tony. Go away, please.'

'Don't get mad, Catarina – get out.'

'And just how am I supposed to do that?'

'Find another apartment?'

'How?'

'Easy. Move in with me.'

It was a good idea, an easy idea, a happy idea. Catarina packed her bags that evening. It didn't take her long – she didn't have much to pack.

39

Catarina's first appointment was with a photographer's assistant at a studio some three blocks away from Eve's. Three blocks could be like three light years in New York. Eve's area wasn't smart exactly, but this place frightened Catarina. There were no apartments, just warehouses that looked abandoned. She was wearing Tony's best frock, tied with an old leather belt around the waist. She wished she'd worn the jeans jacket he'd offered her, too. She felt half naked, walking down those streets. She clutched her book to her chest, like armour.

When she got into the building she walked into the lift, pulled the gates closed and prayed the thing would work. What if she had the wrong address? She passed car parks on the first two floors, then nothing for six floors, then finally the lift stopped. The floor looked deserted. Then she saw a familiar flash of blue-grey light from beneath one of the closed doors and she knocked on that one and someone answered.

There were three other girls inside but they were waiting to see the photographer that owned the place, not his oily rag. Catarina found that out because one of the girls told her quite loudly the minute she sat down. The photographer who owned the place was called Daniel Katz and he was quite a big *fromage*, evidently. His assistant was female – not much older than Catarina. She was polite and friendly and she asked Catarina in a whisper if she would mind slipping into the studio for some Polaroids while Daniel was on his break.

The studio was vast – an airplane would have fitted into

the space quite snugly. It was all painted black, so that it was hard to see where the walls began, and in the middle hung a creased white sheet with a spotlight on it.

The girl motioned Catarina onto the sheet. 'Take off your shoes first – we don't want marks!' she warned. 'There's a cloth there you can dust your soles with.' The spotlight was blinding at first – it was several minutes before Catarina could make out the girl and her camera.

'Are you OK?'

Catarina went to nod but the first flash went off. She shielded her eyes from the light but then put her arm down quickly. The girl peeled the Polaroid off and stuck it under her armpit, counting.

She looked at the result carefully before altering the angle of the light a little. 'You're taller than the last girl. How tall are you, exactly?'

Catarina wasn't sure – the flash went off while she was thinking. A trickle of sweat started to move down her back like snail-slime.

'Just one more, smiling, if that's OK?'

'Don't smile, darling – it wouldn't suit you.'

Catarina shielded her eyes again. There was a man standing behind the girl now – a tall, fat man with long hair and a beard. The girl jumped like a scalded cat. The man had to be Daniel Katz himself.

He stared at Catarina. She felt embarrassed. Her foot went dead. More sweat trickled off her. She felt stupid and naked. She wanted to go to the loo.

'Shall I go now?' The photographer didn't answer.

The lights were burning her skin. She folded her arms and hopped from one leg to another.

'Are you here to see me?' Daniel asked.

'No.' – Catarina's voice got lost somewhere in the back of her throat. Her mouth was too dry and her voice broke in the middle of the word. There was a pause. She could feel herself being watched.

241

'What work have you done?'

'Some jobs in London.'

'You're not British.'

'Russian.'

He took the Polaroid back off the camera.

'You want some experience – some tests, then.'

'Yes.'

'OK.' He stood there in front of her, the long camera lens stuck in his hand like a dick.

'I said OK.'

Catarina stared at him. His face was hidden in the shadows.

'Your job is to model – let me see you work.'

The girl had gone. There was just the two of them. And the other models waiting for their castings. They were just a row of cats' eyes in the back of the dark room, but they were listening – by god were they listening.

'I'm waiting.'

Catarina cleared her throat.

'What would you like me to do?'

'You're wearing a dress – model it. But take off that stupid belt first.'

She undid the belt slowly and it fell to the floor at her feet. Her hands were trembling. She tried to rearrange the dress but it had creased were the belt had been. She looked up at the camera and tried to smile.

'I told you not to smile, you look like a Hallowe'en lantern.'

Catarina stopped smiling. She felt stupid and ugly. Her face had turned red with embarrassment.

'Come on, you soppy cow – let's see some poses. Sell me that disgusting frock.'

She pulled the skirt out with her hand and a flash went off. One. She ran her hands through her hair and there was another flash. Two. She crossed her arms over her chest and turned her head to the side. Three. She looked straight at camera. No flash. He was waiting for something

242

better. The sides of her mouth started to quiver with nerves.

'Catarina,' she told herself, 'Catarina Kirkova.' She thought of the model Klara had invented. What would she do now? What would Klara have done? Would Klara have enjoyed this? Could anyone enjoy it? She felt humiliated — every fluid ounce of her pride had drained away and gone. There was no blood in her hands or her feet and her face felt sheet-white.

How many shots in a film? Twenty-four? Thirty-six? The flash went off again. Four. Four shots. Maybe thirty-two more to go.

'Your expression looks lopsided. Look down, run your tongue across your lips and then look up again.'

She did what she was told.

Five.

'Chin up a little — I said up . . . not that far. OK — eyes back to camera.'

Six.

'Tilt your head a little.'

Seven.

'Not that way — try the other.'

Eight.

'Try to show a little more life.'

Nine.

The tension rose like the temperature in the studio. Catarina saw only blinding light surrounded by blackness. There were blue spots on her vision where the flashes had gone off. The voice sounded surreal, barking out commands from nowhere. Insulting her from nowhere.

'Come on, you lazy bitch.'

Ten.

'Drop that arm a bit.'

Eleven.

She thought about Aimée and the beach. She remembered the wind running through her hair as she rode the pony around the grounds. The white house in the background was bathed in the salmon-pink light of sunset.

Everything was cool. The only sound came from the pony's hooves and the pulse of the sea.

'Close your eyes then open them again and focus them.'

Twelve.

She saw Stephen standing watching her. Klara was at his side, waving. Klara looked beautiful. She was smiling and Stephen was smiling too. When she rode up to them they pulled her off her pony and hugged her, one at a time, while the dog barked around their ankles.

Thirteen.

Fourteen.

Fifteen.

Sixteen.

She was back in Moscow and her mother was still alive. They walked together to the factory to watch her father work. There was a smell of bread and her mother's hand felt warm. She tried to see her mother's face but it was hidden by a book. The hand was Alex's now and he was guiding her off a stage. She felt safe.

Seventeen.

Eighteen – Nineteen – Twenty – Twenty-one.

'Sit down on the floor. Put your head into your hands. Not so low – I can't see your face.'

Twenty-two.

Twenty-three.

She was eating some soup and Alex was wiping her face gently with a napkin. He didn't care what the waiters thought any more – he loved her and he was caring for her. She smelt alcohol on his breath. He was her father now, tucking her up into the hotel-room bed.

Twenty-four. Only twenty-four.

It had finished. He was re-winding the roll. She heard him sigh. He was shaking his head.

'Do you have an agent?'

She told him Beth's name.

'Tell her this, honey. Tell her you're a very nice girl but

you'll never make it in modelling. Tell her to try you out in movie walk-ons or something instead.'

He threw the rewound film at her and she caught it.

'Tell her to get these printed up and she'll see what I mean. There's no life there, honey, no life at all. Without life there is no beauty. With life, beauty comes of its own accord. Look at Patty Skaldi if you don't know what I mean. A dog in the flesh but her beauty comes through the lens. You're lazy too, honey. Models get paid good money to work, not to just stand there.'

Catarina looked at him. The film felt round and hard and cool in her hand.

'I was nervous.'

'So what? Is that like a sick note? Does that excuse you to skip class? Is that why your brain was playing hooky? We're all nervous, honey. Some of us hide it and some of us can't. Life sucks. Life is also short. Don't waste it on something you're not cut out to do.'

'Eve Horowitz has done good shots of me.'

'Eve Horowitz could make a baboon's ass look pretty.'

He went to walk away then stopped and turned, waving a finger in the air.

'Look at those shots,' he repeated, nodding at the film in her hand. 'Even you will be able to see what I'm talking about.'

Catarina waited outside the building until the air had cooled her red face. She was shaking. The photographer's words echoed in her head like a record with the needle stuck. She pulled her purse open to look for a mint to take away the stale taste in her mouth and her money tipped onto the pavement; she grazed her knee scrabbling for it.

When she was more in control – when she could breathe properly again – she looked at her list of appointments. Beth had added an extra one – a casting. She had to be at the offices of Newman and Holt in twelve minutes. She looked at the change in her hand. She had no money for a cab but she called one anyway – there was no other way she would get there in time.

The traffic was gridlocked. Catarina told the driver she was going to be sick and ran up the street before he could stop her. She heard him yelling abuse but the words meant nothing – she had three minutes to cover two blocks. If she didn't make the casting Beth would kill her for sure.

She made it to the building with ten seconds to spare. The ad agency's premises were minimalist modern. A woman took her name then pointed to the waiting room as though her arm might break if she tried too hard. The door opened automatically and about thirty girls turned to look at the new arrival, with faces like badgers whose set has just been invaded by a fox. Beth had sent Catarina on her first cattle-call. The measure of your fame was in how long the other girls stared. They started talking again before Catarina had even sat down. She was fly-dirt to them, she was less than a quarter of nothing.

She looked at the receptionist.

'Are they all here for the same thing as me?'

''Fraid so!' The woman smiled a crack but carried on typing.

'How long will I be here?'

The woman shrugged and looked at her watch. 'They're taking about ten minutes per girl on average. The ones they like take a little longer. Work it out for yourself.'

Catarina looked at her watch. 'I have another appointment in an hour.'

The woman shrugged again. 'Sorry. Everyone is saying the same thing. If you have to go you have to go – only check out with me first so I can take your name off the list.' She looked up at Catarina with an expression that said, I know you're all fucking drama-queens but you won't get the better of me. When you get paid ten thousand an hour you wait when I say so – see? Catarina sat.

She was at the end of a black leather couch – on an arm.

Her knee was still bleeding. All the other girls stared at it. The room was too hot. No-one smiled and no-one spoke. There were a few big names there – very big names, in fact, and the silence came across almost as a mark of respect.

One of the big names rose from her seat and approached the receptionist for the second time. Everyone could tell she was big because she dressed the scruffiest and still looked the best. She bent over and whispered at the woman but her face reflected her anger. The woman shook her head at first but then she looked at her watch. She spoke to someone on the phone. The big name disappeared into the interview room and the other girls started to dissect the situation with their tongues, complaining to one another bitterly.

Catarina had no idea how long it was before she was seen. She had given up looking at her watch because it made her too anxious. She was hungry at first but later she felt sick. If you asked the receptionist she would point the coffee machine out but Catarina had no idea how to work the machine or how much the coffee would cost.

There was a large TV in the waiting room, showing a Newman and Holt corporate promo video. When the video ended it would pause for twenty seconds and then start up again. Catarina had seen the film fourteen times. She tried to turn her head away but then she could only stare at the other models and, anyway, she could still hear it. She thought she would scream if she heard it once more.

Her name was called at last. Her bruised leg felt stiff when she stood. It reminded her of her days with Alex. She was shown into a room that was wide but not very deep. Eleven people sat behind the desk – five representatives of Newman and Holt, a PR, the art director and his secretary and the four clients. The clients were all Japanese. Everyone was smiling. Catarina smiled back. They all looked as though they loved her. She was shown to a chair and her book was taken away for inspection. Everyone was introduced by name while her book was looked through.

247

Everyone took a long time to look at her photos and each person did the same thing — they looked at the first shot then they looked at her for comparison and then they smiled to show they did not mean to be impolite for staring. Then a man in a taupe suit leant forward and asked Catarina if she would please mind trying a pair of the clients' tights on, as that was what she would be modelling in the commercial.

Catarina looked to where the man was pointing. There was a chair beside her and on the chair was a pair of brown tights. She touched them. They were wet with sweat where thirty-odd girls had all tried them on before her. They were also laddered. Catarina wondered if the girl who had laddered them had automatically been barred from getting the job.

'Can I try on a fresh pair, please?'

The ad man's smile faltered slightly, like a brief eclipse.

'I'm sorry — this is the only pair the clients brought with them.'

Catarina looked around for a changing room but there wasn't one. The tights stuck to her legs like damp cobwebs as she tried to pull them on. She stood in front of the panel, hiding her knickers with her hands.

'Turn around please.'

A Polaroid was taken.

'Thank you. Do you have a composite? Only a Xerox of one of your shots? Thank you, that will do.'

She placed the tights back on the chair for the next girl. Tony's frock stuck to her bare wet legs.

They all smiled at her and the Japanese businessmen bowed in their seats.

'Next!'

Tony massaged Catarina's steaming feet when she got back home again and then he made her Camomile tea and sat and brushed her hair until she was calm again.

'That's what it's like, dear,' he told her. 'Welcome to the wonderful world of show business. By the way,' he added, blowing on his own tea to cool it, 'there was a message for you on the answerphone. I left it for you – do you want me to play it?'

Catarina nodded. She felt good again now – safe and warm, like a child.

The tape hissed a little – Tony had it up too loud. The voice filled the room, distorted by the machine.

'Luisa? It's Alex. Forgive me, little one. I love you. Only you know how much.'

Tony laughed. 'Sorry – too loud!' Then he turned and saw the expression on Catarina's face.

40

Stephen wandered into the small gallery in Canal Street, SoHo, clutching his battered black portfolio in one hand and a cheese Danish for Eve in the other. The Danish was by way of appeasement for taking so long a lunch break – the trouble was it kept trying to escape from its bag and great oozing grease stains had broken out all over the brown paper like liver spots.

Stephen licked his fingers before he shook hands, just in case the grease had reached them too. He was a little late for his appointment. He had been early but then he'd somehow got late killing time. It was the sort of thing that often happened – one minute you were kicking your heels and the next you were rushing as though your life depended on it. Newton's law of fucked-up timing – Stephen had given up trying to work out these little glitches of nature years ago.

The gallery owner didn't seem to mind. He didn't look at his watch and he didn't appear impatient, just pleased to see Stephen, which was odd. Stephen wanted some of his pictures hung. The gallery was a good one – the owner should barely have been giving him the time of day, let alone a smile that said, 'Pleased to meet you.'

Perhaps the guy was just terminally polite. Stephen looked around the gallery as they walked towards the office. He saw a couple of Herb Ritts and his hopes dropped to his lower bowel. He should have waited – he wasn't ready yet. What the hell was he doing there? He should have waited ten, maybe twenty years. Possibly forever.

The guy looked friendly enough but that was because he wasn't aware Stephen was about to waste his valuable time. At the moment he seemed to be under some illusion that Stephen might have undiscovered talent. He opened Stephen's book and he was still smiling.

The book contained a photographic essay – Stephen's shots of low life New York. Tramps. Hookers. Kids sleeping in garbage and dealing drugs off street corners. Stephen felt physically sick with disgust at his own hubris. The stuff was hackneyed and clichéd. What the hell was he doing, showing it to an expert? He hadn't even shown it to Eve – he knew he'd find her relentless sarcasm too wounding, as ever. He didn't relish being flayed to the bone – even by someone he liked and admired. The work was his secret – until now.

The gallery owner had rattlesnake eyes – they flicked across each page without expression. He hated the stuff. He was an asshole. Stephen hated him – he would spend his entire life hating him for the blow he was about to execute. Sirens went past outside. A woman was screaming. There was a smell of steam and glue in the air. The window behind the desk needed cleaning.

The guy closed the portfolio. Leant across the desk.

'Mr Van Doren.'

'Stephen.'

'Stephen.' The guy smiled again. 'Talk to me about these shots.'

'Sorry?'

'Tell me their stories – how you came to take them, what you had in mind, what you wish to achieve with them – anything.'

'The shots speak for themselves, Mr Muchnick – they are supposed to tell their own story.' Stephen felt the sweat break out on his forehead. The guy was a complete shit – he had no understanding of art. He was playing with Stephen. His nails were too long.

'Of course,' – the man coughed into the back of his

hand. 'I just wanted to hear you speak about them, that's all. What you said wouldn't matter. I just like to see commitment. I like to spot a masterplan in my new photographers.'

'– Your what?'

The man lifted a desk diary over and licked his finger before turning the pages.

'I have a cancellation for early September. Is that too soon for you?'

Actually the guy's nails were not over-long.

'For what?'

The man smiled. 'For an exhibition of your work. I can give you a week – is that OK?'

Actually the guy's nails were just the right length. And wonderfully manicured, too. In fact Stephen had never seen such nice nails. He had a strong inclination to bend and kiss them.

'– Sure. Fine.' Two totally inadequate words, but they were the best he could come up with. His maiden solo project and he'd hit pay dirt first time. It was unbelievable.

He needed to tell someone badly so he taxi'd across to Catarina's bar. Catarina wasn't there, though, and neither was Tony. Stephen almost didn't mind – he was in a dream. He would have told anyone – as Catarina wasn't there he told a stranger at the bar instead. The stranger resembled a chimp on acid but Stephen didn't mind – even chimps have ears, after all, and that was the only requirement Stephen was looking for in a partner right then.

Catarina and Tony both had the night off. The barman said they were busy decorating their apartment, or something. Gold and violet, he told Stephen with a lift of the top lip. Stephen thought it sounded cool. He imagined the violet paint in Catarina's hair. He saw them laughing together and ordering pizzas to eat among the mess of paintpots and newspapers. Then he got blind drunk for

252

the first time in his life. He had to remind himself occasionally he was celebrating.

Beth studied the shots Daniel Katz had taken of Catarina.

'Don't get upset by what happened, girl — learn!' she ordered. 'Use your own eyes, Catarina. What do you see in these shots?'

Catarina flipped the shots like playing cards but said nothing. Beth could tell she was frightened. She was sulking, like a child.

'Now look at these, Catarina. Do you buy magazines? Do you see what other models are doing? Can you see the difference between these shots and your own?' She held out a copy of *Vogue*. Catarina opened it and flicked through it. She couldn't afford such magazines now but they had always been around at Aimée's.

'Tell me, Catarina. Tell me the difference.'

'These girls are beautiful.' Catarina's voice came out high and small.

'So are you. Now tell me the real difference.'

Catarina looked again. The clothes were different, of course, but it wasn't just the clothes.

'It's their eyes,' she said, looking more closely.

'Go on.'

These girls had life in their eyes — Catarina had none. Their faces were masks of expression but Catarina's was merely blank. Even the fear didn't show any more. Their bodies created expression, too. Catarina was just a store dummy, beautiful but rigid. She felt ashamed.

'Couldn't Eve do more tests of you, Catarina? You look more at ease when she's holding the camera.'

'She's too busy.' Catarina sounded miserable — desperate. 'I asked her.'

Beth took out more magazines and piled them on Catarina's lap. 'How about that boyfriend of yours? The one that used to work as Eve's assistant? Couldn't he work

253

with you for a while? I hear he's doing quite well for him-self these days — he's got his own exhibition at some swanky place in SoHo.'

'Stephen?' Catarina looked confused. She didn't under-stand the bit about the gallery but she understood the past tense when she heard it. 'He has left Eve's studio?'

Beth nodded. 'She took on a new assistant last week. Mad as hell that he left her in the lurch, of course, but she'll get over it. Can't you speak to him, Catarina? Ask him nicely? Huh?'

Catarina called in at Eve's studio to get Stephen's new address. Beth was right — Eve was in a major snit.

'I taught that boy everything he knows, Catarina,' she said over coffee, '— trouble is he hasn't learnt half of it yet.'

'Why did he leave?' Catarina asked. She watched Eve's new assistant setting up the next shot. He looked pretty efficient. She wondered why Eve was so snippy.

'Because he got accepted by some gallery in SoHo for his first exhibition, that's why!' Eve exploded. 'He thinks his name is made already. The boy's a fool, Catarina — he can't see the nose on his own face! He can judge his own work — he's not stupid. He's good — he's learning. He will be really good one day, by anyone's standards. He has to know his own limitations, though, and he's not ready for this kind of move yet, believe me. If you think you're good when you're not then you stop bothering to learn, Catarina, and, believe me, that boy's got a long way to go yet.'

Catarina drained her cup. 'But if the gallery has accepted his work?' she began.

Eve's smile looked strange. 'Sure, they accepted it.'

Catarina watched her face closely.

'She'll kill that boy's career,' Eve whispered.

'Who, Eve?'

'Aimée. The dragon lady.'

'What's Aimée got to do with this?' Catarina asked.

Eve stood up. The chat was over. 'Nothing. I was joking.

Let me know how he's doing, will you? Let me know how he's getting on.'

Stephen had a new low-rent studio in an attic facing Tompkins Square Park, on the easternmost fringes of the East Village. The grey arched window of the studio looked down on the vast tent city that the square had become. He thought the view was apt – he was looking out at the sort of people that had helped him get there in the first place.

The place had a nice empty ring to it. He didn't know how he was going to keep the rent up – low as it was – but he intended to try. Perhaps he would sell some of his work at the gallery.

He had moved out of his apartment and was sleeping at the studio, too. There was a cheap Italian bar below him and it was noisy at night but he didn't mind. He had a friend who worked on a local paper – on the graveyard shift – and the friend had a new girl he was trying to impress so Stephen took over some of his shifts for him and the friend paid him cash, which meant he could at least eat.

The rest of the time he worked in the studio or out on the streets. There was a new enthusiasm in his approach now, not just because he needed to earn, but because he knew he was good. The gallery would never have accepted his work otherwise. He had thought he was good before, but he hadn't known how good. He only wished Eve had shown as much enthusiasm for his work as the gallery owner. He had known she'd be pissed when he told her he was going but he hadn't expected her to be quite so bitter. He thought about ringing her, to see if she'd calmed down. Then he looked out of the window and saw Catarina making her way across the street towards his block.

She looked quite in keeping with the area. She had a short flowered frock on – the sort his grandmother used to wear – and a black leather biker's jacket thrown over the top. Her short blonde hair blew like feathers in the wind. She wore no make-up and her features looked enormous – almost comical – apart from the high sculpted cheekbones, which gave her face a sad kind of dignity. Her legs were bare and she had walking boots on her feet. Whatever else she looked, she looked special.

Stephen watched people turned to look at her as she walked through the square. Most of those people were men and Stephen wanted to punch them. He pulled on his jacket to go out and get her but then he took it off again. She wouldn't want him doing that – it would make her mad – he could tell by the way she was walking.

He had an urge to clean the room and comb his hair but he suppressed that too. He threw some Harpic down the toilet and flushed it instead, as a sort of compromise. Then he hoped desperately that the flushing would stop before she got out of the lift and heard it.

The lift stopped a floor below his. It wasn't her, after all. Perhaps it was just coincidence. Perhaps she had just been walking round the area and not known he lived there. Perhaps she had heard the toilet flushing and decided not to disturb him after all. Then the lift started up again. It was her after all – who had she shared the ride with?

When she knocked on his door he counted off seconds in his head before walking to answer it.

'Catarina.'

He didn't smile and he didn't look surprised. She looked beautiful but that was no revelation, either.

'Stephen.' Why did humans feel the need to identify each other by name like that? Dogs did it by sniffing. Catarina walked straight in, kissing him on the cheek as she passed. She touched his arm. He inhaled silently. She smelt of toothpaste and soap. He didn't know any other women who smelt of soap, except when they'd just showered – after that it was perfume all the way. He preferred soap.

Catarina looked around the studio with all the unchecked curiosity of a child. She didn't know it was bad manners to look about without asking and Stephen didn't care. He said nothing and watched her. She cruised around a while, picking things up and putting them down again. She was surprised at how pleased she felt to see Stephen again.

'You were at the bar, Stephen.' There was a ginger kitten that seemed to have come along with the studio. Catarina discovered it behind a sheet of perspex and picked it up and petted it.

'Yes.' He was worried the cat might have fleas. He hadn't got it to a vet yet. He had been thinking of giving it away but now he knew he would keep it.

'Checking up on me.' The kitten yawned, showing a pink tongue and throat. Catarina smiled delightedly.

'No.'

'Oh?' Now who had the cuter eyes – Catarina or the kitten?

'I just wanted to make sure you were OK, that's all. I needed to know if you wanted anything. Jesus, Catarina – look what happened to you before! You don't know New York – you get a job in a bar – anything could happen.'

Catarina looked at him properly for the first time since she'd arrived. He looked older somehow – he was losing his boyishness. Aimée would be heartbroken – her son was turning into a man. His face looked tired and he hadn't shaved. He wore a creased white T-shirt and jeans and his feet were bare.

'You're looking good.' He'd said what she was thinking.

'Thanks.' She pulled at the skirt of her frock as though she wasn't sure. The kitten was asleep now, its face curled into the nape of her neck.

'What do you call it?'

He had to think of a name. He hadn't called it anything so far – apart from Dogbreath.

'Beryl,' he said. She laughed. It sounded absurd.

'It's a tomcat,' she told him. 'Beryl is a girl's name, isn't it?'

He laughed. 'Albert then,' he said. '– I don't know – Bob? Crispin? Woody?' He stopped smiling suddenly. 'Why did you come here, Catarina?'

She kept stroking the kitten. 'Eve is worried about you, Stephen.'

Eve – not Catarina worried about him – Eve.

His hopes dropped down a couple of degrees, like mercury in a thermometer. He tried to look rakish and devil-may-care.

'Eve? What the hell is wrong with that woman – she's acting like my mother or something.'

'Eve cares about you, that's all.'

– Eve again, not Catarina – Eve.

'I thought she might have been pleased for me, instead she's gone all quiet and moody. Do you think it's her hormones or something, Catarina? Do women of her age go through the change? Can't she get some tablets to make her a more agreeable person?'

Catarina laughed. Her teeth looked white. Her gums were as pink as the kitten's. 'Could you do some more tests of me, Stephen?' she asked suddenly, 'Beth says I need them. I need to learn to be natural in front of the camera. I'll pay you for them. I could be your first client.'

Stephen's mercury dropped to well below zero. So that was why she came – because Eve was worried – because Beth said she needed shots. He became angry and upset.

'Is that all, Catarina?'

'All?'

'– Anything else on your little shopping list? Any other messages you needed to carry? How about one from my mom while you're about it? What about Tony? Didn't he have anything to say?'

'You're angry, Stephen.'

'Fucking right I am.'

'Tell me what I did, Stephen. I don't understand.'

Stephen sighed, 'No, I don't believe you do. You make me feel stupid, Catarina – that's why you make me so mad.

Don't bother trying to work it out. You know how I feel about you. I know how you feel about me – period.'

She was staring at him. 'I hate it when you're angry with me.'

'Then stay out of my way.' He turned his back and tried to look as though he had work to be getting on with. The room was silent. He wondered what she was doing. Was she crying? Was she just standing there? He was too proud to turn round to look.

'Alex never made love to me, Stephen.'

Her voice had changed somehow, along with the atmosphere in the room. She sounded softer and more serious. Things became slower, like in a film. He knew he would turn around any moment now, but he also knew he didn't have to hurry.

Stephen turned around. There was a mist of golden light from the grimy windows. Particles of dust played in the beam of light. The light was so rich the rest of the room looked black by comparison. Catarina still stood in the same spot only now she was naked. Her dress lay at her feet. She had been wearing nothing else.

'Catarina-oh-Jesus-Christ.' It came out a soft groan, a whispered exhalation of air. She looked unreal. She looked so good – so special – that for one terrible, dangerous moment he wanted to photograph her more than he wanted to fuck her. Then he wanted to fuck her more than he'd wanted to do anything in his life – his prick became the giant eraser, deleting any more aesthetic thoughts from his mind.

He hadn't thought she'd look so pleasing without her clothes. He'd thought she'd look bony and slightly scrawny – like a boy with breasts, but instead she was skinny in a soft way. He stared at her. She didn't seem to mind.

He'd become hard at the sound of her voice, even before he'd turned round and seen her like that. There was something in her tone that had told him before he'd looked . . .

now he wished he was naked too – naked in an instant, as she had been.

He'd made love a few times before but never so wantonly. He pulled off his T-shirt and jeans and thanked god he wasn't wearing shoes or socks.

Catarina liked Stephen's body. there was nothing about it she didn't like – nothing she knew she would have to grow to like or learn to love with time. She loved it all right away. He held her by the shoulders and she smiled to show him how OK it was. Then he kissed her and she felt that slight loss of control in him that Alex had always fought so hard to disguise. Alex was always in control. She wanted Stephen to give way completely. She wanted to feel him lose it – to go off entirely and belong only to her. She kissed him back and the response was immediate. She felt his stomach harden and his prick rise up between her legs. She heard the quick gasp of air as he breathed in. His arms went around her, pulling her closer. She wanted to torture him with lust – she wanted him to want her so much he could die. She wanted him to come until it killed him.

She also felt herself wanting to fall in love with him. The thought frightened her. And then it swamped her along with her lust.

They lay on the floor. The wood felt cold and refreshing, like a sorbet after a heavy meal. Stephen was opening a condom but she stopped him before he could put it on.

'Not yet,' she whispered. 'I want to see you.'

She lay him on his back. He was beautiful. She ran a hand down his flat stomach and watched his prick nod in response. He closed his eyes. He had one knee bent and the other leg full out. She bent and kissed his navel and ran her tongue around inside it. There was hair there, soft hair. He tasted of the outdoors. She remembered the beach in Boston. She cupped both his balls in her hand.

'Catarina!' – He sounded in agony. A bead of moisture appeared at the end of his penis. She felt happy. It was as though he were giving her a beautiful present. It was better than the glass snowstorm – he was giving her himself.

The pain was like burning when he finally entered her. When he was inside he lay still there while he kissed her. She let out a small sound.

'It's OK, it's OK. It's there,' he whispered. 'Are you OK?' She nodded.

'Does it hurt?'

'A bit.'

'Too much?'

'No.'

He slid backwards again and she cried out loud because the burning started again and because she thought she was losing him from inside her. He pressed his lips against her ear.

'Tell me if you want me to stop, I don't want to hurt you.'

He pressed back again. She wrapped her legs around him to hold him tighter. He straightened his arms and arched his back. She watched his face. He was moving away from her now, into a world of his own pleasures. He was losing it, he was losing it. The warmth of satisfaction bathed all her burning pain away.

He came with the deepest thrust – pushed in and didn't pull back. His whole body tensed and twisted. She watched his face – she loved him at that moment. He unravelled slowly – he was hers again, concerned, loving.

'Did I hurt you?' He stroked her cropped hair and kissed her eyelids gently.

'No, Stephen, you didn't hurt me.'

He pulled the condom off carefully and walked naked to the toilet. She heard the water flushing. He came back with a handful of tissues.

'Here – dry yourself. Do you want anything? Do you want some wine?'

'Do you have any?'

'No.'

'Then I don't want any. I only want what you have.'

'You've taken it.'

'Have I? Then I'm happy.'

'Are you?'

He poured her a deep bath and, while she was soaking, ran down to the shops to get the wine that she wanted. He came back with champagne. He opened the bottle over the bath and some of the champagne spilt into the water. Catarina giggled as she drank it and Stephen lifted her up by the armpits and kissed her again on the mouth. She pulled him down and he slid, fully-clothed, into the bath with her.

When she was finished he dried her with a soft towel and carried her, still shrimp-pink, to the studio. There he placed her gently on the backdrop and then he took the photos she wanted so badly and this time his camera brought out things in her that had never been shown before.

Clutching the white towel about her, drunk on champagne and sex, she laughed and she flirted and this time the flashes didn't frighten her and she was untroubled by worries about her expressions or her poses. Stephen shot her in black and white, using the available light from the dusty window that looked down on the tents in the square. He said very little as he worked and he only stopped once – to put on a tape of U2 to revive them when they got tired.

Then at last he stopped for good. Catarina was sitting, cross-legged on the floor. Stephen put his camera down, exhausted, and stood over her.

'That's it. We're finished. I'm out of film.'

He watched her eyes refocus on reality. That was good. That was a sign she was learning the trade.

'We're not finished, Stephen,' she said in a low voice. He bent down to kiss her again, picking her up as she was, a tight little ball of arms and legs, and carried her to his bed. They made love again, only this time it was slower and sleepier and this time he made her come, which brought him a monstrous amount of pleasure. He was so proud he thought he might burst.

Stephen slept with Catarina in his arms. When he woke it was dark and she was on the phone, calling a cab. She smiled at him.

'Don't go.' – He caught at her arm as she reached for her jacket.

'I have to – I have to work tonight.'

'At the bar?'

'Of course.'

'So miss a night. Phone in sick.'

She smiled again. 'I can't. I need the money. Tony will worry – maybe call the cops. You know how it is.'

'Come back after then. Stay the night.'

He watched her pull her arms into her coat.

'No. You're tired. It will be too late. I share a cab with Tony. Go to sleep.'

She stopped at the door. 'When will my contacts be ready?'

He ran a hand through his hair. Think. Think straight.

'Tomorrow. Definitely. Come tomorrow. They'll be ready.'

'See you tomorrow then.' – And then she was gone.

41

Stephen contacted the photos that night, as soon as Catarina had left. He needed evidence of what had happened that evening and he needed to look at her again. He watched her face appear slowly on the white paper as it basked in the developing tank. He had never got used to the magic of the process of printing – he knew how it happened – he knew why it happened, but he never lost his sense of wonder as the pictures first appeared.

He had done it. Eve had brought out Catarina's beauty, but he had captured her spirit at last. He smiled at the first shot.

'Hello.' Her eyes looked out at him – it was her – she was there.

He wanted to ring her at the bar, to tell her how clever he'd been, but he knew he should wait, so he hugged his little secret to himself for a few more hours. He ached, he was sore, he was tired, but he was happy – boy, was he happy. He looked out of the window. The darkness was kind to the view. Tent City looked like a magic place, glowing with lights and lazy trails of crimson-grey smoke.

STEPHEN LOVES CATARINA. He wrote it with his finger in the dust on the glass. It was OK – he knew she loved him back now. He was not a fool any longer – he could tell Catarina loved him at last. He thought over every moment of their lovemaking. He remembered the moment she had climaxed and how she had whispered his name and clung to him like a child. But their sex together had not been a release for him – he wanted her at that moment more violently than he had wanted her at any time before they'd made love.

The black sky ruptured and haemorrhaged blood red and slowly it grew light. Stephen shaved, enjoying the smell of the soap. Then he worked a little, preparing some prints for his exhibition. Mostly he just waited, though, killing time until she returned. She belonged there now – it felt right.

She might be hungry. He ran down to the Chinese supermarket and got ingredients for a meal. When he got back he checked his pager but nobody had called. Which meant she was still coming. Chinese was the only food he knew how to cook. His father had lived in Hong Kong as a child and he'd taught him the secrets of Chinese cuisine before he'd taught him about sex. He started to prepare the ingredients, watching the clock, waiting to hear the lift call at his floor.

She arrived at four, which was later than he'd hoped. Her face was pink and flushed. She was wearing denim shorts over leggings and a checked shirt with a tear in the back.

'I'm sorry I'm late, Stephen, I had a last-minute casting.' She threw her book down onto the floor and ran towards the toilet.

'Oh god, sorry. Thanks.' She came out laughing, still apologizing. 'Three hours – one to find the place and then two just waiting and being seen – can you imagine! Nothing to drink and no lavatory in sight – what are you cooking, Stephen? Did you do my shots? Are they any good? How are they, terrible? Did you burn them? Did you feed the kitten?'

She made him laugh at last and then he kissed her. She felt good, but strange. Not so close any more – a little bit of a stranger again. She should have stayed the night – time had put a distance between them. He wasn't worried – he knew it would go. Her eyes were glowing. She found Dogbreath and petted him. 'He's hungry!' she cooed. 'Give me a prawn.'

'I only just fed him . . .' Stephen protested but she stole

265

a prawn anyway and the cat consumed it as though it hadn't seen food for a week. Traitor.

Catarina was smiling at him.

'Your shots are on the table.'

She ran across. Looked at them. Went quiet. Stephen held his breath. It was worse than Eve — far worse. A million times worse — at least.

He bent over her. Stroked the back of her neck. She was still enough to be dead.

She straightened suddenly, making him jump. Her eyes were electric. 'Is this it, Stephen? Is this when they're good?'

He laughed, relieved. 'What do you think?'

'You must tell me first!' She clutched his shirt. He couldn't tease her, he had suffered enough teasing himself, from Eve.

'Yes, Catarina, this is when they're good.'

She let out a whoop of delight. Stephen picked her up by the waist and swung her round so her legs flew out. They were both laughing now. Stephen stopped swinging and kissed her. He pulled her top off and kissed her breasts and she did the same to him. They followed each other, copycat style. He cleared the table with his arms and her pictures fell to the floor in a sweep. He smelt of ginger and lemongrass and fresh garlic. She smelt of patchouli and prawns. She put the condom into her mouth and placed it onto his cock like that. It was a trick he'd never seen before. A cloud appeared in his mind, asking where she'd learnt a trick like that but he kissed her again and the cloud went away.

He looked in the mirror as they made love. They were the same length. She was paler. He watched her skinny pelvis rise and fall like the sea. Her arms fell back. She had a plume of light hair under each armpit. Her spine arched as she pushed against him. She grabbed the sides of the table as she came and then he was lost in his own sweet pleasures.

They lay together in silence when they were finished and

she played with his cock like she played with the kitten, tickling it, stroking it, cooing at it gently. Stephen was hungry but too knackered to cook. Instead he watched the cat finish the last of the prawns and wondered if it would be sick.

'This is a good day, Stephen – the best.'

He yawned and nodded agreement.

'I got a job.'

The kitten had begun heaving under the sink.

'That's good.'

He watched Catarina walk to the bathroom. She had a good back – supple and strong-looking, even though it was thin. She was showering. He heard the water running. She was singing. He had never heard her sing before. The table started to feel hard beneath him. He got up to join her in the shower but she was already out and dressed and standing looking out of the window, staring at the city.

'What are you doing?' He felt stupid now, with no clothes on.

'I told Beth I'd call in quickly. She wants to see the shots and talk over a few things.'

'About the job.'

'About the job. I won't be long.'

'Do you want me to come with you?'

She shook her head. Her hair was still damp. It smelt of his shampoo.

'You'll come back after?'

'Yes.'

'Good. I'll cook supper. Do you like prawns? I'll buy some more. What's the job?'

Her smile grew a fraction more rigid. 'It's a designer – not a big one but a new one, new to the business, like me. He wanted someone different to show his collection. He says I suit his look. He'd seen over a hundred girls, Stephen – I was the only one he picked.'

'Great. What's his name?'

'Marcel.'

'French then?' – Stephen wondered why they were talking like this. Something wooden had happened to his tongue.

'Yes.' She didn't look him in the eye any more.

'Where's the job?'

'Paris.'

'How long?'

'I don't know.'

Stephen's mouth went dry. 'What do you mean you don't know?'

Catarina shrugged. 'All the top shows are in Paris. Nobody likes me over here. Marcel says I have a good look for France. Perhaps I can get some work there. Beth has a deal with a good agent in Paris. If they'll take me on – give me breaks I don't get in New York . . .'

Stephen wanted to touch her but he couldn't. She had moved miles away already.

'You haven't even tried here, Catarina.'

She looked past him, out of the window. 'I'll come back – I'll come back with a good reputation. You don't know what it's like starting from the bottom, Stephen, people treat you like shit.'

'What about us?' He had to ask – he might have heard it all wrong.

Catarina looked at him again.

'I love you, Catarina.' She had been looking at the STEPHEN LOVES CATARINA he had written in the dust on the windowpane.

There were tears in her eyes. 'I have to do well, Stephen, it's important.'

'And I'm not?'

She shook her head. 'You don't understand. There are things I have to do. I need the work, Stephen, I need it so badly. There are things you don't know about. I need to be able to look after myself. All my life I have been dependent on people and terrible things have happened. I have to be dependent on myself. I'm ambitious, Stephen – just like you. You understand that, don't you? You know we're

268

not right for one another. You know that my life has been bad. You deserve a nice American girl, not the sort of trouble I bring with me.'

'We made love . . .' Stephen had run out of words. Catarina had too many.

'You've helped me so much, Stephen – I wanted to thank you – I wanted to please you.'

'You were paying me for the photos!'

'No!'

'You were fucking paying me for them like some fucking whore!'

'No! Stephen! You don't understand! I have to show everyone I can do it! I have to show Alex! I wanted to make you happy, that's all! It made me happy!'

Stephen picked up the contacts – the ones he had knocked to the floor when they made love – and he searched for an envelope to put them in.

'Here!' he said, 'I hope you don't pay for all your test sessions like that.'

She slapped his face. They both went quiet with shock and grief and horror.

'I'll come back, Stephen.' Her face was white.

'When do you leave?'

'Tomorrow.'

The word was worse than the slap.

He heard the door slam as she left and he walked to the window to watch her go. He saw her pick her way across the street but when she stopped and looked up, he ducked out of the way. When she was gone from sight he was still looking after her. Then he saw that she had written something on the glass, too. Under the words he had written – under the place where he had put STEPHEN LOVES CATARINA, she had written CATARINA LOVES STEPHEN. He pulled his shirt over his wrist and wiped both sets of writing off with his sleeve.

*   *   *

269

Tony saw the light under Catarina's door and knocked to see if she was OK. There was no answer. It was late – he felt worried for no particular reason. If she wanted to sleep with her light on what business was it of his? What was he – her fucking mother or something? He pushed the door open gently anyway. She was half sitting, half lying on the floor by the bed. He tiptoed over and did a brief medical check – no blood, no drool, no vomit. No whites of eyes visible, no waxy look to the skin. She was asleep. He could breathe again now. Tony was born worried, though. He bent closer to study the pulse in her neck.

'Tony?'

They jumped out of their skins simultaneously. Tony's was the louder scream by half a decibel. Glass had been shattered by less.

'Catarina! Jeee-sus!'

'What are you doing?'

'I thought you were dead! Oh! Oh! Oh! Shit!' He walked around the room clutching his chest until his heartbeat slowed from a ferocious rhumba to a more genteel cha-cha-cha. His face had turned the colour of Gouda rind.

'Why should I be dead?'

'Don't worry – you're not, I'm not – not for the minute, anyway. What else do I think when you're lying on the floor with the light on?'

Catarina massaged her neck. 'I fell asleep packing.'

Tony looked at the couple of things she had in the case. She must have been a pretty fast sleeper. Two frocks and a cardigan hardly made for exhausting folding.

He sat down beside her. 'What's this?' There were things scattered on the floor beside her – no, not scattered, he noticed – placed, quite carefully, in some sort of order.

The glass snowstorm stood in the middle. Catarina had caught it with her foot when she'd jumped and now the blizzard inside it was calming to a quietly-billowing drift.

Next to it lay a Polaroid – a little creased around the edges. Tony picked it up to see. A girl. A young girl. Giving a blow job. He looked closer, holding the shot to the light. Catarina as a young girl – giving a blow job.

He looked at Catarina's face. 'Where did you get that eyeshadow, dear?' he asked, pointing to the shot, 'It's most definitely not your colour.'

There were more photos on the floor. Tony studied them one at a time. Catarina didn't seem to mind – she seemed to be in a daze. There was a photo of a man – not the one in the shot, this one was dark haired. He looked attractive but a bastard – the sort of man Tony went for himself.

'Your husband?' he asked. Catarina nodded. He needn't have asked. The next shot was of Catarina and Alex on their wedding day. Catarina had long, long hair and a young, confused smile. She clung to Alex's arm with a heartbreaking expression on her face.

The last photo was of two little girls standing in the snow. Tony pointed to the taller of the two girls.

'Is that you?'

Catarina shook her head. 'The other one,' she told him.

There was a strip of red nylon ribbon and a Russian book with a paper jacket.

'I wore the ribbon on my hair when I went to school,' Catarina told him. She sounded tired and she looked as though she had been crying. 'My sister used to tie it for me. She used to smell of aniseed and menthol in the winter. She said sucking cold sweets would keep the germs off. I liked the smell, Tony. I used to complain and wriggle but I liked wearing the ribbons too. I thought they made me look pretty. My sister wouldn't wear them – she said she was too old. The book was our mother's – she had hundreds. My father would never allow us to read them. I stole that one when I left home, to remind me of her. It is the smell that reminds me of home – the smell of old books. I have still never read it – I still obey my father, even now.'

Tony studied Klara's photo. 'I thought you were an only child, Catarina.'

She appeared not to have heard him.

'Why have you got these things out now?' He flicked through the book. The pages smelt dusty and damp.

Catarina looked at him. 'To remind me,' she said. 'To remind me who it is I hate and who I love. To remind me of what it is I have to do. To remind me I can't love Stephen, Tony – not while I have to hate Alex so much. I have my hate and I have my responsibilities and my guilt. I can't live my own life, Tony – it's not possible. I'll go to France. I'll be rich and famous. I'll do it for Klara and for Alex – they are what is important, not me.'

Tony stroked the fine hair at the back of her neck. 'You should only go if you want to, sweetie,' he said.

Catarina turned on him. 'No!'

She picked the things up – the precious objects she had surrounded herself with. Tony tried to help her – he handed her the snowstorm but she turned too quickly and it fell to the floor and smashed.

Catarina stared at it for a second, unbelieving. Then she let out a wail that chilled Tony to the marrow. She fell to her knees with a crash that would have the neighbours punching the ceiling with broomhandles and she pushed the broken glass aside with her bare hands to pick out the unbroken figure of the Russian girl.

She clutched the figure to her chest as she rocked backward and forward. 'Klara!' she whispered, 'Klara!'

Her hands bled onto her shirt. Tony worried that she was having a breakdown. He thought of calling a doctor then he realized they couldn't afford it so he put his arms around her instead and sat there with her until morning.

42

Beth had a new chair. She loved it – it was a power chair – the sort busy executives own – the sort she had always imagined sitting in one day when she had her own business empire. She didn't own an empire as such yet, but she had the chair.

The chair was vastly gruesome and it matched nothing else in her well-designed office. It was black leather while everything else was cream and terracotta. It stood on a chrome base, while all the other metal in the room was faux-vertigrised bronze. No matter, it was the feel of the thing that counted, and this seat felt good – so good it was almost erotic. Like the Soto sports bra she was wearing it supported her in all the right places, whatever she did.

She wondered whether you could have sex in the chair. Of course you could – though the leather might stain. What if she bought some of that stuff you sprayed onto shoes so that you could wear them in the rain without a water mark appearing? She turned horizontally in the chair. The arms were a little high – her legs dangled unattractively and her neck rolled back, making her eyes bulge and her head ache.

Sitting, then – it would have to be done sitting up. Bad news – very bad news. Sitting up was for young bodies only – carcasses her age looked decidedly better lying down – with their arms in the air – and their stomachs sucked in – on white sheets because of the uplight effect. Unless you were screwing an old man, of course and then it didn't matter.

In Beth's book any man over thirty was old and old men made her nauseous. She'd heard they were an acquired taste, like oysters or blue Brie. She'd also heard they could have a lot in common visually with oysters and blue Brie.

She'd met perhaps a couple of older men she could possibly have stretched the rules for but they had always been well swaddled in shirts and ties and suits and suchlike. The thought of what went on below the water line – the fear of grey pubes and veins and stretch marks and so on had been enough to make her turn down several otherwise tempting offers. Her one regret was that it was the oldies that had all the money. Beth's lays were firm and supple and, without exception, poor.

She'd tried counselling for the problem – after all, it had to be related to some little but annoying mental glitch in her childhood. The therapist had been in his fifties, though and, although she had found him otherwise attractive, the moment when he had crossed his legs and unveiled a patch of white skin 'twixt sock and corduroy turnup that had closely resembled a route map of Western Europe had undone all the groundwork they'd so far made.

Did women's pubic hair turn grey? She knew she would dye hers or die herself the moment the problem arose.

The phone rang and she nearly tilted out of her chair answering it. The extension line was useless – the offices were so close she could hear her receptionist talking for real in one ear while she listened to her over the phone in the other.

'Catarina on the line for you.' Sandie was using her classy voice – that meant there were clients waiting.

'From Paris?'

'I don't know – she called collect, though.'

'Shit!'

There was a pause filled with French air and static.

'Catarina?' She could hear the girl breathing.

'Beth?'

'Make it quick, darling, I have clients waiting.'

'Beth, he wants me to shave my head!'

274

'Who does?' – For one moment she thought Catarina had met up with Alex again and he was forcing her into new sadistic practices.

'Marcel. For the show. What shall I tell him?'

It was the sort of decision agents are good at. Usually. Beth floundered.

'How do you feel, sweetheart?'

'Sorry?' Catarina had been talking to someone in the background.

'Where are you?'

'In the hairdresser's – they're waiting.'

'Do you mind having it done?'

'Maybe not.'

Her hair would be cropped anyway. Money always had the casting vote.

'Is Marcel there with you? Good. Put him on.' Beth removed her earring and moved the phone to her other ear. 'Marcel? This is a big step for Catarina. It could lose her money, understand? Good. Let's say two thousand dollars more for the cut and then whatever it costs in insurance in case it goes wrong and the hair grows back crooked, or something? No – I know it won't take long to grow back but she may not be able to work for that period – understand? Nobody may want a girl with bristle for hair. OK? Agreed? Good. Put her back on, will you? They're doing it already? Shit! OK – OK, I know the first show's tomorrow! Send the cheque – OK? Ciao!'

Catarina sat in front of the mirror, watching herself being shorn. They used clippers first and then they shaved what was left, like a man's beard. A photographer took shots for *Paris Match*. They wanted her to smile when she had shaving foam on her head but she couldn't – she was too tense, waiting to see the results.

'You have a beautiful shaped head,' the hairdresser told

her. She was told that with relief – some people were discovered to have strange bumps or scars when the hair was gone.

The salon was hot and the lights made it hotter. Marcel was excited – two newspapers were there, too, and it meant good advance publicity for the collection tomorrow. That was why he was there – waiting for interviews – he should have been in the studio, he had ten garments still left to finish.

Marcel was young – about twenty-six – and extremely small and thin, like a whippet. When he was home he wore Crimplene pantsuits and outside, in public, he wore nylon overalls and plastic aprons. He had pierced nipples and piercing blue eyes. His collection was tasteful in a leatherette-and-velcro kind of way. That sort of stuff kept the press happy, anyway. Dotted between the more *outré* garments were, of course, a few toned-down wearables that he hoped would sell to the shops.

Catarina's head was finished. She went to stand up and she kept on coming. She was nearly six feet tall and, with her head shaved, looked taller. Next to tiny Marcel she looked like a giant. Marcel clapped his hands and the gaggle of hairdressers clapped theirs too. Wonderful. Perfect. Marcel had tears in his eyes.

The show was at seven-thirty in the morning, at an old building site north of the city. To get there, Catarina had to go through a ruined, whitewashed brick tunnel that led across wasteland and she was told the press would have to do the same.

Sheets of plastic tarpaulin had been erected over acres of weed-strewn rubble and in this space had been placed about a hundred dainty gilt chairs, the sort they had in the Paris salons. Marcel considered this a huge joke against the establishment. The chairs faced a long wooden deck covered with sheets of black rubber and it was on this minimalist catwalk that Catarina and four other girls were booked to show Marcel's clothes.

It was raining hard and the tarpaulin sagged dangerously in the middle. Someone said there were rats running among the rubble and Marcel seemed delighted at the news, even relaying it to a journalist who wrote it up immediately in his notebook.

The mainstream press arrived at seven, teetering across broken brick in their platforms, sheltering the tops of their heads with their oversized plastic invites and clutching their skirts and screeching as the rumour of the rats spread like the plague.

By seven-fifteen the place was full and the shrieks had risen to an unbearable pitch. It wasn't the rats, Catarina realized – it was the way the audience spoke – or rather they didn't speak, they screamed. The tarpaulin broke like an expectant mother's waters just as the show was about to start and the first two rows got soaked. Marcel arrived personally to hand out plastic bags for them to stick over their heads.

No one knew the show had started because there was no music, just some knocking sounds that had been recorded in an abattoir just outside Nice and amplified several times over.

There was silence when the first model – a Brazilian girl with hair like a pubic bush – appeared. Catarina watched from behind some plastic drapes. She had never modelled on a catwalk before but Marcel had told her not to worry – just to walk as she did down the street. He didn't want a girl with a model walk, he told her – he wanted his show to be different.

A wind blew up and Catarina shivered. The other girls came off and Marcel nodded at her. She walked on stage and stopped. There was silence. She could feel the faces looking at her. A small explosion that Marcel had set up went off behind her and everyone jumped apart from Catarina. Lights flashed and she set off down the ramp,

277

glowering at the audience because she was concentrating so hard on her walk. The rubber was wet and her feet seemed to stick. She paused on a turn to avoid falling over and stopped to frown and study the bottom of her shoe in case gum was stuck there. Other models often stuck gum to the soles of your shoes – Beth had warned her.

Then the flashbulbs started. The catwalk heaved like something organic as the photographers pressed against it in a mass and Catarina swore loudly at them because she was frightened she might fall off. She looked back at Marcel but he was applauding her, egging her on. Ten more strides and she had reached the end. She looked confused and angry and the photographers loved it.

She wore a leatherette one piece – studded with buttons like an airport lounger – under a transparent lamé shift. Her arms and legs were bound in strips of plastic. The audience forgot about being wet and vermin-infested and started to clap instead. Fashion editors saw other fashion editors taking notes and started to take notes of their own.

When Catarina rushed off stage someone pulled her to the changing area and someone else ripped off her clothes and started to dress her in the next outfit. All around her people were pushing and swearing. Marcel was screaming at a dresser and a guy with a walkie-talkie was throwing a press photographer out of the room by the collar of his jeans jacket.

She went out ten more times and then, because she was wearing the bridal outfit in the finale, she missed the last scene of string hand-knits. Marcel supervised her dressing personally. She wore thirty yards of dyed muslin over a bikini made of flashing white lights. Matching tiny white lights were glued onto her bare scalp and a muslin veil thrown over the top. The veil almost blinded her – she had to be lifted onto the stage.

There was a pause as she posed and then silence as she started to walk. The lights flashed under the muslin but no-one could see anything else. Then, on cue, she pushed the veil back and a ripple of shocked applause turned into a cascade.

Marcel was beside her suddenly, hugging her legs and whimpering like a small humping dog. The audience rose like the sea and prepared to leave – sodden and frozen but relieved to have seen something new.

'What's her name?' An editor from *Women's Wear Daily* poked a pencil in Catarina's direction as Marcel steered her off the stage.

'Catarina – The Cat!' Marcel called back – and Catarina had a new nickname that stuck with her throughout her career.

43

Stephen straightened his picture of a dead tramp on Fifth
Avenue for the sixteenth time and looked at his watch for
the thirtieth. Eight fifty-three p.m. And the gallery opened
at nine. The gallery owner handed him a glass of kir *royale*
and he sipped it and pulled a face.

'What do I do tonight?' he asked.

The man shrugged. 'Oh — the usual things that artists
do — get drunk, insult all the wrong people, throw up, piss
up the walls — anything that takes your fancy, really.' He
put an arm around Stephen's shoulders. 'Or you could be
really anarchic and go round being nice to everyone and
talking them into buying some of your work.'

'What if no-one turns up?'

The man smiled. 'Oh, they will, Stephen — trust me, they
will.'

By nine-fifteen the room was crowded and thirty minutes
later there were queues outside. Stephen had been photographed and videoed and at least twenty of his shots had
been sold. He was drunk on the excitement of it all — it
was unbelievable — only Catarina's presence could have
made it more perfect.

Eve stood in the corner quietly — he had invited her
but was still surprised to see her there. Even her husband
Frederick was there and that had to be some sort of a coup.
Frederick was a medium famous actor who rarely appeared
in the role of Mr Horowitz. He and Eve had been married
twenty years but there were still people in the business who
thought she was single.

'Eve. Freddie.' Stephen shook them both by the hand formally, like the good host he was determined to be. 'What d'you think?'

Eve smiled. 'Great.' – It was not her best smile.

Freddie found lying easier – he was an actor, after all. 'Wonderful, Stephen, you must be delighted.'

Stephen tried to look suitably modest. 'Yeah, well – I am.' He laughed but Eve didn't laugh back. What in hell was bugging her? She couldn't be jealous – she could have filled the place five times over and still had them queuing for more.

'How's the new studio, Stevie?' She sipped at her drink. Stephen knew she wouldn't like it. 'Fine. Great. You must come over and see it some time, Eve.'

'Sure.' She looked about like she was expecting someone. 'How's Catarina?'

Stephen's face blanked out. 'Fine too – I think. She went to Paris. I think she's doing OK out there.'

Eve nodded. 'Beth sent me some clippings. Did you see her hair? Is Aimée here, Steve?'

'Aimée?'

'Didn't you ask her?'

'No. No point, Eve – she doesn't go out.'

Eve nodded again. She was beginning to annoy him. Why didn't she just say what she was thinking? He was pissed off with her spoiling his night.

The gallery owner pulled at his arm. '*In Town Tonight* want to interview you, son. Come over here, where it's quiet.'

'For the TV?'

He was led to where a woman was waiting. She wore black velvet with penis-shaped pearls and a large dopey smile. She asked Stephen a few quick questions about his work and then looked around for her cameraman. They went to the spot where the lights were set up and Stephen's hair was combed and his face touched up with powder for the interview proper.

281

The woman's smile widened as the cameras rolled. Stephen hardly heard her introduction, he was so nervous. He heard his name and then he was barely aware of the first question. He formed his replies about his work by instinct. Then a new question came up.

'Your career as a photographer has taken off quickly, Stephen. How much of your success so far do you put down to your mother's influence?'

The woman's smile somehow widened without splitting. 'What?'

'Your mother was a big name in society in the Seventies – now she is a virtual recluse. You've invited a lot of her old friends here tonight, Stephen – does that mean she's going to show?'

Stephen looked around dumbly. 'The gallery sent the invites . . .' he said.

'And surely you know the gallery is owned by a very old and one-time very close friend of your mother's? Do you think that was why he was keen to try you out at such an early stage in your career, Stephen, or do you think it was all down to sheer talent?'

Stephen looked across to Eve. She looked at the floor. He stalked off the set and confronted her.

'You knew!'

'I didn't know, Stephen, I guessed.'

'Why the fuck didn't you tell me, Eve? Why did you let me go on making a fool of myself? I thought I was good, Eve – I thought that was why they wanted me.'

An elderly drunken man pushed between them. 'What time is Aimée arriving, son? My photographer knocks off at ten-thirty and we need some shots of her to make the little outing worthwhile.'

Stephen pushed him out of the way.

'You *are* good, Stevie,' Eve told him.

'But not that good. Not good enough to do it without my mother's help.'

Eve sighed and shrugged. 'I could have been wrong –

282

anyone can be wrong.' She looked around the room.

'So, Stevie – what do you do now?'

He ran a hand over his face.

'You're launched now, boy – you're out of the closet in a big way – Aimée's son, the one with the silver spoon shoved firmly up his ass. Are you going to fly off in a tizz and try to make it on your own again or are you going to be smart and make the most of a situation that stinks? She'd love to give you the money, Stevie – why don't you just go ahead and take it? Let her buy you a plush studio with all the trimmings and your own little assistant to boot? There's enough guys around who have made it all on contacts and very little else. I don't see why you should be any different.'

'I wanted to be good, Eve.'

'Then you should have stuck with me. You knew you still had a barrelful to learn. You should have changed your surname, too. You might have known this would happen. It's all that Boston high-society interbreeding, boy, it addles your brains.'

'I didn't know there'd be so much interest in her, Eve.'

'Then you don't know the press.'

She looked at him. He had been mad and now he was upset.

'Why didn't you warn me, Eve?' he asked.

Eve whistled through her teeth and shook her head slowly. 'I suppose I tried to,' she said, 'And I suppose I guessed two meddling women in your life wouldn't make things any better. Maybe it was best you learned the hard way. I don't know, Steve – I'm a photographer, not an agony aunt.' She looked at him. 'Do you want to come back to our place?'

Stephen nodded. She sent Freddie off to try and find the car.

*   *   *

283

Catarina's head itched like she had nits. She ran a hand over the bristle that covered her scalp and grinned. She needed a shave, but she had promised Beth she would grow her hair back. She had tattoos all over her body and a fine silver chain running from her nostril to her ear. There was a panther behind her, standing by her bare legs. The panther stank.

'Cat! Cat!' – Catarina looked up at the photographer. There was a bright flash and the panther sounded like it was brewing coffee in its throat. Catarina prayed to any god that would listen that she might not piss herself with fear. The animal's trainer kept smiling at her and there was a vet with a rifle that shot tranquillizers, just in case – though Catarina guessed the panther could get most of her lower leg off if it wanted, before they took effect.

Paris liked Catarina – this was her fourth session in as many days and each one of them had been weirder than the last. Marcel told her she was being booked because she had such an unusual look but Catarina didn't feel unusual – it was only when she looked in the mirror that she saw this alien looking back. She didn't like the look much but had quickly found out that what she liked didn't count. She hoped the tattoos would come off in the bath. She sucked her stomach muscles in and tried not to sweat.

Marcel had taken her to see a couture show before the session started. She had watched the girls on the catwalk and at last she had seen something she liked. The girls were beautiful – stunning. They moved like the panther that lay behind her and they smiled and flirted with their audience. The clothes they modelled were the sort of things she and Klara had always imagined Catarina Kirkova would wear – shimmering silks and rich velvets and golden ballgowns that looked like spring water when the light hits it.

'I want to work here,' she had whispered to Marcel. He wore a short henna-red wig – he had had to be smuggled into the auditorium in disguise.

He laughed. 'You would have to learn how to walk first

284

– these girls are the best – most of them have been doing it for years. Don't you recognize the faces from the papers? Look!'

He called out each girl's name as she passed and Catarina realized she recognized every name, if not every face.

'Who can teach me to walk like that?' she asked when they were out in the air again.

Marcel shrugged. 'Ask your agent – most of them teach their girls themselves.'

Catarina chewed on a nail. 'I want to learn before I go back to New York,' she said – 'I want to do it myself.'

'You could ask one of the girls to teach you, I suppose,' Marcel told her. He lit a roll-up and passed it to her for first drag. She shook her head.

'Do you think they would, Marcel?'

'No.'

'I thought not. Who then?'

Marcel smiled. 'I have a friend – a dancer. He might help. Could you pay him something? He is very good – classically trained, but very poor too, so cheap. His poise is perfect and he moves like a skater across ice. Are you interested?'

Catarina had earned enough money from her work in Paris to pay the Russian nurse and have some left over for herself.

'How cheap?' she asked. 'Lots of money cheap?'

'Not if he likes you.'

Catarina nodded. 'OK.'

Stephen studied Freddie through the bottom of his beer glass. The more he drank the more he liked the man. By that stage he would have allowed Freddie to adopt him, if he'd asked. He was a strange mate for Eve – no wonder they had no kids. Incompatible breeders – like elephants with giraffes and dogs with sheep – that sort of thing. Freddie was tall and dressed like Charles Boyer. Eve

285

was little and looked at best like an upturned toilet brush.

'Women are shits, Stephen,' Freddie was telling him. 'They should be eradicated from the planet, *sans exception*. Save my wife, of course.'

'Of course,' Stephen echoed. He drank some more beer. He had told Freddie about Catarina — he hadn't meant to but he had to tell someone or he knew he would die and Freddie had come across as a good listener. It was easy telling things to strangers and Freddie had sworn from the start not to breathe a word to Eve. Despite the fact he wore a cravat rather than a tie, Stephen had decided to trust him. He'd even told him about Aimée's interference in his career but Freddie had not been keen to listen to that story because he thought Aimée was a remarkable woman and had done for years.

'You've met her?' Stephen asked him.

Freddie shook his head. 'Sadly — no. Don't go on about her, though — illusions are best left intact, as a rule. Let's get back to the girl who dumped you — she sounds like a much easier person to hate.'

'I don't hate her,' Stephen said.

'You should. It would do you good.'

'What would you do about her?'

'At your age?' Freddie narrowed his eyes as he took a trip back on the time machine. 'Oh — get pissed — moan a lot — screw everything that moved for a couple of weeks until I felt better.'

Stephen stared at the floor, trying to imagine sex with another woman. He and Catarina had been good together.

'I don't want anyone else.'

Freddie rose to refill his glass. 'A bad mistake,' he said. 'This may not —' he tapped Stephen's head, '— but *this* soon will,' he pointed towards his crotch. 'That's the wonderful thing about the male sex apparatus, Stephen, it has no memory and no conscience. It is entirely amoral and its powers of recuperation are legendary.'

Stephen closed his eyes and let his head fall back against the chair. 'My career's blown to shit.' he said.

Freddie laughed. 'Only if you look at it one way,' he said. 'I would have said that was a successful exhibition of work we'd left back there tonight.'

'They were there because they thought my mother was coming. My pictures were there because the gallery owner screwed my mother some time back in the last century. He might even be my real father for all I know.'

'So?'

'So?' Stephen was very drunk now – unfocused and close to passing out.

'I only got my first lead because I screwed the director.'

– Did Freddie say that? Or did Stephen just think he did? He didn't care any more – oblivion was settling in.

44

Someone jumped out at Stephen as he left his studio the following night. He kicked the guy in the crotch – it was a knee-jerk reaction.

'Jesus!'

'Tony? Is that you?'

'Who did you think it was – the tooth fairy?'

Stephen helped him to his feet.

'Shit, man – how did you learn to kick like that?'

Stephen shrugged. 'I didn't know I knew until just now. Maybe I saw it in a movie. I was aiming for the gun you weren't carrying. Didn't you ever hear the word mugger, Tony? What are you doing here, anyway?'

Tony wiped tears of pain from his eyes. 'I came to ask you out on a big date, Stephen, only you just blew it.'

'And now the real reason?'

'Catarina.'

Stephen walked off. Tony limped to keep up with him. 'Remember *Midnight Cowboy*, Stephen? People will begin to talk!'

Stephen stopped. 'What about Catarina?' he said.

Tony studied his toes. 'You bought her a glass snowstorm?' he asked. 'I knew it was you. She kept it on the fireplace – it was her only proper possession. She got very upset the night before she left for France. She broke it, Stephen – *we* broke it – it was an accident. She got hysterical – I thought she'd never stop crying.'

Stephen looked at him.

'So?'

Tony looked surprised. 'I thought you might like to buy her a new one.'

'Well, you thought wrong.'

Tony stepped back a little. 'I thought you loved her, Stephen.'

'Wrong again.'

'Sorry.'

Tony went to walk away and then stopped. 'One more thing,' he said.

'Yes?'

'Did you know Alex keeps ringing her?'

A flicker of life passed across Stephen's eyes. 'Alex?'

'Yes. Did she tell you?'

'No. Alex? Jesus.'

Tony looked awkward as though unsure what to do next. 'She doesn't speak to him or anything,' he said. 'He just leaves messages. I thought you ought to know.'

'Thanks.' Stephen nodded.

Stephen felt bruised inside his soul. He watched Tony limp off with total disinterest. He was curled too hard into his own hurt for anything outside to do more than touch the surface. Emotionally winded, he needed time to straighten up. His love and his work – he had been attacked on both fronts – a double kick in the balls. Maybe if he waited the pain would turn from acute to just an ache.

He counted all the losses he was mourning as he waited for a cab: Catarina; his dreams of a career he could quite openly call his own; his youth; he felt uniquely middle-aged now; his enthusiasm; his idealism. In their place – cynicism; a stoop when he walked; fuzzy-edged depression; self-pity, a sudden liking for Leonard Cohen songs and a bitterness he could almost taste. It had been a bad trade by anyone's standards.

Even by his own pathetic standards he had been criminally naive. Galleries didn't suddenly exhibit pretentious crap by unknown photographers unless there was some good reason – like their name happened to be Van Doren.

Women did not have to love you to want to screw you. He saw it all now – why hadn't he seen it coming before? Because he'd been a kid. Because he'd been a kid with such a well-cocooned upbringing that he didn't even know what day of the week it was. He punched out at a nearby wall and his hand hurt. A taxi had slowed but pulled away when it saw what he was doing. Stupid. Stephen knew he would be many more things many times in the rest of his life but he would never be stupid again.

When the bruises faded from liver-red to brown he came out from Eve and Freddie's apartment, prepared and braced to try real life again. He was ready – of that much he was sure. Not to pick up a camera – he needed more confidence for that – but at least to pick up a girl. For sex. He ached for sex. Freddie was right – some parts of a man's body healed faster than others. He was young and duty called.

It was easy. Eve took him to a party – something at a model agency. Girls had always wanted Stephen and with his new bruised-fruit look they wanted him even more. He was no longer polite – he didn't do small-talk and he didn't laugh at their jokes. They were all beautiful but he sought out the best, using his father's yardstick rather than his own: 'Great legs, great smile and an IQ that measures less than her bra size.' This girl talked a lot and Stephen drank a lot and he went back to her apartment without asking her name.

She lived, in some expense, somewhere on the Upper East Side, and she kept her condoms in the fridge – alongside the bottle of Australian Chardonnay they would drink before they made love. She also asked him what paper he liked to read in the morning and he heard her order it by phone when he went to take a pee. He had never seen a toilet that sat two before – or a clear glass cistern that goldfish swam in.

'Always check out the medicine cabinet before you stay the night,' was one of his father's famous pieces of advice. His head dull with alcohol he padded across to do as he'd been taught: Dental floss. Mouthwash. Sleeping tablets. Facial hair stripwax. An eye mask. Eye drops. Nasal drops. Almond oil. Nail clippers. Tablets for menstrual cramps. Tablets for cystitis. Nothing sinister. He shut the door, relieved. Then he saw her standing watching him in the mirror.

'Are you looking for something?' she asked. 'I have some coke if you want.'

Stephen shook his head. 'I needed some mouthwash.'

'Go ahead. Be my guest.'

He went through the motions to maintain the lie. She watched him, smiling, her arms folded.

'You must do well as a model.' He nodded towards the gold taps on the sink.

She laughed. 'I do OK. I get paid more to be a beard, though.'

'Sorry?'

'A beard. I get paid to date the gay actors who want to look straight for the press. I thought you would have recognized me from the papers. I only recently finished with one big name – we told the press we were secretly engaged. I accused him of screwing other women and threw back his ring at Mortimer's – you must have seen the story – oh don't tell me you missed it!'

Stephen shrugged fake regret. She walked across to him and kissed him on the lips.

'The mouthwash tastes good.'

'So do you.'

She winced at the cliché and smiled. Her teeth looked nice.

'Do you like to do anything different?' she asked.

'Like what?' His mouth felt dry now. He looked at his glass of wine but decided the taste mixed with the pepper-mint would make him sick.

'Oh – I don't know. Anything. The last guy I brought up here liked to do it dressed up as Dorothy from *The Wizard of Oz*.'

'Dorothy? Jesus!' – Stephen started to laugh. Maybe he needed the coke after all.

'He's a photographer too. He's famous – you must have heard of him. He's . . .'

But Stephen stopped her before she could tell. 'Don't,' he said. 'I might know him. He might be a hero of mine. I may have to face him some day without laughing.' His shoulders shook. 'Jesus, what did you have to do it as, the Tin Man? Toto? A Munchkin?'

'You're laughing at me,' she looked hurt.

'No! I'm laughing at him. Honestly. I think you're doing a great job. Did he wear the red sparkly shoes? Sorry, sorry. It must have been great, really.'

'He's using me for his next jeans ad.' she said.

'Well that's OK then.'

She smiled again.

'Take your clothes off, Stephen.'

'Now?'

'Why not? I bet you have the most amazing bod. You used to work for Eve Horowitz, didn't you? I heard other girls talking about you – this incredible guy with this great butt who never once tried to fuck them – they had bets on you, Stephen – did you ever know that?

Stephen's brain told him to leave then – while he still had some values left intact – but his body was fascinated – the partnership between body and brain fell awry, like a husband and wife at a late-night dinner party, when the wife gets her coat just as the husband is poured another brandy.

'I want to go now,' Stephen's brain said. 'In a minute,' his body replied, 'Just let me finish this first.'

He finished his treat before he left. Like a waiter in a foreign restaurant she tried to tempt him with more exotic fare but he waved them aside and went for the more homely dish of straight sex on a waterbed instead. She appeared to come four times before he had even entered her and once he did she screamed so loud he had to turn the TV up via the remote control by his feet to drown out the noise.

When he woke in the morning there was the juice he liked on the nightstand by his head and her voice on the phone, ringing her PR.

'He's a photographer, Simon. His mother is famous – surely that's worth a few lines? OK, call me back. *Ciao, bambino.*'

The phone rang a few seconds later – she picked it up halfway through the first ring. Then she came into the bedroom smiling.

'Stephen? Baby? I have a newspaper on the line – I don't know how they got hold of this – but they want to do a little piece on us for their gossip page. They want to speak to you, baby. I told them you were sleeping but they just want a few words. Would you mind? Be nice to them, baby – they're good for a few bucks.'

Stephen took a sip of juice, shook his head and smiled.

'Sure. Here –' he took the phone from her and she kissed him on the cheek.

'Go screw yourself!' he yelled into the receiver and the girl's smile of gratitude froze faster than a TV dinner.

'What are you doing?' she screeched. 'I have to pay my agent to get me publicity like that!' She tore the phone from his hand. 'Jesus, Stephen, what were you thinking of . . . ? Hello? Hello? They hung up. Christ!'

Stephen pulled a few dollars out of the pocket of his jeans as he pulled them on.

'There –' he told her. 'That should just about cover it.'

She screamed at him as he stepped into the elevator. 'Bastard!'

Stephen grinned as the doors slid shut. He discovered he didn't mind that word at all – in fact he quite liked the sound of it.

He got back to his studio before the hollowness in his chest took over and he broke down. He was glad he was alone then – he did not want anyone else to see him making such a fool of himself. What you did in private didn't matter – he kidded himself with that thought, anyway.

45

Asde, Marcel's dancer friend, made Catarina's life hell. He swore at her, he screamed at her but in between the swearing and the screaming he also taught her how to walk.

'Push your pelvis under, you lazy cow – walk from the balls of your feet – who taught you already?'

'Someone at home.'

'Shit! They taught you to walk like a duck! I want you to forget everything – OK? Everything you already know. What have you done with your muscles all your life? We have to start from the first – you will have to learn all about your body.'

'I don't have much time – can you teach me something faster?' – Asde walked out when Catarina said that. She had to phone Marcel to get him to come back. She also had to learn French in a hurry because he refused to speak to her in English any more.

'Look,' he told her. 'I charge little because Marcel says you are good. I am the best – understand? Nobody else will walk like you if you do as I say. If you do what I tell you you will be famous. I will make you special. Is that what you want? Do you want to learn properly and become a star, Catarina, or shall we hurry and mess around? Only I don't waste my time, Catarina. You can – I do not. Eh? Do you understand?'

They began from scratch. He taught her ballet exercises to firm up her muscles because he said without muscle tone her walk would never be good and her turns would be a disaster. He taught her about protein and carbohydrates too and which foods were valuable and which she should avoid. When her walk became fluid she progressed to the turns and it was then that his temper became most vicious because Catarina became most awkward.

She could not keep her balance. Her legs bound together like wet string, knotting as she turned. She nearly fell altogether. Her feet got in the way. She lost eye contact with her invisible audience and looked at the floor.

Until at last she did one right. He picked her up and carried her around the room in triumph.

The next day they went on to full turns and the screaming started over again.

Asde also had contacts in the modelling business. 'Who is the biggest designer in Paris?' Catarina asked him. He looked scornful at her ignorance.

'I like Gaultier or Alaïa. Saint-Laurent is the master, though. He is a legend – famous forever, understand?'

Catarina nodded. 'Where is he?'

'Avenue Marceau – why?'

'I want to meet him.'

Asde laughed. 'What are you going to do, phone him? Ask him if you can call in for tea?'

'What's so funny?'

'Would you go to England and phone up the Queen? Things just don't work like that and you make yourself sound stupid for saying it. Forget it. If you are good you might get to work for Saint-Laurent one day. You don't approach him, though – nobody does.'

Catarina chewed at her thumbnail. She was not prepared to sit around waiting for things to happen to her – she couldn't afford to. What if you waited and nothing happened?

'I need an introduction?'

'It doesn't work like that.'

'Do you know someone who might know him?'

Asde shrugged. 'Maybe.'

'Tell me their name – please!'

'You're sounding stupid again – like a child.'

'Please.'

Asde sighed. 'Brize may know him – I don't know.'

Catarina wrote the name down. 'Brize?'

'Hercule Brize – the designer. He has been in the business long enough – longer than Laurent, in fact. He may know him – I don't know. He's an old man now, but still a great name in couture. He has a salon on the rue du Faubourg St Honoré. He is a sweet old man – an artist, not a dressmaker. We were lovers once. He designed for a ballet I was in. I admired him and I felt sorry for him.'

'Can I use your name as an introduction?'

Asde looked sad.

'If you want. He may well have forgotten our liaison, though – I almost have.'

Catarina's French agent exploded with anger. 'A house model? Look – *we* get the work Catarina, not you. What do you think you are doing?'

Catarina sat there calmly. 'I went to Brize for a job. The manageress offered me a job as house model. I accepted,' she said. 'I will still pay you commission from the money I earn. I don't understand what the fuss is about.'

'Do you have any idea how little the job pays? We have work for you for the next month – do you want me to turn better work down?'

'Was the work definitely booked?'

The agent flipped through her listings. 'No – most of it was provisional – but that doesn't mean you cancel it – you're doing well, Catarina – this is suicide – the old man's stuff is *passé*.'

Catarina smiled.

'Can you get me an interview with Saint-Laurent?' she asked.

'No. You're not ready yet.'

'If I was?'

The agent shrugged.

Catarina's smile froze. 'Then I'm working for Brize.'

Hercule was the old man's first name, which was why he was known by just the one name – Brize. He wore a diamond on each finger and maroon velvet slippers on his feet. He had his face embalmed by Estée Lauder and his body reconstructed via lifts, tucks and liposuction. He drank his own urine and practised Chinese astrology.

His salon was large, with all the antiquated-gilt splendour of an ancient whorehouse, but as most of his clients had grown old and frayed along with the furniture he quite rightly refused to be troubled by the decaying decor.

His workroom, by comparison, was dingy and cramped. He was forced to lift two armfuls of violet cashmere onto a crowded cutting table before he could find a place to rest his elderly but surgically-enhanced buttocks. His face looked as though it were covered with cling-film. A glass of herb tea was pressed into his hand and he was all at once surrounded by a small crowd of people – each one of them intent on pirating his notoriously short attention span.

'. . . I have the music for the introduction, monsieur – listen, it's excellent – if you don't use it I will use it for Lacroix – it has to be used, it is terribly now. Listen, listen – not that bit – *this*! – until there – ignore the rest . . .'

'. . . The crimson chiffon arrived at twelve o'clock last night. I telephoned Madame Jacob to tell her the dress will be ready in three weeks and was informed by her maid she has already taken her order to Jean-Louis Scherrer . . .'

'. . . There are six models outside and another three at ten. The agency phoned this morning, complaining about the wages – Madame Gres pays considerably more, I was told, and Eileen will go to her if we cannot update our rates . . .'

Brize ignored them all, sitting astride his stool, clasping

a dummy between his thin knees as though he was about to make love to it. The dummy wore a half-finished wool crepe dress. He stared at it a while – like an anteater watches an ant – before grabbing a handful of silver taffeta and attaching it as a peplum.

'The appliqué is difficult . . .' he told his assistant through a mouthful of pins, '. . . see how fine the fabric is. Tell Jean to make sure it doesn't pucker like the last time.'

The metal castors on his stool squealed as he pushed himself back to have a look.

'Is Francine still making those tiny felt hats this season? Perhaps you could order a couple in black. Send a swatch of this wool crepe over so that she can get a good match. And give me a costing of the whole thing. Make up the pattern and sent it to the outworker. Where is Philippe? Tell him to order me an iced water and a little salad. No dressing – just lemon. How many are coming on Monday? Do we have enough chairs? Shorten the catwalk if you have to – I don't want my ladies fainting like last year. Where are the evening dresses?'

He looked up as his new house model walked in. He had employed two girls prior to the season – Antoinne, who was shorter and less slim – like most of his clients – and now the new girl who had an impossible shape but who, he noticed, gave new life to his clothes. He watched her walk. She was nervous – her eyes darted everywhere – but her walk was good.

'Stand straight – don't use your hands. You're a house model – you're here to do fittings. If you move too much I can't see the fit of the garment. You see this dummy here? That is your job. Good. Stand straight – don't hold your breath. Relax – your shoulders are tense. Good. Look in the mirror – here. Can you see that? Your left shoulder is a little higher than the right. Can you see? Is that you or is it the way you are standing? Can you straighten them? Does that feel right? Good.'

His hands worked around her body, touching, moving, dusting off creases and straightening seams. He smelt sweet and his breath was warm. Catarina's skin was cold – she had gooseflesh on her arms. No-one had given her coffee and she had been in the salon since six.

'What is your name?'

'Catarina.'

'Are you scared of me?'

'No.'

'Then why are you shivering?'

'I'm cold, Monsieur. Sorry.'

'Cold? This is a sweatshop – how can it be cold? Is anyone else cold here? Keep still or I'll pin you accidentally. You are from Russia, aren't you? You drink tea, then. You should be used to the cold.'

He made her a strong black tea and then poured evaporated milk into it until it was creamy-white.

'Drink it – it's the best. Spill it onto the dress and you are fired.'

The old man said nothing more to her for hours as he sat pinning and fitting his models for the show. Catarina began to ache and her legs felt weak. She was allowed to sit only when she was in between garments, though at times like that she found herself called upon to make coffee and put bags onto the dresses as they were finished.

'Russia.' – She realized Brize had turned his gaze to her again.

'Sorry?' She was almost too weary to speak.

'You come from Russia.'

'Yes.'

He stared her straight in the eye.

'A good family?' he asked.

'The best. Aristocrats. My parents were very wealthy.'

He nodded. 'They sent you to France, then.'

Catarina yawned. 'To England first – from there to America and now to France,' she told him.

'Your English is quite good. Your French is very poor.

It's a pity. If your French had been better, I would have allowed you to sell to my clients during the season. We have some English women, though – perhaps you can speak to them.'

Catarina looked surprised. 'I won't be modelling during the season, then?' she asked.

The old man smiled. 'What makes you think you are good enough?'

'I *know* I am, Monsieur.'

'Let me see.'

He took Catarina through to the salon and told her to walk along the catwalk. She modelled as she had been taught – pelvis forward, head held high, treating the clothes as though she wore garments as expensive all the time. Brize said nothing, just nodded and walked away when she had finished.

The other model approached her as she was changing.

'Are you doing the shows?' she asked.

Catarina shrugged. 'I don't know. He didn't say anything.'

The girl took stock of her figure.

'Do you have a boyfriend?'

'No.'

The girl nodded.

'Watch out for Brize, he's as randy as an old bull and I can tell he likes you.'

'Brize? I thought he was . . .'

The girl nodded. 'I know – everybody does. He's been married three times, though, and sired seven children. He doesn't make much show of them – he thinks they're bad for his business. Just watch him, that's all – he get worse as he gets older. No-one's safe alone with him these days.'

Catarina seemed to inspire the old man as he designed for the new season. He worked with her for hours, wrapping fabric after fabric around her and doing sketches of her

301

for the new range. He had not told her she would be showing for him as well, but she heard he had booked one model
less and she noticed the other house model became more
and more aggressive towards her as the weeks went on.

'Get us coffee will you, Jeanne?' Brize asked the other
model one day as he pinned a hem on Catarina. She came
back with one cup and put it down beside him.

'Where is Catarina's?'

The girl returned with a second cup. When Catarina
went to drink from it she nearly spat it back. She caught
up with her later in the model room.

'You made this with cold water!'

'So? I'm not your slave.'

'It wasn't me who asked for the coffee, you know that.'

'No – it was your adoring lover. When did you allow
him to fuck you, Catarina? He'd never have put you in the
show otherwise.'

'I'm in the show?' Catarina was too pleased to argue.

Jeanne glared at her. 'Don't pretend you didn't know.
Maybe he was going to tell you tonight, at the party.'

'What party?'

'The Clothing Council's ball, Catarina – they hold it
every year just before the season. All the designers get
invited and Brize's told everyone you're going with him.
You must be a good lay, Catarina – nobody's ever seen
him quite so smitten before.'

Catarina laughed. 'He's never touched me, Jeanne.'

The look on the other girl's face told her she wasn't
believed.

When Brize had finished designing that evening he told
Catarina to keep the last dress on as they were going to
an important event. He ordered in a huge plate of bread
and ham and ate the lot first – 'I never eat in public' – he
told her – and then they took a taxi to the Champs Elysées.

The ball was held in the grounds of a large house and

Catarina was disappointed that it was too dark to tell exactly who was there. Everyone seemed to know everyone else and they all fell over themselves to tell Brize how much they adored him — mainly because he was so old they thought he might be dead by the following year's event.

Everyone kissed him — the others just swanned about yelling 'CYK!' at everyone they were introduced to ('Consider yourself kissed,' — the latest greeting among the AIDS hysterics) — and everyone ignored Catarina, save Marcel, who had somehow gatecrashed and who was standing by the toilets smoking an enormous hand-rolled cigarette.

'Nobody kisses me,' he told Catarina. 'They are all scared of me, I turn the whole scene on its head. You see the way they look, though. Fear. Envy. Look — they are threatened by me.'

Catarina looked — no-one was taking any notice.

'You have to screw the old man?' Marcel asked, nodding towards the spot where Brize was last seen disappearing beneath a pile of fawning admirers.

'No.' Catarina was getting tired of the question.

'You wanted to meet Saint-Laurent?'

He asked the question so casually. She looked eagerly down at his face.

He shrugged. 'He won't come. I could introduce you to someone almost as good, though. Mario Salvatore — you know him? Italian — one of the biggest names — everyone loves him and this year he shows in Paris too. It causes a big affair — an Italian showing over here — all the old women are screaming about it — I'll show you to him.'

Mario Salvatore was tall and softly spoken. He watched Catarina as she talked and he listened to Marcel as he praised her. Then he gave her his card.

'I show next week. Come for your fittings tomorrow.'

She looked at the address.

'I'm working for Brize,' she told him. He laughed and she saw his teeth for the first time. 'He's got a nerve, that old man – he's knows you're too good for him. I will pay you double anything he's offering.'

Marcel looked at her. 'Take it, Catarina – Brize designs for old women who are already dead – Mario's clothes will make you famous.' He watched the hesitation that was still on her face and grinned.

'Saint-Laurent will be jealous as hell when he sees how good you look on Mario's catwalks,' he said. 'He may even try to poach you himself.'

Catarina smiled. 'I'll be there for the fittings tomorrow,' she said.

She told Brize the news that evening. He took her back to the salon on the pretext of doing some late work. She allowed herself to be taken there. It was raining, she felt listless after the ball, she needed to return the dress she was wearing. That was all she meant to do. The salon looked strange as the lights flickered on; it was seeing the place for the first time with nobody there – no-one fussing or running about. The place had a certain grace at night, when you couldn't see the dust and the fraying fabrics.

'I always adore the smell of the fabrics,' Brize said, inhaling. He was an old man – she could hear his breath make each inch of its journey – it whistled through his nose and squealed through his lungs. She could smell the fabric – she liked it too.

They walked into his workroom. He had a small TV there that he watched the racing on during the day. He turned it on absentmindedly – there was no station broadcasting – just a grey flickering that lit up the dark room.

'Take off the dress,' he said. Catarina didn't move. He looked up at her in surprise. She was staring at the blank screen.

'Are you alright?' he asked. He put the kettle on for

some coffee and pulled out a bottle of Cognac he kept underneath his desk.

Catarina didn't answer. The flicking screen absorbed her to the exclusion of all else.

'Catarina!' – the old man was annoyed now.

She looked up at last.

'Luisa.'

'What?' Brize frowned at her.

'Nothing.' Catarina looked back at the screen. She was younger again, in another small office with a flickering screen. There was a revolver in her hand, too heavy to lift or use. They were fighting, she was frightened. There was an explosion – she had killed someone. A heavy sense of dread filled up all the hollowness inside her. She had killed someone. How had she forgotten that? She'd been so frightened of reprisals – so desperate to escape from Russia – that somehow it had slipped from her mind. Like forgetting the eggs when you go shopping. She had seen the body on the floor. She had deserved Alex and all that had happened to her since. She had known, of course – but not known at the same time.

'Catarina!' The old man sat on his stool with the wheels on it, waiting. Waiting for what? To design on her? To have sex with her? She stood between his knees. She had killed one man already – perhaps she could kill him, too. It seemed better to think like that somehow – the guilt felt less painful then.

He wrapped a length of purple chiffon around her breasts and tied it in a bow. Then he began to attach a drape of spotted lamé to it. All the time he spoke to himself: 'Topstitching on the bodice – press seams flat – buttons at the back of the skirt – two – gold enamel . . .'

'I'm not doing the show,' Catarina told him. His eyes swivelled up to her face – rheumy eyes, large, like a bulldog's.

'Pardon?'

'Your show. I can't do it.'

305

His eyes refocused – he was listening to her now.

'Don't be stupid – of course you are doing my show. You know it is designed around you.'

'You didn't tell me.'

'You knew – of course you knew.'

He went on pinning.

'I'm not doing it.'

He looked up at her again. His face had become mauve.

'I'm showing for someone else.'

'Who?'

'An Italian.'

'Mario Salvatore.'

'Yes.'

The castors squealed as he pushed his chair back. She though he was having a seizure – his eyes bulged and his face turned from mauve to puce and he fell to his knees at her feet.

'You can't do this to me.' His voice was smothered as he pressed his face into the fabric that hung round her as a skirt.

Catarina said nothing. She stepped away slowly and he fell onto the floor. She offered him her hand and he took it to help himself balance as he struggled to his feet. He wiped his face with a handkerchief and took a deep breath. When he looked at her this time there was hate in his eyes.

'You'll never work in this city again,' he whispered. Catarina shuddered. The room had suddenly become cold.

Two days later Brize was dead. His heart gave out as he took his finale bow at one of his own shows – he keeled over on the stage, right in front of the world's press and the last few words the microphones caught him uttering were full of hatred at Catarina's treachery.

Catarina's photograph appeared on the front page of every French newspaper the following day, alongside a shot of Brize lying prostrate on the catwalk as a team of medics

306

tried in vain to revive him. He had created his final collection around her and she had abandoned him at the very last minute. Any affection the French had for Catarina turned in an instant to hatred. They enjoyed hating her just as much as they enjoyed elevating Brize to the status of a national martyr who had died for his art.

46

Aimée looked at her son in the way that all mothers look at offspring that have returned to the nest: Weight? Eyes? Grooming? Stephen's weight seemed OK – in fact he was filling out a little. His grooming was fine too – nothing unkempt – hair a little long, maybe, but it suited him. He was clean-shaven and his clothes looked pressed.

It was his eyes that had changed – there was something missing there. It was a way he used to have of looking at her – the way any young boy will have of looking at their mom – it had gone completely – he looked at her like she was anyone now, like he looked at everyone else. He looked at the floor a lot, too, she noticed. The floor was rapidly becoming a more popular focal point than her face.

'You should let me repair those jeans for you while you're here,' she said. It was a joke, a well-worn joke. They both knew she didn't sew and she knew torn jeans were the look. Stephen usually laughed at the joke but today he didn't. Instead he studied the tears as though seeing them for the first time.

'Oh, that's OK, thanks.'

He was drinking more too, she noticed. Not a lot, just more.

'What happened to your hair?'

'What?'

'It's sort of flattened, Stephen.'

He ran a hand through it nervously. The hair stayed put. 'I don't know – it just sort of grows like this now.'

'Really? I thought maybe you'd had a root perm or something.'

Still no smile.

'Are you going down to the beach?' Aimée was getting desperate. Her son shrugged. 'Maybe later. I came here to discuss business. I'd like to deal with that first, if you don't mind.'

Intrigued, Aimée leant back in her chair and folded her arms. Had he come to borrow money? At last? She felt a smile of relief begin to spread out across her face.

Stephen looked at his hands. 'I didn't realize you knew so many people, Mom.'

Aimée raised her eyebrows.

'Why don't you go out? I never thought to ask – none of us did. It just seemed normal, you being here all the time.'

Aimée shrugged and looked out to sea. 'I went out enough when I was younger. I did it all, Stephen, everything there was to do and most of it in public. The press loved it and so did I. Then I just sort of finished, that was all. You can finish your life early – you know that – it's not a crime – the crime is not knowing it. I finished and I retired because the real essence of a class act is knowing when to stop.

'Most of them don't know, Stephen – you see them in the papers every day – all the old girls, lifted and tucked like ancient quilts, strutting their stuff like feeble old hens. Marrying young boys because it makes them think they look younger. There's no class in that, Stephen, none at all.'

Stephen nodded thoughtfully. 'So why do you think so many people are still interested in you?'

Aimée chuckled. 'That's just how things are, Stephen. I'm wealthy, I was a society name, I ducked out. People think they're missing something, that's all. They think you're a recluse. They thing you're harbouring some dreadful secret, like your teeth have all fallen out and you've got gout.' She sighed. 'I don't know. People just like the sniff of a scandal, that's all.'

Stephen looked at his watch. Aimée wondered what it was he had to rush back for.

'There was certainly enough interest in you when the gallery exhibited my work. More interest than there was for my shots, as a matter of fact.'

Aimée laughed. 'Don't worry about it, Stephen – use it. If it's good for business use it. You sold your work, didn't you? And I don't mind. Use your connections, Stephen – your brothers always have.'

Stephen smiled for the first time.

'Good.'

'Good what?'

'Good that you don't mind.'

'Why?'

'Because I want to do some shots of you, Mom.'

'OK.' Aimée put her tea down.

'For the papers.'

'No.'

Now it was Stephen who leant back in his chair. 'I only realized after the exhibition. I can syndicate them. I can make money from them. People are interested and I'd have exclusive rights. Using my connections – that's all I'll be doing. It'll help me crack the magazines and that's what I want. Then you can give me more names and I can use your name as an intro to get exclusive shots of them, too. It's the quickest way to the top, Mom, especially when you know you're not exactly shit-hot on the talent side.'

Aimée looked shocked. 'You always said you wanted to make it on your own merit, Stephen.'

Stephen smiled again. 'I know I did. But that was before you started to interfere. You've got to finish what you started now, Mom – you owe me that much at least. If I'm going to make it on my mother's name I may as well do it properly. We can do the shots today or next week if you want to get your hair done. Which do you want?'

Aimée stared at him. There was a coldness about him now that had not been there before. She was suddenly proud of her son – he looked so much like his father.

'You know I don't want to do this, Stephen,' she said. He looked at his watch again.

'Don't make me do it, Stephen. You don't know how it feels. The shots will make me old. I'm terrified of growing old.'

Stephen smiled. 'I didn't think anything frightened you.'

'No – not much, but death scares the shit out of anybody and that's all growing old is, after all – it's dying, however you might fancy it up. I never believed life started at forty, it's just the start of the end. We all know it, Stephen, we just try to bluff it out with collagen and liposomes and silicone and sexercise and buckfucks. It's all so humiliating when you know deep down you're rotting inside like a piece of irradiated fruit.'

She squinted a look at his expression out of the side of her sunglasses.

'Were you always so sure I'd never have the talent to make it on my own?' Stephen asked her.

Aimée sighed. 'Oh, talent doesn't matter, Stephen – take my word for that. You get on because of who you are, not what you can do. The only talent successful artists have is a talent for self-promotion. If you don't know that now you'll realize it one day.'

She leant her head back and closed her eyes. 'Have you seen Catarina recently?' She couldn't help it – she had to throw one little pebble back in his direction. She had only meant it as a glancing blow but when she saw the pain appear in his eyes she was immediately contrite.

He shook his head. 'She's in Paris. Don't you read the papers any more? She screwed up some famous designer's show out there and he died of a heart attack a few days later. The French take their fashion seriously – they said he died of shock when she went to another designer just before the season. It's all crap, of course. I thought you'd have read it. It was great publicity – she even got booed off the catwalk. It got good coverage – they'll be falling over themselves if she comes back here.'

'If?'

'I don't know. I don't know what she's doing. When will you do those shots then?'

Aimée fanned herself with a copy of *Hello!* 'Next week,' she told him. At least it would give her time to lose a couple of pounds.

'Tony?' – She phoned frequently now, always late at night, often when he was asleep. His partner had begun to complain.

'Catarina.' – Always the same sad little voice. It was eerie in the dark, like listening to a lost child that wants to come home. He switched the side-light on and got sworn at for his trouble. He quickly switched it off again. Better eerie in the dark than temper in the morning.

'He died, Tony.'

'Who died, darling?' He tried to think. Who was dead? Was she sitting alone in a room somewhere with her possessions splayed out around her? Then he remembered – the old guy, the designer.

'They all hate me out here now.'

Tony sat up, knocking a metal ashtray onto the floor. Tempers in the morning – mega tempers in the morning.

'Darling, you're ruining my sex life.'

'Sorry.' Did she laugh or was it some electronic hiccup on the line? 'Who is it?'

'Danny.' He whispered the name.

'Danny? The one that wears the trousers so tight you can tell his religion? *That* Danny?'

'Ssh!'

'Sorry.'

More crackling or cackling.

'Look, Catarina, the guy was old – I saw his photo in

312

the paper – Great shot of you by the way – He had a weak heart – that wasn't your fault.'

'They are saying I am a bitch.'

'So? I've been called worse in my time.'

'Like what?'

'Like never you mind, Madame, it's your problems we're discussing here.'

'Sorry.'

Tony sighed. 'That's three.'

'Three what?'

'Sorrys.'

'Sorry.'

'Four.' At least he had made her laugh now.

'What do you want me to do, Catarina? Come over and stitch up your wrists?'

'I just wanted to talk to you.'

'OK, now you're making me cry.'

'S . . .' she began.

'– Five!' he cut in.

There was an expensive silence.

'Look, Catarina, do you want my advice?'

He heard her nod.

'Then play up to it. So you're a bitch? So what? Everyone thinks models are bitches anyway. You've made your name now, kiddo – cash in on it. Give one short interview saying you regret the old fart's death – on TV, if possible, and then forget the whole thing. I served Jack Nicholson in the bar the other night by the way, did I tell you?'

'Who's he?'

'I don't know why I bother. Who *would* impress you?'

'Did you speak to Stephen?'

Tony sighed again.

'I did, yes.'

'How is he?'

'Moody as hell. Fucking beautiful.'

'Did you ask him about the snowstorm?'

'Yes.'

313

'And?'

'Sorry.'

'He hates me too, then.'

'You're becoming paranoid, Catarina.'

'What's that?'

'Never mind. Go to sleep, you'll feel better in the morning. Goodnight.'

'Goodnight.'

47

Only one Paris agent was willing to take Catarina onto his books after Brize's death, as the others told her she had been barred following the scandal. It was rumoured Brize's eldest son, who had inherited the business after his father's death, had threatened to sue her for breach of contract. As no contract could be found, the case was dropped but not after it had run its full gamut of publicity.

'Bitch!' – Catarina heard the word often over the season and once she was spat at by a woman in the street. Two of Mario's other models refused to work with her but then changed their minds quickly when it became obvious it would be they who would go, rather than Catarina. Mario was happy. Catarina on the catwalk meant crowds fighting for his shows and even if they came to boo and hiss they usually went away impressed by his marvellous designs. He had known Brize would be upset when he poached her but even he had not realized Catarina's worth in publicity alone.

'They would have hated me anyway for being a foreign designer but they hate you more and so that is alright,' he told Catarina. 'They hate you so much they forget to hate my designs and so come away loving them instead.'

He was right – his clothes got good press.

At the finale of his show one of the French models, who had been put up to it and paid by a paper, walked up to Catarina and slapped her hard round the face, crying out: 'That is for poor Brize!' Shots of the event went front page the following day and a video made the headlines on the evening news.

Catarina walked into her new agent's offices the following day and threw the papers down in a heap on his desk.

'Phone the designers who barred me,' she said. 'Perhaps they will offer me work now.'

She was right. Catarina had been punished in full view of the press and honour had been restored. By the following season she was booked for four shows a day, commuting across Paris on the back of a Harley Davidson motorbike laid on by her agent. The press loved the story, their photographers following on their own motorbikes as she shot across the city. One day the gendarmes held up traffic in the place Vendôme so that she could make it from Kenzo to Rykiel.

As her fame grew, so too did a fear – that she would be seen in pictures in Russia and recognized as a woman wanted for murder. She would wake in the night and look in the mirror to remind herself: 'You are older, your face is not the same, you have a new name. You were a child with long hair and an ugly nose. Now you are a woman – nobody will know you.' She would whisper this to her reflection until she was calm enough to sleep again.

Eventually she became so sure her identity was an intact secret that she found a new obsession growing inside her. She had money now – enough for a flight back to Moscow. She wanted to know how her father was and, more badly, she yearned to see her sister. The nurse begged for more money each time she phoned. Catarina had begun to have doubts that the woman was keeping her word. She did not sound like an angel these days, she sounded like a greedy woman. What if she were not spending the money on Klara? What if Klara were lying in wretched conditions? Catarina read about her home country at every opportunity. Things were freer there now. Communism had gone. She could never believe it. She saw statues being torn down and Russians queuing for hamburgers, but still she was distrustful. Besides, politics did not affect her own situation, although it might make travelling easier – she had

316

committed a crime in her own country and, if she were caught, she would suffer.

Her longing got to the stage where it overcame her fear, though. She was homesick, she hated the kind of people she worked with. They took too many drugs and they cared about trivia. What did it matter what shade of green was right for next winter? Who cared which American rock stars the girls from the shows were screwing? She watched the models' self-absorption and it both fascinated and sickened her. Was she the same, she wondered? If not, then she must surely become the same, because they all changed after a time.

But, as she watched them eat and vomit and exercise, she felt cleverer than all of them and she felt that cleverness growing like the roots of a tree. It was not hard to be cunning when they were so slowed-down by their neuroses.

'What do you do for a living?' a reporter asked one of the models during an interview once. 'Nothing,' she had replied. 'I am just Me.' Being 'Me' was a full-time occupation. You had to know every inch of your body in a way that others did not. It meant constant supervision and second-guessing reactions to food and outside circumstances: 'If you throw up after a meal open your mouth wide or the acid can damage your teeth.'

'My body can't tolerate lactose – I can only drink soya milk and bottled water.'

'I got a bug in the Philippines and my weight dropped twenty kilos in two days.'

'She haemorrhaged after sex with him and lost ten pints of blood.'

'His skin reacts badly to Tequila.'

'White wine brings me out in hives.'

Catarina missed the snow that covered things and made them all right again. She wanted Klara there to tie her ribbons for her and check her mittens weren't lost. She missed the soft hot dumplings that made your stomach full

317

and on fire and the bite of the tea that you bought in the streets.

She missed everything about her home – even the bad things. She missed the smell of the books that they were never allowed to read. One day she visited an old library in Paris, just to get the smell again but it was too much for her and she came out in tears. She missed the small apartment and huddling in the dark with Klara while their father crashed around drunk in the other room. She missed not being allowed to do things and being ordered and bossed about. She wanted Klara's large hand to put her own in. It was too much for her. The nurse had told her Klara was worse – that she might even be dying. She wanted more money. Catarina had no choice, then. She decided to go back.

Catarina could tell no-one she was going back to Russia – she barely believed it herself. It was as though she had somehow become two people these days – the frightened little-girl Luisa and the clever, crafty and brave Catarina. She modelled Catarina on Klara. It made things easier, somehow, playing at Klara – it was as though her sister was still with her in a little way.

Her disappearance caused almost as much interest as her incident with Brize. She just vanished one day when the season was over. She packed only a few new clothes and her hands shook while she folded them. Klara might die – it was all she could afford to think of. Her fear didn't matter. She was so frightened she was physically sick.

They would know – they would know the minute she landed in the country. She even dreamt about it. All the stories of Glasnost had been lies. They would be there at the airport, waiting to arrest her. She could see the staff of the modelling school standing there, waiting to point her out. She told them who she was now but it didn't

318

matter – to the officers she was Luisa the murderer and nothing else she said mattered.

They weren't there, though – no-one was there, only the smell of her own country which made her weep the minute she stepped from the plane.

Catarina flew economy class, travelling like a tourist to Sheremetyevo Airport, where she sweated for the entire twenty minutes she spent in the queue at passport control. She listened to her own language being spoken all around her and she wanted to be happy but she couldn't, she was too scared.

Someone grabbed her arm as she lifted her bag off the ramp and she felt her heart stop – it truly, totally stopped – she felt it. But when she turned around she found that the someone was just a porter looking out for quick tips, but the fear on her face made him back away without even asking to carry her bags.

When she was through passport control she ran up to the second floor to exchange some dollars for roubles, which took half an hour – and then another twenty minutes was spent negotiating a taxi at the Intourist desk in the arrivals hall. The drive to Moscow centre took forty-five minutes and by the time she had arrived she was shaking with nerves and trying desperately to calm down.

The car dropped her off at the Metropol Hotel and she went straight inside for a vodka. Aimée had taught her how to drink but she had forgotten to eat and the fire went straight to her head. She pulled off her gloves and looked at her hands. They were still now. She closed her eyes and sighed.

The toilets were full of young girls putting on make-up and laughing. It was strange to hear her own language spoken again. She thought of Klara painting her mouth with lipstick before she went to pick up the men in the hotel lobbies. It was a long time before she felt brave enough to look at her own reflection. Her face was white. She had put a red rinse in her hair as a further disguise and then pulled on a hat as well, just in case. Klara would have laughed at the sight she made.

The toilets were too warm, she felt faint sitting there. The girls must have been taking part in some sort of beauty parade – they all helped one another with their hair and the air was thick with sprayed perfumes. Catarina went into one of the cubicles and locked the door and sat there until she felt better. Then she came out and ran a tissue under the cold tap and pressed it against her face.

'Are you OK?' one of the girls asked. Catarina replied in Russian, wondering whether she had an accent now. The girl looked young – not much more than fifteen, though she was heavily made up.

'Are you in a beauty show?' Catarina asked her. She shook her head. No – a fashion show, in the ballroom next door. The best girl would win a place with an agency in Great Britain.

Catarina smiled. 'I know a little about the business. Would you like some tips?' The girl was keen – she had never modelled before.

Catarina took her make-up off with cold cream and washed her face under the same tap. Then she re-applied the basics – just a little mascara as the girl's lashes were fair, and a smear of natural lipstick on her mouth. She brushed the lacquer out of the girl's hair and let it fall over her shoulders without grips or bands. The girl looked worried when she saw herself in the mirror.

'I look too young!'

Catarina smiled. 'They like that – don't worry.'

'Do you think I have a chance?'

'Can you walk OK?'

'Yes, I got a prize at the school.'

'Then you should have a chance.'

She left the girl sitting in front of the mirror and went looking for prostitutes who, she remembered, knew all the best places to eat.

The air still smelt the same. She took off her gloves and

320

the cold nibbled at her fingers. An elderly black limousine drove too close and sprayed her legs with grey slush. The domes of Red Square still looked like whipped ice cream. When they were children Klara had told Catarina that Ivan the Terrible had blinded the architects who built them so that they would never build anything as beautiful again. She never knew if the story was true but she didn't mind because it was wonderful and sad.

In the morning she would visit Klara but first she had to get herself straight again. She no longer had control – she was Luisa – little Luisa the booby, not Catarina Kirkova, the bitch who knew it all.

A bell started to peal and a flock of white birds took off in fright, their wings clapping together like applause. Catarina looked up and smiled for what felt like the first time since she had left Paris. She was home again. The ache inside her felt better, though the fear was still there.

She stayed at a cheap hotel because she felt it would attract less attention to her. There was no phone in the room so she had to call the hospital from the communal phonebox in the hall. The nurse sounded tired at first but then shocked when she heard where she was calling from.

'I will call to visit Klara tomorrow, as soon as I can get a train.'

There was a long silence on the other end.

'You should have told me before you came. I would have put you off. Your sister is very sick, she should not have visitors . . .'

But Catarina cut Olga off. 'I've come a long way. I have to see Klara, it is what I came for. Will she know me? Is she dying? Is she recovering yet?'

'She's still very sick.' Nurse Olga sounded still less like an angel now. 'You will have a shock when you see her. You shouldn't upset yourself like this . . .'

'Tomorrow,' Catarina told her and hung up.

48

Catarina arrived at the hospital while it was still dark. The place had got worse since she was last there. The stench was unbearable and she held her scarf over her nose as she walked past all the wards. There was no money now, she knew that – no money at all. She had read in the papers that diphtheria was an epidemic again and there were even rumours of a case of bubonic plague.

How could she have wondered about the money she kept sending? Even if it was used for other patients as well as Klara it was money well spent.

Klara's old room was empty. Her heart stopped when she saw the rusty bed that was turned on its side and leaning against a wall. Then a hand grabbed her and she almost collapsed again with shock.

'Miss Orlova?' The nurse was like the hospital – she looked the same but worse. Her face had fine lines across it and there was grey in her hair. She stared at Catarina, waiting for her to react.

'Where is she?' Catarina heard her own voice break.

'Another ward. This room had problems – flooding. The ice froze the pipes and when the thaw came they leaked through the roof – look!' She pointed out dark mildew stains on the ceiling.

'Did it happen when Klara was here?' Catarina asked.

The nurse shook her head. 'Don't worry – I look out for her, I told you.'

'Thank you.'

Catarina hoped the woman was telling the truth.

They walked down dark corridors and then suddenly

into the daylight. The sun was coming up over the high back wall and the whole of the rear yard was bathed in a still orange light.

'She's in a special unit over here,' the nurse said. Catarina followed her. She had never been to this side of the building before. There was a small pond, frosted with ice, and a large patch of frozen lawn that crunched as their feet darted across it. Behind a line of fir trees stood a newer wing – a sort of prefab with a tin roof. The nurse unlocked a door and they ran inside. She was nervous – looking all over the place as though she expected to be disturbed. She kept fiddling with her apron.

'You shouldn't be here now. There are no visitors allowed at this time. I am doing this just for you, understand?'

There was a room at the end – a large room with ten beds in it. She walked Catarina to the last bed. It was covered in a plastic tent.

'An oxygen tent – it is how she breathes now. Hurry.'

'I can't see her!'

The plastic was creased and misty. She sat on a small metal-framed chair, pulling it closer so she could see.

'Is this Klara?'

'What do you think? I told you she had changed.'

'But she's not young any more! She's so thin, like an old woman!'

'You can hold her hand if you want – through the plastic – there's a gap – there.'

The hand felt wax-coated.

'How long has she been like this?' – There were tears in Catarina's eyes.

The nurse looked at a small watch that was pinned to her breast. 'They always go like that after a while. The skin dries. She looks better than some. That's because of the money you send, it means I can give her more attention. I put cream on her face every day. They still go like this, though, after a while.'

323

'Can she hear me?'

The nurse shrugged. 'Maybe. You never know. I talk to her a lot, just in case. Some say they have heard things when they come round.'

Catarina looked up at the nurse, her face tear-stained. 'Thank you. Thank you for talking to her.'

She looked back at the bed.

'Klara? Klara can you hear me? It's Luisa, darling. I'm here, here beside your bed. Forgive me for not being here all the time but I can't . . . I . . .' She broke down then and started to sob.

The nurse looked embarrassed. 'Look – you have to go now, they'll be here on their rounds soon.'

'Is she in pain?'

'No.'

'Please. Look after my sister – please! You spoke about God last time – are you religious? You said she was in God's hands. Did you mean that?'

'Of course.'

'Then you must promise you'll care for her. Promise to God, while I'm here. Do it now.'

The nurse looked away. 'This is no place for such things. You've got no right asking me to . . .'

'Promise or I'll sit here until they come. Swear to God, Olga – then I'll send you more money.'

The nurse looked back at her. Her face was red.

'OK. I swear to God.'

Catarina stared at her eyes all the time, trying to tell if she was lying. She stood up slowly. 'I'll go now, then.'

The nurse let out a sigh of relief. She would just have time enough to put the patient's correct name back again before the doctors came round.

49

Moscow, 1994

Rick Palimo knew he hated Russia the minute he stepped off the plane. It smelt of decay and depression. It smelt of something so old he could barely rifle through his child-hood memories to find it but when he did he thought it had something to do with thick heavy clothes and suppressed sexuality. The sort thing that schools smell of. Or maybe it didn't — maybe it was just his imagination.

Rick only liked going abroad if it was to countries that appreciated the finer points of his profession. In Russia he was a nobody — no-one there knew or cared about all the names from London society that were meat and two veg to him. Being in Russia made him begin to wonder just why the people he wrote about were so important and that path led down the road to depression of the greatest kind.

He had come to Moscow because it was a good expense wheeze but once he'd arrived there and stood outside Mc-Donald's for twenty minutes — just staring in wonderment — he knew he was in the wrong city at the wrong time. Still — a lead was a lead and he'd dug up a hooker who was prepared to say she'd seen Catarina on the game once, several years before.

What he hadn't expected was to bump into Alex.

He knew the man at once from his photos. Alex Head. Mr Catarina Kirkova. Mr Fixit — the man who had given The Cat to the Western world and then vanished. Why? Why pull off the greatest coup of your entire seedy career and then leave before the applause starts?

Rick watched the man from a distance. It was hardly a

coincidence, running into him – anyone visiting Moscow would have run into Alex sooner or later. He was a big man out there, a high-profile westerner. Rick wondered how the Russians ever threw out communism with Alex as their capitalist role model.

He watched Alex judge fashion parades and he watched him talk on TV. The more he watched him the more he hated him. When Alex spoke Rick turned down the sound and watched the smug smile instead.

'I'll get you too, you bastard,' he whispered. Suddenly he felt good inside again.

50

Beth was in a shitty mood. Playing a hunch following a chance remark by her NLP counsellor to the effect that the green suit she was wearing was making her aura appear less than *soignée*, she had paid for a second opinion by an independent colour consultant and discovered, to her acute chagrin, that she had in fact been mis-diagnosed in the first place. She was not, nor had she ever been — apparently, Earth Tones. What she *was* was Water Tones, which meant pale pinks, plum, charcoal, baby blue — which meant trashing all her wardrobe, not to mention her entire apartment, which she had decorated to be simpatico to her palette.

She buzzed through to her reception. 'Call Jerry and see if I can sue.'

'Sue? What for?'

'Jesus! You tell me! Wrongful diagnosis? Being prematurely aged by light refraction? Buying a fucking wardrobe full of all the wrong colours? Ask him — that's what I pay him for!'

She collapsed back into her chair, clutching her crystals for comfort. The buzzer went almost immediately.

'Jerry? Baby?'

'No, it's me again. Catarina is here in reception and I have *Elle* on line three and *WWD* on line five.'

Did she spot an element of glee in the girl's voice? As her diaphragm went into overdrive she reached for the brown paper bag in her desk drawer and shoved her nose into it to prevent the onset of a panic attack. Good, old, second breath, stale carbon dioxide — it was exactly what her endocrine glands craved.

'Deal with *Elle* yourself – they only want to check the provis on Dean. Put *WWD* through to Abby – I told them Wanda couldn't double-book for September so maybe they want Kola instead. Try to sell them Nikki – she's got a nasty gap around the seventeenth and I don't want her going off getting married again. Send Catarina through.'

She was better now – in control.

'Hi honey!' – start good, start well.

'Hi.'

Catarina sat while Beth studied her. The girl had splashed out in Paris, or maybe they were freebies. An Important white linen Comme Des Garçons shirt and sassy, whelk-coloured jodhpurs. A Chanel belt, too – or was it faux? Her hair was like a squirrel's tail.

'Don't worry – the red will wash out.' She laughed rather nervously, noticing the path Beth's eyes had taken.

'Good, good.' Beth steepled her fingers.

Catarina unzipped her book. 'I've got some new shots, Beth – good ones, from Paris. And there's shots from the shows; tear sheets . . .'

Beth leant across politely to look at them. She whistled through her teeth. 'Amaaaaazing!'

Catarina smiled. 'You like them?'

'Uh-huh.'

'You think they will get me work over here?'

'Can't do any harm, that's for sure.' She leant across to the lightbox on the wall behind her desk, switching the light on to study some transparencies.

'Do you think I'm ready to see the bigger clients over here now?' Catarina stood up to look at the shots over her shoulder. There was her little face, a hundred times over.

'Mmm – in a way.' Beth snapped the light off and the little faces with their different little expressions all disappeared.

'In what way?' – Catarina sat again.

'In a "yes-you-look-good" sort of a way,' Beth told her, 'In a "your-book-is-up-to-it" sort of a way. In a

"New-York-would-love-you" sort of a way, too. In a "Is-she-professional-enough-yet?" way, no, definitely not. In a "Can-I-trust-her-to-be-a-good-ambassador-for-this-agency?" way, no again.

'You got thrown out of the Paris agency for bad conduct, Catarina. You took work you weren't supposed to and then you let the client down. You changed agencies without even phoning me and then you upped and disappeared without telling anyone where you were going. Do I need to continue or have you got the message?

'I have had people on the phone asking for you and I have had to make up some crap about you needing a complete rest, though I'm not sure they couldn't tell by my voice that I didn't know where the hell you were. I'm your agent, Catarina! I need to know where you are and what you're doing every minute of the day! I need to know when you sneezed and when you last had a pee! I need to be consulted before you make career decisions! We're talking about respect here, Catarina – respect for you, respect for me and respect for my agency. Do you understand? Don't just nod, verbalize – tell me!'

Beth caught sideways sight of herself in the Hammacher Schlemmer mirror by her desk. Her blood-orange safari jacked clashed hideously with her puffball-pink angry face. She staunched the flow of her sermon in mid torrent.

'Can we work together here, Catarina, or are we just scratching our balls?'

'I want to work, Beth. I want good jobs and respect.' Catarina's voice sounded fuzzy. She looked sick. Worried. Beth didn't like her look, after all.

'Well, good.' Beth was all smiles again, 'Let's have us some ground rules, shall we?' She would not have bothered this much had she not thought Catarina to be hot. Luke-warm or even simmering and she would have been on the other side of the door in a nanosecond. She pulled a Xeroxed sheet out of her desk and pointed the key words out with the tip of a built-up nail.

329

'I've had this printed for all the girls who had trouble with the books,' she said. 'It's a sort of precis of the other stuff I gave you on professional behaviour. I want you to read it and I want you to get it framed for your wall, understand? This is your Koran, Catarina — you lead your life according to what you read here, right? Good. Now we can do business.

'I have three castings for you and at each one you have been asked for by name. Dress much as you are now — you look good, only run down to BellaToni's first and ask him to get that crappy rinse off your hair. Get some sleep too, OK? And phone Evie Horowitz — she doesn't have a job for you but she got worried when I told her I didn't know where you were. Off you go, then — I love you. Ciao.'

There was a telegram waiting when Catarina got back to the apartment.

> Phone me — Aimée.

She screwed the message up and threw it into the bin. Eve — Beth — Aimée — she didn't need any of them. They could all go to hell. She had been to hell herself. Her sister's face haunted her constantly — that was all the hell she needed for the moment.

It was several weeks before Aimée tried again. This time the telegram was longer and more astringent:

> Perhaps you mislaid my number, dear — for the record it's . . .

Catarina smiled when she read it. She missed Aimée's company, despite everything.

330

'Catarina?' – Aimée's voice sounded deeper and more hoarse, as though she had been shouting for a long while.

'I got your telegram.'

'Of course you did, dear. Both of them.'

Catarina smiled. 'Why did you want me to ring?'

'I want to talk to you. Come out here for the weekend. Bring that boy you're living with too, if you like – he sounds as though he could do with some fresh air.'

'Tony? You spoke to Tony?'

'Is that his name? Once or twice. Is he as hormonally-challenged as he sounds?'

'Don't be insulting, Aimée.'

'You should hear how he refers to himself. Will you come?'

'I can't, I'm busy.'

The silence sent its own frozen reply. Nobody turned down an invite from Aimée. 'Why don't you come here if it's urgent?'

Aimée's laugh sounded like a wet cork on a glass bottle. 'To New York? You must be mad.'

'Why not? You might like it.'

'You know I never leave here.' There was a proviso in her tone, though.

'I'll be here all day Saturday, Aimée. You know the address.' Catarina put the phone down quickly, before she began to back down.

Aimée arrived in a yellow cab and a cloud of Je Reviens. Spurning the elevator she walked up seven flights to Tony's apartment and then down two because Tony lived on the fifth and she'd overshot.

Tony adored everything about Aimée on sight – from the Southern accent, to the camp sunglasses-in-winter routine, to the metres of duck-egg cashmere she had swaddled herself in. Catarina had never seen Tony act coy before but that day he was positively diffident. Catarina sent him out for Earl Grey tea and hoped he'd get lost on the way back.

'He's a real darling,' Aimée said once he'd gone.

'Don't be patronizing.'

'Why not?' Aimée looked genuinely surprised.

'Because it makes you look ugly – you taught me that.'
– They both laughed.

'You had sex with Stephen, then?'

Catarina stopped laughing. 'He told you that?'

'He didn't need to. He's my son. His hormones sent me little notes when he wasn't looking.'

Catarina studied her shoes.

'Are you in love with him, dear?'

The silence in the room was thick enough to chew.

Aimée sighed. 'You are then. Bugger, Catarina, I thought we had a deal.'

Catarina looked up at her. 'Don't worry, Aimée. I don't mean to marry him. The sex just happened – it wasn't meant to.'

'You hurt him.'

'I hurt both of us.'

Aimée dusted her gloved hand across the arm of the chair and inspected the fingertip.

'Drop him, dear. Without wishing to re-state the obvious you're not good enough for him.'

'I know that, Aimée.'

'I know you do.'

'But I know it for a whole lot of different reasons.' Catarina looked angry.

'Whatever.' Aimée waved her hands dismissively and smiled. 'You know I'm truly fond of you, Catarina,' she said.

'Is that why you came all the way out here?' Catarina asked. 'To tell me that?'

'No,' Aimée's smile darkened. 'I came out here to tell you I'm dying.'

'Of what?'

'Cancer, what else? Halitosis? Psoriasis? You know me better than that, dear. It had to be cancer, didn't it? Cancer still has a certain style to it, unlike a lot of those modern diseases. It even sounds a little *passé*, like me. I like that.' She took off her dark glasses. Her eyes looked dark-ringed.

'You're not dying, Aimée, of course you're not.' Catarina almost laughed.

'Very well, dear – have it your own way.'

'You're telling me this so that I'll leave Stephen alone.'

'Of course I am. How clever of you to have guessed.'

'Aimée?'

'I have to be going now – too much pollution makes me nauseous.' Aimée rose from her chair with a small laugh. She kissed Catarina on the cheek, her lips almost touching it but not quite.

'Aimée – tell me you're lying!'

Aimée stood in the doorway, smiling. 'I'm lying, Catarina – it was wicked of me. Sorry I can't wait for the Earl Grey. Tell Tony I'd like to hear his Garland collection sometime. Goodbye dear.'

51

'Any more shots to show us?' The photographer passed Catarina's book to the client. Catarina shook her head.

'A card?'

She pulled an index card out of her rucksack and handed it across the table. The photographer studied her face and compared it to her pictures.

'How long have you been working?'

'About two years.'

They all nodded.

'You're with Beth?'

'Yes.'

'Why?'

Catarina looked surprised.

'You could do better, you know. Did you see Elite? They could get you the best work. Or Divas – I hear Jack Palitzo is looking for girls like you just now.'

'You don't think Beth is good?'

The photographer pulled a face and sighed. 'She's good but she's not that good. You want someone all the biggest names go to. She'll get there but she's still new. You want someone established – look, take my card. Tell Jack I sent you.'

Catarina read the card carefully. 'Beth has been very good to me,' she said.

The photographer smiled. 'Sure she has, honey, but business is business. She knows she'll lose you sooner or later – none of the girls stay with their first agent – it's a sort of stepping stone. Look at your book – it's good but it's not great. Look at the work she's been getting you –

how much do you earn at the moment? Seven – eight hundred a week? You could be getting two thousand a job right now – more when you're established, much more. You're good – really. Don't take all that 'just starting out' crap – there are girls I work with doing thousand-dollar jobs the day they walk out of high school. Phone Jack – he'll see you OK if he likes you.'

Catarina showed the card to Tony that evening. He agreed with the photographer.

'Phone him. Ring him now. This man is big, Catarina, and you've got the perfect intro. I'll get him for you – give me the number.'

Catarina laughed. 'It's late – they'll be shut.'

'Not if he's as hot as I think he is, he won't.'

The phone was picked up on the second ring. Tony talked for a while then put the receiver down with a smug smile.

'Tomorrow at eight,' he told Catarina. 'I'll set the alarm. Do you want coffee or fruit juice or both?'

Divas occupied two floors of a new block of buildings just off Lexington Avenue. They had their own lift that took you straight to the tenth and the reception area was as big and as quiet as a church.

There was no-one else waiting. At Beth's there were always girls hanging around reception – some who seemed to live there. The receptionist at Divas could have done a *Vogue* cover herself. Catarina sat on a Fifties' black leather Bauhaus chair and looked to check her shoes hadn't marked the white carpet.

When her name was called she was shown through the bookers' hall – a vast room full of long tables, drum files and ringing phones, and into Jack Palitzo's office. Jack was fifty with a pony tail. He looked at her book and he asked about her circumstances. Then he offered to take her onto his books.

'I want less commission than with Beth,' Catarina told him.

'You what?'

'She took twenty-five percent. I want you to take twenty.'

Jack took off his dark glasses and peered at Catarina. He grinned. His body looked older than his face, because of all the lifts. Catarina thought he should do up the top buttons of his shirt.

Jack began to laugh. 'All my girls pay the same. Maybe you don't understand.'

'I understand. I want to pay less.'

'Why?'

'Why what?'

'Why the hell should I?' His voice had become tighter.

'Because I will be earning more.'

Jack fell back in his seat. 'Get outta here.'

He phoned her when she got back to the apartment.

'You earn more than two hundred thousand in your first year and we'll talk about dropping the commission, OK?' he said.

'OK.' Catarina told him. Tony opened the champagne.

She told Beth the next day. Beth said very little but her eyes looked hurt. It was Eve who phoned Catarina to tell her just what she was doing.

'Beth's helped you this far, Catarina, you shouldn't treat her like this.'

'Business is business, Eve,' Catarina said, quoting the photographer.

Eve winced during the pause that followed. 'You're getting a bad name for yourself. I thought you ought to know, in case that's not what you want. Do you care, Catarina?'

'Only if it means I get less work. I need the money, Eve. Jack can earn me more, that's all.'

'You know you might bankrupt Beth?'

336

'Me? How? I didn't earn that much for her!'

Eve sighed. 'Jack's already spread the story to the papers that you've left Beth and gone with him. That means more of Beth's girls will follow suit. Models fly in flocks, Catarina.'

Catarina's voice fell to a whisper. 'I'm sorry, Eve, but it's not my fault.'

'By the way,' Eve told her once the conversation was finished and she was about to hang up, 'Did you know Stephen's mother died yesterday?'

Aimée's funeral was an outrageously lavish event, mainly due to the guests, who were her society cronies from long ago and still famous names in the media. Hoogie brought in the most expensive firm of Boston event planners and left it all in their hands.

The service was held at a chapel that had been specially built inside the Copley Plaza and decorated with one thousand pink orchids. Catarina smiled when she saw them.

The guests drove back to the house after the service to pay their respects over glasses of vintage brandy. An old lover of Aimée's took Catarina's arm as they walked up the drive.

'It was a marvellous service,' he told her. 'Hoogie did Aimée proud. She should have been there – that's all I kept thinking. She would have loved it.'

'Aimee loathed the colour pink almost as much as she hated orchids,' Catarina told him. 'The very smell alone would have made her retch. She also hated going out. The only way to get her there was in a coffin.'

The old man studied her from the corner of his eyes.

'Were you and Aimée related?' he asked.

Catarina smiled.

'No – why?'

The old man shook his head.

'You look a bit like her and you just sounded like her too.' he said.

'Thank you,' Catarina laughed.

Hoogie took Catarina to one side when the wake was in full swing.

'A favour, my dear, for Aimée.'

'What is it, Hoogie?' — she was still trying to see if he walked with a limp. Perhaps that was why he'd chosen the orchids — to get back at his wife after all those years.

Stephen's father looked embarrassed. 'Aimée was very fond of you, my dear — I think she saw some of the spirit in you that she used to have as a young girl. She's left a you a few things and some money in the will — my solicitors will be contacting you in due course — but there's also a little something that she wanted you to do for her. I hope you won't have any objection.'

Catarina frowned. 'Is it about Stephen?'

Hoogie looked confused.

'Stevie? No. It's her ashes, Catarina — she wanted them sprinkled outside Bloomingdales. It was her favourite place when she used to go to New York. She wanted you to do it. I'm sorry, my dear. Here — I put them in something small so you could get them into your handbag.'

He passed Catarina a velvet glove box with 'Ralph Lauren' printed across the lid. Catarina took the box and began to laugh. Hoogie looked puzzled and hurt.

Even stuffed full of people the house seemed empty without Aimée. Catarina patted the glove box affectionately as she left Hoogie's study.

'Come on, girl, let's go and get something to eat,' she whispered. It was then that she first caught sight of Stephen. He was standing by one of the buffet tables near the garden, listening to earnest conversation from one of

338

Aimée's elderly brothers. She watched him quietly for a while. He looked taller and fuller. His jaw had filled out and his hair had straightened, so he could wear it longer and flatter. She had never seen him in a suit and tie before. He looked like a businessman, like his brothers. He looked sad and he looked grave. She wanted him to smile like he used to but she guessed correctly that those days were gone. She felt a pain of regret run through her as she looked at him. She still wanted him – all of him. She didn't want to know if he was with another woman. The pain would have been too much. She was surprised by the strength of her own emotion.

He felt her looking in the way that lovers do and turned suddenly to face her across the room. Catarina felt embarrassed at having been caught so squarely staring. She looked away and then looked back again.

'Stephen.' She mouthed his name silently, watching his hand tighten across the glass he was holding.

He turned back to his companion and Catarina watched him make his excuses politely. Then he was walking across to her and she could do nothing to stop him.

'I'm sorry about your mother, Stephen.' – It was the best she could do.

Stephen nodded.

'How are you doing, Catarina?' His voice killed her.

'OK.'

'Only OK?'

'Great. Things are going well. How about you, Stephen?' He had fine eyes, finer than Hoogie's now. He looked straight at her.

'Great.' He said the word quickly. She knew he was doing well – she had seen his name in the magazines. There had been those pictures of Aimée, too. He had made her look beautiful and young again, standing on the seashore in front of the house. She had been impressed by the quality of the shots. Even Aimée must have liked them.

'Am I embarrassing you, Catarina?' – When had he

become so sure of himself? She had heard he was a bastard to work for but she'd dismissed it as models' gossip until now.

'No, Stephen, you don't embarrass me.'

'You're losing your accent.'

She tried to smile.

'Can we talk somewhere alone? Would you mind?' he asked.

Catarina looked about. No-one looked at them. She wanted to leave before it was too late. Stephen touched her arm and she nearly screamed. Standing next to him she felt as though her body had been turned inside out, with the nerves on the outside.

'Catarina?' His voice was soft now. He led her through the crowds of people, nodding as he went, throwing words of thanks back in return for muttered condolences.

The sun was just setting as they walked down onto the beach.

'I'll miss her, Stephen,' Catarina said quietly.

Aimée was everywhere, watching them. She knew what was about to happen. She would have whipped up a storm to stop them if she could have. Maybe she was trying. A dull wind came from nowhere and Catarina closed her eyes as the sand sprayed her face.

'Are you cold?' Stephen asked. She said no. She had gooseflesh on her arms, though. They walked in silence until it was dark and the house was a small glow-worm of light, wriggling in the distance.

Then they stopped.

Stephen took her by the shoulders and turned her face towards him. She wanted to kiss him. She wanted to be fucked by him. It was a body thing – she couldn't help herself, it was something she wanted badly. She had no control.

He pushed her back against some rocks and her insides caved in like a house of cards.

He didn't kiss her on the mouth, he fell to his knees and

kissed her groin instead. It was like licking your fingers and touching a battery to test it. She jumped as her flesh zinged with surprise.

He was more confident than the last time. He stood again and pushed her dress down over her shoulders and ran his tongue over the tops of her breasts. She whispered his name and grasped his head, her fingers pulling through his hair. She could feel the cold slime of the rock against her bare back and the warm heavy softness of Stephen on her front. He was her love – that was the only thought – her body longed for him.

He pulled up her skirt and she closed her eyes. Then she felt his prick against her thighs and she cried out with relief as he entered her.

'It's there, Stephen, it's there!' Her legs wrapped about him as he pushed deeper inside. It was the best moment – the one to last forever. She started to cry and he called out to her. She saw the lights of boats out at sea and she wanted most of all for them to die there together – to forget everything she had to remember and to live for and to end her life alone in Stephen's arms.

He came quietly, turning inside her, his face taut with pain.

She kissed his face, whispering to him, telling him she loved him until he was still. They became cold and he pulled away from her and she felt a hole of emptiness open up inside.

She felt something on the sand beneath her feet. Aimée's box was lying there, waiting. She had been with them all the time.

'Stephen . . .' she began, but he stopped her. He was getting dressed.

'I'm getting married, Catarina,' he told her. 'I just wanted to say goodbye.'

52

Catarina dressed smartly that day: a Donna Karan skirt suit in neutral jersey, matching tights and a pair of suede-trimmed La Crasia gloves. Tony suggested a hat but she thought that was going too far.

'Aimée wore hats to town,' he told her in the stubborn tone he used sometimes – so then a hat it had to be. She felt like a dork but Tony said she carried it well.

They took the subway to 59th Street, she and Aimée – Aimée travelling in a plastic carrier in case her lid got loose in the wind. It had been blowing since the funeral and Catarina was sure by now that Stephen's mother was responsible.

Tony had played Judy Garland on the stereo in Aimée's honour as they were leaving the apartment. He chose 'Rainbow', which Catarina doubted Aimée would have liked, though she found herself crying buckets with Tony before it came to the end. He offered to make the trip with them but Catarina refused because it was enough of a farce already and she knew he would only cry more if he were there too.

In the end she cried enough for two anyway. She should never have spoken to Aimée en route – it only reminded her how much she missed sparring with the woman.

'Did you know he was marrying?' she asked the glove box. 'I sure hope it's someone you approve of, Aimée, because I can't stand this damned wind around much longer. At least she won't be a murdering little whore like myself. Did you know we made love again, down by the

342

seashore?' The wind blew her skirt around her knees in reply.

'He got me back, Aimée – you would have been proud of your son. He gave me back all the pain I threw at him and then some more. Did you put him up to it? Well done if you did. The trouble is, I don't know if I can stand it. I need you to talk to, Aimée, I need your help and your advice. Why did you have to leave me? Why did you have to go?'

They stood outside Bloomingdales, watching the shoppers go in. Catarina had thought of going at night but Tony had been appalled at the idea – Aimée would only have visited when the store was open. She either went out in grand style or not at all.

She hoped no one would watch her. She felt she looked so furtive there waiting that it was a wonder she wasn't arrested. How much ash would there be in the box? It felt heavy enough. She clutched it to her chest a while as they stood watching.

'Goodbye Aimée!'

The wind took care of the ashes. They missed the store completely and whipped up Lexington Avenue instead, tearing down the street like a bird freed from its cage. Two elderly men spluttered as Aimée blew into their eyes. A wealthy-looking woman got Aimée on her cashmere coat. Then what was left of Aimée blew upward in a spiral and Catarina laughed and didn't stop.

'Goodbye! Goodbye Aimée!'

She shouted it out loud now – she no longer cared if people looked. She couldn't see them anyway – her eyes were too full of tears.

The model was young and new and classy. Her hair was the colour of corn husks and she had eyes and legs like Bambi. She was also nervous.

'Hold the shampoo bottle a little higher, honey. Not like

343

that – closer to your head. Can we get a little more high-light on that fringe? Let's get the suds on her nose now. Don't move, honey – there's a good girl. Don't squint your eyes – I know the soap stings a bit. Good.'

A shot was taken – the first for an hour. Everyone relaxed except the model. She couldn't see beyond the lights. She couldn't see Catarina sitting watching her from the shadows.

'How is she doing?' – the photographer was a friend. Catarina had worked for him a couple of times in the past week. He liked Catarina – she knew how to drink vodka.

'She's OK. A bit scared – you know how it is. Did Jack show you those shots I sent?'

Catarina nodded, biting at her fingernail. Her eyes didn't leave the girl on the set for one second.

'She's very beautiful,' she said.

'Are you hot for her or something?' the photographer asked. He threw himself into a canvas chair beside her and took a slug of beer from a bottle. 'Because I think you'll be unlucky if you are – she's engaged to be wed, my dear – to a colleague of mine, in fact. She's first-generation, no less – you can tell the minute she opens her mouth. His family are loaded – it should be what the rags call "the society wedding of the year".'

'I know,' was all Catarina said. The photographer passed her the bottle and she swallowed some beer and coughed.

Lisbeth Alexander. She'd looked the girl's name up on the files. Lisbeth – not Elizabeth or Lizzie. Soon to be Mrs Van Doren. She was exactly what Aimée had wanted – young, classy, fresh as new-baked cookies.

Catarina walked into the model room and turned the lights on around the mirror. She was beautiful but exotic. Her hair was too short, her neck too long and her mouth too wide. Her dark eyes slanted upward over her cheekbones. Lisbeth was pretty, like a kitten. Catarina looked more like a large wildcat.

'Oh, I'm sorry – are you modelling in here today, too?' Lisbeth stood behind her, smiling and polite.

'No – I just left something from a shoot yesterday. Did you find a packet of edible knickers lying around anywhere?'

Lisbeth shuddered and looked away. 'No. Sorry.'

Catarina smiled at her. 'That was a joke,' she said. Lisbeth laughed politely. Then she held out her hand. Catarina shook it.

'Catarina Kirkova – The Cat. I'm with Jack Palitzo.'

'Lisbeth Alexander – I'm with Jack too.'

'Really? What a coincidence.' Catarina smiled and Lisbeth shuddered a little again. Catarina yawned and stretched.

'I have to go – I've got a shoot in SoHo in thirty minutes. Nice to meet you – I expect we'll see one another again some time.'

When Catarina left the studio she got into the lift and punched the wall till her hand ached. Why? Why did she still want Stephen so badly? Why did meeting that girl only make her want him more? Why couldn't she drop it and get on with her life – that was complicated enough already, she didn't need any more diversions. And why did Lisbeth have to be so nice?

She phoned Jack from a call box in the street.

'Jack? That show I turned down for next week? Who else is in it? OK – can I change my mind? Sure? It's not too late – they didn't book anyone else? Good. Book me in.'

The show was not a big one and the models were behaving badly. None of them were top names yet and so most of them carried on as they thought the supermodels did, disappearing from rehearsals to screw their second-league rock star boyfriends and fighting about which clothes they were going to wear and who was to go on for the longest.

There was no fighting over the finale – Lisbeth was to be the bride. The dress had been specially made for her and it was rumoured to be like the one she would wear at her own wedding.

Catarina arrived early and looked at the dress. It was exquisite and tasteful and she knew she would have looked like hell in it. She thought of her own marriage to Alex and wondered for the first time whether she could get a divorce. Then she wondered why she had wondered that. She didn't plan to get married again so what did it matter? Who could she marry anyway, when she had a past like she did? Alex had been the right man for her – he was the only man who had worse secrets to hide than she.

She sat next to Lisbeth and helped her with her choreography. She discovered Lisbeth was bright, clever and funny, which drilled her through with jealousy, right down to the bone and into the marrow.

'Is your boyfriend coming to the show?' she asked as they went through the final run-through. Lisbeth shook her head and her hair bounced like rubber.

'He's busy. He's on a shoot in the Caribbean. I expect you know he's a photographer – it's been in all the papers.'

'I must have missed them,' Catarina said. She helped tie Lisbeth's necktie. 'Does he go abroad much?' she asked.

'Now and again,' Lisbeth told her. 'He's done really well this year. He inherited some money when his mother died so he can afford staff for the New York studio, which means he can accept commissions abroad. He goes to England in a few weeks. We were hoping to get married before he went but we've had to put it off because some of my family couldn't get over in time.'

She heard her cue then and shot out on stage. She was not a good catwalk model, Catarina noted. Then she remembered how bad she had been before she had had lessons in Paris. It didn't matter about Lisbeth's walk, though – Lisbeth was going to marry Stephen.

Jack Palitzo was trimming his nasal hair when the call came through from Saint Lucia.

'Jack?' – The voice sounded angry.

'Clive?' Jack recognized the voice of Stephen's location manager. ' What's up, mate?'

'One of your girls, Jack – the fair one.'

Jack clicked his fingers for one of his bookers to get him the worksheet for the shoot. 'Zeedee?' he asked, running his finger down the page.

'She's bolted, Jack, fucked off the island. We've got five more days to go and she's vanished. One day she was OK and then she gets a call from some paper asking if it's true her husband's screwing some singer in France. They said they were running it on their gossip page. It's fucked up the shoot, Jack! Sort it out, for Chrissake!'

'I'll send you a replacement, Clive. Don't worry. Relax.' Jack's cool under fire was legendary.

'You'd fucking better, Jack – Stephen's off his fucking head.'

'Don't worry, Clive.'

'Fucking try not to out here!'

'Ciao.'

Jack put the phone down and did a quick minute's chanting. Then he jumped into action.

'Dessie, get on the phone and find out who's available for a trip to the Caribbean, leaving yesterday. Someone as much like Zeedee as possible – is her bloke screwing around, by the way –?' He broke off suddenly. Catarina was sitting in the booking hall, smiling at him. Something was wrong here – Catarina never sat in reception smiling.

'She'll need to have had all the jabs, by the way . . .'

'*I've* had them, Jack.'

'Catarina? How come?'

'Just in case. You never know.'

Jack Palitzo narrowed his eyes. There was a suitcase under her seat.

'What the hell — you'll do. Get Dessie to give you the details.'

53

The location manager met Catarina from the plane in a hired car.

'You just have to be Jack's Cat,' he told her. 'I heard of you before – some scene over in Paris, wasn't it? Some old guy croaked while you were on the job? Any chance on trying the same with a man in the first flush of cardiac youth? Eh?'

Catarina looked out of the window.

'You had Jack yet? I hear he has all his girls. Four at a time is what I heard. You know he's got connections? The name Palitzo means a lot in Sicily, know what I mean? You're Russian, aren't you? You ever seen *The Godfather?* Or *Goodfellas?* You must have seen *The Godfather* – everyone's seen that. Marlon Brando, remember? With the mouthful of lint wadding. Look – I can do it too – lend me your panties and I'll show you my impression.' He laughed loudly at his own joke.

'You work for Stephen?' Catarina asked him.

'Yeah?' – His expression had a 'so what?' look to it.

Catarina shook her head a couple of times. 'He must have been desperate, hiring lowlife dirt like you. I though he would have more taste.'

Clive looked at her out of the corner of his eye. 'You want to watch your mouth, I can get you back on the next plane to New York before your little arse has got so much as a glimpse of the sun.'

Catarina smiled. 'I don't think so.'

'Can't you take a joke?' Clive stopped the car outside a

small beachfront hotel. Two small children ran out to get Catarina's luggage.

'Does Stephen know I've replaced Zeedee?' she asked.

Clive shook his head. 'I did all the arrangements with Jack. Stevie just wanted to know there was a broad coming out here. I don't bother him with minor details like names.'

'Good.' Catarina smiled. 'Get my large bag, will you?' she asked Clive, 'It's too heavy for those poor little children to carry.' She walked into the hotel, leaving Clive cursing in the car.

Stephen was working at a location along the beach. Catarina changed out of her dress and into a bikini and pulled a large straw sunhat onto her head. The white sand burnt the soles of her feet as she walked across to the shoot. There was a model standing on a rock out at sea and Stephen was bent over a tripod on top of a high ridge. Catarina found a dry rock and sat down to watch them.

There was a human chain passing messages from Stephen to the model. The girl looked nervous on the rock with the sea lapping around her toes but as soon as shooting started she was professional enough not to let it show. The long dress she was wearing looked expensive. Catarina wondered what the designer who had lent it would think if they could see the hem getting soaked with salt water.

'Turn your face into the sun!' – Stephen sounded as if he was on a short fuse. The heat was intense and he was stripped to the waist. His back was brown but she guessed his front would be white, like most photographers she knew who spent their time on location bent over their cameras.

The sun hit the reflector boards and everyone was temporarily blinded. Stephen straightened and waved his arms to signal the shot was done. Four men came along the beach, dragging a huge turtle in two canvas slings.

'Thank Christ you found one!' Stephen called out. He

walked across to Clive and the others, his hands on his hips.

'We didn't find it, Stephen, we had it flown in from a zoo in Florida.'

'I'm not sitting on that,' the model said, wrinkling her nose. 'It's filthy, look! It stinks, too!'

'So would you, darling, after a long flight in this heat. Give it a quick scrub in the sea, Damien.'

Puffing, cursing and sweating they dragged it into the sea, where it promptly swam off.

'Jesus! Get the fucker back! Quick! Jesus!'

Clive plunged into the surf in his Stephen Sprouse deluxe label jeans then came splashing out again screaming when he realized what he'd done.

'Do these shrink? Do these fucking shrink?' he shrieked. Everyone else just watched.

'Swim for it, baby,' Stephen said quietly, watching the turtle Olympic-style breast-stroke its way to freedom.

'Oh Jesus, three thousand dollars these jeans cost me!' Clive pulled them off and stood there wringing them out into the sea.

Catarina laughed at the sight of his bare white arse, pock-marked with cellulite.

Stephen turned towards her for the first time, shielding his eyes from the sun. He paused for a moment, staring at her, before walking across the beach in a rage.

'What the hell are you doing here?' – His lips looked pale against his tanned face. His hair had bleached in the sun. Women would have paid hundreds of dollars for a similar frosting effect.

'Stephen.' Catarina stood up. She felt more evenly matched that way. They met eye-to-eye.

'I asked what you are doing here, Catarina.'

Clive heard the anger in his boss's tone and stopped fretting over his jeans to listen.

Catarina looked across at him.

'Ask your pet gorilla, Stephen, he was the one who booked me when Zeedee let you down.'

Stephen turned to Clive. '*You* did this?' he asked. 'Why?'

Clive started towards them. 'We were stuck, boss – Jack suggested Catarina. I didn't know there'd be a problem.'

Stephen looked back at Catarina. He couldn't keep his eyes off her.

'Go away, Clive,' he said. 'Go and get another turtle.'

'But that was on loan, Stevie, they'll never lend us another if they know we lost that one . . .'

'I said go and find a turtle!' Stephen shouted. Clive hurried away, looking out to sea in the hope that the other turtle might return.

'Go and see the stylist about your outfits,' Stephen told Catarina, 'This isn't a holiday – I want you ready on the cliffs over there in under an hour.'

'Yes boss!' She saluted and smiled.

Catarina stood at the cliff-edge, studying the sea that rose up in white wood-shaving curls below her. She wore a long sheer ash-green silk dress and a circle of fresh white lilies around her head. The stylist had left her face bare, apart from the brows, which the make-up artist had thickened with pencil.

The sky had darkened as they clambered over the rocks and Clive said he'd been warned it might rain.

The dress blew around Catarina's legs as Stephen took a light reading and they heard the first complaining grumble of thunder in the distance as he called to Catarina that he was ready.

'Raise your arms. Drop them – slowly. Spread the fingers. Now turn your head around to me. – Do something about that seam, Kate.'

Catarina stood patiently while the seam of the dress was pressed while she wore it.

A huge streak of lightning tore down the grey sky.

'Jesus!' Everyone jumped, apart from Catarina. Clive ran for cover and the stylist and Stephen's assistant followed him.

'Stevie!' Clive called to his boss. They were under a tree, out of the rain, but he'd read trees were the wrong place to be in a storm.

'The dress is getting soaked!'

But Stephen went on shooting in silence. Catarina hung onto her headdress and he shot her looking out to sea.

'Lean towards the wind. Good. Look scared. Bring your arms into your body now. Chin a little higher. Did anyone remember the Polaroid? Your feet – watch your feet, they look clumsy. Better. No – yes, that's it.'

There was another crackling bolt and the crew beat a retreat to the hotel. Stephen continued to shoot, unaware they were alone on the cliff. His voice became quieter but Catarina still heard him.

'Sideways – profile. Arms higher again. Don't worry about the dress. Just a minute . . .' he took another reading as the sky darkened.

'Hold it there – now eyes to camera.'

Catarina looked straight at the camera. And at Stephen. The sky overhead erupted. Stephen stopped shooting. Neither of them moved. Catarina's eyes could not have been photographed – the message they held was for Stephen alone, and he knew it.

He stood up – stared at her.

'Why did you come here?' His voice was quiet now. His hair hung in limp wet curls around his neck. His face was dripping.

Catarina stared back at him. She didn't answer.

'Catarina? Why? What did you want? It wasn't coincidence, was it? Tell me why you're here.' He walked towards her and she backed away a pace or two.

Stephen froze immediately, horrified. He held a hand out to stop her.

'Don't step back, Catarina – mind – mind the edge of the cliff – Christ!'

She still stared at him. Her dress clung to her body like a pair of wet wings.

'Catarina!'

'I came to see you, Stephen.' Her voice was husky and her accent as thick as it had been when she first arrived in New York, so that he barely understood what she said.

'Why?' He was rigid with fear – he suddenly thought she might die there in front of him.

'Why did you want to see me, Catarina?'

Her eyes were frightening. 'You've changed, Stephen.'

'I changed because of you, Catarina. You didn't like me as I was – I figured I had nothing to lose.'

'Did you change because of me or for me, Stephen?'

'Because of you. Why? What's the difference?'

'Don't marry Lisbeth, Stephen. You don't love her.'

Stephen let out a laugh that had no humour in it. 'So that's it. Who do I love then, Catarina? You, I suppose. And what do I do about it? Cancel the wedding just to follow you around the globe whining at your heels like some idiot dumb-brained dog? Will you allow me to fuck you now and again like you did before, Catarina? Will that be my treat for being so faithful? What is it you want? Do you have any idea? Do you even know yourself why you followed me out here? Eh? Tell me!'

Catarina stepped towards him at last, away from the cliff edge.

'I followed you out here to tell you I'm pregnant, Stephen,' she whispered. 'I came out here to tell you I'm carrying your child.'

54

Aimée had relatives in England and, on her marriage to Hoogie, had inherited a large house in Kent. They had spent their honeymoon there and Aimée had discovered something that all Hoogie's family had been aware of for years – when you were left alone with him he was as boring as hell. They had started their family there and then, so that she would never have to be alone with him again.

Stephen had pretty much forgotten the house since his childhood holidays there. Nothing much stirred as he looked at it now. It was big – he could see that it was beautiful, too, but he couldn't feel its beauty inside, where it mattered. He had felt the same about several women in his life.

There was something chaotic about the architecture. The oldness of it all made him feel uneasy. When he looked from the front door he couldn't see any other houses, only lawns and trees. He found all that space chaotic, too. The beach at Boston had been spacious but he'd had the sea there for company. Lawns and trees just weren't the same. The sea had its own life – lawns and trees just stared back dumbly.

'You don't like it here.'

He was down by the lake. It was dark. Catarina had brought him a drink.

'No – it's OK. It's like – I know I should love it but I can't. Do you know what I mean?'

Catarina nodded. 'Like with me,' she said quietly.

Stephen turned to her. 'No – not like you. Not even

remotely like you, Catarina. With you it's always been the other way around. I always knew I shouldn't love you but I couldn't stop myself.'

Catarina watched the black surface of the water. 'You could hate me for that, then.'

Stephen sighed. 'Don't keep picking at it, Catarina. I don't hate you. I hate myself. I feel guilty – I feel angry – I feel as though I don't know myself any more. I was paid to come here to work and now I don't know if I can do that, either. You always act like you want me to hate you. Would it make you happier if I did? Did you love me more when I used to hate you?'

She was so close to him. How could he tell her that each time she got close to him he felt the breath go out of his body? His love for her was awful. He was terrified she would leave him again. He had become pathetic inside and it was a struggle not to become pathetic on the outside, too. Did women want so much love? Insecurity riddled him through like a disease.

He put his hand out to Catarina and felt her shiver as she took it. He pulled her close enough to kiss.

'Aimée would hate what we are doing,' she said.

'So let her turn in her grave,' Stephen told her.

It was late autumn and she only had a thin dress on. He took off his coat and put it round her.

'Are you OK?'

She nodded.

'Sure?'

She smiled at his fussing and they kissed again. Catarina tasted of apples. Everything in England tasted of apples. Or smelt of woodsmoke.

He wondered how she would look when she was fat. The child was his hope of security. When she was fat they'd be OK. In the meantime he tried to feed her up so she'd get fat anyway. He knew he was disgusting but it made him feel better, like he was in charge of the campaign. He'd even tried all the old clichés about eating for two.

Anything. He would stoop that low – he even disgusted himself.

Was he any better than Alex, who beat her to keep her ugly? Was that why Alex had done it, to keep her with him for always? He didn't feel so bad, though. Forcing food down couldn't be as bad as smashing bones.

They'd changed the bed in the house – Catarina had refused to lie down in the one he had been conceived in.

'Were you all made here, Stephen? All your brothers and sisters?'

'Ah-huh. It was a sort of family ritual.' – The story wasn't true, of course, but he liked the way it fascinated her.

Jack had been furious with him for taking her away. He'd called Stephen a scumbag and many other things too. He'd accused him of turning one of his best new models into a fucking housewife. He'd also accused him of screwing up Lisbeth's life. Stephen had tried to tell him he had no choice but in the end he'd wondered why he was explaining his private thoughts to some elderly Al Pacino in a white towelling jacket and lizard shoes, and had got angry instead.

When he made love to Catarina now it was like a sweet pain rippling through his body and he wondered if she felt it too.

He was on a six-month contract but he knew he would keep her there until the baby was born. If he could. The doubt made him shudder.

'Do all these trees ever piss you off, Catarina? he asked. She sounded surprised.

'No. I love them. Why? Do you hate them?'

'No,' he said, covering his tracks. 'I just wondered if you did.'

Of course he grew to love the place eventually and the lake and the trees and he even became comfortable with his love for Catarina after a time. There was sunshine in December and snow and he drove back from London and it just hit him how wonderful it all was and how happy he could be if he'd just stop clinging to the edge and jump in. That was the day Lisbeth had called, though he'd known nothing about her visit as she'd been gone before he got back.

Catarina had been shocked at the sight of her. She'd just jumped out of a cab and stood there in the drive, staring. Grief had made her ugly. Her skin looked as bleak as boiled marrow and her hair had got dull. Her clothes were wrong, too. Jack must've been tearing his hair at the sight of her.

'Is Stephen here?' was the first thing she'd said to Catarina.

'He's in London.' Catarina looked healthy and well in denim jeans and Stephen's T-shirt. She had been trying to cook a Russian meal for his dinner. She stepped back as Lisbeth walked inside the house.

'I was going to live here after we were married.'

She took in the wood-panelled walls and the worn rugs on the floors. She picked up a small *cloisonné* vase and studied it, running her hand across the blue enamel surface.

'I suppose Aimée picked these things.'

'I suppose so,' Catarina told her.

'She had wonderful taste.' Lisbeth placed the vase back carefully.

'Why are you here, Lisbeth?' Catarina noticed the girl's hands were shaking.

'I came to talk to you, Catarina. I came to tell you you're making a mistake. I came to tell you Stephen's not right for you.'

She turned to face Catarina and her eyes were full of tears. Catarina looked away, embarrassed.

'You don't love him enough, Catarina. He was going to marry me. I know you think you want him but I want to know for how long. You're famous, Catarina – I'll never be that good. You've got your career, you don't need a husband, too.

'You didn't even know that vase was there, did you? I

bet you never noticed the table it's standing on, either. It's a New England pine tavern table, Catarina. Hoogie gave it to Aimée on their fifth anniversary. Those rugs are Kazak prayer rugs, worth about two thousand dollars each. They were Aimée's mother's – she never cared for them much, which is why she put them in here. I think they're exquisite. Imagine their history – they're nearly two hundred years old.'

'I didn't know you'd been here before, Lisbeth,' Catarina said. The girl smiled. 'Oh, I never was. I just found out about these things. I was interested – they are part of Stephen's family history. Did you know he nearly died in that lake out the back? Hoogie bought a little wooden boat for him and he took it out himself when he was five and the boat capsized. The gardener saved him and Hoogie gave the man ten thousand dollars. He still lives in the village – I expect Stephen's taken you to meet him by now. His name's Bert Smith, he . . .'

'Get out.' Catarina held the door open.

Lisbeth stared at her.

'You know what you're doing is wrong, Catarina.'

'Get out!'

'Stephen told me you're pregnant.' Lisbeth's heels clicked across the parquet. 'Why don't I believe that? Why do I think you made that one up?'

Catarina closed her eyes and sighed.

'Yes, you're very clever, Lisbeth. I lied to Stephen just to steal him from you. It was the only thing I could think of at the time. I love him so desperately, you see. I would have done anything.'

Lisbeth's face screwed up. 'Dammit, Catarina, tell me the truth!'

'I've told you, Lisbeth, now get out of here. I feel sorry for you but I don't want you here again. Go.'

'Aimée was scared of you, Catarina. She was frightened of what you'd do to Stephen. She knew you'd kill him eventually. She hated you for that – Hoogie told me.'

'Get out.'

Catarina slammed the door on the girl. She was wrong. She was lying. She loved Stephen – more than a kid like that ever could. She would never hurt him again – she was sure of that much.

Catarina clung to Stephen in bed that night.

'Would you have wanted me if I wasn't having your child?' she asked.

Stephen groaned and kissed her face. 'Jesus, Catarina, why d'you ask these things? I thought we were happy.'

'I am happy, Stephen.'

They laid a while in the silence. 'I always wanted you, Catarina. I always will, you know that.' Why could he never remember if she'd told him she loved him?

She heard the trees creaking in the garden and the noise reminded her of her mother. 'I love you, Stephen.'

He kissed her, held her tight. Then he made love to her and, this time, the pain that rippled through his body hurt a little less.

Eve and Freddie spent Christmas alone that year. It was a promise they'd always made themselves: 'One year without all the noise and the shouting and the wretchedness of family. One year by ourselves.' – Now the stress of being carefree masters of their own destiny was getting to them.

Eve dropped the pudding on the floor and wanted to scream out but she couldn't – they were happy. Freddie gave the dog his lunch after she burnt it and she wanted to strangle him there and then but she smiled instead, though he'd done something funny because above all else they had to remember to be happy. It was the relatives that had been causing them grief all those years. Eve was slowly realizing it was them, after all. The realization made her relax a little and she threw an eggnog at Freddie when he told her her hair looked like shit. Then the dog threw his dinner up on the floor and they both laughed properly for the first time that holiday.

The phone rang as they were wiping their eyes and sponging up the dog vomit. They looked at each other: 'No phone calls – remember?' Then Freddie shrugged. 'So what? We're on our knees scrubbing rugs by hand – so what if we break all the rules?'

Eve took the call. It was Stephen – a long way away.

'Stevie?' She always shouted – she never trusted the phone system long distance. She shouted even though Stephen sounded as if he were in the next room.

'Stevie! how are you? Merry Christmas!'

'Merry Christmas, Eve.'

'How's the little earth mother? Freddie says to say hello. Don't ask to speak to him, though, he's doing a very important chore.'

'Catarina's fine, Eve. She's visiting neighbours. She loves it here. She's really well.'

'Good. What's wrong?' Eve didn't need to be an audioanalyst to spot the problem in Stephen's voice.

There was a long pause. Freddie looked curious and Eve shrugged at him: 'Search me!'

'Stevie? You still there?'

A long sigh.

'I need your advice, Eve. Catarina's got a job – a bloody brilliant job, as a matter of fact. She's been offered a top cosmetic account – the photographer worked with her a few months ago and put her face forward. They want someone new. It pays a fucking fortune, Eve.'

'So she got it! I heard she was on the shortlist. That's great, Stevie – you'll both be rich!'

'It's a year, Eve – the contract's for a year.'

'Oh. The baby.'

'The baby.'

This time it was Eve who sighed.

'What does Catarina say? Is she very disappointed?'

'She doesn't know yet, Eve.'

361

'What?'

'Jack phoned through the day before Christmas. I took the call and told him Catarina'd ring him back after I gave her the message. Then we took the phone off the hook for the holiday – Catarina's always complaining I get too many work calls here. I can't tell her, Eve. I can't take the risk.'

'Look – she may be pissed off, Stevie, but she still has to know what she's missed.'

'I can't tell her, Eve.'

'Stevie . . .'

'OK, I know I'm being unfair, right? I do have to tell her.'

'Of course you do. What are you scared of?'

'Nothing. I'll call you, OK?'

He put the receiver down and Eve was left staring at Freddie.

Catarina sat in the hospital, too tired to cry though her chest ached so much with tears she imagined she was having a heart attack – if she cared, which she didn't.

They came and lectured her at first and then the nurse gave her an injection to keep her quiet because she was disturbing the others with her grief. They even made her sign something to say she had been fully counselled before the operation because everyone sued everyone these days and they didn't want any trouble later.

She loved Stephen – that was the problem. She loved him but she had no right to – she had no rights at all – what was she thinking of, pretending to start a proper life? She should have stayed with Alex – he was all that she deserved. They were right for one another. Stephen was not her type. He was too good for her. Aimée was right all along. Aimée knew her for the tramp she really was. She had no choice. There were no options for her. She had known that the minute she had heard nurse Olga's voice again.

Catarina had phoned the hospital.

'You have to get your sister out of here, you know. The place is not fit for animals now. There is diphtheria here, too. Your sister can easily get diseases in the state she is in.'

'Where could she be taken?' Catarina sounded scared.

'To the city, where there are better hospitals. There is even a private hospital now – American-owned. I can get her a place there but I will need money – a lot of money.'

'What is the name of the hospital?' Catarina asked. 'I can find out their fees – maybe pay direct.'

The nurse's voice changed. 'Look – after you came out here I did some checking. I mean, it is a little strange that you should never have visited your sister for so long and when you did you had to be smuggled in like a criminal. I know they are looking for you, do you understand? Do you want them to trace you via your sister? I only need to make a phone call. I don't like having to cover for you.'

Catarina's face went white.

'I think it would be better if I made the arrangements for your sister's transfer, don't you?' – The nurse was pleased her guesswork had been so accurate. She sounded kinder now, as she had done before.

'Look – you don't want to be bothered with all that paperwork,' she told Catarina, 'just send me the money, like always, OK?'

Catarina had tried to snatch one last lungful of air before she drowned forever. She'd phoned New York – spoken to her booker.

'Will they still book me if I'm pregnant? Will they wait till I've had the baby? Can I get some of the money in advance?'

No to everything. Of course.

*   *   *

Eve was shooting in the studio for her new exhibition. The shoot had lasted six weeks already – she had started work straight after Christmas – and her nerves were blown to shreds. When her assistant appeared at her elbow during a particularly tricky moment she let off a stream of loud abuse and then apologized quickly.

'Sorry, sorry, sorry. Look – you should know better by now – what in hell is so urgent?'

'There's someone in reception to see you.' The girl looked embarrassed.

'Who? Jesus, who? A client? The police? Elvis Presley? Who? Who? Give me a name!'

The girl looked at her.

'Do you have a daughter, Eve?' she asked.

'What? A daughter? No – you know I don't.'

The girl shook her head. 'I don't know who it is, then. I thought she sounded like family. It's not that she looks like you or anything, but . . .'

Eve stalked off into reception. She hardly recognized Catarina at first, she looked so awfully ill. Her hair was dirty and her clothes were creased. Her eyes looked red, as though she hadn't slept in days.

'I thought you were in England,' Eve said. She didn't know what to say. Catarina seemed to sway a little before she sank back down onto one of the seats.

'Where's Stephen, Catarina? Is he OK? Is he with you?' – Eve couldn't help but become immediately protective of him.

'Stephen's still in England, Eve. He's OK.'

Eve took the seat beside her. 'He told you about the job, didn't he?' she asked.

Catarina nodded.

'Did you come over here to speak to Jack?'

'Sort of.'

'Do you think he can negotiate something for you?'

'There's nothing to negotiate, Eve, the job's mine.'

Eve stared at her.

'But what about the baby? Stevie said the job came with a long contract.'

'What baby, Eve?' Catarina turned to face her.

'What have you done, Catarina?'

'It was a good job, Eve. All the top names were up for it. Jack says I'll qualify for the title of Supermodel now. Do you know what the money is for this, Eve? Guess.'

'What have you done, Catarina? What happened to the baby?'

Catarina's shoulders started to shake. 'They'll be plenty of time for babies, Eve. You only get one chance at a job like this.'

'What about the baby?'

'I had a termination, Eve. Yesterday. I told Jack I'd take the job and then I went for the abortion. Things happen quick in New York. In Kent it took most of the day just to get a letter posted.'

'What about Stephen?' Eve watched the tear run down Catarina's face.

'I told him there was no baby, Eve. I told him there never had been. I told him I just said so to stop him marrying Lisbeth. He believed me, Eve. Swear you'll never tell him the truth!'

Eve leant her head back against the wall.

'Jesus, Catarina.'

'Swear you won't tell, Eve!'

Eve shook her head slowly. 'He didn't deserve this. He loved you, you know. You could have let him alone – he would have been happy enough with that Barbie doll he was going to marry.'

'I love him, Eve. I love him till it hurts. He would never have been happy with her, Eve – you know that.'

'He would if you were the only alternative.'

'I said I love him, Eve.'

'Well heaven help any man that you hate.'

'Where are you going?' Catarina sounded desperate.

'To phone him – to see if he's OK – to make sure he's still in one piece.'

'Don't tell him I'm here!' Catarina half rose from the chair and the blood went from her face. Eve rushed to grab her as she slid towards the floor.

'Are you alright, Catarina? Do you need a doctor?'

Catarina grabbed Eve's hand. 'You've got to help me, Eve. I know you hate me for what I've done to Stephen but I had no choice, believe me. I've got nowhere to go, Eve – Tony's abroad and he's rented the apartment. I'm frightened, Eve – the press are after me and I don't think I can handle it if all this gets out – please help me.'

Eve looked at Catarina. 'You can come and stay with Freddie and me for a few days,' she said, after a long pause. It was winter – she wouldn't have put a dog out in that weather.

55

London, 1994

A fax came through on Rick's machine.

Rick – you are a rodent.

– Short and sweet. Rick laughed. Oliver's fax was followed by Oliver's phone call but Rick had time to press the RECORD button on his answerphone before the ringing started.

'Rick?' Oliver sounded extra peeved now. Murderous, even. 'Rick, you bastard, I know you're on to something now. You owe me. We had a deal.' There was a pause. Rick leaned closer. Was Oliver crying?

'Rick. I know you're there. Phone me. I want my cut.'

Rick smiled. 'So sue me, sucker!' he whispered, and went back to his work.

56

Catarina fell apart faster than Eve and Freddie could put her back together again. It was like stitching seams with broken thread — emotions kept leaking out like stuffing from an old toy teddy. She drank a lot of vodka and, when she was drunk, she was fun for a while. When she sobered up, though, she became a pain in the ass. Eve got tired of hearing about Stephen — if she wanted him so badly then why didn't she stay with him and have his kid? — so Freddie took over the burden, sitting up with her until two or three in the morning, when the sleeping pills would finally work and she'd slump in the chair in front of him.

Amazingly, she still managed to work and she looked good — which Eve said was a curse rather than a blessing. It would take two hours to get her fully awake and ready in the morning but Freddie would drive her off to the studio and she'd behave herself in a hazy sort of a way. It appeared the photographers and their clients were none the wiser or, if they were, they had obviously seen worse.

By spring she seemed to be getting a little better. Freddie took her to the coast for the day and she enjoyed herself like a kid, eating junk foods and jumping into the sea.

'I think she's out of it,' Freddie told Eve that night. Eve was relieved. Catarina had somehow taken over their apartment and their lives. Eve had become fond of her by default — she would have loved Catarina like a daughter if her neediness had not been so wearing.

'God, I hope so,' she said. She was reading in bed. Freddie was studying a script. He'd been offered a good part in a Broadway play — his best offer for ages.

'You sound rather selfish, Eve,' he said.

'Selfish? No, Freddie, let's just call it relieved. I'll be happy when she gets out of this God-awful depression – happy for her and more than a little happy for us, too. She's dominated our lives for too long. Did you know this is the first night you've got to bed before two? I want us back to normal again. I want my place back and I want my husband back.'

Freddie looked at his wife over the top of his glasses. 'I told her she could stay as long as it takes,' he said.

'Jesus!' Eve slammed her book shut.

'She's like a child, Eve, she needs help.'

'I feel sorry for her, Freddie, but then I feel sorry for myself too. I also feel sorry for you and I feel sorry for Stephen. Most of all I feel sorry for Stephen, though I run a close second, thanks to self-pity. That's too much feeling sorry, Freddie. If Catarina goes, that cuts all that sorry by a half.'

'Did you hear from Stephen?' Freddie asked.

Eve shook her head. 'I tried ringing England again today. There's never any answer. Perhaps he's back in the 'States. I'd hate for him to know we've got Catarina here. That's another reason why she ought to go – it seems like we're taking sides.'

Freddie sighed. 'I shouldn't let it worry you, Eve – Stephen's a big boy now – I'm sure he can take care of himself.'

The following week the papers were all full of Stephen's marriage to Lisbeth. On the day of his wedding Catarina was taken to hospital with an overdose.

It was Freddie who found her. She was late getting up, as usual, only this time she hadn't answered him after an hour. When he looked in her room he found her still lying on her bed, curled into a ball like a squirrel. When he looked closer, her lips were blue and it was then that he panicked and ran to the phone.

His hands shook too hard to punch in the numbers. He was swearing all the time at his useless hands and he cursed the emergency services for taking too long to answer.

He wondered if he should have done something before phoning them. Mouth-to-mouth, maybe, or salt water to make her sick. Perhaps he had wasted vital minutes by phoning when he should have been saving her life instead. Perhaps she was already dead. He let out a huge animal cry of anguish that he had first used as King Lear in 'eighty-two.

They told him at the hospital that Catarina had just taken a few too many sleeping pills. As an oversight it was sloppy to say the least and as a suicide attempt it was grossly understated. Freddie plumped for the understated suicide but he told the doctors he was sure she'd just been careless. Then he phoned Eve and Jack.

Marco – Jack's sidekick – came to sort out the press. It was an everyday occurrence for him to handle – Jack's models were always playing at topping themselves. As an attention-grabber it was no longer effective. Freddie saw him headbutting a journalist in the car park. There was no-one hanging about there after that.

Catarina smiled when she saw Freddie waiting at her bedside. Her smile struck some chord deep inside him and he took her hand and cried real tears for the first time in forty years.

'I'm sorry, Freddie,' she whispered.

'So I should think.'

'I couldn't bear it any more, not when I saw the papers.'

Freddie's lips turned thin.

'Is Eve here? Does she know?'

'She called in on her way to the studio. I told her I'd ring. There was no great drama, really – the doctors said you'd be alright. They said you'd just have a sore throat from the stomach pump. It sounds disgusting. Don't ever try it again — he's not even nearly worth it.'

'Thank you, Freddie. You're the nearest thing to a father I've ever had.'

Freddie frowned.

'I thought your father was some wonderful Russian aristocrat,' he said.

'I hardly saw him,' Catarina whispered. 'He was always away.'

'Oh. Right.' Freddie tapped his knee thoughtfully.

'When can I come home?'

'Today, apparently.'

Eve would have had a coronary if she had heard Catarina call their place home. Freddie, on the other hand, felt rather happy.

Jack sent Catarina off to a health farm to recuperate. She had done the first big publicity shots for the cosmetic campaign but the job would start in earnest the following week and he wanted her looking good. He was proud of the fact that the story of her suicide attempt had not been leaked to the press. He had stifled many big stories in his time and always by the same method. He was a great believer in the phrase: 'Actions speak louder than words.' He also believed violence spoke louder than most other actions, too.

Freddie started rehearsals that week but he still felt oddly lonely. He walked through Times Square on the way back from the theatre one evening and stopped in his tracks when he saw Catarina staring down at him from a giant billboard some four storeys up in the sky. Her face measured two building widths across and her eyes were the size of a bus. He almost got knocked down, staring. It was strange equating that happy, mysterious, seductive face with the poor little wretch they were housing *chez* Horowitz. Pride puffed him out like a balloon and he

371

almost stopped other strangers he saw staring up at her to tell them he knew her.

He remembered her remark about him being like a father to her and in his imagination she became his adopted daughter. He decided that was what he would tell one of these strangers if he happened to catch their eye for long enough.

Her eyes followed him wherever he walked. He tested the idea out, just to see. They were staring at everyone in that square, all at the same time. He wished Eve had taken the photo, so that he could have been proud on two scores. In the end, his legs began to ache from all the walking and he noticed he was not in the best sort of company and that it was getting dark, so he hailed a cab.

'What do you think of the new hoarding?' he asked the driver. They were still within range – the eyes still stared at them.

'What hoarding's that?' barked the driver, slamming on the brakes as a druggie strolled out into their path. Freddie sighed. They'd gone out of sight. He changed the subject and talked about the weather instead.

Jack's limo was waiting at the airport when Catarina flew back from the health spa.

'I'm to take you straight to the agency,' the driver told her. She wanted to argue but instead leant her head back onto the cream leather headrest and relaxed. She wanted to see Tony first – she badly needed to talk to him. She also wanted to see Eve, to find out if she'd heard from Stephen but she supposed going to the agency would do as well.

Jack welcomed her with a hug and a work schedule so full of appointments she could find no space for eating or sleeping.

'I thought the cosmetics firm had me under an exclusive contract,' she said.

Jack laughed. 'No such thing at this agency.'

She pointed to the list. 'What are all these appointments here?' she asked. '"D.F." – the bookings are regular, twice a week.'

Jack folded his arms. 'Doctor Frickstein,' he said. 'I booked them personally.'

'For what?' Catarina looked surprised. 'I'm not sick.'

Jack laughed. 'He's a shrink, honey. You need some help. Nearly all my girls go to him at some time or another. He's the best there is – he'll sort your problems out for you, don't worry.'

'I'm not going to a psychiatrist,' Catarina told him.

Jack leant across his desk. 'He's an analyst and you are,' he said. 'I've got a lot of money riding on you now, honey. You already tried to do away with yourself once. I just want to make sure you don't go trying it again. I sat on the story the first time but we might not be so lucky the next. People don't like 'poor-little-me' models who earn thousands for a job and then try to top themselves. You lose fans that way, honey. Homely housewives who live in trailers with four kids and a debt as long as my schlong start to see that sort of thing in context, understand? They stop buying the products your face is pushing because they figure you're some kind of a ditso. Do you see what I'm saying? It's not that I'm not sympathetic or nothing but we don't want you looking like some spoiled gimpy ratbag now, do we?'

Catarina chewed on her nail.

'You see what you're doing to yourself?' He pointed to her hand. 'Self-mutilation they call that. I've seen it all before, Catarina, next thing you'll be cutting yourself and the scars will show up in the shots. Did they dry you out at the spa? I know a week ain't much but you look better, you look hot. The clients will love you. Did you see the reaction to the shot in Times Square? The whole of New York is hot for you, Catarina, and by this time next week it will be the whole world.'

373

Catarina stared at him, thinking he was a bit mad. She hadn't read the papers and she hadn't driven through Times Square. She asked the driver to take her on the way over to Tony's. She saw her face up there but somehow she didn't believe it. The driver had a grin like a watermelon.

'Fucking great!' he kept repeating.

He parked Jack's limo in view of the hoarding and climbed into the back with Catarina and they both got drunk on Jack's champagne. They were so drunk the driver couldn't drive any more and they abandoned the car there and caught a couple of cabs instead.

Tony poured Catarina a huge bubble bath, like he used to before she was famous and he even made her her favourite sandwich, which was a slab of British milk chocolate between two buttered pieces of sliced white bread.

'Don't eat it all, or you'll be sick,' he warned her. He always said that when he made them for her. Sometimes she ate them all and she'd never been sick yet. The heat of the bath made the chocolate go runny, which was the secret of the truly great chocolate sandwich. Tony sat on the side of the bath, watching her.

'Tell me about your love life, Tony,' she said, smiling at him.

'Tell me about your own.' He dipped a hand in the water.

'I don't have a love life.'

'You're in love, though.'

'You can't be in love with nothing, Tony. There's nothing there for me to love.'

'You've got chocolate round your mouth.'

'So?'

'You're supposed to be a supermodel, Catarina.'

'It's my evening off.' She pushed a toe out of the water and flicked suds into his face.

'I wish you were straight, Tony.'

He looked at her, with her shrimp-pink bath skin and the brown chocolate around her mouth.

'Take my word for it, Catarina,' he said, '*I'm* glad I'm not.'

57

Eve took some black-and-white shots of Catarina, around the apartment. They printed up grainy and natural-looking and were syndicated around the world, to most of the more intellectual magazines.

Jack was delighted — he said the pictures gave Catarina class. They were more artistic than the average model shot and Eve Horowitz and Catarina Kirkova became linked in most people's minds after that.

One of the shots inspired particular interest from the press — it showed Freddie, who had received warmish reviews for his role in the Broadway play, with his arms around Catarina, comforting her while she was crying. Freddie liked the shot, Catarina loathed it and the newspapers loved it.

It occurred to Freddie as he studied the shot that he didn't look old enough to be Catarina's father. He stopped wearing suits *à la* Larry Olivier and started to model himself on Kenneth Branagh instead. He grew his hair a little longer and asked his director if he thought a beard wouldn't suit the character he was playing.

He took Catarina to the Four Seasons one night when Eve was working and was delighted when a colleague at another table caught his eye with a knowing wink and not one of the waiters referred to Catarina as his daughter.

That was the night that Freddie became extremely stupid.

Back at the apartment he plied Catarina with a large vodka. She was foolish to drink it because Jack had made her promise to stay off the booze. Then he drank one himself, which meant they were both out of their heads. Then he snorted coke, which he'd heard everyone under the age of thirty did on a regular basis. He'd seen members of his cast do it at the theatre and felt like the disapproving pater when they'd seen him watching. One of them even hid the stuff when he walked into her changing room unannounced. Freddie desperately needed to be accepted by the younger folk again.

'Catarina?' – She appeared to be asleep. He stroked her forehead and she smiled, which encouraged him. He stripped his clothes off in a trice. His body was good for its age, which was not saying much. Still, love conquered all and he was suddenly unafraid of physical imperfections.

He quoted Shakespeare to her. She needed him – he was sure of that. He was kindly and gentle and he would not break her heart like a younger man might. Like Stephen did.

'Catarina. My darling.'

He looked closely at her face. She plucked a chord of nostalgic longing deep inside him and its vibrations were painful. Like the smell of honeysuckle or baked apples and cloves, she reminded him of his childhood. He felt he had loved her before, in some other life and his prick raised its head in agreement.

'Stephen?' She was smiling as she kissed him. His prick shrivelled to a nutmeg at the sound of the other man's name.

'Catarina – darling – it's Freddie, not Stephen. Forget about Stephen, dear, he's caused you enough trouble already.'

'Freddie?' Catarina turned to face him and he sighed at the sight of her.

'I love you, Catarina. I want to protect you. You're like a darling child to me. Let me kiss you.'

He kissed her on the mouth. She liked being held by him – she felt strangely safe there. She noticed he was naked.

He wanted to fuck her, then. She felt like a whore. She laughed. It suddenly seemed so amusing. 'Freddie! Act your age!'

His face looked sad and huge. 'I'm serious, Catarina. I love you.'

'You're drunk.'

'No. I've loved you since you came here. The drink just gave me the courage to admit it. Don't laugh at me, Catarina. Your laughter will destroy me. Be angry if you like, but don't laugh, it isn't fair.'

He kissed her again. 'Could you love me, darling?' he asked.

'I do love you, Freddie – you've been so good to me . . .'

'No – not like that. Like two adults, Catarina – real love. I'm obsessed with you, I know that. I'm making a fool of myself, I know that, too. Do I frighten you? I'd want to kill myself if I did. I have to know if you could possibly love me back, Catarina. I need to know if there's hope . . .'

'Freddie!'

He was at her feet now. Eve walked in to see her husband's bare ass beaming up at her from the floor, by Catarina's legs. She stood there a while, watching, as Freddie finished his speech. She thought she recognized most of it from a play he had been in but she couldn't be sure. Perhaps he was improvising – it would be the first time in his life if he was. The carpet had left red imprints on his bum.

'Get up, Freddie,' she said. 'You look ridiculous down there.'

Under the circumstances it was amazing Freddie retained as much dignity as he did. He rose to his feet slowly and turned to face his wife with his head held high. He made no move to cover his nakedness, just stood there as though he were fully clothed in one of his tweed suits. Even Eve was impressed. Her working brain wanted to reach for the Pentax to record the moment, it looked so good – the

378

dignified but naked older man with his blank-eyed mistress curled fully-clothed in a chair behind him.

'Get out,' she said. 'Both of you.'

Tony was rather sniffy about the whole affair but he still helped Catarina choose her new apartment. He had to — she would never spend so much money on herself otherwise.

'Eve was a good friend to you, Catarina,' he said. 'You don't go screwing around with friend's husbands — it's bad form. Besides — he's gross.'

'I didn't screw him, Tony, ' Catarina said. 'And Freddie isn't gross — he's very sweet and kind and he's a handsome man.'

'*Was* a handsome man,' Tony cut in.

'He's a friend.' Catarina's voice grew quieter.

'You don't need to fuck all your friends,' Tony said. 'That's the whole point of friends — they're people you don't have to fuck.'

He puckered his lips and wrote down how much she would be paid in total for her cosmetics promotion and he estimated her future earnings on the basis of what Jack was getting for her at that moment. Then he placed the sums in front of her with a triumphant flourish.

'Look, dear. Not only can you afford the apartment right now, in a few months' time you could be moving somewhere better. Jack says he'll be quoting tens of thousands of dollars for each job by then.'

'Jack is full of shit,' Catarina said. She couldn't imagine a better apartment than the one they were viewing. It had more rooms than she'd ever need and a swimming pool in the basement.

'You don't mean that,' Tony said.

Catarina shrugged. 'I don't want this, Tony. It's obscene — who am I supposed to be impressing? There are better things to waste money on.'

'You don't mean that either.' Tony looked aghast at her meanness.

Catarina sat down on one of the disgusting leopardskin settees. 'Tony, do you think I could bring a relative over to live here? Without anyone knowing, I mean? Is there any way someone can just come and live in this country? Is it possible?'

Tony sat down beside her. He couldn't tell if she was serious or not.

'I think you need to marry to stay here,' he said. 'You saw *Green Card*, didn't you? Gerard Depardieu married that woman to stay here and then they fell in love. Jesus, I cried at that ending! I loved him better in *Cyrano*, though – that was a three-tissue weepie. Do you remember that scene at the end where his head's bashed in and he's dying and . . .'

'Would you marry someone to keep them in the country, Tony?' Catarina asked.

Tony stared straight ahead. 'It's illegal, Catarina. You have to prove you've got a relationship. You have to answer questions about one another. You have to practically . . .'

'This woman's ill,' Catarina said. 'She's in a sort of coma, I think.'

Tony smiled and then laughed. 'Jeez, Catarina, I thought you were serious for a moment back there! What a sick joke! Ugh!'

Catarina smiled back at him. 'Sorry, Tony.'

Tony stood again and paced around the empty room.

'Colonial style?' he asked. 'Or Russian Imperial? That would look good when the press come to interview you 'at home'. Could you get some antiques shipped over from Russia, do you think?'

Catarina stood too. 'I'll have to ask Freddie,' she said.

'Freddie? What's he got to do with it?'

'He lives with me now.'

'You worry me, Catarina.'

'I worry myself, Tony.'

380

Tony kicked at the floor with the toe of his boot. 'Look – I don't understand, Catarina – I mean he's an old guy and he's the husband of your best woman friend and . . .'

'Eve kicked him out, Tony. I couldn't let him sleep in some ghastly hotel. You should have seen the state he was in. He looked after me when I was bad – it was only right I should return the favour.'

'But are you two an item, dear? I have a tidy mind, Catarina, you know that. I like to know where things go. Does Freddie fit into the master bedroom with his little mistress or is he consigned downstairs to the servants' quarters? Your public have a right to know, Catarina. Please, dear – we are friends, after all.'

Catarina smiled. 'Mind your own business, Tony,' she said.

He looked as though he had been stung. 'Back in the knife drawer, honey.'

'No offence, Tony.'

'None taken.'

He had barely noticed until now – Catarina was growing claws.

'You should try being nice to people, Catarina,' he said.

'Why?'

Tony sighed. 'Oh – I don't know. I suppose there's the feelgood factor – that has a lot to recommend it. Then there's the fact that New York is an extremely lonely place without friends. You frighten me at times, Catarina. I wonder who will be around to clean you up after the next mess if I'm not here. Sort out your life, darling – do it for me if you won't do it for yourself. You can't be a victim all your life, you know. Every drama queen has a day off occasionally. Take a long look. Take control.'

Catarina took a long look. There was nothing there in her life – no pattern, no meaning. Her sister was the only thing that made sense. She was the why and the what-for in

Catarina's life. She decided not to be scared any more. She decided to bring Klara back home.

She phoned the hospital. Nurse Olga did not work there any more. The news made Catarina feel sick. What was happening? She made herself ask – forced herself to speak to a strange voice. She was enquiring after a patient. The man couldn't know who she was – who was asking. She asked after her sister. Klara was not a patient in the hospital. They had no record of her. There was a mistake, Catarina told him, her sister had been there for years. She had only been moved recently – they must have records of where she had been moved to. Maybe the nurse had transferred with her. The man grew impatient. There was no-one there by that name and the name was not on the past year's records, he was sure. He did not care to be accused of making a mistake.

Catarina offered money – if it had worked with the nurse it might work with him, too. He turned her offer down with dignity but he gave her more information anyway. Nurse Olga had not been transferred. Nurse Olga had been arrested when another nurse accused her of stealing morphine from the hospital. They did not keep such people on their staff, he said.

Catarina put the phone down. She even laughed and swore at the idiot man under her breath. Then she stood up and looked in the mirror. It was she who looked stupid. It was she who was the idiot. How could she have been fooled for so long? What had happened to the money she had sent? What had happened to her sister? A terrible thought pushed its way into her head but she pushed it out again before it took shape. Klara could not be dead. Catarina could never have done everything she had done for nothing. She could not have killed her baby and given Stephen up for the sake of a ghost. She would know if Klara were dead, she would feel it. She made the thought vanish. She would not allow it to be true.

The phone rang as soon as she had put it down, making

her jump a little. She said nothing when she picked it up, just listened.

'Luisa?' Alex's voice.

'How are you, Luisa?' Silence. 'I know you're there. I know you can hear me.'

As Catarina listened to Alex's voice a terrible anger built inside her. They had used her – they had all used her – Alex, the nurse, Jack ... she had allowed herself to be used. What had happened to her? Why had she allowed it to happen? Alex was still talking when she put the receiver down.

'I love you, baby ...'

She hoped he would die. She wanted them all to die.

She liked the anger – it made her feel good.

'Go to hell,' she whispered. 'Go to hell, the lot of you.'

Beth was at home when Catarina's call came – sitting in a mud bath, eating a quart of peppermint-fudge-ripple ice cream with marshmallow pieces and watching her stomach expand from plump to 'when's-it-due?'

Her immediate reaction when she heard Catarina's voice was to vomit the whole bucket back up into the mud.

'Beth? How are you?'

(Shitty, Catarina – how are you? Near death, I hope.) 'Fine, thanks. Why the interest? Did you get bored earning ten thousand dollars a day and decided to have a little sport ringing all your old friends you fell out with?'

There was a pause.

'I'm sorry, Beth, truly I am. I just wouldn't have made it so quickly with you – you know that.'

'Oh, did I sound bitter, Catarina? Well I really didn't mean to!' Sarcasm sounded best on a full belly.

'Could you have done what Jack did for me, Beth?'

'Well we'll never know now, will we? It will be one of the Earth's great mysteries, like the *Marie Celeste* and the corn circles. Perhaps someone will make a fortune one day

383

writing a book about it. Do you mind if I hang up now, Catarina? My mud's getting cold.'

'Wait, Beth – please listen to what I have to say.'

'You said you're sorry, Catarina – apology accepted, if that makes you feel better. Now, you can cross me off that long list of people you screwed along the way and who you now feel guilty about. Did you ring Eve too? I hear you stole her husband from her.'

'Freddie's gone back to her now, Beth – didn't she tell you?'

'Oh good – did you have him giftwrapped and sent C.O.D?'

'Beth – I want you to be my agent again.'

Beth laughed out loud.

'I mean it, Beth.'

'After what you did to me? After what you did to Eve?'

'Eve's OK. She understands.'

'Well good for Evie – I'll wait to read about her sainthood in the papers.'

Catarina sounded patient. 'I want you to represent me again, Beth. I want to get rid of Jack. He's involved in too many bad things and I don't like his attitude. I want some control over my own career. You can have twenty per cent of all my new work once I deal with Jack's contract. The solicitor says I can get out of it quickly if I want to. I checked your record, Beth – you can't afford to say no.'

'Shit, Catarina.'

'Beth, you'll be bankrupt within the week. With this money you'll be OK. All the best girls will follow, too, when the story hits the press.'

Beth said nothing.

'It's business, Beth, pure and simple. I'm not asking you to like me, too. Feel free to hate me as much as you like – as long as you act as my agent while you're doing it. I know you can do the job properly. I also know you've got ethics.'

'Jack's a bastard, Catarina — I don't want him on my tail.'

'I already told the papers, Beth.'

'You what?'

'I knew you'd agree, so I went ahead.'

Beth slammed the phone down and mud splashed up into her face. As she stretched up for the mirror to whip it off she started to hum a little tune. Then she smiled. Jack needed this — he deserved it. And Catarina was right — it was business, after all.

Catarina moved back to Beth the following month. Two weeks later Beth's office burnt down. A note from Jack arrived at her apartment:

Don't let anyone tell you I'm not a good loser.

Eve told Beth to go to the police but Beth was too philosophical — she was insured and she knew there was too little evidence. Besides, with the money Catarina was making, she'd have moved to a better place sooner or later.

58

England, 1994

Gant's Hill hadn't changed since Rick was a boy – that bloody awful roundabout still looked like a toilet in the middle of the road. Maybe it *was* a toilet now – he hoped it was – at least that would mean it served some sort of useful purpose at last.

He looked at the address that was stuck to his windscreen. A soft-top Suzuki Jeep – white, of course – nearly careered into the side of his Citroën and the female driver – blonde, tanned and lycra/leather-clad – leant out of the window with a sneer and made a wank mime with her fist.

Rick turned up Elgar on the car stereo and edged her off at the nearest junction – by the cinema and the hairdressers called 'We Curl Up And Dye'. Then he did a lap of honour round the roundabout, while some local lads jeered and a black cab tooted its horn. Maybe Ilford hadn't lost its old charm after all.

Actually he was almost lost. Almost lost in Ilford was like extremely, desperately lost anywhere else. Landmarks there looked depressingly like landmarks anywhere else up and down the country – Tesco Superstores; gardening centres with World War One Zeppelins moored outside; life-size plaster butchers with their hands missing; pubs that had been lovingly reconstructed by craftsmen in the old style, with hanging baskets and Karyoke (sic) nights.

Dagenham Drive was two past the High Street and then left, according to a kid in surfer's shorts. The road was blandly lower-middle and then some. The Hall was like some overblown tart on the outside, with its stone cladding, double-glazed Tudor-leaded windows and its olde coaching lanterns in the oaken-stained porch. Inside, it had been furnished and decorated exclusively from the *Innovations* catalogue. Rick knew the score the minute he heard the Airsong wind-chimes doorbell set off the fake dog-barking alarm.

Mrs Hall appeared as an undulating pink spectral blur behind the frosted glass of the porch door.

'Back! Back!" she said, waving her arms, and the dog alarm ceased abruptly as she bent to switch it off.

'We don't have a dog, of course,' she told Rick later, over a bowl of St Michael Mediterranean-style black olives. 'But you can't be too careful these days and the alarm might put some people off. I think it was Lucy's accident that really brought it home. Another Prawn won ton?'

She was worried that Rick appeared to have neither a notebook or a tape recorder. 'Do you consign this entire interview to memory then?' she asked.

'Tell me more about Lucy's accident,' he countered. He bit into the won ton and wondered whether it was supposed to be raw. His mind did a quick check over his next week's schedules, just in case. He'd had food poisoning once before, in Malaysia, and he knew he would be looking at a five-day sabbatical at least.

'Lucy was in the drum majorettes, you know, until the accident. She lost interest in it after that. I made all her costumes. We had to take them down to the Charity. I hoped she'd change her mind at the last minute, but she didn't.'

'What exactly were her injuries, Mrs Hall?'

'Cigar burns. Bruising. To her body as well as her mind.'

'And the man was never caught?'

'No. I hope he's punished in hell.'

Lucy came into the room. She was a pretty girl. Rick smiled at her and she blushed but didn't look away. She wore an orange T-shirt and green cycle shorts. Her hair had been tied up on top of her head with a gold scrunchie.

'Did you ever want to model, Lucy?' Rick asked.

She frowned and wrinkled her nose. 'I thought about it.'

Rick smiled again. 'Have you got a recent photo? Something a bit more grown up? I can show it to a few people at my paper – see if they can give you any help.'

She trotted off into the lounge and came back with a studio shot that made her look like a Cabbage Patch doll.

'Thanks.' Rick put it into his pocket. He pulled another shot out, making an expression of mild surprise as he did so.

'Oh – do you happen to know this bloke, Lucy? He's got a few contacts in the modelling business, I believe.'

Lucy stared down at Alex's photo and her expression changed as her face turned crimson. The expression was over in a flash, though the colour took a little longer to fade. Maybe she would have made a good actress.

'No,' she said, looking away. 'I've never seen him before.'

Her mother leant over for a look. 'Let's see?'

Lucy passed the picture quickly back to Rick.

'He's nobody, Mum,' she said. 'You wouldn't know him either.'

When Rick was back in his flat that night he pinned the photo of Alex in among the shots of Catarina. Then he added the picture Lucy-Anne had given him of herself. Catarina, Alex, Lucy-Anne. He looked at the file he had started on Alex. The man had appeared all over the globe. He ran his own model agency in London for a while – not a big-name one but it had had a tidy turnover. One of Rick's ex-girlfriends had been sent along to discover the scam. She'd replied to an ad in the paper and got an appointment for an audition in Maidstone.

There'd been all sorts there – girls, boys, mums with their kids, older types – Alex had been charming to all of them and Rick's ex had discovered he'd offered most of them a place at the agency. After they'd had some shots done, of course – shots that they paid nearly two hundred for – and then there was the enrolment fee – and the money to go onto the headsheet. Alex was taking up to five hundred per person, which more than paid for the charm he was dishing out in return. The newspaper ran a half-hearted exposé but Rick's ex said it only seemed to have increased the interest.

Then Alex had suddenly shut the place and vanished – a girl who used to work for him said he'd scarpered off to the 'States with all the money.

Rick turned slowly back and forth in his chair. Then he sat and watched *Star Trek* on SKY, which helped his thinking process. Then he went back to the pictures on the wall.

The Spring season began and Catarina arrived back in London for the designer shows. She was booked to work for three big names and then, as was the norm, to do a fourth show free for a designer all the models adored and who gave them clothes in lieu of payment.

There were fifteen models in the first show and the biggest names arrived late with either boyfriends, mothers or brothers in tow. Mothers had been last year's accessory and brothers were currently all the rage, as long as they were nubile and had learned to look suitably bored.

Backstage was cramped, even by normal standards and a screaming row erupted when a minion who knew no better tried to evict everyone but those vital to the running of the show.

Catarina emptied her quilted Chanel bag out onto her dressing-table. A stylist tried to put rollers in her hair which was a patent waste of time as her hair was too short. The girl had been told to do it, though, and sheer terror made her persevere until Catarina screamed that her head was getting sore.

'What is the running order?' she shouted. No one looked

and no one answered. Maybe no one had even thought about a running order. The designer seemed unconcerned, but then maybe he was out of his head. Catarina looked at her rail. There'd been no time for fittings and the designer had just worked from the measurements Beth had faxed over. Nothing looked as though it would fit anybody.

The backstage routine at the big shows had become depressingly repetitive. Two of the biggest name models were holed up together at one end of the room and they protected their territory by screaming at anyone who came near – unless it was a magazine with a commission, of course. Catarina was always sited at the furthest point away from these two, in case of fights. The trick was to scream and protest the loudest. The others were in a line in between. Anyone new was treated with fear and suspicion. There had been riots a few years before when the waifs had arrived with their grunge look and some of the older girls had had trouble adapting. There was now a kind of policing policy to make sure nothing similar caught them off-guard again.

The show started before anyone was ready. Everyone shrieked and swore and stubbed out fags and one girl fainted in the heat and the crush. When Catarina got back from her first outing she found a note propped on her table:

We met on a plane – Can we meet again?

– There was a photo of Rick stapled to the side of it so she could remember who he was.

There was a scruffyish little restaurant not two hundred yards from Rick's flat, in what was known locally as The Old Town – a patch of run-down properties the developers had somehow missed during operation Scorched Earth. Maybe the crappy little dwellings – ten houses, a betting shop, the restaurant and a sweet shop – were there as a permanent warning against unwarranted nostalgia. Perhaps when any of the elderlies from the nouveau Ancient Twilights rest home started opining too loudly about the good old days, they were forcibly escorted there with their zimmer frames and made to look at exactly what shitty circumstances they'd been rescued from.

Actually the restaurant wasn't too bad when you got inside – which was where Rick was sitting as he waited for Catarina. The place was owned by an old mate of Rick's – a gay Russian chef who called himself Eno because that was what all the locals dosed up with after they'd eaten there. Rick had reserved the entire basement floor for the evening and, with the door closed, he could almost ignore the sounds from the party of Millwall supporters who were dining above.

'What are they eating, Eno?' Rick asked.

The chef shrugged his shoulders. 'Even I don't know and I cooked it.'

'I hope you've prepared a better class of muck for my guest.'

Eno smiled. 'It is years since I have prepared a traditional Russian banquet – but don't worry, my mother is back in the kitchens and it is she who is doing all the cooking. She's a culinary genius, Rick – a real Keith Floyd when the mood takes her. Don't worry – just worry that your guest shows – she's an hour late already.'

Rick yawned. 'I told you – she's here.'

'Then why don't she come in? You've had me out there five times checking the car's still there. What if it's the wrong car?'

'How many limos do you see in this crap-hole?' Rick asked. 'Don't worry – she's sizing me up. It's a bit of the old cat-and-mouse, Eno. She can't make up her mind what she's letting herself in for. She's a thoroughbred, Eno – I doubt she's set foot in a dive such as this for donkey's years. She's wondering why a dapper little git like myself didn't take her to Langan's or somewhere trendy, like Bibendum.'

'So why didn't you?' Eno perched his rear on the tiny table and lit up a Gauloise.

'I wanted to surprise her,' Rick said. 'I wanted to show her something honest – less glossy. I wanted to make her trust me, I suppose – I know she thinks I'm a mongrel. Could you puff that smoke round a bit, Eno? There's a strange smell in here – a bit like marmalade and chest rub.'

Eno obliged, nodding. 'We had the pensioners' Xmas party down here at lunchtime,' he said.

'Christmas?' Rick coughed, 'But it's only September.'

Eno shrugged. 'We get very booked up,' he told Rick.

Catarina walked in just as Rick was laughing.

She looked like any other girl, except she was taller and she walked better and her face was so near to oddly perfect that Eno could do nothing but stare. She sat down with her coat still on and she pushed her place-setting aside to lean across the table.

'Why did you want to meet me?' she said.

'Why did you come? – Surely that's the more intriguing question,' Rick answered. He felt as though all the air had been squeezed out of his lungs.

Catarina shrugged. 'I remembered you. You seemed nice. You made me laugh. I get a little lonely in London. Maybe it reminds me too much of home. Maybe I am bored.'

Eno handed Catarina a menu and she put it quickly to one side.

'You should read it,' Rick told her. 'The meal's specially prepared by his mother in your honour. It's all traditional Russian – he normally does kebabs.'

Catarina looked at the menu and smiled at Eno. She spoke to him quickly in Russian and then they both looked at Rick and laughed.

'What did you two say?' he asked.

'It's an old Russian joke,' Catarina said, still reading the menu, 'it doesn't translate well.'

392

She put the menu down. 'Everything,' she said.

'Everything?'

'It all sounds so wonderful – I don't want to choose – is that OK? Can you afford it?'

Rick ignored the question. 'Vodka?' he asked – he thought he might get her drunk.

She nodded.

The first drinks arrived and Rick drank his quickly and Catarina followed suit. Rick smiled.

Four shots later and he was beginning to feel it but Catarina was still as sharp as a knife.

'Do you like this dish? Our cook used to make it for my mother when I was a child. I must speak to Eno's mother – she makes food just like I used to have at home.'

'Back in the old country,' Rick said. 'In the mansion with all the acres of ground. When you lived like a little aristocrat yourself and had nannies and your own pony . . .' He thought his words were beginning to sound funny so he had more vodka in an attempt to sort them out. Catarina drank with him, glass for glass. She was smiling at him. They'd finished the bottle, but he didn't know how.

'Eno!' he said, pointing, 'Some more!'

'Do you think you should?' Catarina asked, and his manhood took its hugest, ugliest dent since the day he'd streaked at his school prizegiving and no one had noticed.

He knocked back two more, just for show, and the next thing he knew he was in the front of Catarina's limo, trying not to throw up in the glove compartment.

He managed to stand unaided in the lift and he giggled when she searched him for his keys. He tried to make her a coffee but he got the plunger the wrong way up and so he sat and watched as she made it, instead. He was captivated by her. He couldn't believe she was there, in his flat. She'd thrown her coat over a stool and he liked what she was wearing – it was ordinary, not at all pretentious. Jeans, cowboy boots, a white shirt – it was the sort of thing his sister would have worn. She looked fresh and nice. Was it weird to admire something you were out to destroy?

He went for a pee and when he came back she was by his desk, staring at his wall. The pictures were there – all the pictures of her – pictures of Alex – the studio portrait of Lucy. She had turned on the spotlights and each face had its own illumination. Fuck. How could he have been so stupid? He was instantly sober now. Stupid berk, fucking stupid twat.

'What-is-this?' She turned to look at him. Her face was white with shock. She looked at him as though he was some kind of pervert. A wall of photos of herself. A sort of amateur *This Is Your Life*.

She was struggling into her coat again, trying to get out. Her arm got stuck in the sleeve. She stopped struggling and stared at him again. He could see the fear in her eyes and it made him feel big.

'Who are you?' It came out as a frightened whisper.

He couldn't help himself. His mouth spoke while his brain limped home second.

'Nemesis,' he said. It sounded good. It sounded right. It sounded dramatic. 'Your Nemesis, Catarina. I'm going to destroy you. I'm your fate, your downfall. I'm going to dish your dirt.'

'Why?' Her voice came out as a whisper. She looked so beautiful it hurt. Why? It was a reasonable enough question.

Rick shrugged. 'It's my job – it's what I'm paid for. It's also what I'm good at.'

He didn't like the look in her eyes, though, it was making him feel guilty and he couldn't remember feeling guilty before in his entire life. He was always proud of how un-guilty he usually felt.

'Who are you?' She asked him again.

The question threw him. He felt sick at his own scheming. How much had she told him that evening? How much of it could he use? He felt for his tape machine in his pocket.

'I'm after you, Catarina,' he said, though he didn't feel quite so sinister as he said it. She was so pretty. She looked so hurt, like a child. 'I'm unravelling all of your secrets, one by one. It's taking me a long time but it's worth it. They're big secrets too, aren't they?'

She looked terrified. Then she laughed. Her eyes changed.

'I don't think so,' she told him.

She looked back at the photographs. 'You found him, then.' She folded her arms.

'Found who?'

'Alex, of course. My husband.'

Rick shook his head to clear it.

'How did you know I'd be looking for him?'

She turned around to face him again and this time her smile looked genuine – only it wasn't aimed at him, it was aimed at Alex's file that she was holding in her hands.

'Thank you,' she said, simply.

The fog began to clear from his head.

'You knew,' he said. 'You set me up.' Her smile widened. She looked delighted.

'You fucking set me up!'

'I knew you were the best, Rick.'

'You've played me like a fucking violin from day one, haven't you? You knew I'd find that paper with the article about Lucy on the plane! You left it there for me to pick up, didn't you? You phoned me too, didn't you? You did that to get me going. You knew I'd go looking for Alex too, didn't you?'

'I needed to find him, Rick. He won't leave me alone but I don't know where he is. Have you ever been haunted by anyone, Rick? Have you ever been terrified by someone who just won't go away? I could have hired an investigator but – like I said – I knew you were the best. This stuff looks good, too. Was he really done for dealing drugs in

395

'Eighty three? Did you go and see the girl? How is she? I knew it had to be Alex again when I read about the type of injuries. He nearly killed me, did you know that?'

'What about you, though?' Rick asked. ' What if I found out all about you while I was looking?' He felt sick with anger and admiration at being beaten at his own game.

Catarina smiled again. 'You were hunting me down anyway,' she said. 'How much did you manage to find out?' She flipped through her own file. 'Not a lot? I told you, Rick, there's no point looking for me, I don't really exist.'

She went back to Alex's file. 'You've lost him somewhere in the 'States,' she said. 'Is that all you know?'

As if on cue the fax machine started to hum and the last piece of the jigsaw rolled through. Rick had sent faxes out before he'd left for their meal together. Now one of the people he'd asked had come up with the goods, right bang on time.

Catarina read it out loud: '"Alex Head, aka Alex J. Miller, currently co-owner of an art gallery – Dingwall's – in SoHo, New York." There is an address, Rick and a telephone number. Thank you again.' She blew him a little kiss.

Rick had never sobered up so thoroughly before in his life. He watched her walk toward the door but he would have dragged her back before he would have let her go through it.

'Can we talk off the record now, Catarina?' he asked.

She shrugged in reply.

He sat down.

'Now, you've screwed my balls off and have had them pickled in a jar. *If* (and this is a big if) – I don't present too pathetic a picture, I would like you to tell me if we could ever become lovers. I want you, Catarina – even now, in the pathetic jelly-like state you have left me in, I want you badly enough to ask. Beg even. Do you find pathetic men attractive?'

396

She stood very still, staring at him. 'Do you have AIDS, herpes or thrush?' she asked.

'Don't joke – I'm serious. Would you have dinner with me again? Not Eno's this time.'

'I like Eno's,' she said.

'OK, then Eno's it is – only no vodka next time. I'll get someone to rescind his liquor license, or something. We'll stick to the Evian next time, OK?'

'OK.'

Rick felt himself begin to breathe again.

They ate at Eno's three times that week and then Rick finally admitted he'd had enough and took her to Le Caprice instead. He realized his mistake the minute they arrived. Catarina became uneasy. She saw two other models she knew there and the constant flashing of bulbs told them the paparazzi were lying in wait outside.

'You don't want to be bothered,' Rick told her. 'Most models thrive on that sort of attention. It makes for good publicity, Catarina, being caught coming out of a good eatery looking a thousand dollars.'

But Catarina just shook her head and left most of her food. 'Did you book them?' she asked.

Rick took her hand. 'You still don't trust me, do you?' he asked.

'I never thought I would be expected to.'

'So why do you come out with me?'

'I don't know.'

Rick leant across the table. 'I have a theory. Mind if I try it out on you? Strange as it sounds, I think you might actually like me. Don't look too shocked – it's happened before.'

Catarina smiled. He loved it when she smiled.

'Only you are disgusted by your own taste in men, Catarina – right? You're wondering what you are doing here, enjoying the company of one of the very wolves who have

397

set out to destroy you – right? You don't believe I can have another life away from my job. When you dine with the devil you use a long spoon. Is your spoon long enough, Catarina, or would you prefer a seat at another table?'

'I'm not frightened of you, Rick.' She looked serious all of a sudden.

'Maybe you should be.'

'No, I don't think so.'

He was seduced by her, fairly and squarely, not just physically, because that would have been a pushover, but mentally too, and it was that part that hurt the most.

He watched her undress in the cold light of the early morning and, when she turned to face him, he knew she stood for all he would ever want. He knew what she was doing to him but he didn't want to stop her. He wanted to strap her to the bonnet of his car and drive her around Gant's Hill to show her off to all his old mates. He wanted her to go into every wine bar in Fleet Street with him and every pub in Docklands.

'I can't tell you you're beautiful,' he said. 'You'll have been told it too many times before. I want to be different, Catarina – what is it that no one's ever told you before?'

She laughed. 'You could tell me I'm clever,' she said.

'You are clever, girl – too bloody clever for me.'

'Then tell me I'm fat.'

'OK, you're fat. Only you're not. – Can I take you home to meet my mum?'

'Would she like me?'

'After a bit. I think you'd scare her shitless at first, though.'

'Then maybe we'll leave it. Why don't you take your clothes off?'

He'd been selecting his underpants for weeks. He suddenly thought he'd chosen the wrong pair. Calvin Klein was too posey – he should have stuck to Knickerbox or

398

M & S. He was happy just looking at her body, anyway.

He had never seen anyone naked who did not have anything wrong with them. Not that he'd only been with defectives, but he was thinking of all those picky little things that never mattered in the heat of the moment – things like belly fluff or chicken skin or shaving nicks or the odd spot. Catarina had none of these.

She looked good from every angle, too. Some models looked beautiful when they were still but iffy when they moved. Catarina had no good side because she had no bad side. He realized sadly that fucking her was going to be a problem.

'Rick?' Her voice had changed – she sounded lonely and young. He wanted to hold her and he took her hands and pulled her towards him. She pushed him back onto the bed and suddenly she was astride him and then suddenly he was inside her and it was all alright.

'Oh, Jesus!' he groaned. The worst thing was, when he told his story in years to come, no-one would ever believe him.

Catarina flew off to the 'States with her file and Alex's file packed side-by-side in her case. She had no qualms about screwing Rick to get it – her sister had done tricks for money and now she had done tricks for her life.

Fortunately Rick was good-looking and a good enough lover, too, so she could hardly think of him as a sacrifice she had had to make. She'd almost forgotten how good sex could feel.

She looked at the ring Rick had given her as she'd kissed him goodbye in departures. Was it a real one? It didn't really matter, only the stone was huge and she wondered how much he must earn from his grubby little exposés.

What mattered was that he had given it to her at all. What mattered was that she would make sure she was photographed wearing it when she arrived at JFK and then

399

Rick would see the papers and believe she had meant it when she told him she loved him. What mattered was that he would never meddle dangerously in her life again. What mattered most to Catarina was that she had some control over her own life at last.

59

Dingwall's Art Gallery was a long glass and chrome studio on the second floor of a small mall of chi-chi dress shops and interior horticulture design stores. The floor of the gallery was of varnished cherrywood and there was a notice requesting visitors to remove hard-heeled shoes before entering.

Alex had an office to the rear of the studio, with a spyhole in the door to keep a subtle eye on clients who preferred to browse without, apparently, being observed.

He was peering through this spyhole when Catarina walked in. He was not surprised to see her — she was his wife — he knew she'd come some day. He enjoyed the luxury of watching her surreptitiously for a while. She wore a black Jasper Conran trouser suit with a soft knitted wrap thrown over the top. She also wore dark glasses, which he supposed were *de rigueur* among the members of her set.

She saw the gallery was empty and went across to study the paintings. He wondered what she made of them — they were mostly abstracts, done by known artists. Had she acquired a sense of culture, along with all that money? If he'd never met her before he would have guessed her to be an upper-class bitch.

She stopped in front of a medium-size canvas, covered in scarlet paint, with a large gash through the middle.

'This looks like your own work, Alex,' she said loudly. So she knew he was watching. He paused before opening the door. Long enough to get a smile on his face.

Catarina could feel his presence in the room without even seeing him — she could feel his breath before it touched her face. The terror was mesmerizing. He stalked her like a great dog. She hid her fear from him as much as she could but she knew he could sense it there inside her and she knew it pleased him. He was her husband – he knew too much. She turned to face him. He had grown a beard. At a quick glance he looked like Barry Gibb. A longer look, though and it was just Alex again – Alex in an expensive suit and Alex with a tan that looked as though it came from the ski slopes at Sun Valley.

He studied her face. She wondered if he was admiring his handiwork. What did he think when he looked at her? Did he see something he had destroyed or something he had created? All her old wounds came to life again at the sight of him, causing her real pain that made her flinch.

'I'm pleased to see you,' he said. He looked almost as though he meant it.

'Why?' She kept her voice steady.

'Because I still love you.' He sounded surprised at her question. His voice was low and intimate. They were the only two in the world again. Alex and Luisa. Alex the destroyer.

'I'll always be pleased to see you,' he said. 'You know that. I think perhaps you know me better than I know myself. I know I know you in that way. I don't believe we were ever apart, Luisa, not in our souls. It would take more than what happened to kill the love that we had for one another. You were my creation – I will always feel that, even if we are no longer lovers.'

'That's quite a speech, Alex.'

'I've been waiting a long time to say it.' He smiled.

Catarina cocked her head to one side, watching him. The change in her was remarkable, he thought. She had confidence now, and wisdom.

He waved a hand towards the door. 'You didn't come mob-handed then? You haven't brought the police with you, baying for my blood?'

She shook her head.

'No.'

'Why not? It's no more than I deserve.'

Catarina looked away. 'So why did you come back to New York?' she asked.

'Hoping you'd find me after so long – hoping you'd come looking for me. Hoping you'd see me and realize how much I've changed. I had to keep in touch, Luisa, but I knew I had to leave the rest up to you. I'm not a monster any more. I didn't care what happened to me as long as you found that out.'

'What are you now then, Alex?'

'Oh –' he puffed thoughtfully, '– a normal sort of man, if I'm lucky.' Catarina almost laughed out loud at the lie but Alex went on.

'. . . A man who has been blessed with the ability to recognize his sins and make amends before it is too late. It was Jesus Christ who showed me the way and I believe I have been offered a path to salvation. You were my only dark spot, Luisa, and now you've come to me. I knew you would if I prayed hard enough. Now I have to keep praying for your forgiveness.'

Catarina moved closer to him. She shuddered. He had never sounded so sinister. His eyes grew larger, drawing her in.

'Jesus Christ?' She had only heard him utter the name as a curse before.

'Forgive me, Luisa,' he repeated. His eyes were hard, though, like stones.

'Of course I'll forgive you, Alex,' she said, looking away, 'only first I intend to ruin you. I mean to make you suffer, Alex, in any way that I possibly can.' She looked at the painting. 'I'm glad that you've learnt religion – now I have something else to teach you. It's called misery, Alex – I want to see you learn the sort of pain I felt when you almost killed me. I want to see that look of fear in your eyes that you instilled in mine.'

She pulled the Polaroid out of her bag – the one she had

403

taken from the porn session in London, the session Alex had made her take part in. 'I want to see you feel shame, Alex – the sort of shame I felt when I had this shot taken.'

Alex took the photo from her and studied it. When he looked back at her, he was smiling.

'And I want to share that pain, little Luisa – believe me,' he said. They were evenly matched now – his lies and her resolve. Their eyes met and glued together. Without the interruption they would have held that stare forever.

A woman walked into the gallery with two small girls, and Catarina snatched the photo from Alex's hand and pushed it into her bag. The woman walked up to them. She was small and attractive in a strong, motherly-looking way. She wore a Burberry raincoat over a beige cashmere rollneck and chinos. Her hair was cut into a sharp bob that gave her ordinary-looking face character.

The child in her arms was still a baby – a beautiful thing with curled toffee-coloured hair and wide cornflower eyes. The other girl, who was several years older, pulled away from her mother's hand and ran off into Alex's office.

'Where are my sweeties, Daddy?' she called. They could hear her opening drawers in her hunt.

Catarina looked at Alex. He still stared and he still smiled and his stare and his smile were totally untouched by any sense of pity or shame. God was his scam now and it was a good scam – Catarina had to admit it.

'She calls me Daddy, though I'm really more of a stepfather,' he said. 'This little one is mine, though. We called her Luisa – I hope you don't mind.'

The woman held a hand out to Catarina.

'It's Catarina now, isn't it?' she asked. 'I would have known you anywhere. My eldest daughter is a great fan of yours – she has your pictures all over the walls of her bedroom. I'm Charlotte Raphael-Scott – my husband was a senator. He died two years ago. We've been living with Alex for a year now – he's my husband in all but name.' She smiled.

'I know what you must be thinking, Catarina. Alex has told me all about his past, including what he did to you. I can understand that you would never want to forgive him and I wish he would not suggest that you do. He is a different man, though, Catarina. He truly repents all that he's done. It was I who bought this gallery and I who introduced him to Jesus Christ for the first time. I love Alex, Catarina, he is a fine man now and a good father to both my children. I believe all men have a right to salvation, however terrible their crimes. I only hope you can see that, and see that he is truly sorry.'

Catarina looked at the child in her arms and she thought of her own child – hers and Stephen's – the one she had had to give up for her sister.

'She's beautiful,' she said.

Charlotte beamed. 'She was named after a beautiful woman.' She touched Catarina on the arm. 'I know how your life must have been destroyed and I'm glad you have managed to build it up again. Please don't hate us – that's the most I feel I have the right to ask you.'

Catarina looked at Charlotte and then at Alex. They were both smiling at her and Alex's smile was one of pure victory. She felt as though she were suffocating.

'I must go,' she said. Alex showed her to the door while Charlotte cooed over her baby.

'Please – come to see us again,' Alex whispered as she left. The whisper felt cold, like a draught from hell. The flesh on Catarina's arms dimpled in protest.

Eve watched Stephen working in the studio. Like most big-earning photographers he barely bothered to take shots these days, but just hung around while his minions set up, adding enough clever ideas to give him the right to his byline.

That day he was doing a cover for *Rolling Stone*.

'I'm impressed by your technique,' Eve told him. He

looked up from the camera. At least he hadn't forgotten how to blush. She bit into a cream cheese bagel. 'How's Lisbeth?' she asked.

'Fine.' He bent back over his camera again.

'Just fine?'

'No, Eve, she's great.'

'What about the baby?

Stephen sighed. 'It was a false alarm. No problem. It was too early, anyway. I think she just wanted it for the company.'

Eve studied him. 'Get her a dog, then.'

'Sure. Good idea.'

Eve hopped down from the table she had been sitting on. 'No, Stephen, it's a shitty idea, actually. What's wrong with you? Can't you hear the way you sound?'

The look of surprise on his face made her grin.

'You used to be such a nice young boy, Stephen.'

He almost grinned at that, too. 'Sure.'

'No – really. You used to buy nice Danish pastries for me.'

'I bought you the bagel.'

'I'd have preferred a Danish. Anyway, you didn't buy the bagel for me, you bought it for yourself. I just happened to get to it first.'

Stephen put his hands on his hips. 'Eve – I'd love to discuss bagels all day with you but I'm working.'

'I spoke to Catarina,' Eve said.

Stephen threw his hands in the air. 'Christ!'

'Christ I spoke to her, or Christ I shouldn't tell you while you're busy?' Eve asked.

'Christ you should speak to her at all after what she did to you and Freddie,' Stephen said. He stopped work, though, and poured them both a coffee.

'Freddie did it to Freddie, not Catarina,' Eve said. 'All actors are like children – it's the insecurity of their profession.'

'You don't believe that crap,' Stephen said.

Eve pulled a wise face. 'No – I think he was just feeling his age and fancied screwing someone young and beautiful,' she said. '– But then don't we all? Who am I to throw stones, Stephen? Given the same circumstances . . .' She stared into space and took a long sip of her coffee.

'She's been to see Alex,' she said.

Stephen stared at her. There was a long, disbelieving pause. 'Pea soup for brains,' he said.

'She hasn't,' Eve told him, 'that's the whole point. Lord knows what she thinks she's up to.'

'Where is he?' Stephen asked. Eve was surprised by the sudden anger in his tone.

'Alex –' he said, staring at her, '– where did Catarina find him?'

'This doesn't involve you now, Stephen – she's not your responsibility. She says Alex has changed – he's got a family now. Leave it alone – you'll only end up getting hurt.'

'The address, Eve,' Stephen said.

Eve looked at him. 'Dingwall's Gallery in SoHo,' she said – unfortunately it was an easy one to memorize.

Alex saw Stephen standing in the gallery and he figured he looked good enough for at least a couple of thousand dollars. Alex prided himself on being able to judge a man's spending ability from the cut of his clothes and the posture of his body. In this case he forgot to look at the face. Even if he had, he might not have recognized Stephen in time – he had been a young boy the last time they'd met.

They were both the same height now and, although Alex was the stockier, Stephen had the element of surprise on his side.

'Leave her alone, you bastard!' were the last words Alex heard before a fist smashed into his face, knocking two caps off his front teeth.

In a moment of blinding clarity, Alex realized who his

407

latest visitor was. He tried to say Stephen's name but he couldn't, because the fist was back and this time he managed to raise an arm to ward it off. Then he changed tactics. He stood stock still, his arms at his side and blood trickling from his mouth.

'Go ahead – hit me all you want,' he said. 'I deserve all that and much worse.'

Stephen tried to hit him again but his knuckles were sore – maybe even more sore than Alex's face and it was difficult to hit a man who was smiling at you in such a way.

He paused and Alex wiped the blood onto the sleeve of his Armani.

'I'll kill you if you hurt her again,' Stephen told him.

'I don't doubt you will, son,' Alex said.

'What the fuck are you up to, Alex?' Stephen asked. The man's smile sickened him.

'Oh, the same as you, probably,' Alex told him. 'I still love her and I want her back. Strange, isn't it, how two grown men can make such bloody fools of themselves over one woman. I never stopped loving her, Stephen, not for one minute. I know you can understand that – you above all people.'

Stephen wished he was somewhere else – anywhere that he didn't have to see that Jesus-loves-you smile.

'You've got a family now, Alex,' he said.

'So have you. Doesn't seem to make much difference, does it, my old mate? You can't keep away from her any more than I can, can you?'

Stephen stared at him.

'I'm not the bad guy any more, Stephen – I'm a reformed character. Charlotte – my lady now – helped me see the light through the ways of Our Lord.'

'Don't give me that crap!' Stephen said.

Alex shrugged. 'As you like, Stevie. I don't expect you to believe me. Go and see Luisa, though – she does. She still loves me, too – I know it's a miracle but miracles can happen and I've prayed long and hard for this one.'

'And what about Charlotte? Does she know about all of this?'

'Of course – I tell her everything. She understands, Stevie, but then she's a wonderful woman like that. More than I deserve and then some.'

Beth looked at her watch nervously. It was after midnight. If the press party was to be a success it depended on The Cat showing up soon. She would have loved to tell herself that the turnout was just for the launch of her new premises but, then, who was she kidding? They'd eaten the sushi, drunk most of the champagne and now the natives were getting restless in a big way.

'. . . Jesus, I mean who does she think she is, some fucking star or something? Ten more minutes and I'm going, OK? *Absolut*. No two ways.'

'. . . There's no way she'll show, darling. She's in Dubai – I told you – on a shoot for the summer collections . . .'

'. . . Beth, you promised my editor some shots of The Cat. Now how can I go back empty-handed? I've got a whole page reserved for tomorrow's issue!'

'. . . I heard Jack's bribed her back to his stable. Did you see Beth's expression? It didn't look good.'

'. . . Beth, look, Sondra and I and the rest of the girls are a bit pissed off, actually. I mean, it's not as though we're second-league or anything but you'd think so tonight – the only photos so far have been by that little wizened guy by the door and Deelite says you paid him yourself anyway. And you know we can't eat raw fish because of the allergy problems . . .'

Beth tried smiling and turning off at the same time. The faces quickly became a blur. It was a trick she'd learnt on the new Visualization programme she was attending.

They'd begun by juggling balls – or taking part in Spherical Appropriation Programming, as the instructor called it – to understand and maximize their true potential as achievers. Then they'd gone on to the practical visualizations. Beth had been told to imagine she was a small fat brown slug, and she found the technique surprisingly functional for her current predicament. Slugs didn't have to speak and everyone just hated them and trod on them. Once you'd visualized your place on the world's stage it was easy-peasey adapting to your role. Just smile and be sluglike – no problem.

'Did you invite Stephen, Beth?' Eve's was the latest in a long line of cross faces. Beth's slimy brown flesh rippled silently. No need to explain – no need to reply.

'That wasn't a smart move, Beth!' Eve looked pretty sluglike too, when you studied her closely. Only she wouldn't shut up.

'Maybe you'd better hope Catarina doesn't show after all – Jesus, didn't you think when you were writing out the invites? Don't tell me – your mailing list is computerized. Who else do you have on it? George Bush and Saddam Hussein? Donald and Ivana Trump? Popeye and Bluto? Jesus!'

Beth blinked at her slowly and turned her head towards the door. There was a crush there and the room had suddenly tilted on its axis by forty degrees. Catarina had arrived. At last.

'Excuse me Eve.' – A slug no more but a social butterfly, fluttering past the press, stamping, pushing, biting, kicking – anything to be in her rightful place as hostess, which was in those first few shots when the guest of honour arrived.

'Catarina! Darling!' She launched herself at the girl, kissing her in the air next to her cheek and whispering fondly into her ear, 'You shit! We nearly lost them!'

On cue the room went dark and twenty video screens lit up like candles, all showing Catarina's face. Half of them showed stills from her cosmetics campaign and the other half showed her modelling on catwalks in Milan and Paris.

The sudden semi-darkness gave Beth enough time to

assess her star model's appearance. She was sober, she had slept well and she was magnificently, expensively attired. Beth breathed a deep and extremely soulful sigh of relief.

They arranged a quick line-up near the agency's logo — all Beth's top girls, with Catarina in the middle. They squealed and played like kittens for the press, hugging one another and playing happy faces, but mostly they resented Catarina for arriving late and for standing in the middle — they were all out to kick her off her perch, just as quickly and as permanently as they could.

She saw Stephen as she posed for the thirty-fifth shot and the minute she saw him she walked straight out of the line-up and over to where he stood. The press followed her, leaving the other girls standing.

They stared at one another and the flashes began to blind them. Catarina saw a grey floating dot where Stephen's head had been. Perhaps she had made a mistake after all. She looked up at the bank of video screens that all displayed her face and then back at the man who stood in front of them. It was Stephen — of course it was.

The photographers were still hovering. Catarina half smiled for their benefit. They took a few snaps and started to drift away.

'I read about your wedding,' she said. 'Congratulations.'

'Thanks.' He sounded very angry and looked angrier than he sounded.

She saw Eve trying to fight her way across the room. 'Catarina?'

'Yes?' She looked back at Stephen.

'Why do you have to be so fucking stupid?'

'Stephen . . .'

'You went to see Alex.'

'Who told you?' She looked surprised.

'Eve told me. Why? Was it supposed to have been a state secret? What did you wear — a headscarf and dark glasses to disguise yourself in case anyone saw you mixing with lowlife again? What's the matter with you, Catarina?

Didn't life with a wholesome boy like myself provide you with enough kicks? Do you have to go back to your psychotic husband to get the kind of treatment you need? What were you hoping for, Catarina? That he'd beat you up again? Is that the kind of thing you like? No wonder you were bored with me, then!'

Catarina struck Stephen hard on the face. The photographers started a stampede back in their direction. Beth tried to cut them off but got pushed back down onto one of her own settees.

Stephen went to walk away. Catarina followed him.

'I'm sorry, Stephen, I didn't mean to do that!'

'Don't worry about it.'

'Alex has changed, Stephen – he's not like he used to be.'

Stephen stopped then, and faced her.

'You fell for that?'

'I didn't fall for anything.'

He pulled her into Beth's office, away from the photographers.

'Tell me why you find such scum irresistible, Catarina?'

Her face looked serious in the darkness.

'Maybe because I know I don't deserve any better,' she said.

'That's the most stupid, pathetic thing I think I've ever heard,' Stephen told her.

'You don't know me, Stephen – you don't know anything about me.'

'I know you used to love me. I know that you walked out on me. I know you nearly killed me.'

'Stop it, Stephen.'

He grabbed her by the arm.

'Alex says you still love him – that you always have.'

'Don't be stupid.'

'Is that true, Catarina?'

'Let me go, Stephen.'

'Is it true?'

'No.'

He let go of her arm slowly.

'Did you ever love me?'

She looked straight at him. If he had taken her photo at that moment he would have seen himself reflected in the orbs of her eyes.

'I have to go back,' she said, 'Beth will be worried.'

60

Alex dressed the young girl up like an angel and then he asked her to read aloud from the Bible while he watched. She was sixteen and an experienced hooker but she looked about twelve in the white dress and silver scarf.

When she got to the bit about the Good Samaritan he tore the dress off her and bit at her bare buttocks until she screamed. His office at the gallery was useful, though. Not only was it locked and dark but it was also soundproofed especially for such purposes. It was Alex's dearest dream to be screwing a hooker while Charlotte stood a few feet away with their child, unaware.

'Bite me back,' he ordered. The hooker looked dubious. There were more germs in a human bite than in an animal's. She dug her nails into his arm instead. At least it stopped him biting her when he might break flesh.

The letter arrived the following week. It was postmarked London and double-sealed with cheap Christmas tape, as though someone had been afraid its contents might burst open in the post.

Catarina cut through the tape with scissors and two colour photographs fell out, followed by a letter written on wafer-thin airmail paper.

The photos had fallen face down on the table. For some reason she turned them over slowly one at a time, like tarot cards. Had she known what they would be?

Nemesis. Her past *was* catching up with her. As she looked at the photos she shivered as though they had arrived along with cold London air. Just two shots. She picked one of them up and turned it towards the light. It was similar to her own shot, only it was a print instead of a Polaroid. The angle was slightly different as well. The badly made-up face was the same, though, and the great dick it had shoved into its mouth.

The letter with the shots was simple:

> I know who you are. Two million dollars or these will appear in the press.

There was no forwarding address – presumably the black-mailer would be in contact again.

Catarina tore the note to shreds and then she burnt it in the sink. The small flames started the fire alarms off and the persistent noise did much to drown out her howls of anguish and rage.

Rick Palimo turned on his TV and poked a fork into the cold remains of a biriani take-away. How could food that looked so good when you bought it look so much like crap a mere two hours later? It hadn't changed texture or shape. What was it that turned drooling so speedily into gagging? Perhaps it was like sex with an ugly woman – maybe your needs sometimes overcame your visual judgement.

He looked up at his TV screen. *Ed the Duck* – highlights from his private video collection. Rick had a thing about Ed – he figured he could actually tell what the puppet was saying before the announcer/sidekick translated. He watched Ed a lot and sometimes he was wrong when he guessed but most times he was right on the button.

The doorbell went just as Ed's own puppet Ted appeared. Rick swore under his breath – Ed and Ted meant classic comedy and he was annoyed at the interruption. The bell went again. Rick flicked off the screen and turned his chair back to face his computers before he went to answer it. No need to let visitors know about his secret little vices.

Catarina flew into the room like a hairball from hell.

'Bastard!' – He'd been called the name a million times before but never with such vehemence.

'Hi, Catarina, great to see you,' he said. He slammed the door behind her. 'I thought you were in New York.'

'I was,' she said, 'Until I got your little letter. What the hell are you playing at, Rick? Did you really think I'd pay one penny for these photos? Or am I supposed to think you dug up worse in your pathetic little research? Send them to who you want, Rick – then you can go to hell!'

She threw the shots in Rick's face. He bent down slowly to pick them up from the floor, where they had fallen. Then he looked at her.

'You thought I sent you these?' he asked.

'Who else?'

'How much did I want for them?'

Catarina folded her arms. 'You tell me. You know the limits of your own greed, Rick. Who else have you blackmailed, eh? Do you save up all your really juicy stories to earn you real money? How much have you made over the years? I thought this flat was too good for someone with your type of job!'

Rick sat down on his computer chair.

'I didn't send these,' he said. 'I could have – I unearthed this session from the files months ago – but I didn't, and you know why.'

Catarina stared at him. 'It has to be you,' she whispered.

Rick shook his head. 'Think,' he said. 'Who else knows about these shots?' He handed them back to her and she looked down at them.

'Let me answer for you, Catarina – there was the photographer, wasn't there? Only he's dead – I found that out when I got them. No one else would begin to recognize you from them, now, would they? Nose job – different hair – different name. I dug up more than you knew, Catarina, but there's someone who knows a whole load more than me.'

'Alex.' Catarina sounded calmer now.

Rick spread his hands. 'Why not? Why didn't you think of him first?'

Catarina ran a hand over her forehead, as though she had a headache. 'What about these, Rick?' she asked. She threw a couple of newspapers at Rick's feet, open at the gossip pages. Rick didn't need to look at them – he already knew what they contained. Catarina Kirkova and Rick Palimo. A coupling made in hell. Juicy news.

'Oliver Zweinfeldt's revenge,' he told Catarina.

'Oliver Zweinfeldt?' Catarina looked even more confused. 'What's he got to do with this?'

'He interviewed you after a show once, remember? Then he got on to me. It was his idea I dish the dirt on you, Catarina. When he found out I was still chasing you he wanted half the money from any story. This is his revenge for my telling him to piss off, that's all. Don't let it worry you. This other stuff is serious blackmail – this is the stuff you should be worrying about. Tell me about your husband.'

'I don't know . . .' Catarina said. 'I only met him again recently . . . he said he's turned to religion . . . he's got a nice wife and kids. He's got too much to lose now. How do I know you're telling the truth, Rick? The letter came from London . . .'

Rick smiled.

'Do you think I'd be that stupid?' he asked. 'I might at least have got it sent from somewhere less obvious.'

Catarina sat down slowly. It had been a long flight and she was veering between hyper and comatose.

'Oh God, I don't know any more,' she said. It had all seemed so clear cut in New York. Rick was the man with the info and Rick was rat enough to try and get it published. She'd thought she had him tamed, though – and then the blackmail.

But Alex was starting a new life. He had a beautiful child he obviously adored and was living with a woman of integrity. Would he be stupid enough to risk all that for some half-baked blackmail scheme? He must know she had enough information on him to fight back. From what Charlotte had told her he had obviously croaked about a few of his major crimes – but not all of them. Charlotte was obviously under the impression that he had ceased living the life of a sadistic bastard the moment he set foot in her church. She wondered whether Charlotte knew about Lucy.

Rick wondered the same thing at precisely the same moment.

Alex stretched and yawned and took another bite of his fried-egg sandwich. It had taken him three goes to teach the guy in the deli how to cook it exactly as he liked it and then another four day's wait while the HP sauce was shipped over from the UK.

The yolk had to be cooked on the outside and runny on the inside and the white had to be cooked without any brown edges. The bread had to be white thin-sliced and covered with salted butter. When the insides leaked as you ate it you had yellow yolk and brown sauce running down your chin onto your Turnbull and Asser shirt.

Poor little Luisa. He saw her face again. Not loving. Not bruised and scared. Proud and confident. That look had said she no longer belonged to him. Alex smiled. Her expression had changed, though, when she'd seen Charlotte. That had surprised her. Now he had a new surprise for Luisa, and this little secret would wipe that confident look away for good.

He stood and peered through his spy-hole. He'd done the trip to the hole and back more times than usual that morning because the paintings he was showing that week were more valuable than most. There was one in particular

— a vast oil-on-canvas that would fetch more than half a million by the end of the week, when it would be sold off. When he had looked the last time, the gallery had been empty. Now Luisa was there, standing in front of the canvas, admiring it like any other visitor.

As though she knew he was watching she reached into her bag and pulled something out. It looked like a photograph — a large colour shot — twelve-by-ten at least. She pulled out something else too — a roll of masking tape. Before Alex could move she had taped the photo onto the middle of the canvas and, with one quick glance towards the office, she left the gallery.

Alex was appalled. He ran into the room and stared at the damage. He was so horrified by all the tape that it was a few moments before his eyes focused on the photo glued there in front of him. It was a picture of a girl — quite a young girl. The face meant nothing to him. Then it did. Lucy. Little Lucy. The girl from London. The girl he . . .

'Shit!' Alex tore the picture down and large strips of canvas came with it. He stared at the girl's vacant face for a second and then he tore it into shreds.

'Shit! Shit! Shit!' The fried egg sandwich rose into the back of his throat atop a sudden wave of fear and he barely made it to the waste bin in time before he stared retching.

'Did you do it?'

'Yes.'

'Did he see her?' — Rick was desperate to hear their plan had worked.

'I'm sure he did.' Catarina sounded confident.

'You're positive he was there?'

'Of course. Anyone else would have come running out to serve me.'

'He must be shitting himself.'

'Very likely.'

'So now what, Catarina?'

419

Rick heard Catarina sigh.

'Now I go and get back the rest of the photos and the negatives. I go and see what else he thinks he's got to hold over me. I'm going to his place tonight.'

Rick felt a sudden panic. 'To his place? Can't you see him in the gallery?'

'I want to see where he lives, Rick. I want to see what it looks like.'

'So go past in a cab! Why go inside? Will the other woman be there?'

'No, Charlotte's away with the kids. She phoned a couple of times to see if we can be friends. She told me they're attending a memorial for her late husband in Seattle.'

Rick tried to keep his voice level. 'Catarina, you know what Alex is like and you're going to his house all by yourself. Can't you at least get someone to go with you? What about that waiter you told me you're friends with? What about that photographer you used to live with? Don't go alone, Catarina – he could kill you this time.'

'I'm not frightened of Alex any more, Rick.'

'You should be! At least take a gun.'

Catarina shuddered. 'I couldn't,' she said. 'Maybe I'll take some Mace.'

'Anything. For me – please.'

Catarina laughed. 'You sound like my mother.'

'Oh yeah – what was her name again?'

'Get off my trail, Rick.'

'Sorry – force of habit.'

He really was fond of her, he thought. He had never been so scared on behalf of someone else before.

'I could come out there, Catarina. I could travel by Concorde. You could wait and let me go with you.'

'Go to sleep, Rick.' She hung up on him.

*   *   *

Alex and Charlotte lived in a large house in a beautiful tree-lined street in Brooklyn Heights. The area seemed quiet and peaceful and the only building that Catarina passed that was not a house was a church.

Despite her conversation with Rick, Catarina had planned the evening carefully enough. She told her driver to park one block away and told him to wait until she came out. She also told him to come in after her if she had not paged him after thirty minutes and then again another thirty minutes after that. Catarina was not armed but her driver was.

The house had to be Charlotte's. It was grand and tasteful and Alex would never have chosen it – given the money, she knew he would have opted for a glitzier place nearer the city's main artery. A butler answered the door when she rang and showed her into a large waiting room off the main hall. As she waited, she studied the collection of bronzes Charlotte had displayed in a beechwood cabinet. Then the butler came back to show her into Alex's study.

They walked across a vast floor of antique marble, past a sweeping stairway that Gloria Swanson would have died for and into a large and dimly-lit room. The door was shut behind Catarina and it took a few minutes for her to make out all the shapes in the darkness. The only light came from an open fire and the smell of it reminded her of Russia.

'Alex?' She was annoyed with him for staging all this amateur drama. She felt along the wall for the light switch but then turned again quickly when she thought she heard a noise behind her. She refused to be spooked. It was obviously exactly what Alex wanted for her. In a way she felt flattered that he had gone to all that trouble just to frighten her – in the old days a smack round the ear would have done just as well. Perhaps he was learning some subtlety in his old age.

There was a high-backed chair in front of the fire, covered in a deep-red tartan print. Catarina almost laughed at the effect. It was the sort of chair Vincent Price might have used in one of his Edgar Allan Poe films. She wondered if it would turn around slowly to reveal him. She wondered what expression he had rehearsed – friendly or malevolent?

In the end she could wait no longer, it was too ridiculous and she refused to play along. She found the light switch at last and turned it on. The main light was brighter than she had expected and she winced a little as the entire room was illuminated.

Then she saw the mirror on the wall facing the chair. In the sudden light she had a clear view of the chair's occupant and she thought that she might faint for the first time in her life and then she thought that she might die of the shock.

'Klara!'

Her sister sat curled into the chair, her hands on the wide arms and her eyes on Catarina's reflection. The blood drained from Catarina's face and her struggle for consciousness was like a swim against a strong tide. Her hand covered her mouth. She wondered if she were awake or asleep. Klara stared at her hard and then she slowly smiled.

61

Strangely enough it was Alex who came to Catarina's rescue, running into the room when she screamed and catching her before she collapsed to the floor. She felt his arms around her and thought for a while that she was back on stage in Russia again, unable to move until he helped her off.

"Luisa! Luisa, listen to me! There's some goon round at the front door and he's threatening to break his way in unless you call him off! He says you promised to buzz him through, or something – look, will you just tell him you're OK – that I haven't killed you, or anything? Catarina!"

His words sounded foggy – she shook her head to clear it.

'Klara's here,' she told him.

'Just deal with this first, will you?' he asked.

Catarina walked unsteadily into the hall and told her driver to go back home. Then Alex led her back into the study. Klara was still there in the chair. She unfurled her long legs and stood as Catarina walked in.

'Luisa Kuznetzova,' she said, and it was then that Catarina realized her sister was no ghost.

She walked towards Klara with her arms outstretched and her throat seemed to fill suddenly with tears, so that she thought she was choking.

'Klara!' It was impossible but she threw her arms around her sister's neck and Klara was real – she could feel her – there was warm flesh and a smell like before – that wonderful smell she had had back in Russia. She kissed her sister

423

on the cheek. Had she ever done that before in her life? She couldn't remember. She didn't care.

'Klara! How are you here? What happened? I thought you were still in the hospital! Did nurse Margolis send you here? I didn't know whether to trust her, you know, and yet here you are! Why didn't she tell me you were better? Klara – I can't believe it's you!' She spoke Russian without even being aware of it. She thought her heart would burst apart with the pleasure of seeing her again. She had never been so happy, not even with Stephen. All the sacrifices had been worth it for that one wonderful moment – the baby, Stephen, the country she loved – none of them mattered now that Klara was well and back with her again.

'How did you get here?' She leant back a little but could not let go of Klara's arms for fear she might vanish again.

Klara was smiling at her – her face was wet with Catarina's tears. 'Alex brought me here,' she said.

Catarina looked at Alex. He was sitting in the chair that Klara had been in, staring at them. He looked shaken, as though he needed a drink.

'When? Why didn't I know?' Catarina had too many questions. All she wanted to do was hug Klara forever.

'Last month, Luisa. I came here last month.'

'A month? Why didn't you find me before?'

'I did.' There was a pause. Catarina looked at Alex again. He was staring at the fire.

'You did? What do you mean?'

Klara smiled. 'I wrote to you just recently, Luisa,' she said. 'Didn't you get my letter? Why didn't you reply?'

Alex looked really shaken now.

'You wrote?' Catarina sounded dumb. 'You wrote to me? Where? When? Why didn't I get it? I would have come to you straight away, Klara! It must have got lost in the post.'

'No, Luisa,' Klara said. 'I didn't sign it, that was all. I'm teasing you – you wouldn't have known where to find me.'

424

Her face looked funny suddenly. Her mouth was smiling but her eyes weren't.

Catarina laughed nervously.

'Didn't you guess it came from me?' Her voice had gone cold.

Catarina stared at her sister.

'Did you bring me the money, Luisa?'

'Klara?' The nervous laugh appeared again, 'What are you talking about?'

Klara looked at her as though she were being stupid.

'I wrote and asked you for money, booby – money that you owe me.'

'But it was Alex who sent that . . .' Catarina began.

'I stole the photos from Alex, Luisa.'

Alex stared mutely into the fire. He seemed to be in shock.

Catarina's hands dropped slowly to her sides. '*You* sent them, Klara? Why? Why didn't you just come to me?' This time she ran out of questions altogether.

Alex cleared his throat. 'I tracked Klara down in Moscow, Luisa, on a trip I made there last year. She was living in poverty with your father. I couldn't believe you would want to treat your family like that. Klara didn't even know where you were or who you were or if you were still alive. I told her you were my wife and she told me your story up until we met.

'There's a slight gap in the middle of that story, though, so perhaps you would like to fill it in later, when you're over the shock.'

Klara stepped forward and grabbed Catarina's arm. She spoke in English now and her accent sounded strange.

She dragged Catarina spitefully to the long mirror on the wall and made her look in it. Catarina's face was white with shock. Klara's had turned red with anger. She spoke in Russian again and she spat as she spoke. Catarina could only watch the face as it spoke – the words had no meaning

425

for her any more. Her beloved Klara was angry — and angry with her — that was all she knew.

'You left me there in the hospital, Luisa,' Klara was saying. 'You ran off with my boyfriend and you abandoned me. I couldn't believe you would do such a thing. At first I thought I must be mistaken but as the years passed I realized it could be the only truth. Were you frightened of me, Luisa? Were you scared to face me because you had stolen Rudi from me?'

Catarina struggled. 'Rudi? Klara what are you talking about?'

'Did you think I would be angry? Was that why you went? I wouldn't have minded so much, Luisa. I was sick — I needed you, you were the only person I had in the world. When we were little I looked out for you, Luisa. When I was sick you should have looked out for me.'

Catarina was in hysterical tears. 'I did, Klara! I sent money to the hospital! I phoned the nurse all the time! I even went out there and saw you! You were there in the bed!' A sudden terrible doubt crossed her mind as she spoke. Could she really have been so stupid? 'I did all that I could! I know nothing about Rudi — he drove off and left me!'

Klara lifted her chin so that she looked back into the mirror. 'Look what you did to me, Luisa! I couldn't believe what Alex told me but then I saw the magazines and I knew it was all true. You stole my life, Luisa! You took my face, my name and my ambitions! *I* was Catarina Kirkova, Luisa — not you! You stole it all from me and now I want it back.'

Catarina looked at their reflection in the mirror. It was true, they looked almost like twins, standing side by side there. She did have her sister's face now and the sight frightened her. It was she who was the more beautiful now, though — little Luisa — instead of the ugly duckling she had been before.

'You stole my face,' Klara kept repeating. 'I hate you, Luisa.'

'I didn't plan to look like you, Klara,' Catarina cried. 'I stole nothing from you! I didn't even want my career, except as a way to get money for your hospital bills!'

'What bills?' Klara said. 'I was only in the hospital for a few weeks — just long enough for you to run off with Rudi, in fact.'

'A few weeks?' Catarina thought she had gone mad. 'What do you think I have done, Klara? I did everything for you, believe me! I don't know what you're talking about! A few weeks — you have been in that hospital for years!'

Klara let go of her. 'I thought you loved me,' she said. 'You have no idea what I have been through these past years.'

'I *do* love you Klara!' — Catarina was desperate, 'I would do anything for you!'

Klara's face was hard.

'You don't have to, Luisa,' she said. 'I don't want your charity. All I want is what's mine by rights. You owe it all to me, Luisa — all I want is for you to repay all that you owe me.'

Catarina's driver had waited after all — in fact he had been about to call the police. He'd decided to count to a thousand and Catarina came out of the house like a bullet from a gun on nine hundred and eighty-two.

Alex came running after her, looking scared. The chauffeur reached under his armpit. Alex looked crazy but he didn't look armed.

'Luisa!' Alex was screaming and Catarina was crying. She climbed into the car and locked the door. Alex started beating on the tinted glass. The chauffeur was unhappy — he had cleaned the car that afternoon and Alex was making marks. He rolled his own window down slowly.

'Piss off,' he said. 'Before I run you over.'

427

The guy was either deaf or stupid – possibly both. He just kept screaming and banging on the glass. The chauffeur took one look at Catarina and pulled away anyway. He didn't like Alex's face. He didn't care if he ran over his toes.

When the car had gone, Alex ran back into the house. 'What the fuck was that all about?' he screamed at Klara.

Klara sat silently, staring at the floor.

'You let her think I was blackmailing her?' Alex paced in circles, running a hand through his hair continuously. 'Jesus, I thought maybe she'd be pleased to see you! What the hell has gone on between you two?'

Klara looked up. 'You knew she would not be pleased, Alex. Don't pretend you ever thought that.'

'Jesus!' Alex stopped pacing. 'I thought we might just get a little something going, Klara! I thought we could launch you on the modelling scene on her back! Make a few million dollars, understand? Of course, I thought she might be pissed about it, but I never knew you were going for the jugular too! Blackmail! Christ! Do you know how much she's got on me? You destroy her – she destroys me. Understand? Only all she loses is a bit of a reputation. She can put me in jail with what she knows, you stupid, fucking cow!'

Alex phoned Catarina non-stop. She listened to his messages on her answerphone but she didn't pick it up once. He phoned for a week – she knew because she was in her apartment, listening. She had the drapes closed and she sat there in darkness. She didn't eat except for a few disgusting bits she found in a cupboard and she didn't wash.

She didn't go out – she couldn't.

Other people managed to phone between Alex's calls – Stephen, Eve, Rick, Beth, Tony – all sounding increasingly

428

worried. They all gave up though, except Tony. It was Alex's begging that drove her crazy, though. Was she mad? Had she imagined it all? Maybe Klara had been in the hospital all the time. She had been fooled once – it could easily happen again.

People knocked on her door and some even opened the letter box to peer through. She hid behind the door to the kitchen. One time she even picked up a knife. Someone would call the police soon. She picked up Alex's call. She had forgotten how much she hated him but she remembered again now.

'What do you want, Alex?' Her voice sounded hoarse.

He didn't know what to say to her now he'd got through but he couldn't let things go without saying something.

'What will you do?' Alex sounded angry and scared.

'Klara,' Catarina said. 'Klara – it was her, Alex? That was my sister? She hates me. You did that, didn't you? What did I do to you? Why, Alex? Why?'

'Look . . .' Alex began. Catarina liked the scared note in his voice. It gave her a strength she didn't know she had.

'. . . You tried to manipulate things one time too many, didn't you, Alex?' she asked. 'This time you got caught in the crossfire. So what do you do now? You saw me with Lucy's photo last week, didn't you? You know what I'll do to you – would that be worth it, Alex?'

'I'll get the shots back from Klara,' Alex said, 'I won't let her blackmail you. I'll drop her, honey – she no longer exists for me. Don't do anything, promise me you won't.'

'You'll have to,' she told him. 'If you help Klara you'll end up in jail, Alex. I can promise you that much.'

The porn shots and their negatives arrived in the post the following day.

Catarina phoned him back.

'Alex, is Klara with you?'

'No.' He sounded pleased about that fact.

'Where is she?' Catarina had to know – she was

429

desperate. She thought she could still see her sister and that somehow everything would be alright after all.

She heard Alex sigh and she heard him flipping through some papers. 'What about my stuff, Luisa?' he asked. 'What about the things you have on me?'

'That'll be our secret, Alex. Nobody need ever know.'

Then he gave her the address.

Klara's hotel was shabby and sad-looking.

Catarina went round to visit her sister a couple of days after talking to Alex, when she felt stronger and looked halfway decent and when she'd had time to think. She looked up at the place and she cursed Alex for being mean enough to have Klara put up in such a doss-house in such a neighbourhood. Klara would not have known any better but Alex did. Maybe Charlotte kept him short of pocket money after all.

All the way up the stairs Catarina told herself that Klara would be out. By the time she had reached the landing she was so strongly convinced that she jumped in surprise when the door to the room opened and Klara's face appeared in the thin gap.

They stared at one another and then Klara stepped back and Catarina walked past her into the small room.

Klara's room was tiny and dirty and she had a small cardboard suitcase with only one spare dress folded inside it. She sat on the bed while Catarina took the only chair.

They stared again without speaking, Catarina's hands were shaking but Klara's lay still in her lap.

'It's so good to see you . . .' Catarina whispered.

Klara shook her head.

'More lies,' she said.

'Don't hate me, Klara – I can't bear it.'

Klara rose from the bed. Catarina thought she was going to hit her.

'Alex won't speak to me now, Luisa. He was the only

friend I had here. You did that, didn't you? Were you frightened he might fall for me? Do you have to take everything? You have to give me money, Luisa — what else will I live on?'

Catarina sighed.

'I can support you, Klara — I'm your sister — I love you. Alex only wanted to cheat you. He's a wicked man, Klara, you should never have trusted him.'

'He's your husband, Luisa.'

Catarina shook her head.

'You don't understand, Klara. I'm sorry.'

Klara paced the room. Her legs were bare and her suit was shockingly out of date. Catarina suddenly felt ashamed of the expensive clothes she was wearing.

'I brought you some money, Klara,' she said. 'There's enough cash here to get you a room in a better hotel. You won't have a bank account yet so I'll write a cheque for an apartment for you when you've found one you like. Or you can live with me. I'd like that, Klara, I'd like that most of all. Are you going to stay here still? I'll give you as much money as I can but you must understand that I thought you were in hospital all these years and I sent most of my money out for your keep. Don't worry, though — I earn good money now, enough to pay for both of us . . .'

She stopped when she heard Klara laughing.

'You are such a good liar now, Luisa. Who taught you to lie in this way? You sound as though you believe yourself. I could have taught you to lie just as well, though. Do you remember all those men I had to screw just so we could get away from our home? I had to lie to all of them, Luisa. Is that how you learnt it? From working as a whore here?'

Catarina put her face into her hands. Her skin felt hot, as though she had a fever.

'Do you expect me to forgive you, Luisa?' Klara asked. 'Do you expect me to forget how you abandoned me in the hospital and took all my dreams and stole all my life? You were such a docile little thing. Were you planning it

431

all along while we were growing up? Did you plan to look like me and act like me and live the life I wanted to live some day? Why did you leave me in such a way, Luisa? Why?'

Catarina looked up at her.

'Klara, I have the most terrible secret,' she said.

Klara sat down on the bed again. Her face was pink too and her eyes seemed to glitter.

'I had to leave you,' Catarina said. 'I had to leave Russia. I had no choice. After your operation Rudi was mad and said we were to take revenge on Samuel Lorenz for what he had done to you. We went to his office and they fought, Klara. I was so scared – I had never been so scared before in my life. Samuel was hurting Rudi, Klara – I thought he might kill him.' She stopped for a second to get her breath. 'Something awful happened then, Klara. Rudi had given me a gun – I can't remember why. I was scared and next thing the gun went off and Samuel Lorenz was lying on the floor. We killed him, Klara. That was why I had to leave you. We were scared we would be caught. Alex didn't know – nobody knew, apart from Rudi and he left me to fend for myself. Klara, I would never have left you otherwise, I swear it.'

She looked up. Klara was staring at her as though she were mad.

'You killed Samuel Lorenz?' she asked. Catarina nodded.

Klara let out a strange laugh. 'You *are* mad, Luisa,' she said. 'You're mad and you're a liar.'

Catarina tried to catch her hand. 'No, Klara.'

Klara laughed again. 'I can't believe you'd make up such stupid stories,' she said. 'You must realize I would know if Samuel Lorenz had been murdered or not. If he's so dead, how is it he still runs his school in Russia, Luisa? What do you think he is these days, a walking corpse?'

Catarina watched her sister's face. Was she lying?

'Samuel Lorenz is alive?' she asked. Klara shook her head at her.

'Samuel Lorenz is alive so you couldn't have killed him,' she said, 'I was only in the hospital a few weeks so you couldn't have been paying money for me all these years, and Rudi is married and working as an accountant out in Tashkent, or so I was told by his grandmother last year. He's not some desperado on the run, Luisa, he's a boring accountant with a wife and a small child. Either you're a bad liar, Luisa, or you're living in a fantasy world and about to go mad.'

'I'm not lying, Klara!' Catarina said. Had her life been so wrong for all these years? She tried to straighten her thoughts up in her mind but they kept shuffling out of order, like a pack of greasy cards.

She saw Samuel Lorenz lying on the floor of his office. Had he just been wounded when Rudi hit him? Her bullet must have missed. She saw Klara being released from hospital, fit and well and then she saw the nurse's face and realized she had been lied to.

There was nothing she could say to Klara. Klara hated her and that was that. She rose from the chair and clung to a little dignity. She smoothed her jacket down and walked towards the door.

'Will you stay here?' she asked her sister.

Klara nodded. 'In New York, yes. Not in this hovel, though. I won't stay here while you live somewhere expensive, Luisa.' She picked up the cash from the bed.

'Can I find you a good hotel?' Luisa asked.

'I can find one myself. I bought a guidebook at the airport.'

Catarina felt tears sting her eyes. Klara's guidebook was old and out of date.

'You'll look for a good apartment, though?' she asked.

Klara nodded. 'I'll send for the money when I've found it.'

'Klara, you can't live here like this.' Catarina moved across the room towards her. 'You don't know anyone, you don't speak much of the language . . .'

433

'I said I can manage.' Klara took a step backwards. They were both crying now. Klara opened the door for Catarina to go.

62

Beth was working on a damage-limitation exercise.

'The fact that you have a sister no-one knew about is bad but not fatal,' she told Catarina, 'Everyone has a member of their family they'd rather keep under wraps. Did I ever tell you about my cousin Valerie? Remind me some time when you have a week or two to spare.

'Now – the fact that she decides to launch her career in this type of paper with these types of pictures – that's a little more serious. What do you think she was doing, Catarina? These shots are crap and this newspaper stinks. We all know Catarina Kirkova as a class act and now her sister sells some exclusive in the most downmarket rag it is possible to imagine.'

Catarina sighed. 'It was probably the first paper she bought,' she said. 'She doesn't have any contacts – she wouldn't have known any better.'

Beth looked back at the page spread out in front of her.

'She looks like you,' she said. 'She doesn't have your nose quite or your hair and she's obviously older but no-one would say she wasn't your sister.'

She pointed to the small article that accompanied the photos. 'What's the worst thing here?' she said.

Catarina shrugged. 'She says I got rich while she was poor in Russia. She says I didn't send her any money. There's not much, Beth.'

Beth looked at her. 'Will she say any more, Catarina?'

'I don't think so. I'm not sure. I don't think she has much more to say now.' Alex said he hadn't told Klara much – just showed her a couple of shots. Catarina prayed he was telling the truth.

'She needs help, Beth,' she said. 'I want you to take her on your books.'

Beth's lips narrowed. 'She sounds like trouble, Catarina.'

'I'll keep an eye on her.'

'You told me she hates you.'

'I can still keep an eye on her – she doesn't have to know.'

'What's her number?'

Catarina smiled with relief.

Beth phoned Catarina late that evening.

'Bad news – seriously bad news,' she said.

'What is it?'

'Klara won't be joining the agency. Jack got to her first.'

For Jack Palitzo it was like Christmas had come early hand-in-hand with the fourth of July. Firecrackers went off in his head the minute he saw Klara's photos in the paper. It was all so perfect he thought someone was kidding him.

Klara Kirkova was not a bundle of laughs – he discovered that when they met – but then neither was her sister, so that was no problem. She needed a little work done, too, but then Jack was known for his polishing up of rough little diamonds like her. A quick trip to Loehmann's and a little subtle face-paint and he was looking at a thousand dollars an hour, even if she didn't have her sister's talent to go with the looks.

It was the sweetest thing. Jack smiled and leant back in his chair.

Rick Palimo took one look at Klara and the hairs on the back of his neck stood up like corn-shoots. What was that, he wondered, some sort of an animal reaction? It happened with dogs, too, he knew that much.

It was just like looking at Catarina – only different. Same eyes, but with a different expression. Same features – only not quite so fragile. It was weird. He smiled and tried to look normal.

Klara looked at her watch. 'Jack said you are from *The Times*.'

Rick nodded. What was a lie between friends?

Her foot swung backwards and forwards, marking off each second like a metronome. 'Jack said fifteen minutes will be enough for the interview. I have to go and get ready after that. I have a photo-shoot in an hour.'

Rick nodded.

Klara began to look edgy. 'So what is it you want to ask me?' she said.

Rick leant forward in his chair. 'Nothing,' he told her. 'I want you to listen to me . . .'

It was several weeks before it occurred to Catarina that she had achieved a strange kind of freedom with her sister's arrival. Samuel Lorenz was alive. She had been too busy mourning the years she had lost to guilt and fear to appreciate the fact that she was no longer wanted for murder.

She was not a killer and she had no sister to keep alive, either. She had lived with these two burdens for so long that she was still stooped with the weight of them long after finding out they no longer existed. She could do what she wanted and she could go wherever she wished.

Then she realized that she actually wanted to model. Once it was no longer a necessity she found enjoyment in it at last. She had sacrificed so much for the career.

Jack got Klara several features in magazines and a few spots on the TV. Interest in her grew as it became obvious she hated Catarina. Catarina read all the interviews, nervously at first but then with a measure of relief when she realized Klara was not going to brand her a liar.

Klara had obviously decided it was in her own best interests, too, if she carried on with the story about the aristocratic parents. She was quoted as saying their money had been mostly taken by the communists but the essence of the story was still there.

Then Jack started pushing Klara for editorial work. The quality magazines were slow to pick her up, especially as she would never be photographed with Catarina. They mostly wanted 'sister' interviews or fashion shoots, with both women modelling side-by-side in friendly loving poses. With that out of the question she became a slow burner.

She was not as good in front of the camera as Catarina but she looked a lot like her. The public like the buzz of a good feud. Jack broke the rule of a lifetime and cut her price to steal some of Catarina's work from the less wealthy magazines. Beth wanted to fight back but Catarina told her to continue just as normal.

'I don't understand you,' Beth said. 'She's taking your work and you're letting her. You even had a contract for that job last week – you could have sued her for that one – and Jack, come to that.'

Catarina shook her head. 'She deserves a lot of it,' she told Beth. 'I want to see her do well.'

Beth whistled through her teeth. 'You'd both do a lot better if you'd work together,' she said. 'Can't you give her a call and make it up or something? Jack's out to screw us and you're letting your sister help him. What about all that 'blood's thicker than water' stuff? Can't you just give her a ring?'

Catarina tried. She phoned Klara but Klara would not answer her calls. She went round to her apartment but the doorbell always seemed to be ringing in empty rooms. In the end she wrote a letter but Klara, of course, never replied.

Jack did phone Beth, though. 'Klara's a pain in your ass, Beth, am I right?' he asked. Beth just blew him a kiss down the line.

'Two million to get her off your back,' he said. Beth laughed and hung up.

The following season Catarina lost shows in Paris and Milan because Jack was playing silly buggers – trying to hassle work from designers by telling them Klara would work with Catarina and then threatening to sue when they discovered she wouldn't and tried to cancel. One designer even booked Klara, thinking he'd scored Catarina at a cheap rate.

Then, finally, it was Klara who phoned Catarina.

'I thought you should know,' she said, 'our father is dying. Grandma just phoned me – his liver has given out at last. I'm going out to see him.'

'I'll come with you,' Catarina answered without hesitation.

Two limousines pulled up outside the airport and a woman stepped out from each – both wearing headscarves and both dressed top-to-toe in black.

The flight was delayed by bad weather. Catarina and Klara sat in the departure lounge, staring and wondering but not speaking. It was snowing outside – it was as though they were already in Moscow.

Catarina still hated flying. She wondered whether the knot of fear in her stomach was down to that or the dread of seeing their father again. How would he look? She tried to see his face in her mind. She also wondered how Russia would look now she was no longer eaten with fear of discovery. She looked across at Klara. Her sister had barely moved in two hours. Someone touched her on the arm and she jumped out of her seat, thinking their flight had been called.

'Stephen.' He looked older and wiser and she loved him

again the moment she saw him. He sat down beside her. Klara's head moved to watch them but then moved back again quickly when she saw Catarina looking.

'Eve told me you were going back to Russia.'

'I have to – my father's ill.'

Stephen looked at the floor between his knees. 'Catarina – don't stay out there,' he said.

She closed her eyes and leant her head against the back of the seat. 'Stephen . . .'

'I knew I shouldn't come but I just needed to tell you some things, Catarina. I also need to hear some things from you too. I couldn't bear it if you went off and we'd left things unfinished. I just want to talk to you for a few moments before your plane arrives. Do you mind?'

Catarina shook her head. Until Stephen had mentioned it she hadn't thought she might be going back to Russia for good. Now she realized it was something she might do.

'Do you love me, Catarina?' Stephen asked. He placed his hand over hers. His hand was warm and felt comfortable there.

'Stephen, you're married . . .'

'Catarina,' he stopped her and turned her face toward his own. 'Let's pretend you are going to Russia forever. Let's pretend I'm going out of this airport in a few minutes and back to my wife, whatever happens. Let's pretend those two things are fact – totally irreversible. Do you love me?'

She looked far into his eyes. 'Yes, Stephen, I love you.'

His whole body seemed to slump a little.

'Now tell me why you left me.'

She groaned. 'Even if my flight never came I wouldn't have time to tell you that.'

'You *were* pregnant, weren't you?' he asked. She nodded.

'I knew you were. I knew you were lying when you said you'd made it up. Yet I still loved you, even with all that. I loved you when you left me and I loved you when I

440

thought you must hate me. I even loved you while I stood there in church, saying my vows.

'I've spent my whole marriage loving you, Catarina – I feel as though I've loved you my entire life. It's a pain I have to live with – I'm used to it now but it won't go away and I know it won't stop if you go.

'I feel as though I've wasted years loving you but it won't be such a waste if I know you loved me back. It will be a tragedy then, Catarina, but it will have been something precious to cherish all the same.

'Don't go – if you do I'm afraid you'll never come back.'

Catarina kissed him gently on the lips. 'I have to go, Stephen, Klara needs me.'

He hugged her to his body and rocked her gently against him.

'Do you remember how good it was in England, Catarina?' he whispered, 'That house I hated so much and then finally fell for? Remember the lake and the trees? Why did we waste so much time when we both knew we loved one another?' He sat back suddenly. 'Here – I bought you this.'

Her flight was called and they both stood up as she took the gift-wrapped box from him. It was large and square and wrapped in silver paper. Stephen kissed her one last time.

'You know what the present is – don't open it until you get to Moscow.' They ran toward the boarding gate and Catarina thought she might suffocate if she tried to get onto the plane.

'Stephen!' She saw him through a gauze veil of tears and then he was gone.

She wanted to stay with him. But she boarded the plane instead.

63

The two Kuznetsova sisters walked through the snow in Alexandrovsky Gardens, both still dressed in black because they had been attending their father's funeral that day. The sky above them was the colour of wet pebbles and the air smelt of kerosene and snow.

They walked in silence – Luisa could hear Klara breathing. Klara stopped to throw a stone into the Moskva for luck. It was as though the stone broke the skin of the river and then the sky broke open too and the snow started to fall.

Luisa stared at the water long after the ripples had vanished. She carried a large leather folder in her arms. As the snow began to settle on her eyelashes – before her fingers had quite frozen through after keeping still for so long – she opened the folder up and began to throw its contents, sheet by sheet, into the river.

'I wondered what the hell you had in there.' Klara was watching her. It was the first time she had spoken to Luisa since they had left New York. 'That's Alex's stuff, isn't it?'

Luisa didn't need to reply. A photo of Alex floated away alongside one of Lucy's battered body.

Klara looked around. 'Stop it Luisa, you'll get us arrested.' But the papers had all gone by then and no-one was watching anyway.

Luisa turned to her sister. Her face looked like a little peach, with the cold.

'You are an idiot,' Klara told her. 'You should have saved that stuff. The man is a bastard. He deserved to be punished.'

Luisa just shook her head. 'I want to start again, Klara. Leave it all behind. Besides, there are others who will remember for me,' she said.

Klara tutted. 'What do you mean, booby?'

But Catarina wouldn't say any more.

They shoved their frozen hands into their pockets and when they sat down at a bench it was near the spot where they had seen the English model, many years before.

'Look at us,' Klara said. 'We're dressed up like a pair of old babushkas.' She stretched her long black legs out and studied her boots.

Luisa smiled. The snowfall started to get steadier. Klara had snow on her nose. Luisa wondered why she never brushed it off – surely it must tickle? People stared at them as they went past – two tall blonde women dressed all in black, sitting in the snow as though enjoying the first sun of the spring.

'Are you going back to that man?' Klara asked Luisa.

'Which man?' Luisa knew who Klara meant but she just wanted to hear the sound of her sister's voice again.

Klara stretched her arms and coughed. 'The one at the airport of course, booby. He looked nice – better than most of the men in New York. He loves you, too, didn't he say?'

'You were listening!'

'So? What else was I supposed to do, sitting there?'

Luisa took off her gloves and blew on her fingers. The gloves were only thin kid and her fingers were dappled grey and white, like fish-skin.

'*I'm* not going back, you know,' Klara said – maybe as an incentive. 'I didn't really care for it much, to tell the truth. There's not a lot of difference between modelling and whoring, when you give it some thought. Either way, it's your body you're selling. Agents are only like pimps,

443

don't you think? Jack even looked like a pimp. Why did you work for him in the first place, Luisa?'

She sniffed and looked about. 'Maybe I'll become a fat old babushka after all. They eat what they like and they have some self-respect – that's enough in basic dignity for me, Luisa. I feel as though I have been starved for half my life. Don't you miss food?

'Did you know there are girls you can work with who live on powder that they make up into drinks? Or some that are sick as soon as they've eaten?' She laughed. 'Do you remember the doughnuts, Luisa? Or the stew with fat brown dumplings rolling in it?' She got up from the bench and held out her hand. 'Come on – let's eat.'

They bought hot blinis stuffed with everything and oozing with sour cream that ran off down the greaseproof they were wrapped in and onto their fingers. They drank cups of black tea and they ate their blinis as they walked through the park. Klara made noises of pleasure as she ate.

When they had finished and their stomachs were full like balloons she threw the paper into a bin and licked the last cream off her gloves.

'It should be the basic right of any human, don't you think?' she asked. 'To eat when you are hungry – to eat until you are full – to eat until you feel sick.' She breathed in a lungful of air. 'It's a good feeling, isn't it, Luisa? Eating until you are sick. Eating until you get fat. Look – look at my stomach already! Do you know I bought this dress too small so that I could starve my way into it? Look at it now – it hates those blinis! Any minute now it will get so angry with me for eating them it will split apart and the buttons will all drop off.'

She turned to Luisa. Her face was pink and happy. 'Look at you – you're cold! Here, you booby!' She did up the top button of Luisa's coat and pulled her hat more firmly onto her head.

Luisa looked annoyed at the fussing but inside she beamed with pleasure. 'Klara – about the hospital . . .' It

444

seemed a good time to talk – her sister was in a good mood at last.

'I know about it, Luisa,' Klara said.

'You know?'

Klara looked out across the park.

'The English journalist – that friend of yours – he came to see me in New York. He knew everything about you, Luisa, did you know that? He even had copies of your bank statements showing the money you had sent to that nurse.'

Luisa looked shocked. 'You knew, Klara? How long have you known?'

Klara shrugged. 'A month, maybe.'

'Why didn't you tell me? We could have been friends again.'

Klara smiled. 'Oh – I thought you were enjoying the competition, Luisa,' she said. 'Besides – it was good for business, wasn't it? I would have told you some time, booby. I'm telling you now, aren't I?'

When Klara turned to Luisa there were strange bright tears in her eyes and her face looked red. 'Will you stay here, Luisa?' she asked.

Luisa studied her silently. 'What will we do?' she said.

Klara whistled through her teeth thoughtfully. 'Oh – I don't know. We could just get fat together, I suppose, maybe. Or we could start a modelling school – only a proper one – and put that bastard Samuel Lorenz out of business. How would that sound to you? "The Orlova Academy" – it has a nice ring to it, doesn't it?'

She put out a hand and Luisa took it.

'By the way – what was in that box you were given at the airport?'

Luisa had almost forgotten Stephen's present. That evening, when she was alone, she opened the box. Of course it was a glass snowstorm, and the sight of it alone made her start to cry.

There was a note with the present: 'Sorry it's not exactly

the same — love forever, Stephen.' She pressed the note to her lips and then she looked back at the snowstorm. It was not the same, but it was perfect, nevertheless. The old one had just one figure inside it — Klara by herself, lost and alone in all the snow. In this one there were two figures — two small girls, waving side by side. Klara and Luisa. Together again forever.

Epilogue

Her photograph was still on his wall. One day he might even go out to Moscow to visit her — if he could get the trip on expenses somehow. Her face was amazing. He had trouble believing he had ever fucked her. But it was the truth.

His cursor blinked at him. Ready and waiting. Two exposés to write up and one more simmering on the back-burner. Lovely-jubbly. He gazed at his new headline: MINISTER IN LONDON ZOO SEX SCANDAL. A little frisson of glee sloshed through his bowels like an ice-cold colonic irrigation. He was so rapt in what he was doing he barely noticed the knock on the door.

'Sign here please.' The messenger thrust a clipboard into his hands. Rick signed and the clipboard was snatched away and replaced with a package. A corner of the parcel was ripped already so he could peek inside to check it wasn't explosive.

Papers. And some photos. His file on Alex had finally found its way back again like a bedraggled homing pigeon. Rick emptied it out onto the desk. There was no covering note with it but Rick didn't need one. He could smell Catarina's scent just as surely as if she were standing in the room next to him.

A lot of it was photocopies. He wondered what she'd done with the originals.

Why had she returned it? He thumbed through the papers and Alex's face in the shots made him shudder. Then he spotted some new stuff — photos and cuttings he'd never seen before. He started snuffling through with more interest. Cuttings of Charlotte, the clean-living American icon, smiling with her kids; then Alex, her lover – Rick turned a shot around for a better angle – was that not illegal? Or physically impossible at least? And why did he go screwing such dogs, when he had such a smart lady at home?

Rick looked at the shots again. Catarina had done her homework thoroughly. There was a good story there. One he could syndicate to the 'States for a few thousand dollars, too.

Alex Head – to expose or not to expose? Rick was sitting on a backlog . . .

He pulled a coin out of his pocket. Heads, Alex. Tails, the minister and the gorilla. The coin landed tails. Rick stood for a minute, staring at Alex's little pile of sin, then he thought of Catarina. Bruises, cuts, burns to the stomach. He looked at her luminous face in the photo above him.

Rick shrugged. 'Sorry, Minister.' He shoved the coin back into his pocket and set about composing the downfall of Alex Head.